MW01518862

HERETIC

THE GRAY ASSASSIN TRILOGY BOOK THREE

HERETIC

GREGORY A. WILSON

Detroit, Michigan

HERETIC

Copyright © 2024 by Gregory A. Wilson

Cover Illustration by Peter Tikos
Interior Design by G.C. Bell

Edited by E.D.E. Bell

All rights reserved.

Published by Atthis Arts, LLC
Detroit, Michigan
atthisarts.com

ISBN 978-1-961654-14-3

Library of Congress Control Number: 2024941057

✦

THREE small fenners flew in a circle, cooing and trilling as they spiraled down from the azure sky above Tellisar. None were native to the area, of course; fenners mostly lived in warmer climates. Yet impossibly, here they were, their wings tracing white streaks against the blue backdrop of the cloudless sky as they descended. Their singing was calm, peaceful ... almost tranquil. Only if one were close up, and then only if they were observing every detail intently, might they notice a slight rigidity in the angle of the wings, a slight strain in the curve of the fenners' necks, a certain wild, staring quality to the eyes.

Down they flew in their inexorable spiral, down toward Tellisar and the center of the Armor Quarter, toward a building of polished white marble and ebony pillars. They circled around the building's roof and made for the open area right next to it, a section of white marble flooring and two large fountains, set in a square, in the middle of which two robed figures stood waiting. One of the figures lifted a hand, and the descent accelerated, the fenners straining against the resistant air to go ever faster. In a few moments, they lit upon the robed figure, each of the three spaced precisely over the length of the outstretched arm, where they sat motionless, almost silent except for an occasional coo.

"Lovely creatures, fenners," observed the figure watching the birds on his arm. His voice was deep and sonorous, like the

To the ones who blazed the trail:
Thanks for showing us the path to follow.

sound of metal vibrating after a bell has been struck, and he was dressed in robes bluer than the sky over Tellisar. His face was clean-shaven and unblemished by the advance of years, with dark hair above deep blue eyes; he could have been thirty years old or ninety. But his hand, exposed at the end of the blue-robed arm, was curved, clenched as if in some mild exertion or palsy.

The similarly blue-robed man standing next to the speaker, brown hair over thin eyebrows, brown eyes, and a sandy brown goatee, nodded. "It has been years since I've seen any," he said, voice slightly higher and less resonant than his companion. "I had not expected to see any here."

The blue-eyed man chuckled. "Expectation is a weakness of yours, Father Rennix. It anchors you in the past." He leaned over the three fenners, their feathers shivering slightly. "There are many things we do not *expect* to see, or experience . . . yet we do. Eventually we come to realize the only thing we can expect is the unexpected." He glanced at Rennix, the slightest suggestion of a smile playing on his lips. "But then, I suppose expectations are part of what the Service needs. Rules, regulations—predictability."

Rennix smiled without mirth. "It is part of my charge, Eparch Kaenath. Our Acolytes work best with an understanding of what truly is."

"Indeed," the Eparch replied, stroking the feathers of the largest fenner, sitting in the middle of the row. "Then what do we understand about our new arrival?"

Rennix's jaw worked slightly. "Not enough, Eparch." He took a few steps away, gazing at the fountain. "We know his name. We know he arrived in Tellisar about three months ago, before the first snow. We know he has companions with him—though who or what they are remains uncertain. I've heard everything from cats to children to giants to dragons, but getting any real details we can confirm has been . . . difficult." He sighed. "But that's temporary. We'll find him one way or the other."

"I'm less concerned about finding him," Kaenath said, eyes narrowing slightly as he leaned closer to the large fenner. "I'm more concerned with stopping him."

"We'll do that too, Eparch. He hasn't appeared in any of our reports, and so wherever he is, he can't be doing much for the moment."

"And what, Father Rennix," Kaenath said as he raised an eyebrow, "would give you that idea?"

Rennix blinked. "I know this city, and I know my Service. We've had enemies before, and all of them have felt Argoth's Hammer in the end. This Grayshade will be no different."

Kaenath leaned back from the fenner, whose head was beginning to swivel back and forth as if the bird were looking for something, and turned to face Rennix. "You're forgetting your recent history, and this person's place in it." He turned to face the fountain, the fenners shifting slightly on his arm as he moved. "Cohrelle's history, for one."

"The Order's High Prelate in Cohrelle had ideas about him, Eparch, and if he could have been—"

"The High Prelate," Kaenath said, cutting Rennix off, "was as arrogant as he was stupid." He looked up at the darkening sky and shook his head. "He moved far too quickly in Cohrelle, with no understanding of the variables at play, putting all of his faith in his Acolytes without seeking outside allies. He had no control of the political situation outside of the Order. He had no control over Grayshade." He looked at Rennix, blue eyes cold and fathomless. "He was a fool who deserved his fate."

"Even so, Tellisar is not Cohrelle, and Grayshade is one man, Eparch," Rennix objected. "Surely there is a limit to what one man can do."

"This one man," Kaenath replied, "thwarted our efforts in Cohrelle, and ended any chance we had of controlling it for years. The Order will be lucky to run a market stand there by the time the Governor has completed his purge. This one man almost singlehandedly tipped the scales in the war between Calarginn and Arginn, essentially ended our influence with Arginn, and weakened our authority here. And this one man," he went on, turning away again as the fenners on his arm were becoming increasingly unsteady, "has eluded all your efforts to find him for the better part of three months since he supposedly arrived here, or even to discern what he's been up to. In short, this one man Grayshade has done more than his fair share to hamper, undercut, and harm the Order of Argoth since he became a renegade. And now he has come here—unless I am very much mistaken, because he has decided to go after us. I am ... *disinclined* to underestimate him again." He took several slow steps forward, watching as the fenners began to shuffle and bump into each other, the one on the far right nearly falling off of his arm. "I am disinclined to let him destroy any more of the Order, especially not now ... not when we are so close. Do you understand?"

Rennix nodded. "I do, Eparch. Then we must find him. But if he is as skilled and dangerous as you say, it will be difficult."

"Begin with his allies," Kaenath said, looking at the fenners curiously as, their eyes wide and beaks opening and closing silently, they began to flap their wings, banging into each other. "Find them, and you will find him. End them ..." Suddenly he relaxed his hand, and without a cry or call, the three fenners toppled off his arm and fell to the ground with a loud thump. There they lay, in a heap, motionless and staring. "End them, and you'll end him," Kaenath said, turning his blue-eyed gaze to his companion. "Can you do this, Father Rennix?"

Rennix swallowed and bowed. "As you say, Eparch. We will find them, and him."

"We are so close," Eparch Kaenath said softly, turning and walking away with Father Rennix close behind. "So close to the time when none of this will matter." The two men exited the Garden of Argoth's Forge, in the Armor Quarter of Silarein's capital city of Tellisar, without a single glance back at the three small white birds which would never move again.

PART ONE
APOSTASY

Do not seek alternatives. One will never find the way
after turning from the straight path of righteousness.

—The Seventh Rite of Devotion

CHAPTER ONE

WHEN I was a child, the markets of Cohrelle always fascinated me, the sights of bustle and stir, the sounds of trade and barter, the smells of food and sweat blending into a complex tapestry of sensation as I passed by stalls with all manner of goods for sale, the merchants standing near them shouting the quality of their contents. I suppose I could have found it overwhelming, too ... but for some reason, there was a life in that place which energized me. And I remembered someone with me, holding my small hand in her cool, pale one, tall and gentle ...

No. That time is long past, and memory is treacherous. It will turn you if it wants, betray you when it can. Focus on now.

Still, the excitement of the markets had never left me, and as I stood inside the door to Carver's General Goods, in the middle of the Gauntlet Quarter, the eastern section of the great city of Tellisar, I listened intently to the calls and responses of merchants and customers coming from Lantern Street. In here it was much quieter; most customers seemed to know what they wanted, and the store's owner, a burly man with a thick mustache, stood behind the counter at the back of the room with his arms crossed, staring at the people browsing his wares. But one person was not looking to buy: a young child of ten, with an earnest expression on their smooth brown face, who was making their steady way to the counter.

"Excuse me," they said, their high voice clear, almost musical.

The burly man's mustache twisted. "Aye," he said gruffly. "All the goods we've got are out there. What d'ya want?"

"Well, I guess I'm not looking to buy anything, or not anything on the shelves, anyway," the child said easily. "I'm looking for information, actually."

"I ain't a guide, nor a tale-swapper," the man replied. "Don't go bothering merchants at work. Be on your way to the Helm Quarter, or the Sabaton Quarter. Some of what they'll sell you there might even be true." He chuckled without smiling. "Now, go on, child."

"It seems like you've been here a long time," the child said. "I'd guess you know most of the people around here . . . give them advice, maybe, counsel when they need it. They already trust you enough to buy from you; why wouldn't they trust you to give them news of the city?" They smiled, but the man pursed his lips, his mustache bristling.

"Ain't about being trusted. It's about what I do and don't sell. I don't sell information. Too dangerous, and too expensive." He glared down at the child. "Now go tell whoever you're working for to keep you out of here before it starts trouble."

"Oh, I'm not working for anyone," the child responded. "My name is Caron, and—"

"Don't care what your name is. Be on your way."

"Oh, of course, as soon as I get the information I need. It's about a religious order, actually . . . I'm sure you've heard of them."

"Don't hold with religion," the man said, turning away. "Waste of time."

"Well, this one is pretty important. It's the Order of Argoth, and—"

The burly man spun around, his eyes wide. "The Order—" His mustache twisted violently. "I'll thank you to get out of my shop."

Caron blinked. "Well, I—"

"I said get out. Don't want no trouble with any religion, and especially not the Order. You can go babble in the Helm Quarter with the other mad ones for all I care, but don't do it in my store. Out."

Caron raised an eyebrow, then nodded. "I'm sorry to have distressed you, sir. I hope sales are good for you today." The man said nothing, just staring at them before Caron nodded again, turned, and left. Suddenly I saw the man, gazing after Caron, exchange glances with three customers at the front of the store who were looking at him, then subtly but definitely nodded in the direction of the door. Immediately the two men and one woman exited . . . but not alone. I waited a moment for the burly man's attention to shift elsewhere, then slipped out after the three customers. Caron, it appeared, had attracted attention of a less than welcome kind.

Outside on Lantern Street I quickly looked in both directions, heading to my right as I saw the slight figure of Caron making their way down the street, followed by the three people from the shop. Caron had not set a fast pace, and their pursuers seemed in no hurry to overtake them. But I could see their focus on Caron, slipping around peddlers and passersby on the street, and they were slowly gaining ground. I ducked around a wagon being dragged to the side of the road and past an older man holding the hand of a young boy, counting the alleys as we went. Three ... two ... one—and then, past a stack of crates, Caron turned into a small alley on their left. The three followers glanced at each other, then drew next to the alley's entrance and peered around the corner.

"Nowhere to run," one of the men hissed, "and nowhere to hide. I'll head down the center; flank out behind me." The other two nodded, and I saw a flash of metal as both drew daggers from their belts while the man entered the alley. They waited a few moments, glanced behind them, then followed.

So did I.

The alley was narrow, running between two fairly ramshackle buildings the roofs of which extended over the alley and cut further into the limited space and light. It was fortunate it was daytime, in fact, or it would have been nearly impossible to see. As it was, it took a moment for my vision to adjust and make out the two figures in front of me, one on each wall, slowly and silently moving forward. "Look, child," I suddenly heard a raspy voice say, and peering into the dim light I saw the third figure stopped and staring at something in front of him. "Don't be scared, we're just here to talk."

"I don't mind talking," I heard Caron's voice say as the two other figures drew to a halt not far behind their companion, with me in turn dropping to a crouch behind them. "But it doesn't feel like you want to talk."

"Why would you say that?" the man responded, perhaps with a slight chuckle.

"Well, I don't know why you wouldn't just talk to me in the store instead of following me here. And I don't know why your friends behind you have daggers drawn. And most of all," they said as the man drew himself up, back straight and rigid, "I don't know why you'd be so nervous if you just wanted to talk. Nervous . . . and angry."

The man and woman in front of me glanced at each other, though I couldn't yet make out their expressions, as the man near Caron laughed again. "Now, why would you think we're nervous or angry?"

"I can feel it," Caron said simply.

The man was silent for a long moment as his two companions stepped forward to stand right behind him. "You were asking questions in Carver's a little while ago," he finally said. "Now, in Tellisar, you ask questions, people notice and start asking questions about you. We ain't seen you around before, and you're pretty young to be that curious. I'm betting you're not that curious for free, and you didn't think up those questions on your own. All you need to do here is tell us who put you up to asking what you did, and you can be on your way."

"I don't think so," Caron replied. "Whether or not I tell you anything, or whatever I tell you, you're not planning on letting me leave this alley and tell people who and where you are. Which means there's no reason for me to tell you anything."

The man sighed. "There is," he said, drawing a short sword from his belt as the man and woman behind him readied their daggers. "Because now we're going to bring you to heel, the way you do any stubborn puppy that doesn't do what it's told. Same amount of pain, but not doing what you're told makes everything take a lot longer. Sad, really, but you've made your own choices."

"That's true," Caron acknowledged. "But we've both made

choices today. Are you sure you don't want to rethink yours? If you stay here, you'll get hurt."

The man barked a harsh laugh. "Too bad Carver didn't have the chance to talk to you himself . . . you could have taught him about having a sense of humor." He lifted his sword. "But that's all over now."

"Yes," I said. "It is." I drew my cucuri as I leapt toward the man on the right, who hadn't even fully turned in my direction before the hilt of my blade raked across his skull. He slid to the ground with a sigh as his companion slashed wildly in my direction, but the blade went well over my head as I was already low to the ground again, sweeping my leg around to catch her as she stood. She went backwards in a heap, and the sound of her skull impacting the stony ground as her blade clattered away from her told me she wouldn't be a threat for a while. I turned to face the other man—but found I was looking at Caron instead, around whom the man's arm was twined, his blade at their throat. Now that my vision had adjusted to the dim light, I could see his eyes were wide, his shadowed face covered in sweat.

"This one yours?" he growled. "Then back off, or they'll be done permanently."

"You talk too much," I said, balancing on the balls of my feet. "Talk less and do more, and you wouldn't be in this spot."

"Thanks for the advice. But I don't take lessons or orders from a sneak in an alley." I saw his arm tighten around Caron's chest; Caron's eyes were wide too, but their expression was otherwise calm, their breathing steady.

"I'm not a sneak, and I'm not giving lessons or orders," I replied. "Just some advice. If you see someone take out two of your men in a few seconds, you might want to consider your own situation carefully. You won't get anything from this child. But keep holding on to them, and you'll get more than you want from me."

"Now who's talking too much?" he said with a sneer, but I could feel him drawing back slightly. My gaze flickered down to Caron, who looked at me briefly; their eyes shifted, and I knew they had understood. "Here's how this is going to go," the man went on. "You're going to walk backwards, slowly, right to the edge of the alley. Then you're going to lay your weapon on the ground and move well across the street while I bring this one out and back down to Carver's. We'll let him decide what to do with the child." He placed the flat of his blade right underneath Caron's chin, so they had to look up to keep from getting cut. "No one gets hurt, no one loses."

I pursed my lips. "That's a fair deal," I said, "if I trusted your word. But I've already seen you lie to this child, and if I hadn't been here they would have been more than hurt by the time you were done. I think you're lying now." I drew myself up slowly, watching as he took a step back, dragging Caron with him. "Here's what's going to happen instead. You're going to let the child go. I'm going to stand aside, and you're going to leave this alley alive . . . and go learn how to tell the truth."

His eyes narrowed. "You don't have the leverage here, sneak. Get out of my way, or the child dies. We're done talking."

I looked at Caron. "Yes," I said, deliberately building a sense of anticipation, concentrating on my readiness, actively feeling my tensed muscles, my hands loose and open near pockets in my cloak, my slightly accelerated heart rate. "We're done talking." Caron nodded, and I waited as the man just slightly lowered his arm holding the blade at their throat. I watched a bead of sweat roll slowly down his cheek. Suddenly his muscles tensed, and just before he could pull his blade back up, I threw a spray of kushuri darts as Caron pushed back into him, hard. He reflexively lifted his free arm to block the darts, but simultaneously staggered back from Caron's unexpected push, and three darts landed in his neck. He released Caron and fell to one knee, clutching at the darts, but I was on him in seconds, and with one slash he was gone.

Caron and I stood above his body, looking down in the half light of the alley. "Are you all right?" I asked Caron.

They nodded, their expression serious. "Are you?"

I nodded but said nothing for a long while, gazing at the man's face, remembering. "I'm sorry," I said at last. "I didn't want to do that ... especially not in front of you. But he was going to ..." I trailed off and shook my head. "I'm sorry," I repeated.

"I understand, Grayshade," Caron said quietly. "I could feel his anger, his fear. He would never have let me go. I'm sorry he grabbed me ... I didn't have anywhere to go. If I could have stayed away for another few seconds ..."

"It was my fault," I said. "This was the alley we agreed that you should go into if you were followed; I didn't think about how little room there would be for you to avoid being grabbed while I was eliminating the other threats. It was a foolish mistake. I gave him plenty of chances to walk out alive, but ..."

"He felt trapped," Caron said. "He might have been just as afraid of what would happen to him if he walked out without me as he was of you." Their expression softened. "Feeling that amount of fear—the sense of helplessness ..." They shook their head. "It's not pleasant."

There was a time when I would have laughed at such words, or dismissed them as the weak mutterings of someone with one foot already in the grave. But that was before everything else over the past six months had happened, before I had lost my livelihood, my faith, and nearly—multiple times—my life. That was before my world had changed forever.

Now, I felt the weight of what Caron said. I wasn't a sensate like them, and couldn't viscerally feel the emotions of those around me as they could. But now I knew what it was to inspire fear, and to feel it myself, and now I knew what it was to feel trapped and helpless. How might I act in a dark alley, desperate, out of hope and time, when I had just followed orders to make a marginal living? Would I have thrown away my leverage and walked out, trusting in the stranger who had taken out my companions with ease to let me go?

Looking at the man's dead face, I thought I knew the answers to these questions . . . and took little comfort in the knowledge.

Suddenly someone's hand slipped into mine, and I looked with a bit of surprise to see Caron looking at me. "Learning from the mistakes of the past is one thing," they said. "But to remain blanketed by those mistakes, weighed down by them, is another."

"A lesson from your teachers?" I asked.

Caron smiled. "A thought I had myself."

I smiled back. "And a good one. Let's go home." And with one final look down at the body of the man who could no longer learn from his mistakes, we turned and left the alley together.

Home was, of course, a relative term. We had been in Tellisar for nearly three months now, but that was a fraction of the time we would need to fully explore a city of this size. It was twenty years before I felt truly at home in Cohrelle, twenty more before I understood how it moved and breathed and changed from day to night, season to season. For Tellisar, larger, taller, and ever-shifting, it would take more years than I could count to know it that well. Still, we had at least been here long enough to know the basics ... and, I hoped, not look entirely out of place.

We had spent much of the last two weeks in the eastern area of the city, known by its residents as the Gauntlet Quarter. Most of the general stores and merchant residences were here, and anyone who spent any time gathering information knew that outside of informants and innkeepers, merchants knew more about what was happening around them than anyone else. But there were many merchants, and progress had been slow—most of the ones we had spoken to were no more helpful than Carver, though he was the first one that had sent anyone after us.

This had always been a risky strategy, of course; we needed to gather information about the Order of Argoth, but had limited options for how to go about doing it. Neither Rillia nor I had any real contacts in Tellisar, nor familiarity with its traditions or customs, but we knew that the Order was strong here—though much less public than it had been in Cohrelle, which in some ways made it even more dangerous. Trying to track down informants like Rumor would have exposed us completely, and even in a city of Tellisar's size, we wouldn't be able to hide once the Order had fixed upon us. They almost certainly knew we were here already—the situation with Arginn and Calarginn from a few months ago would no doubt have warned them of our arrival. And the Order was still the Order, with ways of finding things out. But even for them, finding a specific individual or small group among a hundred thousand or more would be a challenge no matter who the target was, and when the target was *us*, it would be even more difficult.

Still, the relative obscurity in which we lived was a double-edged sword. If they couldn't find us while staying hidden, we also couldn't find out much about them in the same state, and as I said, we had no allies to whom to turn. It was Caron's idea, a few weeks after we arrived, to start asking the questions themself, reasoning that their slight frame and open affect would help put others at ease and their sensate abilities would help them pick up on how the person being questioned was feeling, and of course I had to agree that these things were not insignificant advantages. But I refused to allow them to go out on their own; for all of Caron's wisdom and growing powers as a sensate, they were still very young, and had little experience with cities, especially ones in the Cloud. So we agreed that I would follow them on these fact-finding expeditions, to keep them safe and look for details they might otherwise miss, and we discussed protocols to follow if they were ever threatened. In the end, that caution had been life-saving . . . at least Caron's life. For the life of the man who had threatened them . . .

Don't be weighed down by your mistakes, Caron said. But I was used to that weight, and old habits were sometimes hard to break.

"Do you think Carver knew more than the others?" Caron suddenly asked, startling me from my reverie as we walked. After making sure we weren't being followed, I had settled more into my own thoughts than I realized. We were nearly out of the Gauntlet Quarter now; the bright signs and beautiful houses of the merchants had dwindled, and as we turned on to the Lane of Renewal I could see the road of healing houses stretching out before us, at the end of which was the Sabaton Quarter, South Tellisar, and our current home.

"I don't know," I said, glancing down at Caron, who was looking around with their usual expression of curious interest as we walked. "You told me you didn't sense any real fear from him, and he didn't strike me as a power broker, or someone with a great deal of hidden knowledge. But he sent people after you; even if he didn't mean for you to be killed, he has to be dealt with one way or the other. We can't go back there now, after what just happened. But I'll pay him a visit soon, and we'll see what answers we can get from him."

A cry of pain came from within the small building next to us as we walked, a wooden sign with the classic image of a cloaked figure tending to a prone figure carved on its surface. The healing houses of Tellisar were much more extensive than those in Cohrelle, regulated by the city and completely decoupled from any religious orders. Churches and temples here were allowed to provide basic medical care to their parishioners, but anything more serious had to be referred to the healing houses for treatment. Coming from a place where religious structures were of equal importance to governmental ones, this arrangement still felt strange to me, but it made sense; on the surface Tellisar seemed to be much more driven by its military and merchants than its religions, and it put a premium on making sure these basic services were managed properly. Soldiers themselves were treated for injuries elsewhere, mostly in the Sword Quarter where most of the barracks were found, but almost everyone else, from the poor to some of the wealthiest in the city, came here for healing.

Caron looked at the building as we passed and shook their head.

"Can you sense anything from within?" I asked.

"Yes," they replied, the expression on their face sad. "Fear, and a great deal of pain. The same thing I felt in the—" They glanced at me and fell silent, but I could complete the sentence internally: it was the same thing Caron had felt in the alleyway, from the man I was forced to kill. And there was more where that came from, for if all went as it had to, we would be facing death, our own or others, more than once. The Order had to be stopped, but even if it could be—even if, against all logic and reason, my companions and I could bring down something as well organized, disciplined, and focused as the Order of Argoth—it would not go quietly. The fact that I could see no alternative didn't make things any easier.

We reached the end of the Lane of Renewal and turned slightly left onto Central Street, the widest road in all of the Sabaton Quarter. This was easily the largest part of Tellisar; almost everyone but soldiers, merchants, and government officials lived here, and both taverns and temples—*one for the body, one for the soul*, I thought wryly—had been built here to accommodate them. The Poor Markets were crammed in here as well, the bustling, dirty home of haggling and unregulated goods which made the activity from the general stores in the Gauntlet Quarter seem like prayer services in a church. All of this was, ostensibly, to support the operation of the Docks, the massive array of wooden platforms where countless ships arrived and departed every day, into the Glacalta and from there to the Labyrinthine Sea and the nations beyond. The trade to and from and through Tellisar had made it the richest and most powerful city in Silarein, and well beyond; it was a greater city than Cohrelle in more than just population. But for a city so reliant on trade, it certainly seemed anxious to keep the people and goods responsible for making it so at arm's length, until it could properly organize and direct them.

Still, there was no better place than the narrow alleys and turning lanes of the Sabaton Quarter, and the thousands of residences and residents found there, to pass through without notice. When we first arrived in Tellisar, I had thought that staying in or near the governmental areas would be the most efficient way to gather information, since there was no separate district for the churches as there was in Cohrelle, and from what I could tell, the organization of the churches throughout Tellisar was much more haphazard anyway. But I soon realized I had assumed too much too quickly. Religion was, in its own way, just as important in Tellisar as it had been in Cohrelle, but here it was driven much more by individual needs than by the demands of groups or organizations. Religion here catered to the people, so it was to the people we needed to go.

"The people are restless," Caron said as we made our way through the press of workers, merchants, and travelers heading from or to the Docks, squeezing past carts filled with overflowing sacks of grain and wagons laden with raw metal for the forges.

"I could have told you that," I said, glancing at Caron as I narrowly avoided two people yelling at each other over a tipped wagon and a smashed pile of plates and glasses.

Caron smiled. "Yes," they replied. "But there's more. They feel ... worried, I think, unsure about what's happening in the world around them. They're on edge."

"So am I," I said as we ducked out of the path of a terrified seabird's flight as it shot past. It must have ventured too far from the Docks and was now trying to get food and escape with its life ... and I knew that feeling all too well. "This way." We slipped into an alley extending off of Central Street, leaving the noise behind, and followed as it wound around several buildings before exiting onto the much calmer Street of Sixes, named after The Sixes gambling den at the street's far end. But we were headed to a smaller building before that, a ramshackle structure of wood and stone which somehow fit two stories within its frame. Stopping in front of the crooked wooden door, I knocked three times, waited, then knocked four times more. After a moment the door opened, revealing a woman and, behind her, the silent form of Caoes, the panther.

"Come in," Rillia said. "Hurry." Her dark hair was tied back into a single ponytail, and she was wearing her usual gray tunic and pants. But her forehead was sweaty, her eyes angled in deep worry.

"What—" I began, but she shook her head quickly.

"Not now," she said. "Just come in." I glanced down at Caron, who looked back at me, their expression one of mild surprise. "Hurry!" Rillia said again, her tone impatient as I looked back at her. "I overheard one of the soldiers heading to The Sixes, some fool in their cups. Said there was talk that some people were making trouble, that it was getting some others agitated. They said they'd got word to keep an eye on things with the Just God." She stared at me, gaze intense and searching. "It has to be the Order, Grayshade. I think they're on to us."

CHAPTER TWO

EVEN with only four creatures in residence—two adults, one child, and one panther—there wasn't much room in either floor of our makeshift home in the Sabaton Quarter. When we first found it, it had been abandoned and condemned . . . not surprising, given its filthy condition and resident population of vermin. But somehow arrangements for the building had fallen through the cracks of Tellisar's bureaucracy, and Rillia soon discovered that the plans to tear it down had been put on "temporary hold" many years ago, and may well have been completely forgotten. Keeping up appearances was of little concern in the Sabaton Quarter, which made it perfect for us.

We took a week to clear and clean the place when we found it, and at least a month more to make it vaguely livable. Rillia had insisted on making sure we had plenty of shelves, while I wanted the walls to be reinforced and largely silent. The result was a mixture of my old room at the Cathedral in Cohrelle and Rillia's old shop there—not even remotely compatible, but despite everything, reasonably functional. We had a kitchen and multipurpose living/dining room on the first floor, on which the only really soft surface was Caoes's bed . . . something both Rillia and Caron had insisted on, though knowing what sort of surfaces we had used for beds during our trek across Silarein, I doubted Caoes really needed it. At the moment we entered, he was curled up in his bed near the hearth, eyes apparently closed, but I knew better than to trust appearances with him.

A fire was crackling in the hearth, not overly large or particularly warm, but still a welcome respite from the chill of the early spring weather outside. Caron and I sat down on two wooden chairs, as Rillia brought over a jug of water and two cups. "Are you okay, Rillia?" Caron asked, concern in their voice. "I can—"

"Never mind, Caron," Rillia said, setting the jug and cups down on the small table in front of us and standing straight again. Watching her tight-lipped mouth and narrowed eyes, I didn't need to have Caron's abilities to know that Rillia was angry ... and even more than that, frightened.

"All right," I said, filling Caron's cup and my own. "So you've heard a drunkard talk about people making trouble, and something about the Just God. And you think that means us?"

"Who else would it mean?" Rillia responded, voice intense, arms folded as she stood watching us.

I took a deep drink from my mug and shrugged. "Not sure. But Tellisar's a big city, and we already know the Order is a big part of it, even if it's a lot lower profile here than in Cohrelle. Could be there are others looking into the Order the same way we are, and it could be they're the ones in trouble."

Rillia scowled. "It could be that they've decided to disband and spend the rest of their miserable lives serving the poor and destitute, too, but I didn't think you liked fairy tales."

"You of all people should know I wouldn't minimize the Order, or our risk in investigating them," I said with a frown. "But you're basing this on something you overheard from some soused soldier, and we both know the dangers of relying on the words of either drunkards or soldiers."

Rillia shook her head. "This was more than that. I heard his voice, Grayshade; this didn't sound like boasting to me. And with the chances you've been taking lately, it's not surprising that the Order might have finally caught wise."

"But isn't that what we want?" Caron asked. "Don't we need the Order of Argoth to get closer to finding us if we're going to find anything out about them?"

"It's not what I want," Rillia replied, furrowing her brow. "What the two of you are doing is . . . foolish, Caron. It's putting yourself in unnecessary danger, and this proves it."

"Oh, I've been in worse danger than this," Caron replied promptly. "I was even in more danger earlier today." Rillia slowly looked in my direction as I glanced at Caron, but I already knew it was pointless; Caron's honesty was as consistent as it was, occasionally, annoying.

"So," Rillia said after a moment of silence. "What kind of danger are we talking about, Grayshade?"

I took another drink from my mug and sighed. "One of the merchants in the Gauntlet Quarter got hot under the collar when Caron asked the usual set of questions, and when Caron left, they didn't leave alone. A few lowlifes followed, and I dealt with them."

"They were going after Caron?"

"They were," I said quietly. "But it didn't happen."

"But it could have," Rillia said, eyes flashing, "and if it had, you would have been responsible."

"No," Caron said, "because I—"

"No, Caron," Rillia said, cutting them off. "This isn't about what you suggested or wanted. It's not even about your training, or your powers. It's about pushing the line from risky to foolish, and Grayshade knows, maybe better than anyone else, what that line is. He let both of you cross it, and you're both still crossing it now. What if these 'lowlifes' decide to track you down?"

"They won't," I said, thinking about the dead face of the man in the alley. "Two of them didn't even see what hit them, and they won't be interested in finding out when they wake up. The other one . . ." I trailed off while Rillia, seeing me shake my head, narrowed her eyes.

"Are you serious? You're leaving bodies unconscious in the streets and you think no one will notice? And what about the merchant?" she demanded. "He's just going to let everything go? Or are you going to 'deal with him' too?"

"What's the alternative, Rillia?" I asked, looking at her intensely. "How would you suggest we find our information about how the Order and the Service functions in Tellisar? Should we wait for them to jump us in a dark alley? Take out each one of us one by one trying to move through a crowded marketplace, in the broad daylight? Or maybe you'd rather they track us down here some evening, wipe out all of us—" I stopped as Rillia broke my gaze and looked at Caron, who was now watching Caoes as he slumbered by the fire.

I pursed my lips, then sighed and put my mug down on the table. "All right. I suppose there's enough darkness outside without bringing it here. The point is, the longer we stay here, the more at risk we are. We have to find the weak spots of the Order, and that means we need information. Neither you nor I can get enough of that information safely; if either of us gets caught, that's the end, and the one of us left has worse odds. But Caron is a random element. The Order isn't looking for them—"

"A random element? This all started because the Order had the Service send you to assassinate them," Rillia pointed out, folding her arms as she looked back at me. "They were a target before you were!"

"Yes," I replied. "But that was in Cohrelle, and the people involved are all dead. And even if the Order here was in charge of the one there—and that's another reason we need to learn more about it, by the way—Caron is much less likely to attract attention in Tellisar, a larger city with thousands of people coming and going every day, with even more trade than Cohrelle has. Besides, you're forgetting about their powers."

"Are you serious? Which of us saw those powers up close while the other was traipsing across Silarein?" Rillia looked again at Caron, who had turned away from Caoes and was focused on our conversation. Caron smiled, and Rillia's eyes softened as she returned the smile. "Obviously I haven't forgotten," she said after a moment. "I've seen what they can do, and so do you. And if the Order also sees it, and if that interests them . . ."

"You said yourself that the Order wanted Caron dead," I said. "Even if it knew about Caron's powers, it clearly saw them as more of a threat than a potential asset. And as I said, the only ones who could know for sure one way or the other can't tell anyone about it, because unlike Caron, they *are* dead."

Rillia glanced at me sharply. "Even if you won't listen to me, Caron is clearly still at risk, as your little experiment in the Gauntlet Quarter proves. And for all of this risk, we've still learned nothing."

"Not nothing," Caron said at last, and I looked at them in surprise. "Rillia's right that we haven't learned much so far . . . but that's been useful too, because we know the places *not* to look now, except maybe for Carver's shop."

"The merchant from earlier today," I said, answering an unspoken question in Rillia's glance. "But we'll deal with Carver soon."

"So outside of that," Caron went on, "we've already been in most of the rest of the Gauntlet Quarter, and not found much. We've been through much of the Helm Quarter, but there are mostly government offices and houses there, and not all that many people who aren't rushing from one place to another; unless we start going into every building, there isn't much we can find there either. The Sword Quarter is all soldiers and, well, swords, weapons and things like that; we mostly talked to soldiers or weapon merchants there about making swords and axes and hammers. And the Armor Quarter has the armor, mostly—"

"We're not sure about that," I cut in. "There's something odd about that part of the city . . . as if there's more that's not visible to outsiders. Even Cohrelle had layers, and this city is older."

"All right," Caron agreed, "so maybe we still have to look there too. But there's one place we haven't really examined much at all, except when we first got to Tellisar, to find a place to live."

"You mean here?" Rillia said, sounding incredulous. "The Sabaton Quarter?"

"It's the biggest part of the city. Most people live here."

"And we can't investigate them all, Caron," Rillia replied. "Besides, the Order isn't going to be running the Service out of someone's home."

"There are a lot of temples and taverns, too," Caron said, "and the Docks."

I shook my head. "I looked into the temples, but they're all small, no real political power that I can tell, and none of them affiliated with Argoth. I checked out most of the taverns when we arrived, too, but people there were as tight-lipped as they were anywhere else in this city, especially about religion. They're much less interested in talking about their faith, any faith, over a drink . . . and I can tell you the Order has never been interested in taverns or pubs anyway. In Cohrelle I was one of the only Acolytes who ever spent any time in one, even if I was doing it mostly to hear about the city from another angle. As for the Docks, maybe ships docking are carrying things for the Order and maybe they aren't, but either way, most of the sailors there won't know the first thing about any of the cargo they've got in the hold, and the captains aren't going to talk to us."

Caron's expression turned thoughtful. "Then we can't find out what we need all by ourselves," they said. "My teachers always said that wisdom comes from more than just yourself. Maybe we need more friends."

I sighed heavily. "Caron, we can't trust—"

"Maybe not on the surface you can't," they said, cutting me off. "But people are more than just what they show on the outside. Some people may want to help—in a city this big, there have to be some who would want to, some who know the city better than we do."

"We can't take you around to sense every person, Caron," Rillia said. "Even with the risk, the pattern would be unmistakable."

I was surprised to hear Caron's voice waver. "Maybe, Rillia.

So let's be people." They looked between our confused expressions. "You're people," they replied, watching us earnestly. "People like them, with hopes, fears, doubts." They watched as Rillia and I exchanged glances. "Didn't you both leave the Order because it thought you were servants, slaves, not people?" they finally said. "Didn't you connect with each other, and with me, because we thought differently? Because we understood each other? So give them, and you, a chance to do the same thing."

Rillia hesitated, looked at me again, then shrugged and nodded. "I suppose you haven't been wrong much before. If you think it makes sense, I'd rather do that than keep you next to the assassin's blade."

I sighed again, but with a slight smile. "Fair enough, then. So the Sabaton Quarter: where do we try first?"

"Well, there's one place you didn't mention yet," Caron said. "If there are too many houses to search, and the temples and taverns don't work, or the Docks . . . there's still a pretty big part of the Quarter left over."

Rillia snorted, loudly enough to cause Caoes to stir in his sleep. "The Poor Markets? The Order's never cared about criminals or merchants, much less the poor and destitute."

"Exactly," Caron said with a grin. "The Order doesn't like criminals and merchants . . . so where could we find better friends to help us against the Order than the place that has the most criminals and merchants in the entire city?"

I found myself smiling along with Caron, and I looked at Rillia. "It's ridiculous, isn't it?" I said. "But it's better than anything either of us have come up with. It's late afternoon; no better time to see who the regulars are. This time you should come with us . . . but not alone." I rose from my chair and walked over to the fire, kneeling down by the bed where the panther was sleeping. Ever since meeting Caoes months ago—or being "chosen" by him, as Caron put it—I had learned to pay close attention to his condition, to draw a measure of calm from his stoic demeanor. I had named him as both a tribute to my former Trainer and a nod to the chaos of my life at the time, but in truth, few creatures helped keep my world more stable than Caoes did.

I took a moment to admire his sleek, lithe body, somehow radiating agility and grace even in rest, before leaning over and speaking. "Caoes!" I said quietly, then louder as he stretched his front legs so they were hanging over the edge of the bed. "Caoes, you've rested enough for the moment." As if in answer, the panther yawned wide, revealing two rows of teeth flanking a pink tongue, and opened his eyes, which glowed yellow in the light of the fire as he blinked slowly. "Sorry," I said, more quietly again. "But we need you, Caoes—at least, we need your ears and eyes." I looked up at Rillia, who still had a slight frown of evident concern on her face, then at Caron's thoughtful smile, before turning back to Caoes, whose yellow eyes were now gazing at me.

"We have too many questions," I said, looking back at him. "Let's go get some answers."

✦

As Caron had said, the Sabaton Quarter was the largest part of the city, and given the size of Tellisar, that was saying something. So getting to the Poor Markets was not the shortest journey, especially since we were trying to stick to the main thorough-fares, crowded with people as the day gradually gave way to early evening. I had considered taking us through the smaller back streets, which had always been the safest paths to use when I was in Cohrelle. But if the Order had indeed begun to focus their search for us, those were exactly the paths the Service would also be using, and even with Rillia and Caoes alongside, I didn't relish the prospect of dealing with a silent ambush against one or more Acolytes in the shadows of an unfamiliar alleyway. As uncomfortable as it was given my usual habits, in the midst of colorful crowds was the safest place for us to be at present.

So we took our slow, careful way, pressing through squares and crossroads swelled with people and other creatures, children and adults, cows and goats and pigs, letting the laughter, crying, yelling, and grumbling blend together into one general rush of sound as we moved along. I was in front with Caron, eyes shifting left and right as I searched the sea of faces for expressions of recognition … or expressions of searching like my own, telltale signs of the training of an Acolyte. About fifty feet behind us were Rillia and Caoes, weaving around people, animals, wagons, and wheelbarrows as they kept us in sight. In a smaller or more isolated place I would have been more concerned about people's reactions to Caoes, but I was less worried in Tellisar, where animals of all kinds were a common sight and even wild creatures were not unheard of, though I had yet to see another panther uncaged. In any case, Caoes had his ways of avoiding notice, padding quietly along below the sightlines of the travelers clogging the city streets, and most people against whom he might brush would probably assume a large dog had gone by.

In Cohrelle, crowds like this would have included a number of merchants hawking their wares among the passersby, but I had heard that this practice had been abolished some time ago in Tellisar after an argument over the cost of a set of daggers had led to a near riot, with many people hurt and trampled. Now all mercantile activity was confined to officially sanctioned places within each Quarter, with the city's notoriously inflexible Varan Guard enforcing the restriction. In the Sabaton Quarter, that meant the Poor Markets, which had started as separate stalls on different streets and had finally grown together into the largest place for sales and barters in the city . . . both legal and illegal, and ranging from barely suitable for the poor to supplying the wealthiest shops in the city. From what I could tell, there wasn't much distinction drawn between these conditions, and there were no fences needed in the Poor Markets. The Tellisarian authorities had apparently decided not to take action . . . or perhaps, as Rillia suggested, had decided to take its cut through taxation, which was fairly high in Tellisar, again enforced by the Varan Guard.

Either way, the Poor Markets was the place for buying and selling in the Sabaton Quarter, and as we finally came within sight of the first stall, its bright yellow flag waving as the sounds of buying, selling, haggling, curses, and commitments washed over us, my memory slipped for a moment into the merchant stalls of my youth. I remembered little of my childhood before the Order, covered in a haze of loneliness and pain, but the street festivals—the sights and sounds, the smells of fresh-baked spiced rolls drifting by as I hurried along, stomach rumbling—these held firm in my consciousness, and even if I had wanted to, I doubted I could shut those memories out. I never liked crowds, never felt comfortable around the masses of people found in parts of every city … except in a market, where something beyond my natural suspicions and concerns took over.

"This doesn't bother you," a voice said, and I blinked as I looked down at Caron, who was smiling up at me. "You seem … calm, peaceful. Maybe even content."

"Let's not take it too far," I said with a frown as I looked back around again, watching a woman lift a blue fabric banner on which *New Shipments Arrived* was embroidered in sparkling gold thread. "I'm more likely to be calm when there's no obvious knife at my throat, or yours, but that situation could change swiftly."

"Still," they said, "it's not your usual emotion."

I glanced at them sharply. "Are you still spying on my emotional state?" I held up a hand as I saw their brow furrow. "Sorry. I know it's not *spying*, exactly; I'm just still not used to the experience of being so … easy to read."

Caron's brow smoothed over as their usual smile returned. "Oh, you're definitely not easy to read," they said as their grin widened. "You just happen to have some consistent emotions. Something like this stands out."

"I'd rather that none of us stand out, Caron," I replied as we moved into the first row of stalls, flags and signs flanking our path. "Less focus on me and more on the people around us would be helpful."

"Oh, yes," Caron said, their expression quickly growing serious. "So far I don't really sense anything that—"

"No, no, no!" a loud voice near us suddenly said, cutting above the noise of the crowd. "You've already done enough to bankrupt me, Nuraleed." We looked in the direction of the voice to see a

short, rotund man wearing a gold and purple tunic with match-
ing pants, hands on hips, standing in front of a stand on which
rolls and loaves of bread had been arranged. His outfit gleamed
in the light of the setting sun, but he was staring at an even more
extraordinary figure. An enormous man perhaps six and a half
feet tall stood looking down at him, olive-skinned with a dark
mustache and twinkling green eyes; he wore a sleek turquoise turban, a gold caftan over a bright red tunic, and a purple sash, with a
curved, jewel-encrusted sheath at his belt. The sunlight reflecting
from the sheath was almost blinding, and the shimmering gold
caftan looked ridiculous—but there was something about the
eyes which made me pause.

Suddenly the man broke out into laughter, a deep, rumbling
sound which seemed to move the ground beneath our feet.
"Bankrupt you, Castiun? I've bought enough of your rolls to keep
you and your beloved family in the best house in the Gauntlet
Quarter for years to come," the man said, voice deep and rolling,
with an accent the origin of which I couldn't place.

"Never mind the jokes," Castiun replied, scowling. "You're
not a beggar, and I'm not a poorhouse. Three equinnes for one of
my loaves would be a bargain; three equinnes for ten is an insult."

The man called Nuraleed grinned widely as he opened his
arms and bowed slightly. "To insult an artist like you would be to
do violence to the art itself, and that I would never do," he said.
"I am seeking a way to demonstrate my appreciation in a way
which will both uplift you and provide me with a way to more
fully experience your artistry."

Castiun folded his arms. "You're seeking to rob me by giving
me a ridiculously low offer for my bread, which you will then

resell at a markup, or trade for other goods which you can in turn sell at a profit," he said sourly.

"Come on, Caron," I said. "Just two thieves squabbling."

"Wait," Caron said quietly. They were watching the exchange intensely, looking back and forth between the two men as the conversation continued.

Nuraleed laughed again. "My stalls have stood next to yours for nearly a year, Castiun, during which time I have had to suffer the exquisite torture of being wrapped in the scents of your exceptional bread every day. I have simply chosen to end that torture through a fair and reasonable offer, a sign of my admiration for your work. Surely any objective person, like these people," he said, suddenly sweeping his arm in a grand gesture in our direction, "would agree that such an offer could never be seen as an act of robbery. It is a sign of deep respect."

Castiun sighed. "This is how you operate, Nuraleed: flatter and cajole, convince the other party that you find them enthralling and extraordinary, then fleece them for all they're worth."

Nuraleed's eyes widened, and his mouth opened in apparent shock. "I'm deeply wounded," he said after a moment, "that you would so impugn my reputation, or my intentions. From a generosity of spirit and a dedication to our close connection, I was prepared to raise my already substantial offer to five equinnes. But it appears there is no reason to demonstrate my full commitment to an honest and fair arrangement for us both."

"Five equinnes is still half of what this is worth," Castiun said. "Nine equinnes is more than honest and fair, but I'm willing to take nine simply to keep you from plaguing me."

"Would that I could empty my purse so completely," the

larger man countered, "but alas, I am in no such position. I have only six equinnes remaining."

"Seven."

"One more than I have, sadly. It seems I will have to remain in my state of torture."

Castiun's eyes narrowed as he studied Nuraleed's face, perhaps looking for a break in the man's placid demeanor. Finally he shook his head. "Fine, six it is, you thief," he growled. "But one payment; no installments this time. And if—" Suddenly he stopped and turned, and with a swift motion he stepped behind his bread stand and reached down, prompting a high-pitched yelp from an unseen figure. "I won't be robbed twice in one day, gutter rat," the merchant hissed as he pulled up, none too gently, a child of perhaps seven or eight years old, dressed in a brown tunic, pants, and hat; their face was filthy, and the matted dark hair extending below the hat didn't look much cleaner. In one of their hands they clutched a roll.

I glanced at Caron, but they were still staring at Nuraleed; behind me, I knew, Rillia might well be staring just as intensely at me. For his part, Nuraleed was silent, watching the scene unfold.

"You see, Nuraleed," Castiun said, holding the child by the shoulder, "this is what happens when people believe they can take things from others with impunity. And this is what should happen when they get caught. Guard!" he shouted. The child did not struggle or protest, but looked up at me with dark, hollow eyes I understood all too well. I had seen it before, from the desperately hungry and poor, from those who had given up on everything but the grinding drive to survive, whatever the cost. Yes, I had seen it before.

When I was young, I had felt it.

I stepped forward, but hesitated, gaze still on the child. To expose us for a memory, for a young thief who would probably be dead within the month anyway, was more than foolish . . . but still—

"Perhaps that is not needed, Castiun," a deep voice said, and startled out of my reverie, I looked up to see Nuraleed, arms by his sides. "How much is that roll? I'll pay the child's debt."

Castiun snorted. "Now you're in the mood to be generous? I don't think so. We've already had our discussion." He looked down at the motionless child. "This one's for the Guard."

Nuraleed frowned. "Perhaps an . . . alteration to our original deal is in order."

The other merchant looked up slowly, eyes narrowed. "Ten equinnes," he said slowly. Nuraleed's mustache twitched, but after a moment he gave a tight nod. Taking his purse from his belt, he tossed it to Castiun, who caught it with his free hand.

"You got lucky," he said to the child. "Don't count on your luck saving you again." With a push, he let the child go. "I assume you can take care of the stock, Nuraleed," he said with a chuckle, before turning and vanishing into the swirling crowds. The child stared up at Nuraleed, but only for a moment, as the massive man sank to one knee, bringing his eyes level with theirs. I could not hear what he said, but after a few words he rose, went to the bread stand and collected several rolls and loaves into a brown paper wrapping, then came back to the child and handed them over. The child stared for a moment at the bundle in their hands, then up at Nuraleed, then glanced for a second at us before turning and darting into the crowd, where they were quickly lost to sight.

I heard a small laugh, and glancing down I saw Caron watching the child vanish. Then their eyes twinkled. "But see: where better to find a friend?" they asked as they turned. And following their gaze, I saw Nuraleed looking at us with a quizzical expression, his arms folded over his gleaming gold and red-clothed torso.

CHAPTER THREE

"WHILE I appreciate your consideration of my talents, friends, I'm not sure I understand what use I could be to you," Nuraleed said, a wide smile on his face. We were sitting (all but Caoes, who had slipped into an alley as we headed out of the crowd of people) in a tavern near the Poor Markets—called, without a trace of irony, *The Fair Deal*—to which the merchant had brought us right after the incident with Castiun and the girl. "I am a merchant, skilled in the arts of trade and bargaining. It is clear to me that you are . . . something else. What value could my knowledge have for you?"

"Oh, a lot of value," Caron replied promptly with their usual smile. "We need to know more about how Tellisar works—all of Tellisar—and you would be a perfect person to help."

"Mmm," Nuraleed replied, mustache shifting. "And you?" he asked, turning to me. "You seem to let your child do most of the talking." I glanced at Rillia, who was sitting next to me, a bemused expression on her face. Caron had not explicitly said we were their parents, but had done nothing to correct the merchant's assumption . . . and since Rillia had not done so either, I had little choice but to go along. I tried not to think much about what I would have said if I had been asked directly.

"Caron speaks for themself," I said briefly. "I—we trust them to know their own mind. And they seem to think you could help, if you're willing to do so." I glanced at Rillia, who nodded tightly.

Nuraleed laughed suddenly, the sound rumbling through the wood of the table around which we were sitting, then drank from the mug in front of him. "Not everyone trusts children to have their own minds ... or adults, for that matter," he said after setting the mug back down. "It is quite a risk to think for oneself." He winked. "The authorities don't like it, for one thing. And in this city, there are few things which an honest person of business can engage in which the authorities *do* like. Other places are more ... forgiving."

"So you've been to a lot of places?" Caron asked.

"Of course," Nuraleed replied, tilting his head slightly as if he were trying to appraise the worth of an offered barter. "Merchants seldom succeed by staying in one place, at least not until they've established themselves. Even then, why would one want to stay, when the wide seas beckon and the opposite shore invites?" He threw his arms as wide as his smile. "The world, my friends, is much larger than the walls of Tellisar, or the borders of Silarein, can contain. One must embrace all of it if one is to truly live."

"Then where did you come from originally?" I cut in before Caron could reply. The man had charm to spare, but I had heard pretty words before ... words which, coming from merchants, could easily be twisted to whatever purpose the speaker chose. "What parts of the world have you embraced?"

Nuraleed's green eyes glittered. "Ahh, there is a tale," he said slowly, his smile undaunted. "But one too long for this most fortunate meeting, I think." His eyes narrowed as he considered me. "But if you would have the overbrief summary: I am a humble citizen from Al'Estra, far to the south. I have only been in Tellisar for a few months ... long enough to miss my own climate and people," he chuckled. "Still, the market is quite good here, and I do have a certain ... fondness for the people of your country. If only more of them understood how to properly bake a roll, I wouldn't have to barter my way to a halfway decent meal." He gave us a mournful look as he took a long drink from his mug.

"Al'Estra," I said. "I don't think I've heard of that."

"It's a city on the coast of Cartevis," Rillia said, breaking her silence at last.

"Ah, she knows ... and she speaks!" Nuraleed said, his smile returned. "I had wondered whether your silence was a permanent state."

Rillia frowned and folded her arms. "I've been a merchant for quite a while, and goods from Al'Estra were always highly prized ... especially silk and other refined fabrics. And I speak when I need to. I don't like to waste words."

"Sadly, I have the opposite problem. Words are part of my stock in trade, and in some ways I spend more time buying and selling language, you might say, than physical goods. Conversation leads to commitment, you see. Yet how many of my words have I ... how did you say it ... 'wasted' over the years?" Nuraleed shook his head. "I could not count them. I must make more to compensate for their tragic loss." He raised his mug with a flourish, before setting it down. "In any case, my city of Al'Estra is as subject to a desire for power, as at risk for corruption, as anywhere else. Yet my people seem less driven by it than the people in Tellisar. I suspect it is the weather."

"The weather?" Rillia asked, raising an eyebrow.

"Why, naturally. The winters here are desperately cold. How can anyone concentrate on anything but avoiding death by freezing?" Nuraleed gave an exaggerated shiver as he picked up his mug again. "Not even this brew can keep up with what the people here describe as their 'weather.'" He drank deeply, then pulled an enormous red and gold silken handkerchief from a pocket at his belt and wiped some of the leftover foam from his mustache. "Narlend!" he roared, causing an old man in front of him to stumble forward in surprise. "Another, my friend, if you have enough of this swill to go around!" He chuckled, then looked back at us. "But if it is not the weather, then it is the way the city, how can I say this . . . imagines itself, let us say. There was a time not so long ago when Tellisar was driven by military honor and financial return. But for the last few years, it has turned its attention to other matters: expansion. Control of territory. Power." He shook his head. "Tellisar still wants money. It is what it wants that money for which has changed."

I exchanged a glance with Rillia. "We haven't been in Tellisar for long. Why has their motivation changed? Has a new leader come to power?"

Nuraleed gave me a searching look. "The leaders here come to power only with the consent of the noble families who support them, and those families are the same which founded Tellisar centuries ago. Leaders come and go, but the families stay." He nodded as the barkeep Narlend, a thin man with a perpetually fixed smirk, put down a fresh mug in front of Nuraleed and took away the used one in one swift motion, vanishing into the crowd between our table and the counter on the other side of the room.

"And religion? The church?" I asked, trying to sound casual.

Nuraleed's eyes narrowed. "There are many faiths here. But the main religion, the one to which all subscribe, is profit. That, too, has not changed."

"Except the Order of Argoth," Caron said promptly. "They're stronger than they used to be, right?"

Nuraleed nodded slowly. "Argoth, yes. I must admit that my spiritual interests are not overly developed; I am more concerned with the work of this life before I take up the labors of the next. Much of Tellisar seems to be the same way. Yet I have heard of this Order of Argoth more than once, as quiet as they are. It sounds as if you have some familiarity with them, then?"

Caron nodded. "Yes. We've . . . met some of them before."

"Merchants elsewhere in Silarein, even elsewhere on the continent, deal with them a lot," Rilla put in. "They control much of the trade where they are more active."

"Of course," Nuraleed said, though I wondered if his resilient smile had wavered just a bit before drinking from the fresh mug. "In any case," he went on with a sigh, "though I would dearly love to discuss politics and economics and selling, I must again say with some sadness that my time is limited. What, then, could an exceedingly engaging merchant, husband, and child, wish from me?"

"A new start," Caron said, grinning at me as Rillia stared, probably still processing Nuraleed's use of the word "husband."

"Er . . . yes," I said after a moment's hesitation. "I suppose it could be put like that."

I hesitated, not sure where to go next, but from the smile on Caron's face I had a feeling they already had a plan.

"Well, we're not from here, or even from a large city," Caron said, an expression of perfect innocence on their face. "We come from a small village, a long way from Tellisar. This is Carrnisk, and this is Rivinnea," they went on, pointing to myself and Rillia in turn. "As Carrnisk said, we haven't been here for long, and we need . . . help. Not money—just knowledge."

I risked glancing at Rillia, who looked as stunned as I felt. Caron was honest to a fault. They were the opposite of foolish, but asking them to maintain a convenient fiction was liable to produce a pleasant smile and a reference to a lesson from their teachers about the dangers of disingenuous language. Yet here they were, making up a story about us from whole cloth as easily as any honey-tongued thief asking their mark for directions while getting in position to pick their pocket. I wasn't sure whether to be proud or profoundly troubled.

Nuraleed pursed his lips. "Knowledge?"

"Yes. In our old village we got kind of a . . . well, not the best reputation."

Nuraleed raised an eyebrow. "Reputation?"

Caron's expression grew troubled. "Yes. While working for Carrnisk and Rivinnea, I found out that the other merchant in the village was being dishonest—cheating people out of their money for basic needs, milk and cheese and bread. Carrnisk has a very strong sense of duty, and felt he needed to say something." They looked at me, apparently for confirmation.

"Yes . . . well," I said. "I . . . didn't want the people to get hurt."

"Of course," Nuraleed said. "Commendable." He smiled, but I was pretty certain I didn't just imagine his gaze holding mine for a moment longer than necessary before turning back to Caron.

"Well, the merchant was extremely angry about being found

out, and threatened us. Carrnisk and Rivinnea were both worried about me—about all of us, really. As an orphan, now with a mark on me, they offered for me to stay with them, and continue to help. So we left and came here. We thought a big city with a lot of people would be a good place to be for a while until things were better back home." The bang of a mug hitting the ground near the front of the tavern, followed by loud laughter, pulled me from my admiration of Caron's story—one which, while an abject false-hood, was as close a metaphor for my actual situation as I could have imagined. Even Caron's lies seemed rooted in fundamental truths.

"A powerful tale," Nuraleed observed with a slight bow of his head, "reflective of a good conscience and courageous demeanor. Truly inspiring! But I think you have come to the wrong place if you're trying to find more honest people. As I said, I have a cer-tain fondness for Tellisarians, but I cannot claim that they have a greater sense of, how shall I put it, *morality* than anyone else. Given a good and fair deal or a better and scurrilous one, they will wink at the misdeed and take the fatter purse, as sorry as I am to say it."

"Oh, we're not looking for more honest people," Caron said with a smile. "We'd be happy to learn better ways to figure out if someone is honest or not. We need to learn how to, um . . ." They trailed off, looking at me, then Rillia. "We can't stop selling things completely, if we're going to get enough money to survive," they finally said, returning their gaze to the merchant. "So we need to learn to blend in, I guess. Especially in the merchant areas, the ones here and in the other quarters. Just in case the merchant from our village comes looking for us."

Nuraleed nodded slowly. "And you think that I can, in some extraordinary way, help you to 'blend in'?"

Caron looked at me again, and I cleared my throat. "We were ... impressed by how you handled that situation with the girl who stole the bread. And because of that, Caron believes that you can be trusted to be honest."

Nuraleed's mustache twitched furiously before he threw back his head and laughed uproariously, rattling the mug on the table. "Honesty!" he finally managed after catching his breath. "To accuse anyone of 'honesty' here is, my friends, a most terrible insult."

"We mean it," Caron said.

"That makes the insult even more terrible," Nuraleed laughed again. Then he caught sight of Rillia's and my stony expressions and grew serious again. "A thousand apologies, friends. Mine is the curse of an experienced nature. In truth," he said as he leaned forward and dropped his voice, as if he were in a silent sanctuary rather than a loud tavern, "I *am* honest, though I will deny it completely if you say so." He winked. "But even then, I am at a loss as to why this fact is of value to you."

"Because you can teach us without cheating us," Caron responded. All of us stared at them.

"Teach you ..." Nuraleed finally said.

"To blend in, as we said," Caron said. "To be one of the merchants here. To seem like we belong in Tellisar, and in the markets. To gather information so we can blend in even more easily. To, I guess you could say ..." They hesitated. "To disappear. If we need to."

Nuraleed leaned back in his chair and rubbed the back of

his neck. "I am flattered by your trust, Caron. Indeed you are as extraordinary as I had guessed. To teach you without cheating you!" He shook his head and chuckled, then spread his hands wide. "But I am no teacher. I have no skill in instruction, at least not in terms which the untrained might easily understand." Something struck me about his use of the term "untrained," but I couldn't quite decide what it was as he continued. "And again, my time is limited. While I would like nothing better than to help you in your fascinating pursuits, I have responsibilities—"

"We'll pay you," I interrupted, knowing I would be the next to be stared at. But I had decided that Nuraleed might indeed have value to us ... though not in the way Caron seemed to be imagining.

"Carrnisk," Rillia started, the false name sounding unfamiliar in her voice. "Shouldn't we—"

"We'll pay you well," I went on. "You would be helping three innocent people avoid harm. You would be discovering more about our ... fascinating pursuits, which I'm guessing you're more interested in than you're willing to admit. And you'd be compensated." I paused, then added, "After all, you have a whole new bread stand to pay for." I studied Nuraleed's face carefully as his mustache shifted again, his eyes wide.

Finally he laughed again, quietly at first, then louder and louder. Then he grabbed his mug from the table and downed what was left in it with one long pull. "Extraordinary!" he said, beaming at us as he set the mug down. "Never did I imagine this morning, when again preparing to experience the particular charms of this frozen wasteland some whimsically call a city, that I was to encounter an individual, indeed, a whole group of people as astonishing as the company with which I am currently graced. Indeed the Spirits are at work in even the most unexpected conditions. Narlend!" he roared again, voice rumbling through the noise of the crowd like thunder. "If you want to be paid for this swill, you robber, come forth so I can pay you before I change my mind."

He winked again at us as the barkeep made his way toward our table. "Very well, friends. I agree to your intriguing proposition. Only a few—let us call them 'lessons,' if you will, in return for your stimulating presence and the promised reward. Being rewarded 'well,' if I recall your words correctly, Carrnisk." He drew an outrageously flamboyant purse from his belt, covered in golden and red flowers, and counted out several coins which he handed to Narlend, who bowed slightly and vanished as quickly as he had come. "And now it is time for me to return to my shop before the Poor Markets close," Nuraleed said as he rose from the table, displacing as he did so several workers, slightly unsteady on their feet, who had stumbled a bit too close to the merchant's chair. "I will not be much good to you, as a teacher of mercantile talents, if I bankrupt myself through missing easy sales at the end of the day."

"Where will we find you?" I asked.

"The same place where you found me before," Nuraleed replied. "What better place to learn how to be honest and dishonest—and when to choose each particular condition?" He chuckled. "Timing, friend Carrnisk, is everything. The difference between a prosperous merchant, such as myself—" he spread his hands wide, apparently emphasizing the richness of his attire— "and those who have been, let us say, less fortunate, is often quite small. Good judgment, and good timing, is the key. If you have chosen your humble instructor properly, I will teach you about both." He turned away and took a step, then stopped. "Tomorrow, in the Poor Markets, near my stand," he said. "Do not be late to class, my most unusual students." He laughed and headed off, the crowd parting around him as he went, the sound of his rich and merry voice audible over the noise of the tavern until he was well and truly gone.

I leaned back slowly. "Interesting."

"Interesting!" Rillia said, voice tight as she looked around. "This isn't interesting, it's stupid—stupidity of the highest order. This man can't be trusted, and even if he could, this is a dangerous waste of our time. We're exposing ourselves to discovery and attack for certain. You saw what he was like; a volcano would have more discretion."

"A volcano couldn't have helped the child Nuraleed did," Caron replied, looking into the crowded room as if they could still see the merchant. "Most merchants think only of their own purses. You taught me that, Rillia."

Rillia pursed her lips. "Yes, I did. And this merchant didn't even ask your price for these 'lessons.' There's no reason to believe he isn't thinking of his own purse now, by selling us out when he has the opportunity. The child could have been working with him, for all we know, or the one who owned the bread stand. And even if he isn't trying to set us up, what exactly are we supposed to learn from his galumphing around and bowing and scraping? Either he's as single-minded and ridiculous as he seems, in which case we won't learn anything useful from him, or he's smart enough to play us for fools, in which case we're walking directly into a trap with our eyes blindfolded and hands tied behind our backs. In either case we lose." She paused, looking at me. "I understand Caron's take on this . . . don't agree with it, but it's consistent with what they believe. But you?" She shook her head. "I don't understand you at all, Grayshade. You've had informants much closer to you than Nuraleed could ever be, and you didn't trust them. Now you see an opportunity to shape things here in Tellisar, and you've decided to throw every caution to the wind and put everything you care about at risk, with a man you don't know, for the sake of proving some point I can't fathom."

"Coming to Tellisar was a risk from the beginning," I pointed out. "And every moment we delay compounds that risk. I still think we made the right decision to push that merchant earlier today. But say that I'm wrong, Rillia; say that I've lost my edge, that Caron and I are wandering around in the dark. How do you propose we step into the light?" Rillia's glare intensified, but she said nothing, and after a few moments of silence I sighed. "But in any case, I don't trust Nuraleed any more than you do, and considerably less than Caron does." I glanced at the child, whose forehead was furrowed as they looked at me. "You think he can get us information—reliable information," I said.

They nodded. "I sensed his interest in us . . . and his surprise. I don't think we're what he expected. And the merchant he managed to talk out of punishing that girl in the market was genuinely angry; I could sense that too. That situation was real, and Nuraleed handled it with kindness. It's a good combination."

"Unless he's lying to us now," Rillia said. "You can't sense that yet."

Caron nodded. "Not yet. But I can sense hesitation, uncertainty, doubt. He didn't have any of that. I think we can trust him, or at least trust him to teach us some of what he knows."

Rillia turned her gaze back to me. "But you say you don't trust him. So what's your play?"

"It's because I don't trust him that we *have* a play," I said with a small smile. "I think Nuraleed may have information ... or, more specifically, his sources can, if he's not who he says he is. The Markets should be closed within the hour, along with his shop. I'm going to tail him when he leaves, and we'll see what 'responsibilities' he goes to attend to then."

"What if he sees you?" Caron asked.

"He won't."

Rillia sighed. "And in the meantime, we're supposed to wait quietly at home?"

"Not at all," I said, rising from the table just after Narlend passed us again, heading for a newly arrived group of eager drinkers on the other side of the room. "I need you to gather any information you can on Nuraleed, whether it's in the Poor Markets or elsewhere. Maybe we can get a sense of what other people who deal with him all the time think of his 'mercantile talents,' and your story of being a merchant will cover you if someone gets suspicious. Caoes can stay with Caron to protect them while we're away."

Caron frowned. "And what should I do?"

"You," I said, "need to think, and talk to those teachers of yours. If Rillia and I are right, and Nuraleed isn't on the level, we need to know why he's as interested in us as you say he is. Maybe we're just marks to him ... or maybe we're something more."

"My teachers always said," Caron replied slowly, "that people tend to become what they're treated as, good or bad … even in the Cloud. If you see him as suspicious, isn't it more likely that's how he's going to be, at least toward you?"

I sighed and shrugged. "Maybe. Someday, Caron, I hope our world of the Cloud is more like the world of Varda's teachers. Until then, I must deal with things as I find them, suspicious or not."

"So long as you can try to make them better along the way," they replied. I nodded as I turned to go, but made no reply. As always, my problem was never about knowing the real world, filled with people like Rillia and me. It was about knowing how it could be different, if only it were filled with people more like Caron.

CHAPTER FOUR

I paused just outside *The Fair Deal* and glanced around quickly, scanning the street and passersby, of which there weren't many; most people were probably still at the Poor Markets or in other quarters of the city, not taking a late afternoon trip to a tavern. While the people I did see walking by didn't seem to take any particular notice of me, the best way to attract unwanted notice is to spend too much time in one place. I drew my cloak around me, but before I could take a right onto the small street which led back to the thoroughfare on which the Poor Markets sat, I heard the tavern door open behind me.

"Wait," a voice said, and I turned to see Rillia, who had stepped outside and was looking around just as I had been.

"I thought we were leaving separately," I said.

"We will; I'll bring Caron home with Caoes before heading out myself. But first I wanted to talk to you without anyone else nearby to hear . . . tavern goers or merchants." She turned her gaze to me, but it was not angry as it had been inside. She looked . . . thoughtful, perhaps, or even a bit sad.

"Or sensates?" I asked.

She nodded slowly. "Maybe especially them. I'm worried, Grayshade. Caron has been . . . uncertain, lately. If I didn't know them better, I'd say they're even a little confused once in a while."

I furrowed my brow. "I haven't noticed that."

"I'm not surprised." She held up my hand as I was about to respond. "I don't mean you're not paying attention; you probably know them better than anyone besides their teachers. But you've been so focused on the Order that you might not have noticed anything closer to home. And Caron certainly wouldn't tell you."

"Why?"

"Because they want to help, and they don't want you distracted by them."

"I can do two things at once. More, if needed. And they should know that."

Rillia frowned. "Not indefinitely, you can't, and they know that too. In fact, they know both of us—how we're feeling, how we're managing—as well, or better, as we do ourselves. But we don't have to be sensates to tell if something's off about Caron, and I'm telling you there is."

I nodded. "All right . . . I'll keep it in mind."

"One other thing," she said. "When we got to the tavern, I told Caoes to wait in the alley for me . . . but he didn't go right away. He hesitated at first, then growled at something. I looked myself, and I thought I might have seen something, but not clearly—the alley is narrow and covered in shadow, and there was too much noise coming from within the building to make out any quiet sounds. I thought about going in myself to check, but you were in there alone with Caron, and I wanted to hear what Nuraleed had to say myself . . . and besides, after a minute Caoes went in there anyway. It was probably nothing."

"But?" I asked.

She hesitated. "I don't want to jump at shadows, but I don't want to ignore them either," she finally said. "And what I thought

I saw . . ." She swallowed. "Whatever it was vanished immediately. But it might have been a person. A person . . . in a cloak."

———————◆———————

The crowd in the Poor Markets was thinning out when I arrived there, the sun already set and the lanterns lit for the evening. But as I made my way toward the stand where we had first met Nuraleed earlier that day, I didn't pay much attention to the people hurrying home in any case. My thoughts were elsewhere . . . on Rillia, Caron and Caoes, and cloaked figures in the shadows.

I had talked a good game with Nuraleed and Rillia in *The Fair Deal*, but it had become clear that the slow and steady path we had been following since getting to Tellisar wasn't leading anywhere, except further into danger we weren't prepared to handle. And even if I could manage that kind of risk myself—and I had learned over the past six months that pretending I was the only one who could change the world in which I lived was a fool's bargain—I wasn't prepared to expose any of the others to what might happen. We needed to push things further, force our enemies into the open.

It sounded right. But there were still too many variables I couldn't control. Rillia was more than capable of taking care of herself; in fact, she was clearly better at that than I was. Had it not been for her, I would never have made it out of the Cathedral in Cohrelle . . . or made it, even for a brief time, out of the darkness into which my soul had fallen. But like me, she was a newcomer to Tellisar, and had not been trained, or corrupted, by the Service for nearly as long as I was. She had been an excellent Acolyte, but as a renegade, like me? I had no idea how either of us would us hold up . . . or, if I was being completely honest, how *I* would hold up if anything happened to her.

And then there was Caron. No doubt it was true that they wanted to help, had always, since I had met them, wanted to help in any way they could. Why they were so determined to help me, the man who had been sent to kill them before coming to his senses and recognizing the difference between faithful obedience and dogmatic fervor, was even now unclear. Yet I had to accept it as true, after all I had seen and felt from them. Still, even if I had learned that underestimating Caron was a mistake, I knew that even they had their limits. If Rillia was right, and something was wrong with Caron, I had to ask them about it, before it became a problem even they couldn't handle. I was used to physical targets, not intangible feelings. But I needed to adjust, grow sensitive to things beyond what my training and senses revealed. If I had done so earlier in my life, things might have been different.

More by instinct than awareness, I ducked out of the way of an awning above one of the larger stands being closed for the night, and brought my attention to the moment. *The past and future are bookends*, my old trainer Caoesthenes had once said; *they hold things together, but sometimes you need to focus on what you're reading in the present.* As for what I was meant to read with the cloaked figure . . . I shook my head. *Control what you can*, I thought, *and focus on what's in front of you.*

I slowed my pace and moved behind several rows of closed stands, careful not to stand out as I did so. Most of the merchants had already left by now, and only a few guards remained, wandering slowly up and down as they looked for opportunistic thieves hiding under stalls or behind stands. But they were looking for street urchins, children like the girl we had seen earlier, desperate people trying to survive. I had been desperate too, more than once. But I had learned to hide it, to bury it down deep, where only I could feel it, and only I would pay the price . . . or so I had thought, until I had learned that others I cared about would be forced to pay it too.

Still, old habits die hard, and years of training were not undone by six months of reassessing the values by which I lived my life. So no guards noticed me as I passed by the last row of stands before the one in which Nuraleed kept his shop, crouching down behind the furthest stall and peering out cautiously. Sure enough, even in the lantern light, the combination of turquoise, gold, red, and purple was unmistakable, as Nuraleed bent over his stand, securing something on its end. After a moment he turned around and headed in my direction . . . but I had already ducked out of the way and slid back a few feet, counting the seconds before the merchant passed my position and out of the row. I watched as he left the square, waving to a guard as he went, then waited for the guard to turn away and continue their rounds while I quickly moved to the edge of the square, then slipped into an alley to follow Nuraleed.

I had followed more than my share of targets over the years, some fast, some slow, some oblivious, some drunk. But I couldn't remember the last time I had followed someone quite as cheery as Nuraleed. He spent most of his time whistling loudly, occasionally breaking into snatches of some song about a merchant who sold stolen trinkets, became fabulously rich, and then had everything stolen back from her. In Nuraleed's rich, bass voice, this was somehow more a fun tale than a tragedy. If Nuraleed himself had been trying to summon every thief and cutpurse in a mile radius, he could scarcely have done more than he was doing. A *ralaar* would have made less noise than the man did, and might not have occupied much more space; he seemed to fill every alley and street down which he was walking, beyond even his imposing physical stature.

I could have followed someone like this if I were blinded and deafened, and Nuraleed's presence was so overwhelming that anyone coming across us would have paid little attention to me, even if they had noticed I was there. But I remained cautious. For all his bluster and noise, there was a casual grace about Nuraleed which set off warning bells, and besides, I had my own concerns about discovery. So I trailed at a respectful distance, sliding from shadow to shadow, as I had once done in another city far from here, and far from who I was now. Still, if I closed my eyes, I could picture the streets of the Merchant District in Cohrelle, an inattentive merchant who had crossed the Order of Argoth wandering down Commerce Street, me in silent pursuit, my blade drawn and ready for purpose.

My eyes remained open. I was in Tellisar, not Cohrelle, and I needed information, not blood, from the man I followed. If that changed ... well. I put the possibility in the back of my mind where it belonged as we continued our course.

Nuraleed made his way from street to street at the same relaxed pace, greeting guards and the occasional startled resident hurrying home before a growling voice and notched blade could divest them of their property. Soon we passed from the Sabaton to the Gauntlet Quarter, where Caron and I had been earlier that day ... though not in quite the same place, as the merchant headed toward the residential part of the Quarter, where most of those who ran the stores and shops of the area lived. As we moved along, our way lit by lanterns hung on curved poles above us as we went, I began to doubt myself. I was increasingly feeling like I was following someone on their way home for the night, not a mark tracing a careful course to a secret meeting or forbidden group. At best, I might have simply wasted time which could have been used to much better effect.

I had just about decided to give up the pursuit and return home, working out what to report to Rillia along the way, when Nuraleed abruptly veered from his course, turning sharply left into an alley. I crouched behind a barrel a few feet away and peered around and above me. Nothing about the area seemed particularly exposed. There were a couple of small, squat houses along each side of this narrow, roughly cobblestoned street, and the roofs were mildly sloped; I could see most of them from my vantage point, and other than a few gabled skylights, nothing was on top of them that I could see. Waiting a moment longer, I emerged from behind the barrel and walked slowly up to the edge of the alley down which Nuraleed had just gone. Looking down it, I saw it was quite short, quickly widening into a larger, open space in the middle of which stood a house ... and as I watched, a flash of gold and red vanished through the door beside which two lit lanterns hung.

I paused for a moment, looking behind me at the deserted street before again focusing my attention on the house. There was nothing particularly unusual about it from the outside; it was a single floor structure, perhaps a bit shabby by the standard of typical merchant homes in the Gauntlet Quarter. But I had spent years looking for details that others missed—specifically in this case, the fact that it was set back from the street, and with a definite space separating it from other buildings. Most thieves would happily rob a home with roof access, but they would think twice about having to leap a ten foot gap from a standing position . . . especially when that position was at the precarious edge of one of the sloped roofs which surrounded the area, which also made a running jump impossible. There were no windows to be seen on the front wall, and I knew if I circumnavigated the building I wasn't likely to find any windows on the other walls either.

No, this was a building intended to prevent easy access from the outside. But defenses only work against the tactics they're designed for . . . and Rillia and I had been rebuilding our weapons and other useful items since we arrived in Tellisar. Neither of us had Caoesthenes's ingenuity or consummate skill in fabricating tools for those trained by the Service, but together, we had a good idea of what we might need—including, fortunately, fly hooks.

I made my cautious way down the alley, looking in all directions for silent watchers or potential traps as I went. It had only taken Nuraleed a matter of seconds to traverse the alley and the space beyond it to the front door of the building, but I had not seen him do it, and had no idea what secret signs or hidden tokens he might have used to pass by. Yet I heard and saw nothing, and after some tense seconds I reached the edge of the open space within which the building sat. I put my hand on the right-hand wall just inside the alley and closed my eyes, letting the quiet rhythm of my heartbeat and the muted sounds of a city gradually sinking into sleep recede to the back of my consciousness. Through the wall, I felt the regular vibrations of someone snoring, heard the nearly silent creaking of the floor as something small—perhaps a cat—took a few steps, then turned in place before lying down, purring softly. Beyond that was the sound of two people talking, while a teakettle sang out, ready for its water to be poured in preparation for an evening tea. All was normal, quiet . . . boring, just as I had hoped. Soundshifting had many benefits, not least the confidence of knowing where safety lay.

I opened my eyes and stepped back from the wall, and after a visual appraisal of the roof above, leaped up and grabbed the edge, pulling myself up onto the sloped surface. I might have had a harder time doing this near where we lived in the Sabaton Quarter, where the roofs were thin and, after a few years of wear, barely able to hold out rain and wind, much less the weight of someone larger than the one who fashioned it in the first place. But here the buildings were sturdier, and with little effort I was up on the roof. Reaching inside my cloak I pulled out Rillia's and my version of a fly hook: a crude copy, really, three metal prongs surrounding a metal weight attached to a length of thin, strong rope. From the outside it probably looked ridiculous, more a child's toy than something intended for serious work. But it was the mechanism which mattered, and I knew that it would function well enough for my purposes. I took a quick look around to confirm there were no rooftop watchers, then whispered a few words and spun the hook above my head slowly before releasing it toward the roof of the building opposite. It arced lazily up and over the intervening space before landing on the middle of the slope without even a hint of sound—as the words I had whispered to it, part of a modified soundshifting technique to temporarily silence any noise on a given object, were designed to do—then, as I slowly pulled the rope taut, embedded in the surface of the roof. I hooked my end into the tiles of the roof on my side, pulled on the rope again to make sure it was secure, then stood. After one more look around, I began to cross, one foot after the other.

I had always enjoyed the experience of maintaining balance in the air, of using my knowledge and skill to, even for a little while, pull free from the hardness of the ground below. But the feeling this time was both familiar ... and unpleasant. The last time I had done an aerial entry like this had been in Cohrelle, many months ago, and the result of that mission had eventually changed everything for me, the Order, and the city. Given what I knew now, would I have done what I did then—throw away my sense of order, stability, and purpose, all in exchange for the truth?

Of course I would, I thought. *I would always rather know.* But another part of me was not so sure. *Knowledge is the foundation of action*, Caoesthenes always said; what he hadn't told me was that some knowledge was also the foundation of fear, of doubt ... of self-loathing. Which foundation I would ultimately build the rest of my life upon was still an open question.

I was now in the middle of the rope, moving steadily along as I took slow but sure steps. I wasn't too far above the ground; I wouldn't be badly hurt if I fell. But I had taken this approach to avoid any notice from below, where it was most likely to be, and a sudden arrival on the street from above would do the exact opposite of what I hoped. And though I hadn't seen anything obvious, I hadn't had much time to survey the area, and I felt exposed here in the open. I focused my attention on the last stretch of rope. *A*

*few more steps, and information you need on the other side. Stay in
the moment.*

In less than a minute, I stepped slowly and carefully on to
the roof of the building where Nuraleed had entered, bending
low and keeping my stance wide to minimize pressure points of
weight where the surface could bend or creak. There was no sky-
light or window on the roof, but I needed none . . . just a surface.
With some difficulty I managed to shift into a prone position,
facing down the roof's slope in the direction of the street, lay my
head flat onto the surface of the tiles, and closed my eyes, reaching
out with my senses as my breath stilled.

". . . no," a thin, reedy voice was saying. "I don't see it at all.
And even if you're right, we can't just assume he's reliable."

"I am right," a deep, familiar voice said—Nuraleed for certain. "And we don't have to assume anything, Markas. It fits the
timeline we already had; he's been in the city for enough months
for it to fit."

"If it's the same person. But anyone with a similar description
could have been in Tellisar for the same length of time."

There was a long chuckle. "What do you take me for, my
love?" Nuraleed finally said. "You think I do not know the difference between people in this city?"

"I think you haven't been in Tellisar as long as I have,
Nuraleed," came the reply. "This city is larger than you think, and
some of its people more cunning than you'd like to believe. What
worked elsewhere won't necessarily work here." I certainly hadn't
heard this voice before . . . but both the cadence and the content
reminded me of more than one conversation from my past, of
two supremely confident people each certain they were right,

while the fate of someone else hung in the balance. But who the "someone else" was ...

"It is because the city is larger, and some of its people cunning, that I know I am correct," Nuraleed said. "It takes time to establish a foothold, and this man has done so in a remarkably short period of time. And we are not the only ones who have noticed that he and his friends are most unusual."

There was a long sigh. "Argoth, you mean," the voice said, and it took all of my training to keep from starting and possibly giving myself away. I opened my eyes and blinked several times, then shook my head and laid it back down, refocusing on the conversation.

Nuraleed laughed. "Yes, indeed. From what you told me, the Order has been asleep in Tellisar for some time. Now it appears they have awoken again; something has stirred them up, something more than just a desire to reacquaint themselves with city politics."

"And you think this man is the one responsible?"

Nuraleed chuckled. "Who can say? It would seem unlikely that one man can outthink and outmaneuver the Order, or indeed any elite organization here. But many things have seemed unlikely which turned out to be true. That's one of the reasons I'm here, remember."

"I won't take that from you," said the reedy voice, now agitated. "It wasn't cheap to get you here, and we need you ready when the moment comes, not chasing after phantoms and angering the common people. Now is the time to be cautious, for *all* of those reasons." At the end, the voice softened.

"I know, I know," said Nuraleed. "But I haven't angered

anyone, and the common people have nothing to tear down in any case. Besides, this isn't a phantom. It is a real, flesh-and-blood human being, yes? He is within our sphere of influence now; we cannot ignore him."

"Then what do you propose to do?"

"First, study him, to see if we can get a better sense of his motives and what he's planning. Second—" Suddenly Nuraleed stopped talking.

"What?" the thin voice asked.

"There," Nuraleed said. "Up there. Something on the roof."

My eyes shot open, and more by instinct than conscious thought I swiftly pulled myself into a standing position, then hopped onto the rope and ran across as fast as I could while still maintaining balance. Once on the other side I drew my cucuri and swept down with the weapon, severing the rope in one cut, then, dislodging the fly hook from my side with a quickly whispered word and concealing it back within the folds of my cloak, I sheathed my blade and dropped from the roof into the alley below. I ducked into the safety of the shadows just as the door to the building where I had been listening opened. Nuraleed stepped out, expression serious, and looked around, then up at the roof; someone was standing behind him in the house, but I couldn't make anything else out about them. Then Nuraleed stared directly at me—or at least, at the shadows in which I was concealed. I held my position under that gaze, barely daring to breathe, for what felt like an age. Then, slowly, the merchant turned and re-entered the building, closing the door behind him.

I remained motionless for a full minute, staring at the closed door, before exhaling and turning to leave. I had gained at least some information already, and I dared not chance any further surveillance now, though I was sorry to leave my improvised fly hook behind. A severed rope and a three-pronged hook wouldn't give away much information when it was eventually found, other than confirming that someone had indeed been on the roof ... but even a device like this had not been easy to make, and I was none too enthusiastic at the prospect of having to refashion it. But being caught would be far worse ... since, as I had suspected, there was more to Nuraleed than he had let on.

As I retraced my steps down the streets of the Gauntlet Quarter, I replayed the encounter in my mind, trying to pick up details I might have missed. No one should have been able to hear me on that roof, certainly not over the noise of a conversation. The fact that Nuraleed had been able to do so, or sensed me in some other way, was a sign of considerable skill ... though I couldn't be entirely sure of skill in what. I had dealt with enough merchants in my time to know that the best ones had a kind of sixth sense; not something like Caron's power, which extended beyond normal human limits, but something more grounded, more driven by experience and intuitive insight. A few of them could appraise people as well as they did merchandise. But to sense an unseen, trained assassin on the roof above a room—to sense *me*—was a whole different matter.

"Maybe you've lost a step, Grayshade," I murmured to myself as I turned onto the final narrow street which would lead me back into the Sabaton Quarter. "Gods know you've made more than your share of mistakes." Yet even for me, I knew this was untrue. Perhaps I hadn't succeeding in sabotaging a military camp while I was traveling from Cohrelle to Tellisar, nor in saving all of those who had thrown in their lot with me along the way (as I considered this, a brief memory of Alarene's smiling face and cackle flitted through my consciousness, but I cast it aside). But I had been well out of my element in those circumstances; I had to rely on my reactions and instincts, not my experience. Surveilling a target in a city environment, gathering information in shadows and silence without anyone noticing my presence? That was my bread and butter, and even Caoesthenes would have had a hard time discovering me in those situations.

If it wasn't a failing on my part, it meant that Nuraleed had some method or mechanism of sensing potential intruders. And the conversation itself between him and the one known as Markas was just as concerning. Though they hadn't mentioned my name, everything suggested they were discussing me—the timeline of my arrival, whether or not I was reliable, and of course, the Order of Argoth. Unless they were trying to throw me off their scent— the possibility of which I couldn't completely dismiss—Nuraleed and Markas were part of some other organization, some group separate from the Order. It was good to get independent confirmation that the Order had indeed been stirred up by our arrival, at least. But until I knew what organization Nuraleed and Markas belonged to, I couldn't know what they wished for us, and whether we suddenly had more to worry about than just the Order and the Service.

"More variables," I muttered, slowing as I reached the end of the alley and prepared to enter the Sabaton Quarter. "More things I can't control. And if—"

Suddenly there was a cry from behind me, immediately cut short, and I drew my cucuri and whirled, blade held horizontally to block an attack. But no attack came, only the dull sound of metal clattering against stone. I looked down, and in the dim light of the alley saw a body lying facedown on the ground, only a few feet away. I waited for several seconds, eyes and ears straining for any sight or sound, before moving to the body and kneeling. It was a man wearing leather armor, his bearded face streaked in sweat, probably not much younger than me. A short sword of standard make rested near his hand as he lay motionless on the rough stone of the alley. But of greater interest was the dagger in his back, its black-cloth wrapped handle sticking out. He had meant to kill me, and someone had killed him first. And as I looked around fruitlessly for sign of the one who had intervened, I realized that the list of things I could not control was growing more rapidly than I could have possibly imagined.

CHAPTER FIVE

MY search for my apparent rescuer did not last long; when one tried to kill me, others would presumably follow, and I needed to go to ground and consider my options ... especially when I could not be any more sure of the motivations of the rescuer than the would-be assassin. As I had suspected, there was little to identify the dead man, no crests, badges, or identifying adornments on either armor or sword. In all likelihood he wouldn't have succeeded even if no one had intervened; this was obviously no Acolyte, and I would have heard him if he moved any closer. But that he had gotten as close as he did was already a failure on my part ... and if he had used a thrown weapon, it could have been a deadly failure. I took the dagger which killed him with me, though; even if there was nothing obvious on it, perhaps Rillia could recognize an element of the weapon's design. I couldn't be sure Nuraleed's people (whoever they were) were behind either the attempted killing or the rescue, but based on what I had heard on the roof of the building earlier it seemed reasonable that they were involved somehow. If so, we needed a new plan before we were used for purposes other than our own and cast aside ... something I had dealt with before.

My senses were on high alert, but fortunately the rest of my journey home was uneventful. Perhaps this was understandable; at this time of night, the Sabaton Quarter with all of its taverns and residences was considerably more populated than the Gauntlet Quarter, and finding an easy moment to attack me without anyone noticing would be much more difficult as a result. People were still passing by, some less steady on their feet than others, as I turned onto the street which led to home. But I was still on edge as I reached the front door and did my customary knock: three short, three long, one short, two long. Almost immediately the door opened, and I saw Caron looking at me with their usual calm smile. I didn't return it, passing swiftly in before closing and locking the door.

"How long has Rillia been gone?" I asked as I double-checked the locks. After a moment I felt something bump my leg, and looking down I saw Caoes had padded his way over to me. I kneeled down and scratched behind his ears as his yellow eyes blinked slowly.

"About as long as you were, I think . . . maybe an hour," Caron replied.

"Has anyone come by, knocked, anything?"

"No . . . we haven't had any problems. Caoes didn't even need to growl," Caron said with a grin. But their smile quickly vanished. "Outside in the city, though . . . things feel different."

"How?" I asked, tossing my single fly hook onto a shelf and moving to the seat closer to the fire as Caoes padded back to his bed and lay down with his head between his paws. "You sensed a specific change?"

"Yes," Caron responded. "I was at lessons with my teachers—I figured it made sense while I was waiting for you both to come back. I was meditating, and then . . . I felt it."

"What, exactly?"

Caron shook their head, expression troubled. "I don't know. A kind of change in the air . . . sadness and anger suddenly mixed together. It was so strong that I couldn't concentrate on my lessons, and my teachers had to stop."

I raised an eyebrow in surprise. "Has that happened before?"

"No, not really," Caron admitted. "I've had times where it was hard to hear them, but that was because I needed to concentrate more, to focus. This time, though . . ." They stopped for a moment, their expression of worry deepening, before continuing. "They said they were having trouble connecting to me. It only lasted for a few seconds, but—I can't remember the last time something like that happened. I don't think I ever remember it happening, actually."

I nodded slowly, remembering Rillia's earlier words about Caron. "I sometimes forget that you still haven't been in the Cloud all that long. It can be . . . unpredictable."

Caron's smile returned. "Well, that part hasn't been all bad. I haven't been bored for a long time."

I smiled back, but my feeling of unease remained. The Cloud, the people of Varda's term for the world outside the boundaries of their Chapel—what I had long considered the "real" world—had been a place of possibility and learning for Caron since they had left the Chapel with me, after an encounter which had changed both our lives forever. Whether dealing with assassins, merchants, or the Sewer Rats, they had managed every environment and challenge with steady calm and compassion. They weren't just a sensate; they were an exceptionally gifted one, deeply intuitive and insightful into the emotions of those around them, and over the past six weeks their power had steadily increased. They could now feel the emotional conditions of not just the people in front of them, but of whole sections of the city . . . and they had learned self-control from their teachers, enough to keep them from being overwhelmed from the press of emotions from tens of thousands of Tellisar's residents all at once. If that self-control was now beginning to waver . . . if Caron was losing their connection with those who guided them from beyond the Cloud . . .

"I'm fine, Grayshade," they finally said, and I blinked. "So much of this is new to me, and it's a lot to take in. But this is what I was trained for . . . what I'm training for. You don't need to worry about me."

I nodded, though in reality, I *was* worried, and not just for them. Caron's ability to deal with anyone, to smooth over deep suspicions and raw feelings, was an enormous asset in a city like Tellisar, especially when we were trying to gather information quickly and (at least until recently) quietly. Rillia wasn't terrible at diplomacy herself, but she was now just as much a potential target of the Order as I was; Gods knew my ability to manage conversational niceties was about as good as Caron's ability to assassinate targets from the shadows. And even the smartest and steadiest-tempered panther, in a city more used to them than in Cohrelle, wasn't going to be much for small talk, which left Caoes out. Besides, out of all of us, only Caron could not just guess but truly know the emotional state of another person—invaluable both to understand them empathetically and to warn others when danger was brewing.

And most of all, yes . . . I was worried about them. *They can probably sense that, too, damn it all.*

Suddenly there was a knock on the door: three short, three

long, one short, two long. I went swiftly and silently to the door and, my hand on the hilt of my cucuri, drew it open. The sight of Rillia's face, the expression a mask, greeted me, and a faint smell of quirvill spice reached my nostrils as she passed by. I closed and locked the door and turned to face her as she knelt down to pet Caoes lying near the fire. "Market or tavern?" I asked.

"How about both?" she asked with a small smile. "Or, to be more exact, one inside the other?" She shifted into a sitting position, knees drawn up, as she continued to stroke Caoes's fur. The panther's eyes were closed, his breathing regular. "I've been to The Heron's Wing," Rillia went on after a moment.

"Other end of the Sabaton Quarter," I said. "Seems pretty new, though I've only seen the outside of it. Not a very big place."

"No, but a busy place for merchants," Rillia replied. "And the place may be new, but the owner certainly isn't: a man named Rannis Carndan runs it, and he's been in Tellisar his whole life."

"I've heard of him . . . and not kindly."

Rillia snorted. "That's an understatement. Rannis is a bitter old grump, and it's a minor miracle he isn't already dead or bankrupt. But he knows this city and its people, especially its merchants, as well as anyone in Tellisar . . . and he won't serve anyone else, for any amount of coin. He'll tell you what he thinks."

I nodded and folded my arms. "Thinks about what?"

"About a large, flamboyant man neither one of us trusts. I asked him about Nuraleed."

"Do you think you can believe what he says, Rillia?" Caron asked, a slight frown on their face. "Wouldn't one merchant have a reason to lie about the other?"

"I didn't, when I was one," Rillia said. "And besides, if you go into any conversation with Rannis knowing he's going to growl and spit and mutter about 'stupid robbers and thieving fools,' you won't be disappointed by what you get."

"I know the type," I said with a sigh. "At least he's likely to be honest about his own opinions, then. What did he have to say about Nuraleed?"

"Distrust and racism, for starters," Rillia replied, gazing into the fire. "Rannis thinks foreigners are ruining Tellisar; 'the more trade we do with these people, the less like *us* we're getting,'" she said, narrowing her eyes and making her voice gravelly to match Rannis's. She glanced at Caron, who grinned, before going on. "There was a lot more of that, but you get the idea, and I don't much like bigots or the things they have to say. He as much as said he didn't think I'd fit in here, if not in quite those words; to Rannis, I'm just as much a foreigner as Nuraleed is."

"I didn't think you would suffer fools like this, Rillia," I said. At her sharp expression, I suddenly remembered yesterday's talk with Carver.

"I don't. But I nodded and murmured some things about changing times, and I guess I relaxed Rannis enough that eventually he let down his guard. Turns out he does know Nuraleed; he's not much for the man's choices in clothing or his attitude—'never trust a man who smiles as much as he talks,' Rannis said—and he's a competitor, too, and I guess Nuraleed has been more successful than he'd like. But for all that, he admitted he didn't know and hadn't heard about any dishonest dealings from Nuraleed either. 'Probably just a matter of time before he gets to be as much of a thieving rat as all the rest of 'em,' Rannis said, but still … if I had to guess, I'd say he even sort of, I suppose, respects him. He'd never admit it, but there it is." Rillia looked at me, shadows from the flickering firelight playing on her face. "As for being part of some bigger group or organization, I didn't get the sense that Rannis thought Nuraleed would be part of something like that either. What you see is what you get, at least as far as what Rannis believes. A couple of others had joined us by then, and they said more or less the same thing: big personality, ridiculous outfits, but, from all they could tell, reasonably honest . . . and a good salesman."

"If they all say the same thing, I guess Nuraleed is who he says he is," Caron said, expression thoughtful. "And I didn't sense any doubt or fear when we were talking to him."

"I can't say what you did or didn't sense, Caron," I said. "But I've known some awfully confident liars in my time . . . some who had lied so much, they might even have come to believe their own deceit eventually. Just because Rannis and a couple of merchants said Nuraleed seems trustworthy doesn't make it true."

"You did tell me to get information about him from the merchants he deals with every day," Rillia pointed out.

"I did . . . and it's good information, Rillia." I sat down on one of the chairs near the fire and began to stroke the fur on Caoes's neck, watching as the panther's yellow eyes slowly narrowed, then closed. "I just don't know if it's enough to counter what I found out during my own excursion."

Rillia took a deep breath. "Okay, then. What did you find out, exactly?"

I glanced at Caron, watching me closely, and sighed. "First of all, none of what I'm about to tell you definitively means anything. Something is wrong somewhere . . . but whether it's with Nuraleed, or the people he works for, or someone else entirely . . ."

I shrugged unhappily. "I don't know. All that I do know is that Nuraleed is more than he's presented himself to be." And I proceeded to explain what had happened from the time I left *The Fair Deal* to when I was returning to the Sabaton Quarter. Caron sat listening silently, their expression mostly calm and open as usual; Rillia also was quiet, though a frown which began with my description of crossing over to the roof of Nuraleed's building grew deeper as I explained how I escaped the area.

I had a feeling the frown would lead to something much stronger when I got to what happened when I was leaving the Gauntlet Quarter, and in that regard I was not disappointed. When I described seeing the dead man behind me, she leaned forward, knuckles white as her hands gripped her knees, her gaze intense and unwavering. "He had nothing on him?" she cut in when I paused. "No marks, no colors, nothing?"

I shook my head. "Simple leather armor, boots, and a dark cloth cloak, and carrying a normal short sword. But in his back I found this." I drew forth the dagger with the black cloth-wrapped handle and held it out. Rillia stared wordlessly, then took the dagger from me. For a long while she just held the blade in her hand, turning the hilt around and around as she gazed down.

Finally she looked at me again. "You were careless . . . careless and stupid."

I pursed my lips. "He wasn't close enough to me yet for me to notice him. A second later I would have sensed him, and would have turned—"

"—much too late, if he decided to throw something at you," Rillia cut in, eyes flashing. "What if the weapon in his hand and the one in his back were reversed, and this was what he was using?" She held up the dagger. "At best you would have taken this to the chest instead of your back."

I glared at Rillia, but in truth, she wasn't saying anything I hadn't already berated myself for on the way here. So after a moment, I sighed and shook my head. "Fine. I made a mistake. It could have been a serious one. Happy?"

"No," she said, surprising me as her expression softened. "We came here to stop the Order, Grayshade. Something happening to you while we do that wouldn't make me happy. Either one of us." She glanced at Caron, who nodded, before looking back at me. "Anyway, this dagger doesn't seem familiar—it's just a generic blade."

I nodded. "Which means we're not dealing with a gang of thieves marking their territory."

"You're sure they weren't aiming for you and ended up hitting the other one stalking you instead?"

"Then why not try again? I never saw anyone; they could just as easily have thrown another dagger from the shadows if they missed the first time."

"Maybe they didn't want a fight," Rillia pointed out.

"What if the person who died," another voice said, "was trying to protect you?" Rillia and I turned to see Caron, their eyebrows raised.

"It's possible," I finally admitted. "We still don't know many of the players in this city. But they took this dagger in the back; whether they meant to kill me or save me, they didn't see it coming."

"So we don't even know if this is related to Nuraleed," Rillia said.

"No. But you don't believe in coincidences any more than I do, Rillia. Given what I heard in that conversation, Nuraleed has to be more than he claims; and then, less than ten minutes later, a mysterious assailant—or protector," I said, nodding at Caron, "is killed by an unmarked dagger thrown from the shadows? Paranoia was part of my old life, but even now, ignoring a connection like that is foolish in the extreme."

"So what do we do?" Caron asked.

There was a long silence. "If Nuraleed is there at his stand tomorrow," Rillia finally said, "and if he's dealing with customers like he usually does, it means either that he wasn't involved in this at all, or that the group he's with, whatever it is and whatever it's trying to do, has taken its shot for now. They won't challenge you in the Poor Markets in the light of day, in full view of guards and citizens. If they would, they would be tracking you already. Which means," she added, nodding at the covered window, "they could have broken through there and made quick work of us already."

I thought for a few moments, then nodded. "Probably right. Then it makes sense to keep our appointment. And if Caron's with me, they can help give me a sense of what Nuraleed is feeling—perhaps anger or fear, if he missed his chance to be rid of me last night, or something else if he wasn't connected to what happened. Can you manage that?" I asked, looking at the sensate. But Caron's face was troubled, their eyes shifting to the left and right as if looking for something.

"I ... yes," they said after a moment, just before I was going to ask what was wrong. "Sorry. Yes, that's fine, I can come. I'll see what he's feeling." Their brow smoothed, and they looked up at me with their usual calm smile. But I had seen the first reaction, and as I glanced at Rillia, I saw from her worried expression that she had seen it too.

For the moment, though, I decided to let it pass; the discussion of what was wrong with Caron was likely to be a long and complex one, and I needed to plan how to best approach it. So I simply nodded. "All right, then. We do need more information about what happened, though—and it almost certainly is related to what we came to Tellisar to find out in the first place. So while we're with Nuraleed—"

"—I need to track down something about the one who tried to kill you, and the one who protected you, whichever one of them it was," Rillia said, finishing my sentence.

I nodded. "I'm afraid so. We could send you with Caron to meet with Nuraleed instead, but that's bound to raise his suspicion if he is involved in this, and besides, I'm the target; whoever's after me isn't as likely to mark you."

Rillia sighed, running a hand through her black hair. "Not until after I've proven myself to be a threat by looking for them, I guess. But you're right; it's the safer play. And I'll take Caoes with me," she said, looking down at the slumbering panther. "I doubt he's going to be part of anyone's calculations. And besides, he's getting soft here, with all of this city living." She smiled as she watched his sleek sides peacefully rising and falling with every breath, then yawned. "He's got the right idea, though . . . it's been quite a day. We could all use some rest." She looked at Caron, smile vanishing as she laid a hand on their shoulder. "That means you too, Caron. No staying up with your teachers for more lessons."

Caron smiled. "They would agree with you. I'll sleep too, Rillia. Don't worry." Rillia returned the smile, but I didn't need to be a sensate like Caron to know how she was actually feeling. I had known her for too long not to know the tenseness around her dark eyes, the slight furrow in her brow, meant she was very worried indeed . . . and she wasn't alone.

———————◆———————

I was in a world of dark green, the slight shimmering of pools of water reflecting off the leaves above me as I rested near the trunk of a tree. The mosslight of the Bloodmarsh was dim, but in its own way better light than any lantern or torch by which I had navigated elsewhere; even the faintest light could illuminate the darkness, and mosslight was consistent and unwavering, steady, reliable. It was what I had always hoped to be myself . . . until events had changed my view of my world and myself forever.

Yes, there was peace here. It was an uneasy and imperfect one, but then, when had my life ever been anything but imperfect, at the best of times? What could I expect out there—there, where the world still sold death as faith and blind obedience as devout service? "Maybe just a few days more," I murmured, closing my eyes against the brilliant light. "Just a few more, to catch my breath." In the far distance, I heard the slightest sound of splashing, drifting lazily through my languid thoughts.

Suddenly there was a high, keening shriek, abruptly cut short. I gasped as I lurched forward, eyes wide and staring in the faint green glow. Then a whisper next to me, in my voice, or

Caoesthenes's or Alarene's, or Jant's: "You're too late, Grayshade. You were always too late to save him, and her, and everyone else you cared about."

The shriek sounded again, and I leapt up and ran wildly into the glow. Somewhere in the back of my consciousness I dimly remembered having a companion with me . . . an animal, perhaps? A . . . panther? But I quickly forgot about anything other than reaching the source of the scream in time, to stop whatever was happening, to keep the piercing wail, which sounded over and over and over again, from driving itself into my skull like a dagger. Everything around me looked the same as everything else, the same trees and bushes and pools of fetid water all cast in a green glow, and as I leapt over fallen trees and ducked beneath low hanging branches, I began to fear I was simply running in circles while the screams grew more deafening by the second.

Finally, my lungs burning and head pounding, I made one final leap over a natural basin of brackish water and slid to a stop in the muddy ground on the other side. Another deafening shriek sounded, and I looked up to see the open door of Alarene's shack in front of me. A dim, low light shone from inside.

I drew my cucuri and bolted forward and onto the path. But just before I reached the front door, I saw something glinting from within. Even as I tried to slow down, something in my memory knew what would happen next, but somehow I also knew I could do nothing to stop it. I heard an audible click as I stepped on the threshold of the shack, and with no time to throw myself clear, closed my eyes as I waited for what I knew must happen next. Several long moments passed, the sound of my heartbeat booming in my ears.

"I guess whatever happened next must have been really terrible," a familiar voice said.

My eyes opened to see, sitting in Alarene's rocking chair, Caron. The leader of Varda's people was rocking back and forth in front of a small fire in the hearth, and the shadows flickered on their watching face as they smiled. I took a deep breath and looked around. This was indeed Alarene's shack in the Bloodmarsh, just as it had been. But in reality, the shack had been torn apart, the outside ripped up from the explosive trap on which I had unwittingly stepped and the inside in shambles from whoever had killed . . .

Alarene. I could still remember the old woman lying on the ground, a huge slash in her side, leg twisted beneath her. But she was not here, nor was her house destroyed . . . nor, now that I thought of it, was Caoes anywhere to be seen. It was me and Caron, and I understood, somehow, that I was asleep.

"You're really here, aren't you, Caron?" I asked, sheathing my cucuri and sitting down on the edge of the bed on which I had spent many days in the Bloodmarsh during my convalescence. Most of my dreams were hazy and indistinct in some areas, terribly defined and sharp in others—but for some reason this one was clear throughout, even though I knew I was dreaming. "I haven't had a dream this clear since the woman who lived here helped me," I said, looking around.

"Alarene, you mean?" Caron asked.

My arm twitched at the casual mention. "Yes. I drank from a mug of some kind of tea she had brewed . . . it gave me a kind of shared vision with her." I looked at Caron directly. "But this isn't a vision, is it?"

Caron shook their head, still rocking back and forth slowly in the chair. "No. My presence changes the shape of what happens next, makes it so that we can both be present within this experience. But it's still your dream, or at least the first part of it. I'm just visiting."

Instead of comfort, I felt irritation. "Why?"

Caron's smile faded. "I was ... curious. You've always had a tinge of darkness, but in the past several weeks it's been harder for me to sense it. And I wondered how you were feeling down deep, beyond what you allow yourself to show on the surface."

"I see," I said, the irritation growing. "And you thought it was all right to simply enter my dreams and discover those emotions yourself, without asking, without permission?"

Caron frowned. "I've searched for feelings before, and I didn't think—"

"Of course you didn't think," I snapped, uncomfortably warm from the fire in the shack. "Why would you think about the feelings of others? They're just notes for you to read, after all, secrets to pore through and sort and accept or reject as you will."

"They're not notes, and they're not mine," Caron said, their eyes slightly widened in apparent concern. "I don't accept or reject the feelings of others; they're just there."

"Some of them are there. Others are behind walls, walls which protect them ... walls which are there for a reason, walls which aren't meant to be breached. I know something about being an unwelcome intruder, Caron. Your teachers are training you well, and your power is growing. But you can't just increase that power without thinking of how it will affect others. I thought you, of all people, might best understand why the desire to keep certain things safe should be respected."

Caron's face fell, and I felt a tinge of regret color my anger. But they nodded before I could say anything else. "You're right, Grayshade. I'm sorry. I've felt a little . . . off lately, a little confused, I guess. I wanted to help, but . . . I can't just do that without asking. This," they said, gesturing to the inside of Alarene's shack, "is part of your story, not mine. I won't come in to that story again unless you ask me to." They rose from the rocking chair and walked past me to the door, then paused and turned just before exiting. "This dream—the original version of it, before I came in. You don't have to answer this, but I was wondering . . . is it what happened, in reality?"

I didn't speak, but as I looked at Caron I knew that my expression said enough, and they sighed. "I can't know this for sure, but I don't think this is anything you could have stopped. You've done so much to try to change . . . eventually you're going to have to accept who you were before, and who you are now, the way Rillia and I have."

"All actions have consequences," I replied, Alarene's scream still echoing in my mind.

"Yes," Caron agreed, expression thoughtful, "all of them, good ones and bad. And my teachers say that not even a sensate can predict the future, or how we can change it, and us, with what we do. You're still writing your own story, Grayshade. The last few pages are just as important as the first ones." Then they turned again and left the shack, and I was left alone with my dreams . . . and my doubts.

CHAPTER SIX

THE next morning Caron and I said nothing about my dream from the night before. In a way, there was little more to be discussed, and if Caron seemed a bit more thoughtful than before, I was probably the same. Rillia looked at us doubtfully during our breakfast, me carefully segmenting eggs and ham and Caron's hands still warming against a bowl of split pea soup. She had probably noticed our more reserved demeanors and was trying to figure out what could have happened, but gave no voice to her possible suspicion. And Caoes, eating his own slices of ham in front of the still warm embers of last night's fire, was as placid as ever. Even if he could have talked, I doubted he would have said anything, content to eat and observe our own silent meal.

We left Rillia and Caoes at home, preparing to head out in search of the groups to which my assailant and protector both belonged, and made our own way to the Poor Markets. We arrived at Nuraleed's stand right before the ninth bell, and though I had been wondering what I should do if the merchant gave any obvious reaction to my arrival, I quickly saw I needn't have worried. As we approached, we saw the gold, red, and purple attired man (today wearing a black turban) apparently fully occupied by a haggling session with a tall, thin man with a thin mustache, dressed in rich golden robes.

"Perhaps my business isn't good enough for you anymore,

Nuraleed," the man sniffed, his thin, angular nose twitching slightly. "Or perhaps you've taken leave of your senses. But trying to sell me some low quality fabric a master tailor would have a hard time working with seems a bit of a stretch, even for you."

Nuraleed laughed, his chuckle warm and welcome as ever. "And calling my merchandise 'low quality' is more than a bit of a stretch, *especially* for you, my friend. You know that given the state of supplies right now, with multiple conflicts in Silarein, we have many new challenges before us." He widened his arms, an expression of wry acceptance on his face. "What can be done? But for all of those challenges, I continue to provide the highest quality fabric available to clients of refinement and taste . . . chief among them, naturally, yourself."

"Naturally," the thin man said, expression even more sour than before. "I've known you too long to fall for threadbare flattery, Nuraleed. Whatever you're selling me here is trash compared to your usual stock, and you know it."

Nuraleed's mustache twitched. "Trash? Now you offend me beyond words, Kaltir. I would never sell—" Suddenly he noticed us standing nearby, and with barely a second of hesitation turned to face us, a wide smile on his face. "But here. Perhaps others besides me can convince you. Carrnisk, this man Kaltir has insulted my merchandise and, by extension, myself. Yet I understand that even the most experienced and knowledgeable merchants can, on occasion, be led astray by an honest misapprehension. I trust you can lead him back to a clearer course." He turned back to the thin man. "Kaltir, this is my nephew Carrnisk, a trader of considerable knowledge just arrived in Tellisar, and his child Caron. I must attend to a quick matter; while I am gone,

Carrnisk can help clear up your undoubtedly unintentional misunderstanding." And with a quick nod to Kaltir and what seemed like, though I couldn't swear it, a wink to Caron and me, he turned and strode off through the aisles of the Poor Markets, customers and merchants parting to accommodate him as he passed by.

I stared after him for a moment, mind whirling, before turning to face Kaltir, who now looked as if he had bitten into a lemon. "I, uh," I began after a moment. "I'm most . . . pleased to meet you. I understand you have some concerns about Nura—uh, *my uncle's* fabric here?" I waved vaguely in the direction of the stand containing bolts of brightly colored silks, linens, and other materials I had no hope of identifying.

Kaltir regarded me in stony silence. "I am not *concerned*," he replied at last, biting off the last word. "I am angered. I am enraged. I am *appalled*." He stabbed a finger into a bolt of cream-colored fabric, which looked to be made of some kind of sheer material. "This is an insult. Your uncle is thought to be one of the finest fabric merchants in all of Tellisar, and perhaps beyond. Yet the best he can bring to the Poor Markets is this junk, barely better than a canvas sack, and then has the gall to ask four silvers a bolt—four!—when he'd be lucky to get a copper or two from some wretched outlander who can barely hold a needle, looking to make a horse blanket."

It appears we're not quite on the same page, I thought wryly. "Well," I began, "of course honest appraisals can differ, but I—"

"Appraising *this*," he cut in, still pointing at the offending fabric, "as anything other than material barely suitable to make a carnival tent is not 'honest.' It is a foolish joke, and I don't deal with fools."

Healer, mend thyself. But I held my tongue and simply nodded. "Certainly," I said, keeping my voice as level as possible. "But my uncle's reputation, as you said, is quite high, and he is neither foolish nor inclined to make jokes . . . when business is concerned, in any case. Clearly he has his reasons for setting the prices he does. Anyone with customers as discerning as you can't afford to behave dishonestly, or they'd quickly be out of the Markets, possibly even out of all of Tellisar. Surely you don't consider yourself to be undiscerning, do you?" I glanced at Caron, fairly pleased with my approach, but my smile vanished as I saw their face—eyes wide, mouth closed in a tight line. They were looking at Kaltir, and if I could judge Caron's expressions by now, they weren't sensing anything positive.

I looked back at the thin man to see him staring at me, his eyes narrowed. "I am indeed discerning," he said after a moment. "I've discerned that Nuraleed's nephew is as buffoonish as him, if this is your approach to haggling."

Well, then. I felt my face growing a bit prickly, my heart rate increasing slightly, but I knew I had to maintain my composure. "Be that as it may," I said with what had to be an unconvincing smile, "I assure you that the price he's established is a reasonable one under the circumstances. And of course, we have other options for you, if need be. As you can see, our inventory is quite substantial."

"A substantial amount of garbage is still garbage," he shot back. "If I gave you a silver for the whole stand, I'd be doing you a favor."

"Now, to be fair—"

"Nothing about any of this is 'fair,'" Kaltir snarled. "You're robbing people, most of whom will be too stupid to realize it at first. By the time they figure it out, I suppose you think that you'll be long gone from Tellisar. But reputations last much longer in people's minds than you think, Carrnisk. In the end, both you and your uncle will be known in this city as the thieves you are."

"My father is just trying to work with you, sir," Caron suddenly said, stepping forward with their usual disarming smile. "I can tell you're angry, but I promise he didn't mean to offend you. Maybe if we could start again, we—"

Kaltir rounded on them. "No one's spoken to you, child. Until someone does, you keep your mouth shut and let the adults speak."

So much for maintaining composure, I thought, heart pounding as I took a menacing step forward. "The child speaks wisdom. And you won't speak to them at all. This conversation is between you and me."

Kaltir's eyes widened. "What did you say?"

"You heard me, you insufferable fop," I growled. "You won't speak to my child that way, if you ever want to speak again."

"Well!" a deep voice exclaimed as Kaltir's eyes widened even further, and I turned to see Nuraleed, teeth gleaming as his hands rested on the purple sash around his waist. "I see our transaction has not yet been resolved to either of our satisfactions. This is truly regrettable."

"Regrettable!" Kaltir spat as his shock passed enough for him to speak. "Regrettable that your nephew here has insulted me and threatened my life? What is regrettable is that neither you nor he will see the sky over Tellisar again, once I'm through with them. When I speak to the guard—"

"—you'll say nothing of any of this," Nuraleed finished, his smile unwavering. "In fact, my friend, you won't speak to the guard at all."

Kaltir snorted. "Why?"

"Because if you do, the guard will hear from me next. And he will hear, in exquisite detail, how exactly you have bought and sold goods within the Poor Markets."

"I don't understand," the thin man said, voice uncertain.

"You understand a great deal, actually," Nuraleed replied. "You understand that the city of Tellisar has grown rich from its trade . . . trade which can be relied upon to be honest. If that reputation of honesty fails, so, eventually, will this city. That is why the laws against theft and extortion are so strict. That is why you will say nothing: because those laws will be applied to you, and then it is you who will not *see the sky over Tellisar again.*" His mustache tilted. "Such a delightfully fascinating phrase."

Kaltir glanced at several people passing by Nuraleed's stand, then glared at Nuraleed, his face now a mask of hatred. "Filthy outlander," he hissed. "You think they will believe you, or that other outlander scum you call family, over a citizen of Tellisar?"

I stepped forward with my hand on the hilt of my cucuri, but Nuraleed held up a hand. "I believe you won't want to take the chance, Kaltir. I believe your common sense will override your bigotry. And most of all," he said, his grin widening, "I *know* you are a coward. And like all cowards, you will run in the end."

Kaltir stared up at the merchant, mouth working. Then he spat on the fabric on Nuraleed's stand, turned on his heel, and stormed away, shoving his way through several startled customers and another fabric merchant as he went.

There was a long silence before I finally took a deep breath and spoke. "Is that the usual type of customer you deal with?"

Nuraleed made no reply, and assuming he had either not heard me or had no response to make, I shrugged and turned to Caron, who was still looking at the crowd into which Kaltir had disappeared. "The better question," Nuraleed suddenly said before I could ask the child what they were feeling, "is whether that is the usual way in which you deal with potential customers. Were you really forced from your village because of your sense of duty, as Caron here has said, or because you decided to insult, belittle, and threaten people with whom you were doing business?"

"I haven't usually needed to threaten people with whom I did business," I said with a growl as I turned away. I could already see where this conversation was leading, and I was in no mood to be lectured.

"Perhaps you simply dealt with them in more permanent ways?" Nuraleed said, an edge in his voice, and I turned back like a shot. But he wasn't even looking at me, attending instead to the fabric which Kaltir had befouled. "However you have managed your affairs elsewhere, Carrnisk, you should know that it is not the way things are done here," he went on, carefully cleaning the fabric with a handkerchief and a small vial of clear liquid. "Here both merchants and customers are plentiful, and if a customer decides that they would prefer to go elsewhere for the material seek, they will find another merchant."

"I can think of worse outcomes."

"I, however, cannot," Nuraleed said sharply as he looked up from the fabric. "And since I am the one from whom you are

supposed to be learning, what *I* am thinking of is considerably more important."

I was immediately reminded of Caoesthenes, whose early lessons with me had held much the same tone. Though what my mentor would have thought of my decision to become a student of fine fabric sales ... "So I am expected to simply take abuse, to nod and bow and scrape, to accept any attack with a smile?" I asked.

Nuraleed sighed, drawing several pieces of silken fabric over the cleaned one with practiced ease. "You are expected to remember that your customer is not your adversary, no matter what they may do. When they become an adversary, they can no longer be your customer."

"Then why did you say what you did to Kaltir at the end?"

"Because he is now a lost cause, and I needed to make sure I would lose only his coin, not the coin of anyone else he would tell about what happened. Kaltir has always been a sour, prickly man even on his best day. But his worst days have happened more and more frequently of late, and truth be told, I do not know how much longer he will be a buyer in this city. The more people he sees, the angrier he gets."

"Then why did you foist him on me?" I demanded, narrowing my eyes.

"Because you asked me to teach you to—what was the delightful way in which you put it, Caron? 'To blend in? To seem like we belong in Tellisar, and in the markets'?" Nuraleed's mustache twitched. "Seeing how you would manage Kaltir was a good way to see how much work you have to do. At the moment, you blend in here about as well as a piece of weathered canvas among the finest vellinin. Berating and threatening your customers will not end well for either them or you, and you can be certain they will remember the experience either way."

"And I shouldn't want that?"

"No," Nuraleed said firmly. "You want to be remembered as a purchase, never as a man. Blending in means you are not remembered, except in the familiarity of a returning customer to please again."

"It's hard to imagine Kaltir forgetting us at this point, after how angry he was," Caron said.

"Indeed," the merchant replied, nodding. "But he will not challenge us, or at least not for a while. Even if he does stay in Tellisar and remains a buyer, I will have some time to—how do they put it here?—smooth the waters, I think is the phrase, make it so that you become just another minor annoyance in the tapestry of his experience in the Markets. But his money is lost for good, and that," Nuraleed said, pointing at me with one eyebrow raised, "is your doing. Either you must learn to lock away your pride, or you will have no hope of being anything more than a target here."

I glanced sharply at Nuraleed again at his use of the term "target," but he seemed unperturbed ... unlike me. I had plenty of misgivings about this whole arrangement to begin with, and what I had discovered (and not discovered) about Nuraleed since yesterday had only increased them. And besides, I had doubts that I could keep my temper if I was to have to cater to arrogant fops like Kaltir, who a year ago would have more likely been my targets than sources of "learning."

"Carrnisk," a voice said, and I turned to see Caron looking up at me. "I know this isn't easy for you. And dealing with someone like that," they said, nodding in the direction of the crowd into which Kaltir had disappeared, "must make it worse. But we need to learn how to do this if we're to get the information we need. And it's not just you doing it; I can help with the customers too." They put a hand on my arm. "We can do it together." I looked at Caron, smiling calmly as usual, and was suddenly reminded of the limits of my former life ... of how, for all the time I had spent in my own thoughts, for all the comfort I found in solitude, in the end I couldn't do everything on my own. More than that: perhaps in the end, I had learned I couldn't do *anything* on my own, not completely.

"A wise child," Nuraleed observed with a cough. "One well worth listening to."

I looked from the child to the merchant and back again, then sighed and shrugged. "Fine. To blend in. What must I do?"

———————————+———————————

What I must do, as it turned out, was practice; practice, again and again, working with the seemingly endless stream of buyers to Nuraleed's stand. There were occasional customers who would be using the fabric directly, tailors and homemakers and the like, to make clothing for their clients or their families. But most of the people who came to Nuraleed were wholesalers, merchants themselves who would bring the goods they bought at the Poor Markets to their own stores in the Gauntlet Quarter or elsewhere in the Sabaton, where they would sell them at a no doubt considerable markup.

When I asked Nuraleed if this situation bothered him—why he wouldn't simply sell the goods at the markup price himself, and keep the profits—he simply laughed. "In this way I would make more money in the short term, yes? But then in the long run I would have to rely on the customers who chose to come to my stand, and others could easily undercut my prices and take them. This way I am above all of that. One person sets a price, another undercuts it, still another sells under them, they squabble, they fight . . ." He shrugged. "What does it matter to me, so long as all of them must come to me for their merchandise, and I must only compete with a few others like me? And I can see the market from a distance—what trends have taken hold, what will be bought next season, what fabric I must hold onto, what fabric I must turn into scraps for the ragwoman. That is an advantage I would be foolish not to maintain."

It made sense, but I was not wholly convinced. If there were fewer people in Nuraleed's position, it meant each of them—including him—must be a greater target, as I had seen for myself with some of the merchants in Cohrelle. But Nuraleed seemed not to think of himself or others as targets, or even rivals; in fact, he seemed completely unconcerned about the business of others, beyond general comments about the state of the market. I never saw him frown at a customer, or shout at the owner of a nearby stand, the way everyone else in the Poor Markets seemed to do. Yet the line of buyers never seemed to lessen, and Nuraleed somehow managed to talk to all of them in turn, giving each of them plenty of time while never making anyone wait too long. Watching him looming over his customers, a vision in gold, red, and purple, smiling broadly while his green eyes glittered as he searched for what would help him land the next deal, was an odd experience—like watching Acolytes of Argoth spar, looking for an opening, a weakness which they could exploit in their opponent. Though I could tell that unlike a sparring match between Acolytes and despite the incident with Kaltir, almost all of Nuraleed's buyers walked away from their interactions apparently satisfied with the result.

I asked him about this phenomenon a couple of days later, right after I watched Nuraleed negotiate a particularly contentious arrangement of a regular fabric supply to one of the more prominent stores in the Gauntlet Quarter, turning a buyer's scowl into a vaguely smug smile. "Unless I've been asleep in the last several days, you just managed to mark up the price of that cetellin fabric with her," I said, nodding in the direction of the red-haired woman who was now strolling through the crowd of buyers and sellers surrounding the Markets, holding one of the bolts of indigo cloth, "and yet she's acting like *she* won. What happens when she finds out the deal isn't as good as she thought it was?"

The merchant's mustache smirked. "She won't," he said with a wink as he stacked a few new bolts on top of the gap created by his latest sale. He laughed as he saw me raise an eyebrow. "Ah, Carrnisk," he chuckled. "Your—shall we call it paranoia?—is both charming and utterly absurd. I mean no insult, my friend. But for someone with such a keen and discerning attention to detail, you have a remarkable capacity to underestimate human experience."

"Is that so?" I asked, trying again not to be thrown by Nuraleed's blunt assessments, as charming as they were direct.

Nuraleed laughed even more loudly, clapping me on the shoulder so hard I almost stumbled forward. "Yes, it is so!" He turned to look at the red-haired woman, now almost out of sight in the crowd. "Now Yenachia, there. She is one of the more successful fabric merchants, and tailors, in the Sabaton Quarter ... skilled and astute. She also *knows* herself to be these things, and she does not suffer fools gladly. Assume for a moment I approached her as you have approached others: someone with whom I am in competition, someone who could take my customers and eventually my livelihood. Someone who is a *threat*." His smile grew narrower, more thoughtful. "In that situation, yes, one must win and one must lose, one must succeed and one must fail. I must defeat her if I am to survive, yes? But that is not the only way. Yenachia had a need for a delicate yet strong fabric, one which will move with the body and not restrict it. She had a need for something beautiful and functional, in rich shades of blue, purple, indigo. She had a need for my cetellin. And I have a need for buyers, especially successful ones who will sell what they have and will return to me to buy more, while making the same calculation with their own customers. No one wins or loses. They discuss, they share, they exchange. We are all enriched by the interaction."

"Inspiring," I said, trying not to let the cynicism in my voice overwhelm the other sentiments. I had heard pretty words like this before, beautiful lies like glittering images carved in ice, all melting when the light and heat of reality poured in. And yet, there was an echo of Caron's philosophy here, and they had long ago demonstrated that reality was not as harsh and unforgiving as I had been taught in the Order.

Nuraleed, though, neither frowned nor laughed. "It can be," he said quietly, watching the crowd and the next buyer, a robust-looking, copper-skinned man with staff in hand, heading in the direction of his stand. "Or would you prefer to manage your goods like assets and your customers like opposing sides in a war? That, my friend, is inspiration of a very different kind." Without another word he strode off toward the buyer, arms wide in his usual gesture of welcome.

I frowned. If I was to be authentic and connected with the customers, didn't I need to be true to myself, to be forthright and clear instead of burying my intentions and myself in the shadows and vague rumors which were the tools of my past? And how was Nuraleed being any more honest with customers than I was, if he was able to change prices on the fly, alter the cost of items to fit the monetary resources and specific situations of the buyer? How was any of this fair?

No, I thought as I watched Nuraleed talking to the buyer with the staff, at least a foot taller yet somehow not intimidating, slightly crouched, body language simultaneously confident and deferential. *This isn't about fairness. It's about the interaction, the connection between two people.* I had always envisioned these connections as asymmetrical, transactional: *I flatter, cajole, bribe, threaten, kill, while they ignore, resist, deny, rebuke, and . . . die.* For much of my life I had viewed most of the people around me like the tools I used in my profession: things to be either feared, used, or destroyed. All until I met Caron, when something in me had helped me decide to mutually connect rather than determine the difference in power and act accordingly.

All until I decided not to be a thing to be used, either.

And so the lessons continued. Learning to put myself in the shoes of another, to imagine their life, their hopes and fears, as my own, was as hard as any training I had ever done with Father

Esper or Caoesthenes . . . harder, in a way, since these lessons were as much about my feelings about myself and others as they were about techniques and physical challenges. But Nuraleed proved to be an able instructor, endlessly patient and generally amused by my rough and uncertain attempts to engage the customers. And in spite of my own doubts and my manifest unsuitability for the task, I slowly began to respond. None of the buyers were as obnoxiously arrogant and offputting as Kaltir, but many of them were less than pleasant. But I didn't permanently anger anyone, and when I managed to convince a hesitant customer to purchase not one but two bolts of vestile cloth, a transaction concluded with mutual smiles and an assurance that the buyer would return, I knew I was making progress.

Caron was just as busy training as I was, though their work was in sensate skill rather than sales technique. The Poor Markets turned out to be an ideal space for them to feel the emotions of others—both the obvious ones, from sellers and buyers accusing each other of every version of fraud imaginable, and the more subtle ones . . . the boredom of the guards patrolling the area, the doubt of the merchants running out of resources and time, the worry and frustration of the beggars trying to survive . . . though even I could see that, and what came next: a hollow acceptance of what was. But I could see it with one person at a time, while Caron had grown powerful enough to sense these things broadly, the moods of many people in concert, or competition, with each other. Yet their growth was not all smooth. A portion of the center of the city, the Armor Quarter, was "shut off" to them, as they described it . . . a kind of dead zone where they could sense no emotions at all. And they had several more incidents of confusion, along with a second time where they struggled to connect with their teachers. With the exception of the problems sensing the Armor Quarter, none of these moments lasted for long, and Caron shrugged all of them off as a result of fatigue and adjusting to their process of growth . . . but I hadn't forgotten Rillia's words outside *The Fair Deal*, and I was starting to grow worried. We needed Caron's insight and wisdom . . . and most of all, we—I—needed them to be all right. But where did one find a healer to treat a sensate? I doubted the Gauntlet Quarter would have the kind of medicine for this kind of illness, if that was what it was.

In the meantime, Rillia was conducting her own investigation throughout the city, backed up by Caoes. I didn't know if she would be as much on the minds of the Order—or whomever had decided to come after me—as I was. But in the Poor Markets, between the Varan Guard presence and very public environment, I was fairly confident I was going to be a much harder target to deal with than in the isolated alleyways I was used to, like the one in which I had been attacked. Given Rillia's skill and Caoes's presence—and, I hoped, their lower profile—they might have more success than I would in finding answers. But night after night, we reunited at home in disappointment: the Order had a very low profile in Tellisar, which if anything had grown even lower in the past few months, and information about them was spotty and unreliable at best. Religions here held much less sway than they did in Cohrelle, at least on the surface, but that didn't prove anything: it could just as well be that the Order was even more powerful here than in Cohrelle, unfettered by competition or rivalry from other religious factions . . . and even more secret than the Order I had worked for in my native city. As for Nuraleed, Rillia continued to hear the same story: he was affable, charming, and both cunning and discerning. No one was particularly close to him, but no one had a bad word to say about him either—even his fiercest rivals had a grudging respect for his ability. If he was some evil mastermind, he had covered his tracks exceedingly well.

One evening about a week after I started training with Nuraleed—just after I closed a deal with a particularly frustrating buyer without losing my wits or temper—I turned from the transaction to see Rillia standing nearby, a worried expression on her face. "Rillia?" I said. "What—"

"I need to talk to you," she interrupted me. "Alone."

I blinked, then nodded. Nuraleed was deep in conversation with the final customer of the night, Caron alongside, and after making sure they were both occupied, I moved with Rillia to the other side of several stands already closed. "What's wrong?" I asked as soon as we were out of earshot. She seemed agitated, a thin sheen of sweat covering her face. "I thought you were in the Helm Quarter today."

"We were," she replied, drawing the sleeve of her cloak across her face. "I had a lead about a couple of government officials who might be in the bribe business, and I figured they might either know something or could tell me about someone else who would."

"And?"

"And I tracked one of them from outside her home to the Great Hall in the center of the Quarter . . . she didn't talk to anyone or stop along the way. When she went into the Hall, I turned to tell Caoes to wait there while I did a bit of surveillance. And when I turned . . ." She hesitated, and my stomach went hollow.

"What?"

Rillia sighed heavily. "He was gone."

"He does that sometimes—if you go home, he'll—"

"I looked at home," she cut in. "And I looked in every place I could think of to go safely without backup. But I came up empty. Now it's been four hours, and no sign of him." I looked at her, eyes wide, as Caron joined us, gazing up at Rillia. She sighed again. "Caoes is missing, Grayshade. And I have no idea how to find him . . . or where to look."

PART TWO
HERESY

The path of truth is straight, unbroken, and undeniable. To deny, to doubt, is to be deceived. You must believe, or you will fall.

—The Eighth Rite of Devotion

INTERLUDE

THE private office of Eparch Kaenath had taken some time to furnish properly. There were the curtains to consider, as richly blue as the robes worn by the members of the Order, made of fabric not easy to find in Tellisar or anywhere else. There were the chairs, feather-soft pillows covered in dark velvet. There was the vaulted ceiling, from which a golden chandelier hung and upon which was painted, in exquisite detail, a hammer striking an anvil. There was the desk, made from jadeheart wood worth as much as half of the stands in the Poor Markets, which still exuded the faint scent of the forest from which it had been harvested. And there were the windows, arched windows looking out to the garden and the two white marble fountains below, which were cunningly cut and angled so as to allow maximum light from the outside, even during the rising and setting of the sun.

It was this light which made Father Rennix blink, though he resisted shielding his eyes as he stood, ramrod straight, on the other side of the desk, waiting for Eparch Kaenath to turn and acknowledge him. The dark-haired man was staring out the window, his hands clasped behind his back, looking down at the garden below. He had shown no sign of noticing Rennix's entrance, but Rennix knew better than to clear his throat or otherwise try to get the Eparch's attention. Kaenath knew he was there. Kaenath knew everything.

Finally the Eparch nodded, as if satisfied of something, and turned to face the younger man. "Father Rennix," he said, in a tone of simple acknowledgment.

Rennix bowed. "You wished to see me, Eparch?"

"I wished to hear your report on the man we have been seeking. The report you assured me I would have on my desk three days ago."

"Yes," Rennix replied, straightening up and keeping his expression as neutral as possible. "We have made progress, Eparch. We've heard that Grayshade is making inquiries about the Order, and have confirmed several places where he might have been present. We've learned more about his allies: he has at least two people accompanying him, one of them a child. There are rumors that he also has a pet of some kind, but we haven't been able to confirm those yet. Still, it's only a matter of time until—"

"Time?" interrupted Kaenath. "It has been a month since we last discussed this Grayshade. In that month, you have come no closer to knowing where he is, right now, than you did before. You know almost nothing about his allies, other than the fact that he has 'at least two' of them, one of them young. You have learned nothing about his motives. If it is indeed a matter of time, the Service has already wasted a great deal of it."

Rennix swallowed and gave a tight nod. "I am sorry progress has not been swifter, Eparch."

"I am sorry your definition of progress is inaccurate, Father Rennix," the Eparch said, his smooth face contorted into a scowl. "The only progress we've made with this man has come from outside sources, not you." He turned away again, silhouetted in the light from the window. "What of the assassination attempt?"

Rennix blinked. "Assassination attempt? On whom?"

"On Grayshade, obviously."

"But—but I was not informed—"

"You did not need to be. I ordered it, from someone outside the Service," Kaenath replied.

"What?" Rennix said, stunned. "You ordered—an assassination?" Then he remembered a report he had received from one of his Acolytes: the strange discovery of a man in leather armor, dead with a dagger wound in his back, in an alley right near the Sabaton and Gauntlet Quarters. He had thought little of it at the time ... a theft gone wrong, or a minor skirmish between rival guilds, no doubt. But if this was the person Kaenath had ordered ...

"Is there a problem?" the Eparch asked, gazing out the window. His voice had an edge of iron in it, an edge with which Rennix was all too familiar.

Rennix swallowed again. "I—why would you go outside the Service? Argoth's will—"

"—is my concern, Father Rennix, not yours," Kaenath cut in, his voice deep and final. There was a long, deadly silence before the Eparch spoke again. "Your Acolytes have found almost nothing in the four months since Grayshade arrived. It's quite likely that he knows more about us at this point than we know about him, despite the fact that he is a stranger to Tellisar, with few allies to rely upon. For all his training, Grayshade is not a god, but a man—one single person, one you have been utterly unable to track down." He turned away from the window, eyebrows angled as he stared at Rennix. "He was an Acolyte, and that means he knows our means and methods, even in Tellisar. I chose to go outside of those methods to bring him into the open, to force him to make a mistake."

"But the assassination failed," Rennix objected. "In all likelihood, it didn't come close to succeeding. All it's done is make him more cautious."

"No. It's made him more paranoid, more uncertain, more on edge. It's made him more vulnerable, and that is exactly what we want. It's exactly what your Acolytes would never have been able to do, had I given them years to try."

Rennix opened his mouth to reply, but someone knocked on the door to the Eparch's office first. A nervous-looking Apprentice opened the door and entered, bowing low. "Excuse me, Eparch Kaenath, Father Rennix. Eparch, someone has come to see you. They say they are expected."

The Eparch nodded. "Send them in." The Apprentice bowed again and exited, and a few moments later a dark-cloaked figure entered the room, slightly shorter and a bit bulkier than either Rennix or Kaenath, a hood covering their features. They came to a halt next to Rennix, only slightly inclining their head. The Eparch returned the nod. "You made good time," he said.

"I work quickly," the figure replied. The voice was low and gravelly.

"Remove your hood in the presence of the Eparch," Father Rennix said sharply, but the cloaked figure neither responded or even looked in his direction.

The Eparch waved the demand away. "Never mind. What of your charge?"

"I've been ... tracking him since I arrived here," came the hoarse reply after a few moments of silence. "I need a little longer.

But I'll find him." The cadence was slow and halting, as if the person was searching among words to find the right ones.

"Who?" Rennix asked.

Again, several seconds passed. "Grayshade," the cloaked figure finally rasped.

Rennix's eyes widened slightly. "Grayshade. You know him?"

A guttural sound, something between a cough and a laugh, emanated from beneath the stranger's hood. "I know him . . . very well. Better than anyone else."

"But I don't know you," Rennix replied, before looking at Kaenath. "Eparch, we can't be sure this person is who they say. They could just as easily be one of his friends, or some ally he's managed to seduce to his cause here. To bring someone in from the outside is dangerous at best."

The Eparch's gaze flickered in Rennix's direction. "Are you questioning my judgment, Father?"

Rennix took a deep breath and shook his head. "Never, Eparch. But I've spent many years assessing the worth and value of people in Tellisar, and I know the difference between discretion and suspicious behavior."

"You haven't . . . found him," the cloaked figure said, turning their head slightly in Rennix's direction. "And you won't."

"You don't know this city," Rennix replied with a glare.

"And you . . . don't know him. He's better than anyone you have . . . in the Service." The figure took a long, hoarse breath. "He's better than you."

Kaenath spoke before Rennix could reply. "Enough. The Service is Father Rennix's charge . . . and mine. You'll speak with respect when you refer to it. You have work to do. It is time for you to do it. And be aware: you are answerable to me, in success or failure." He took a step forward and rested his hands on the desk, staring at the stranger.

The cloaked figure inclined their head ever so slightly, turned away without looking at Rennix, and departed.

"In the future, Father," Kaenath said, still looking at the space where the stranger had stood, "you will keep your concerns with my decisions to yourself."

Rennix bowed. "My apologies, Eparch. My role requires my obedience . . . but also my suspicion."

"You should remember them both," Kaenath responded, finally turning his gaze back to Rennix, "since I had already planned to indulge your suspicion. Set two Acolytes to watch the stranger."

"Watch them?" Rennix said, surprised.

"Yes. That one will lead us to Grayshade," the Eparch said, nodding at the closed door, "and if all goes well, will rid us of him without our direct involvement. If it does not go well, we will be there to clean up whatever remains." He turned away, almost vanishing into the overwhelming, merciless light flooding in from the window.

CHAPTER SEVEN

OVER the last months, I had learned to divide my worries equally. In the beginning I had only been concerned with my mission and my faith; attend to the one and I would strengthen the other. Then my faith was taken from me, and without that, any mission seemed of little consequence. I had replaced those jagged voids in my soul with new things: the protection of those who had thrown in their lot with me, like Caron, Rillia, and Caoes, the commitment to learn how to exist in a world not shaped by the capricious will of a false god, the conviction that the end of one truth was not the end of all truth and hope. But with every new item I added, every new reality which I acknowledged and accepted as my own, I had more to concern myself with. I could no longer throw pieces aside as if they were useless rags; every part of who I was now mattered, one way or the other.

Of all my worries, though, Caoes had been lower on my list for a time . . . because, at least in this city, he seemed as much a part of the fabric here as the rest of the citizens. Despite his agility and freedom, Caoes had a way of disappearing into the background when he wanted to, and most people seemed to ignore him. He was such a constant presence in our lives now that the thought of not seeing him somewhere in the background, quiet, steady, comforting, was almost impossible to fathom.

"I don't like it," Rillia said for the third time since returning home after the Poor Markets closed, staring into the fire. "He doesn't just vanish like this."

"Not lately," I agreed, leaning against the wall with my arms folded. "But when I traveled with him across Silarein, he vanished more than once, usually on a hunting expedition, and always returned. He's not a cat, you know; it's not that surprising that he might need more food than we've been able to provide him so far."

"Then he would have been hungry before this," Rillia argued. "Why now, just when the weather is growing warmer? And you're bringing food home from the Poor Markets now, anyway; he ate when he had to, like always. He hasn't lost muscle tone or energy since he's been here."

I frowned, looking at the empty bed on which Caoes would normally slumber in the evenings, silently outlining the space his body usually occupied. But I had no easy answer. Caoes could take care of himself, but he was not immortal, as the incident in the Bloodmarsh had proven; without Alarene's medical skill and some considerable good fortune, he would have died. If someone had indeed taken him . . .

"Caron," I said, looking at the sensate, who was sitting on the chair near the fire, not unlike the way they had been when I first encountered them in Varda's Chapel in Cohrelle. "I know you can't sense most individuals yet, or at least not easily . . . but with Caoes, perhaps there is an element that you can detect but not pinpoint . . . a signature, or a song, or . . . a piece of clothing which stands out from everything else?"

Caron shook their head slowly, smooth face focused, eyebrows angled in a worried expression. "Ripples in a pond." They looked up and saw my curious expression. "It's how I can describe it ... kind of like a ripple in a pond, one which you know you made yourself by dropping a stone into the water. I can feel his emotions slowly rippling outward ... or I could." They sighed. "But ever since Rillia found us and explained what happened, he's ... not there."

Rillia turned to face Caron. "What do you mean, not there? You mean he's gone? Dead?"

"No," Caron said, shaking their head more vigorously this time. "At least, I don't think it would feel this way. When we were walking past the healing houses, I felt fear ... fear and pain."

I nodded. "And this is different?"

"Yes. It's more like—a gap, a space. Like I can't see him, even if he's there. And not just him; it's anyone. If I sense in a particular direction, they're just ... vanished. Or hidden, or ..." They frowned. "I just can't feel them, where they are. And I want to!" A note of something crept into their voice, and as I exchanged a glance with Rillia I could tell she had heard it too, something which we never heard from Caron: fear ... and frustration. Even, though this seemed impossible ...

Anger.

"All right," I said, raising an eyebrow at Rillia in the hope she would know not to pursue the concern right now. "Let's take this in a different way. Caoes isn't a tame panther; we've never fully understood what drew him to me in the first place. He's not our pet to be kept on a leash."

"Are you saying he's decided to leave us?" Rillia demanded, folding her arms.

"No. I think he would have done that a while ago if he had planned it. I'm saying that he sees things none of us do. And he may have seen something which needed attention, something which we'll need to know sooner or later. When he comes back, we need to be ready to follow wherever he leads."

"So you think we should wait for him, just assuming he's fine?" Long experience had taught me to know when Rillia was more worried than frustrated ... and, on certain occasions, when she was both in equal measure. She was now quite obviously in the final category. "And assuming you're right, how long exactly do we wait? How long does he sit, thinking we don't care?"

"So you believe he must have been taken. Perhaps even taken to get at us."

"It's more likely than assuming he just decided to pick this moment to leave without warning, and more sensible than acting as if we have nothing to worry about!"

"I do think we have something to worry about," I said. "But if you're right, what exactly do you expect the kidnappers to do with him ... except hold on to him and wait for us to seek him out? To draw us into the open, where they can choose how and where to engage us? What can we do to help him that won't endanger us all?"

Rillia glared, then shook her head and turned away. "Maybe. But we can't do nothing." She grabbed her cloak from one of the hooks on the wall. "I won't put myself into the light, but at least I'm going to see what I can find in the shadows."

"Rillia," I said, stepping forward. "I told you, I'm worried about him too. But if he has been taken, the worst thing we could do is get picked off one by one. Without Caoes to watch your back, if someone gets the drop on you—"

"They won't," she said, pulling up her hood and opening the

front door. "But even if they did, I'll be armed and ready, instead of sitting at home waiting for the blade to strike. I'll be back tomorrow afternoon . . . with Caoes, hopefully." She hesitated and turned her attention to Caron, who was regarding her with no trace of the anger their voice had betrayed a minute ago. "It'll be fine, Caron. Stick close to Grayshade and listen to your teachers." She walked over to Caron and kneeled down, putting a hand on their shoulder. "I'll find him. And I'll be back soon." Then, with a brief but searching glance at me, she stood, turned, and departed, closing the door behind her.

I watched the door for several minutes, the crackling of the fire in rhythm with my own restless thoughts. To stay or to go: to act from passive fear, or cautious wisdom? I could not know. All I knew for certain was that my worries were no longer divided. They had multiplied, and I now had more than enough to go around.

———————+———————

There was little else we could do that night but rest as best we could, hoping to hear the opening door and the familiar sound of Rillia's boots hitting the stone floor, perhaps followed by the near-silent padding of Caoes's paws. But night passed to dawn with no sound or sign, and sooner than I had hoped, the bit of light creeping underneath the bottom edge of the door, slowly lightening the gray ashes of the now cold and lifeless fire into which I had been staring for several hours, proved that morning had arrived. I sighed and turned to wake Caron, but they were already there, dressed and facing the door.

"Caron?" I said. The sensate's head moved at the sound of my voice, and after a moment they looked at me, lips slightly parted as if they had just been speaking. Their eyes had dark circles underneath, and the lids dropped with apparent weariness. "Are you all right?" I asked quietly.

"Yes," Caron said, voice catching a bit before growing stronger. "Yes, I'm okay. I was trying to sense Caoes, or Rillia."

"All night?"

They blinked, then nodded. "Yes . . . I guess so. I was talking to my teachers, and they thought I could try again—if I still couldn't sense Caoes, I could at least find Rillia and see how she was feeling." They frowned. "But I couldn't sense her either. I can sense so many people . . . so many happy, or sad, or frustrated, or afraid. But I can't sense either of the ones I'm looking for." Again there was a tinge of annoyance, if not full anger, in Caron's tone, though much milder than the night before.

"None of this is easy," I said. "You're learning fast, but nothing happens that quickly . . . especially in a new place, and one as big as Tellisar. Give it time."

Their expression shifted again. "Rillia doesn't think we have much time to find Caoes. You don't think we have much time to find the Order."

I shrugged. "It's true, Caron . . . we don't. But for all of our training, Rillia and I were trained to be patient and careful once we had a mission and knew our targets. Before those times— before we knew our objectives—we could be just as impatient as anyone else, probably even more. And we're setting our own objectives now, and old habits die hard."

"Old habits," Caron repeated, their gaze slightly unfocused.

"Yes. That's one of the reasons you're so important. Because *your* habit is patience, care, time, whether you have a mission to complete or not, and Rillia and I need those qualities as we learn to do things differently. We're learning from you too, you know."

Caron smiled, the familiar reaction temporarily erasing their tired expression. "Everyone learns from each other, whether they know it or not, so I guess that makes sense."

I put a hand on their shoulder. "More sense than you know. Rillia will be fine, and Caoes didn't make it to me—and survive once he met me—without having wits and instinct. He'll be fine too, and I'm sure we'll see him soon."

Caron nodded, smile lessening only slightly. "All right. Then I guess we need to head to Nuraleed's stand, like usual?"

"Yes . . . for a few more days, anyway. Even more lessons." I smiled, but felt no mirth or comfort. I had been trying to convince myself as much as Caron with my words, but as much as I believed that patience mattered, I had little of it now. Rillia could take care of herself, and I had seen Caoes do extraordinary things. But Tellisar was no ordinary city, and the threats here were amorphous, uncertain. I had to watch over Caron, and get a better read on Nuraleed, but what I wanted to do most was seek out the panther and former Acolyte who had both thrown in their lots with me. And as I closed the door to our home behind us, I again wished with every part of my soul that my duties and desires were not so perpetually opposed to each other.

The day's lessons with Nuraleed were uneventful, but I took no solace in the routine; my mind was elsewhere, and although I did nothing to obviously offend any customer or neighboring stand's owner, I could tell that the merchant was aware of my distraction. "That is the third time you have folded those same bolts of cloth, Carrnisk," he observed in early afternoon, just after we had finished our noonday meal and returned to the stand. "They are not likely to get any more neat, or saleable."

I nodded, putting on what I hoped was a sheepish expression as I shifted the slightly textured fabrics into place and turning to face the larger man. "Yes, Nuraleed ... sorry. I've been trying to be focused, I suppose."

"Then you have succeeded, my friend!" Nuraleed said with a laugh. "Indeed, I have rarely met anyone so focused when engaged in a task. That kind of discipline is most unusual. You have obviously had a most productive early education." For the briefest of moments I thought he might have raised an eyebrow, his expression more probing, but it was gone so quickly in favor of his usual beatific grin I wondered if I might have imagined it. "And your child Caron, there," he went on, gesturing toward them as they were speaking earnestly to one of the merchants from a stand a few rows down from our own. "Now they are a truly extraordinary discovery: a person who genuinely seems to care about the needs and wishes of others, so deeply it is as if they know the desires of those people more than the people themselves. It would be a most valuable talent for this profession, if not married with an uncomfortable tendency to put those other's desires above one's own." He sighed dramatically. "Alas, I am afraid the utter lack of selfishness will put Caron at a disadvantage. You will have to fill in that gap for them."

I stiffened, but Nuraleed simply winked. "Yes," I said, trying to keep the sour tone out of my voice. "I suppose I have enough of that trait to cover the both of us."

"Now, now, Carrnisk, let us not take easy offense," Nuraleed replied, holding up one large hand. "You have less of that—how shall we call it?—self-focus than most men within this city. I speak more of Caron's unusual nature than your own. Though I have noticed," he went on, rubbing his chin, "that they have been somewhat more distracted of late . . . troubled, even. Today they seem particularly divided in their attention. Like you." This time I knew I wasn't imagining Nuraleed's searching gaze.

"Nothing to worry about," I said carefully. "Just a temporary concern."

"I wonder if our dear friend Rillia shares that concern," Nuraleed responded. "I wonder what she might say if we were to ask her."

Hells, I thought. I hadn't wanted to get pushed into a corner, but it looked like the decision had been made for me, and my only real option now was to shift tactics—to go on the offensive, no matter how risky it might be. I glanced briefly at Caron, still talking animatedly with the other merchant, than took a deep breath and focused my attention on Nuraleed. "I wonder about that too, Nuraleed. I wonder what she might say if she knew that our instructor has taken an interest in our private affairs . . . that a small group of merchants from a small town has intrigued him much more than necessary for his task of instruction. I wonder if she has the same questions about those things that I do." I drew myself straighter. "Or whether she would do the same things to answer those questions as I would."

The sounds of the Poor Markets, music and laughter and arguments and an occasional shout warning off a customer getting too free with the merchandise, continued. But they seemed to fade slowly in the long, heavy silence between Nuraleed and me, his smile vanished, his green-eyed gaze boring into mine. After what felt like a year, Nuraleed nodded slowly. "Yes, just so." With a sudden movement he grabbed a folded piece of purple vestile cloth, opening it with a snap, and tossed it over one of the tables in his stand, repeating the process with the other tables in his area before turning back to me. "You and Caron should follow me," he said as Caron, finished with their conversation, joined us, a quizzical expression on their face. "It appears the time has come to answer all of our questions, yes?" Without waiting for an answer, he turned away and headed off to the south, in the direction of the Gauntlet Quarter.

I hesitated. Had I pushed too far? And could I afford to take a chance on being wrong, either about Nuraleed's motives or his masters?

I glanced at Caron, who nodded. "We should go. He's not angry," they said, "or nervous. He's calm . . . focused."

I sighed and shook my head. "So was I, once. Right before every kill I had to make." Burying my fears in the need of the moment, I set off, followed by Caron, in pursuit of the merchant.

Nuraleed took the same route he had taken several nights before, when I had followed him through the streets of the Gauntlet Quarter. On that evening he had shown no particular hurry, wandering along, hailing guards and passersby alike with his usual cheery greeting. But tonight he was entirely focused, moving swiftly around and past people on the street, even those who seemed to know him, with steady momentum. We followed at a similar pace, not needing to avoid his notice this time—though he paid little obvious attention to us, once or twice glancing back in our direction but otherwise content to keep moving. My own attention was divided, looking both at the back of Nuraleed's golden caftan as he strode along and the surrounding rooftops and alleyways for potential spots of ambush. It was true that an attack seemed unlikely here; there were still too many people on the streets, including a reasonable number of guards, not to attract notice, if not a full out fight with a panicked group of regular citizens caught in the middle. Even if my concerns about Nuraleed were justified, he didn't strike me as someone who would want that kind of chaotic, uncontrollable situation. It would have been much easier to just poison us, or have his associates follow us home the way I had followed him home, and do the job there.

But I was working from assumptions, not facts, and doing so with someone who had been hard to get a clear read on from the beginning ... and there was the attack I had already survived. Given the circumstances, and the fact I was having to do all of this without backup from either Rillia or Caoes—while still trying to protect Caron—I had no choice but to remain vigilant. So I continued to watch the shadows, even if my main focus was the billowing gold charge of the merchant in front of us. Caron, however, was even more focused, staring at Nuraleed's back, almost leaning forward as we walked along. Again, I felt a twinge of worry. Caron was usually calm and peaceful, even when sensing the emotions of others, and even if they had several moments of anger over the last few days, this level of intense scrutiny was not normal. What was happening to Caron ... and what could I do about it?

After only a few minutes more, we arrived at the short alleyway which led to the building to which I had followed Nuraleed a few nights earlier, and without a pause or a glance Nuraleed turned into it. As we slowed down to enter the alley ourselves, Caron looked at me for the first time since we had left the Poor Markets, their expression softening into its more usual form. "Are you sensing anything else from him?" I asked, watching as the merchant approached the open space surrounding the house.

Caron shook their head. "No," they said. "Just the same calm certainty he's had the whole time. Grayshade ... when you followed him before ... is this what he seemed like? Did it look like he was this focused?"

I shrugged. "No. He seemed ... unconcerned, carefree. Not worried. It wasn't until he was in the house, and I was listening to him from the outside, that things changed."

"I guess we'll see, then. But either way, we should be careful of someone that sure about anything."

I nodded, though the warning was unnecessary. I didn't need Caron to tell me to steer clear of absolute conviction; I had learned, more times than I could count, of how powerful, even deadly, that state of mind could be. We walked down the alley in silence, and though I saw nothing obvious, something felt off as we crossed into the space between the house and the alley. The area seemed empty, and the bright afternoon sun made it impossible for anyone not actually invisible to hide on a nearby rooftop. Then I realized the problem: my improvised fly hook, and the rope hanging from it, were gone from Nuraleed's meeting place. I should hardly have been surprised at this; anyone would have checked around their home when suspecting, as Nuraleed clearly did, that they were being spied upon by someone. Yet I still silently berated myself for leaving it behind. I wasn't sure what information anyone could get from trying to figure out how the device was put together, but at best it would reveal some measure of sophistication; at worst, if the person knew anything about the Order, or the Service . . .

What's done is done, I reminded myself as we stopped in front of the door behind which Nuraleed had just disappeared. *Focus on the moment instead of the mistakes . . . especially if you don't want to make more of them.* I sighed, took one last look around us, and reached for the handle, but before I could grasp it the door opened suddenly, and I heard Caron give a small gasp as I took an involuntary step back. Nuraleed was standing there, his large frame nearly filling the doorway, green eyes glittering. But I was drawn to another set of eyes, the yellow eyes of a four-legged creature standing in front of him and looking up at us silently.

They were the eyes of Caoes.

CHAPTER EIGHT

FOR a moment no one said anything as merchant, child, assassin, and panther all stared at each other. It was Nuraleed who finally broke the silence with a theatrical cough. "Yes," he said, mustache twisting. "He is most friendly, Carrnisk. And he appears to know you quite well."

I looked at Nuraleed, who was regarding me with a bemused expression. "What's your point?" I asked, holding his gaze with mine.

He shrugged. "The same point I made in the Poor Markets, my friend: there are questions to be answered, and the time has come to answer them. I suggest we do so inside." He turned away, but took only a step before looking over his shoulder. "You can see for yourself that he is unharmed—and, moreover, that he is not being held against his will. In fact, he came to me . . . a most fortunate occurrence for you, as it happens."

I bent down and gently stroked the back of Caoes's neck, feeling the velvet texture of his fur, his shoulder muscles slightly tensing and releasing at my touch. "So," I said quietly. "Are you all right, Caoes? Not hurt, or sick?" The panther remained silent as usual, but the tilting of his head to one side at the sound of my voice was unmistakable; this was Caoes for certain, and as I glanced at Caron I saw from their expression that they had been sensing the same thing.

"He's fine, Grayshade," the sensate said. "Calm . . . and happy."

"Very much so," Nuraleed agreed.

I nodded as I stood. Whatever was going on here, it wasn't the setup for an ambush . . . at least not yet. We still needed answers, and we were going to get them one way or the other. With a deep breath, I entered the building, Caron and Caoes falling into step behind me.

Nuraleed's home, if it was such, was as impressively opulent inside as it was unremarkable, even underwhelming, outside. The windowless room into which the merchant led us was decorated on every wall with tapestries and silken fabrics, many of which I had seen in the Poor Markets and some of which I did not know, a riot of color and texture to rival even Nuraleed's wildly over-wrought outfits. In the back of the room was a small fireplace, though I had seen no obvious chimney outside to exhaust the smoke. In any case, it was currently dark and cold, swept clean of any lingering ash. Hanging on each side of the fireplace was a large cloth map, the various geographical features done in some kind of full color needlework; the left one looked to be of the cit-ies surrounding the Glacalta, from Sullbris, Tellisar, and Arginn on the water's northern edge to Calarginn in the south, while the right one appeared to be a larger view of Silarein and the seas and continents beyond. A magnificent oak desk sat on the right wall, covered in papers, scrolls, books, and inkwells, matched with an equally impressive chair, made of a strange darkwood and dark purple plush cushions, which sat in front of it. Four other such chairs sat around a round table in the center of the room. The whole thing boasted unthinkable wealth and easy opulence. It was very much what I might have expected from Nuraleed . . .

and very much a message about what resources he could bring to bear if needed.

The room's owner gestured to the chairs around the table, and Caron and I each took a seat as Caoes padded to a richly textured cushion in front of the cold hearth and slowly lay down, yellow-eyed gaze fixed upon us. Nuraleed went through the only other exit, a sturdy looking oak door in the left side of the room, and was gone for less than a minute before returning with a tray of three mugs and a saucer. He placed the tray down on the table, then removed the saucer and laid it in front of Caoes; it had some kind of oily liquid which Caoes quickly began to lap up with his pink tongue. "Namirs do not typically like the company of others once grown," Nuraleed observed as he sat down at the table, "but then, this is no typical namir, yes?" He stroked the panther's back, which arched slightly at the touch. "You have taken good care of him," the merchant went on. "We are grateful ... and eager to hear how he came to be in your company."

"And by 'we,'" I said, nodding slowly, "I assume you don't mean 'we merchants of the Poor Markets.' What other organization is eager for this knowledge, Nuraleed? Is it one to which you personally belong ... or one to which you have sold your information about us?"

Nuraleed's mustache twitched. "Your use of the term 'information' is illuminating, friend Carrnisk. It is reflective of a certain state of mind ... a mind which is not used to being open to the questions of others." He drank deeply from his mug before continuing. "I knew from the moment we met that you were most unusual, and not long afterward that you were also not being truthful. Your story was much too convenient and unbelievable;

the idea that you had ever survived by buying and selling goods was laughable on its face. Once we followed up with our own investigation, I knew I was right."

"Investigation?"

"You suspected this yourself," Nuraleed replied, "so I am afraid that any expression of disbelief is not credible, my friend. You did not follow me several nights ago out of concern for my welfare, nor did this namir keep company with you out of coincidence."

"What is a namir?" Caron asked.

Nuraleed turned his gaze to the sensate. "Namir is our word for what you call a panther. As for our word for what we would call you . . ." His eyes glittered. "That, you must teach me."

"This discussion is about us, Nuraleed . . . not Caron," I said, leaning forward.

"It would be more correct to say it is about both," Nuraleed replied, looking at me. "For it is clear that you are bound to this child in some way, and much will be learned once that bond is understood."

I pushed my chair back from the table. "We are not research experiments. You'll have to do your work on other subjects." Caron opened their mouth to say something, but Nuraleed raised a hand first.

"If there is anything you have learned from me so far, Carrnisk, it is to control your impulses when dealing with others. You are remarkably insightful . . . but your insights have limits." He watched as I let my hands slowly relax their grip on the edge of the table. "This is good, yes," he said after a few moments. "Now we may discuss things more reasonably. You can explain what you know, I can explain what I know . . . and together, our knowledge will be expanded."

"No one wins or loses. We are all enriched by the interaction," I said, my gaze steady.

Nuraleed laughed loudly. "So you see, you have learned something after all. Then I will begin." He took a long drink from his mug. "It was immediately obvious to me that you were not a merchant, and your name was most certainly not Carrnisk. Our people confirmed that Rivinnea, on the other hand, *is*, or *was*, a merchant . . . among, perhaps, other things. And they learned that a namir accompanied you throughout the city, though you were most careful not to reveal his presence." He paused, looking at us as I kept my expression as neutral as possible. "Last night I heard that same namir had been seen elsewhere, in the Armor Quarter, and I decided the time had come to see him for myself. I found him there . . . and, as you can see, we swiftly became friends."

"What did you do to him?" I asked, my tone much calmer than my actual feelings.

Nuraleed raised an eyebrow. "Nothing, except remind him of his home, perhaps. Namirs are common in Al'Estra, and indeed the whole nation of Cartevis; my people have worked with them for centuries. Though, as to that," he said with a chuckle, stroking the back of Caoes's smooth neck again, "this namir is not as common as others might be. But, blessedly, I know how to deal with even the uncommon ones."

"You and your people," I said. "All right, Nuraleed. You've told us who you think we are. You haven't told us who you are—who you truly are."

Nuraleed leaned back and threw his arms wide, breaking into

his usual wide grin. "But I am exactly as you see me, one whose name is not Carrnisk."

I returned the smile grimly. "I see you . . . but not exactly as you are. No more secrets." I pulled my chair back toward the table, glancing at Caron, who was still watching the merchant.

Nuraleed's gaze bore into me. "No more secrets for me, or for us all?" As I did my best not to react, he nodded. "We came here to be honest with each other. So, since you—whoever you may be—are by nature a suspicious man, we will engage in a mutually beneficial transaction, yes? You will give me something, and I will give you something in return. We will begin with something simple: names. Though I am singularly amused by the name Carrnisk, you do not wear it well, and it is clearly not yours. What is your true name?"

For a tense few moments there was complete silence in the room. I looked again at Caron, who turned their attention to me. Their expression seemed slightly troubled, but they simply nodded once. I sighed and turned back to Nuraleed. "My name is Grayshade, for whatever good it will do you. And this is Caron, just as we said before."

Nuraleed nodded, expression thoughtful. "Grayshade," he repeated slowly, as if he were examining the name for imperfections. "I see."

"And now?"

Nuraleed paused before he grinned again. "I have the advantage on you here, my friend, as Nuraleed is indeed my name. But fear not; as you have no doubt learned by now, I do not cheat. And it is my turn to give you the first bit of information." He took a long drink from his mug, wiped his mouth, and set the mug down on the table with a resounding *thunk*. "So. As I told you, I am from the country of Cartevis, and its capital city of Al'Estra. As Rivinnea—we will refer to her by this no doubt inaccurate name for the present—told you, my city is known for many things, particularly refined fabrics like silk. And, with all respect to the wonders of Tellisar—" he waved vaguely in the direction of the front door— "they pale in comparison to the spectacular nature of Al'Estra. Beauty is the birthright of the jewel of the Labyrinthine Sea. But for all of that luxury, our true power has never been in military might, or the control of natural resources; indeed, we must import some of those resources from elsewhere, relying on trade to make up the difference. No, the true strength of Al'Estra lies in its wealth ... and the intelligence necessary to keep that wealth flowing toward us, and not toward jealous neighbors with dangerous ambition."

"Intelligence?" Caron asked, watching Nuraleed closely.

"Just so. Knowledge of the actions, and intentions, of others, you might say."

"And I might say," I broke in, "that I've heard of such things before. But no country or city has enough resources to follow the machinations of everyone else. There have to be gaps, breaches."

"Indeed," the merchant said, smiling broadly. "It is our job to fill those gaps."

"Whose job, exactly?"

"Mine—and the people whom I work with." Nuraleed leaned forward, voice dropping slightly despite the fact we were the only three people in the room. "I am the leader of the Silken Order."

I raised an eyebrow. "I've never heard of it."

"Most in Silarein have not, and those who have might not

admit to it. But it is an ancient organization, founded centuries ago. Originally it was what you would call a trade guild, yes? A sort of loose association of merchants and tradesmen who came together to advocate for their common interests, when Al'Estra was closer to a fishing village than the jewel in the crown of the Estranian Archipelago. When they first began to organize, they were dedicated to maintaining honest and fair trade for all of their members . . ."

". . . who wouldn't do it on their own," I said.

Nuraleed snorted. "It is unsurprising to me, friend Grayshade, that someone so anxious to conceal his own name and purpose believes everyone else to be as covered in shadows as he is. In truth, most merchants in Al'Estra are honest . . . or honest enough so that their, shall we say, slight bending of traditional regulations causes no permanent injury to anyone involved. But as they say here in Tellisar, 'one rotten fruit, one rotten bushel,' yes? And even an enlightened metropolis like Al'Estra has a few rotten fruit. So the organization of merchants was intended to seek out and, as it were, clean the rottenness."

"Were they able to do it?" Caron asked.

"Why of course, after a fashion," Nuraleed replied. "In many ways it was a great success."

"But it didn't stop there, did it?" Caron said. "I mean—it wasn't the Silken Order yet."

The merchant looked at Caron and adjusted his turban. "Again, Caron, your insight is most intriguing to me. I wonder whether you could give some of that understanding to our newly named Grayshade." He laughed as I managed to hold back a scowl. "Yes, it changed," he went on after a moment. "Soon enough the merchants realized they could no longer simply concern themselves with trade and profit, for the government of Al'Estra had grown powerful and greedy, its leaders desiring an ever-larger part of the money its citizens were attracting. In and of itself, there was so much wealth that it might not have mattered what Al'Estra demanded. But the city did not stop there. It became increasingly protective of its own money, belligerent toward other cities and trading partners. It built its military power, developing a wildly expensive armada and field army. Soon enough it was threatening to sink other countries' ships, raid them, and the government of Cartevis was helpless to stop them." Nuraleed paused to shake his head, then drank deeply from his mug. He put it back on the table and sighed. "As I told you, the merchants of Al'Estra sell fabric, not swords and shields and cannonballs. A war would have been disastrous. And so the decision was made to shape the organization of merchants in a new direction, using their contacts and resources all along the Labyrinthine Sea to recruit the best from among their number."

"The Silken Order," I said.

"Just so. It was quite small at first, but over years it grew, always in secret, training the members of the Order in the most advanced techniques of espionage and, when necessary, combat. The Order did not want open warfare with either other cities or Al'Estra itself, and so it worked carefully, cautiously, undermining military preparations when needed, thwarting potential ambushes, gathering intelligence on the actions of Al'Estra and revealing that intelligence to its potential targets."

"Wouldn't that leave Al'Estra vulnerable to attack?"

Nuraleed chuckled. "One would hope not. But I suspect the

Order in those days knew that if it overreached, it would bring down a city whose trade was fundamental to the Order's existence." Inwardly I flinched a bit at the use of the term "Order"—I had long been used to it referring to something quite different—but outwardly I simply nodded as Nuraleed continued. "In the end, Al'Estra's belligerence was mitigated, and the city has grown increasingly wealthy and powerful since that time. But the Silken Order has not disbanded, for we know all too well that humanity will always be seduced by power and greed. So we remain in the shadows . . . and watch."

I pushed a sudden memory into the back of my mind, where it belonged. "And you? How long have you been in the shadows?"

Nuraleed grinned and took a long drink from his mug before responding. "But you have forgotten our agreement, friend Grayshade. I have given you information about where I am from and the group with whom I am associated. Now you must return the favor and tell me something more of yourself than your colorless name." He rested his forearms on the table and leaned forward, the wood creaking slightly beneath his weight.

I shrugged. "I'm not sure I ever made an agreement with you, Nuraleed. I'm grateful for the information you've provided so far, so . . . I'll answer what I can. But I still have more questions of my own."

"Let us focus on the transaction of the moment, then," Nuraleed said with a nod, "as I have taught you. So. The namir. How did you come to have him—and train him?"

I glanced down at Caoes on his cushion, whose eyes were closed as his head rested lightly on the plush surface, then looked at Nuraleed, bemused. "I didn't train him . . . and he came to me, as I was traveling across Silarein. At first I thought it was just chance; he had no real reason to join me in the first place, or stay with me when he could have left. But eventually I decided there must have been something to keep him connected with me, something which made him want to help."

"Help with the dishonest merchant in your village, I would imagine?" Nuraleed asked with a tilt of his mug.

"Something like that," I said, rubbing the back of my neck. "But I wasn't expecting help of any kind, especially from someone like Caoes."

"Yes," Nuraleed mused. "What of his name?"

I hesitated. "It was . . . a tribute, of a kind, to an old mentor of mine. Perhaps overly sentimental, but it seemed to fit him."

Nuraleed nodded slowly. "Indeed. Perhaps it does. As I said, my people have worked with namirs for many decades. There are a few here, mostly maintained as starving novelties for the people to goggle at." For the first time since arriving here I thought I detected a touch of anger in Nuraleed's tone, and a quick glance at Caron, leaning forward with rapt attention, suggested he was noticing the same thing. "But in my city, a number of them wander the streets, companions of choice who are nourished and respected by all. To kill or even hurt a namir would be a grave offense, in part because they are so important to the smooth operation of the city. The belief of many, even many of Al'Estra's own citizens, is that all namirs are like this naturally. Only a few—including Al'Estra's leaders—know that the reason they are so useful is because of us."

"The Silken Order?" Caron asked.

"Yes. We have trained namirs for many years, raising them

from cubs to full grown adults, teaching them all of the tasks which we will need from them."

"Such as?" I said.

Nuraleed shrugged. "Information gathering. Carrying messages from one member of the Order to another, without being noticed." His eyes glittered. "Of course, fighting. As you might have noticed, the namir is quite skilled in combat."

I nodded, thinking back to the battle in the Bloodmarsh and the fight against Merynne. "I noticed. But why did he come to me?"

"That was what I hoped to hear from you," Nuraleed sighed. "He is obviously one of our namirs, and must either have been brought to Tellisar or somehow made his way on a ship from Al'Estra to Tellisar. But why he left after that is a mystery, yes?" He stroked the back of Caoes's ears again. "Yet it is said among my people that the bond of a namir is the truest sign of friendship. If he found you, and decided to stay with you, it means you were worthy of his trust. For us, that is a significant mark in your favor."

"So without it, you wouldn't have trusted me?" I asked, folding my arms.

Nuraleed chuckled. "Without it, friend Grayshade, we would probably not be having this discussion—for you would already have been dealt with."

I raised an eyebrow. "Is that so? I appreciate your confidence, Nuraleed, but you may not know all of what other people can do . . . even strange merchants from out of town."

"Perhaps not," Nuraleed replied with a grin. "But I know what we are capable of doing, and I know if someone is or is not a merchant." He leaned back again. "I know that you have never bought or sold goods before arriving in Tellisar. And I know that you are a gifted combatant . . . and, presumably, an assassin."

I stiffened and stared at Nuraleed, whose hands were now resting lightly on the edge of the table in the manner of someone ready for whatever might happen next. "I would have thought the leader of the Silken Order would choose his words with more care. There is a difference between confidence and arrogance."

Nuraleed rubbed his chin. "Just so. And there is a difference between defiance and bluster, Grayshade. So let us not continue this dance, you and I. I know you are a trained fighter, gifted at tracking and infiltrating. I know you are a dangerous man, who carries himself with the air of one who is at ease with danger, though not at ease with himself. And I know that your companions are both mysterious and unusual—in part because they do not seem to view themselves as such." He glanced at Caron, who gazed back, expression again serene. "And then there is the namir," Nuraleed went on, looking back at me. "But whatever it is you seek here, Grayshade, you must know by now that you will have little luck in finding it by yourself. And you will soon learn that a person who cannot trust in anyone else will have difficulty in getting anyone to trust them . . . and no matter how dangerous or mysterious, a friendless soul will not survive long in Tellisar."

"So I must trust the Silken Order, with your own interests and city at stake?"

"No," Nuraleed responded, suddenly serious. "You must trust *me.* The man who could have killed you by now, many times . . . and did not." Suddenly Caron started, and I looked over to see them staring up at the ceiling. I followed their gaze to see something odd—a dark corner, within the recesses of which something was glinting . . . light reflecting off the metal tip of . . .

A crossbow bolt.

I turned my head slowly to see, at every other corner where the wall met the ceiling, the same telltale glint. I would swear there were no such installations when I first walked in, but weapons could be concealed, even if I had never encountered concealment of such skill before. I looked back at Caron, who seemed to have composed themself—though their initial reaction was as surprising to me as the suddenly apparent crossbows—and finally turned my attention back to Nuraleed, who was watching me closely.

"Trust at the point of a crossbow bolt isn't likely to last," I said slowly, hand inching toward my cloak, considering my options. *A spray of kushuri darts as I threw myself into Caron to knock us both to the ground, maybe . . . and if we could roll under the table to avoid the crossbow fire . . .*

"That is true," Nuraleed said, gazing at me steadily. "But I am not asking for your trust at the point of a crossbow bolt. I am showing these crossbows to you because I could have used them any time I wished . . . and did not. I am asking for your trust because I did not kill you when I could have. I did not disarm you when you entered the house, nor confront you when you came to visit me the first time. I am asking for your trust because I did not push you into a situation which would make escape or defense impossible. I did not report your existence to any but my closest confidant, whose job is to be . . . interested in such matters. I am asking for your trust because I respect secrets and individual desires over many things . . . perhaps even, at times, my own best interests, or those of the Order which I lead." He glanced at my hand. "And I think you know that those bolts are faster than any weapon you might be able to wield."

In spite of the tension, I couldn't help a grim smile. "It's more about the wielder than the weapon. And I don't think you know how fast this wielder is."

Nuraleed grinned widely. "Quite so. Perhaps it would be in our best interests not to test our mutual theories, then?"

The greatest danger of leaving an ideology behind, especially when that ideology has determined the nature of your life for so long, is not the loss of community, or belonging, or even identity. The greatest danger is you will never feel certain again: that you will never feel the comfort of knowing the best, the only path which remains to be taken. I had walked across uncertain ground for months now, never sure which step might be my last, and I was weary of having to survive in this uncanny darkness. And here I was again, making decisions in the dark.

But they're your decisions, I thought I heard a voice whisper. *And there is nothing to fear in darkness but what you bring to it.* I looked at Caron, who was looking at me ... but he was simply smiling as usual, and it hadn't sounded like his voice. Perhaps I was speaking to myself, and perhaps the time had come for me to listen.

I sighed, nodded, and turned back to Nuraleed. "All right. My name is Grayshade. I'm from the city of Cohrelle, to the east of Silarein, along the Silver Coast." Nuraleed said nothing, large hands resting lightly on the edge of the table, his green-eyed gaze intent and focused. "But I was more than just a citizen," I went on. "For ten years I was the best Acolyte in the Service of Argoth.

I was their greatest assassin." I glanced briefly at Caron. "Then one of my missions went sideways, and instead of killing my next target as I was intended to . . . I saved them instead, and defied the Service. I became a target of the Order of Argoth which I had once served without question. Rillia—the true name of the woman you know as Rivinnea—was a merchant, as she told you, but also a former Acolyte. With her help, and the help of Caron here, I managed to stop the High Prelate, the leader of the Order in Cohrelle."

Nuraleed nodded slowly. "I assume that was not the end of it."

"No," I said. "The Order wasn't destroyed, and I couldn't stay until it was. And it became clear the High Prelate couldn't have been working on his own. Something or someone larger, outside Cohrelle, had to be making decisions. So I went cross-country, across Silarein to Tellisar." I paused, then decided there were some details Nuraleed didn't need. "It was . . . a difficult journey. But I found Caoes along the way," I said, gesturing to the sleeping panther, "or rather, he found me, as did Caron and Rillia. We stopped another Acolyte who had been sent to take me down . . . and in the end, the trail led us here, to Tellisar. And here is where it's going to end, one way or the other. For the last months we've been tracking down information about the Order of Argoth here in the city."

"And when you have that information?"

"I'm going to go to where it leads me—to the leaders of the Order, whomever they are." I leaned back and took a deep breath. "And then I'm going to kill them."

There was a heavy silence, which Nuraleed finally broke. "To get your revenge?"

"To end the threat. Forever."

Another silence ensued. Finally the merchant leaned back and rubbed his chin. "And you, Caron," he said, not breaking his gaze with me. "Do you approve of this plan?"

"I . . ." Caron said, then hesitated. "Grayshade has to follow his own path."

"Then you do not see this Order of Argoth as a threat?"

"Oh . . . they're definitely dangerous," Caron replied.

"But you do not agree with their destruction?"

Caron frowned. "Even if I didn't . . ." They looked at me and pursed their lips. "My teachers tell me that my decisions are my own, as are everyone else's. In the end, the Order is threatening everyone in the Cloud. Something has to be done to stop them."

"Before," the merchant said, turning his gaze to Caron, "they stop you."

Caron nodded. "And Grayshade. And everyone else."

Nuraleed looked from Caron, to me, then to Caoes. "Very well," he finally said. "Then we must find your Rillia, and make plans. There is much to discuss, and you must each decide what to do."

"And what about you?" I asked.

"I must decide what the Silken Order should do," Nuraleed replied, then grinned slowly and leaned forward. "Another transaction, friend Grayshade. A chance for us to help each other, yes?"

CHAPTER NINE

A slight stirring behind me caused me to turn swiftly and silently in that direction, but in the reflected light of the lanterns from the street I saw only the end of a tail vanishing behind a barrel. At least that was one way in which Tellisar was similar to Cohrelle: even the mice could act as a distraction, if focus was lacking. I shook my head; perhaps it was understandable that my focus wasn't entirely where it needed to be, given the events of the last week, but if anyone had told me six months ago that I would need to improve my concentration so I could do proper surveillance on a simple storefront . . .

"As if you're incapable of making mistakes," I muttered, turning back to my task. But it would have to be a pretty big mistake to miss something like this. The store I was observing from across a narrow street in the Sword Quarter was small—probably no bigger inside than Nuraleed's stand within the Poor Market, though at least this building had two floors—with one door and window on the bottom floor and one barred window on the second floor, with a sloped roof leading up and away from the street, and two small alleys to either side of the building. I supposed it could technically be called its own building, but I doubted that a few feet of space all around provided much of a buffer for either sound or movement. And unless there were extensive cellars below the store—not impossible, but unlikely given the rest of the layout—there wasn't much more room inside the building to store material. All told, I had seen far more impressive places than the establishment of Yanner Fris in my time.

But this was where Nuraleed had sent me, and this was where I had to be. And, after a few more weary hours, I'd be rid of the place and my duty within it, if all went well.

I continued to watch the alley to the right of the building until I saw a pair of yellow eyes gleaming in the darkness, only for a moment before they were extinguished. Caoes had held his position as I had wanted him to . . . not that I would have expected any different, even more now that I knew his background and the training he had gone through before coming to me. I blinked and rubbed my eyes. Even with the disruptions of the last few days, it might have been easier to stay focused on my objective if I believed in the necessity of all of this, in the way I had always believed in my missions in Cohrelle. Of course those missions were based on a lie—but a lie in which I believed could be more effective than a truth which I found underwhelming.

At least the Silken Order found our task important . . . important enough that it would not help further until we had succeeded in it. "I am sympathetic to your urgency, friend Grayshade," Nuraleed said after I revealed the circumstances under which we had arrived in Tellisar. "But the Order of Argoth is much quieter here, it seems, than they were in your city. No one really knows their intentions, or, beyond the foothold they have with some of Tellisar's military elements, what they intend to do with the presence they have established here."

"I've told you—"

He waved my words away. "I have no doubt, friend, that you

are their target. Even we noticed their activity escalate within recent months . . . right around the time you arrived, in fact. You seem to have aggravated the hornets even before you began to poke at their nest, yes?"

"Aggravation is indeed one of my talents," I replied grimly. "But these hornets seem to sting in silence."

The leader of the Silken Order shrugged. "Perhaps. But the two main leaders of the Order of Argoth in this city—a man named Rennix, who seems to be the leader of what you describe as the Service, and the Eparch Kaenath, who is apparently his superior—have a most strange way of preparing to sting. We have not had many encounters with Argoth's people, but they seem disciplined and cautious . . . not the sort to act impulsively."

"That makes them the more dangerous," I said. "When they do act, they will have prepared for almost any eventuality. It is their way; it was mine, for many years."

"But until then, I have little to go on," Nuraleed said, spreading his arms wide in a gesture of resignation. "Suspicions and rumors are a poor way to determine one's future course of action, yes?"

"I told you about the cloaked figure following me after I left your home the first time, and the way he met his end. That doesn't trouble you?"

"It would trouble me more if I knew that the Order of Argoth was responsible for it."

"Then you don't believe me," I said, folding my arms. "You'd rather wait for the knife to be at your throat before acting to protect yourself?"

"I would rather know whose knife I must protect my throat

from, my friend," Nuraleed replied with a wry smile. "Listen, Grayshade. I do, indeed, believe your story. Both your own behavior, and that of Caron, confirms your tale, as does your relationship with the namir. But my belief is not enough. We have not been active in Tellisar long, nowhere near as long as the Order of Argoth you have described. And we are foreigners here, from a distant continent. Accuse without proof, condemn without evidence, and we will not only be a target of this same group you have spent considerable time convincing me is dangerous, we will most likely be forcibly removed from Tellisar. The consequences of that—and of losing our trade contracts—are too great to risk. I am not a king among men; I am the leader of an Order which works to advance the interests of its members and head off war which might threaten the Order or Cartevis as a whole. I cannot simply snap my fingers and provide you people, resources, and support. The danger to the Silken Order, and the people of Al'Estra, would be greatly increased if we were to be discovered and targeted here."

"So instead you will do nothing."

"What we will *not* do," the merchant said, eyes flaring, "is go to war with a group of what you tell me are elite assassins, solely on the word of an elite assassin who once served that same group. I have much respect for you, friend Grayshade; have the respect for me to understand that such a request would be impossible to grant." He grinned as he saw my reaction. "Yet I forget that the people of Silarein and the Silver Coast are an impulsive sort, swift to react and slow to listen. For I have said the Silken Order will not oppose the Order of Argoth *solely* on your word. But I have also said your word does carry weight, and I have my own concerns about a group so suddenly flustered, even if you are to blame for their agitation. So we have begun our own research into this regrettable situation, and we will decide whether—or perhaps how—we will assist you. If, that is, you can assist us with a small matter first."

I raised an eyebrow. "I won't kill for you, Nuraleed. I'm not a blade for hire."

He shook his head. "Fortunately for both of us, I do not need a blade for hire. But I do need what your people might call 'suitable distance' from the execution of a task." His green eyes glittered. "I need a response to, let us say, unjustified bigotry against outside trade. I need a bit of—how do your people put it? Sabotage."

It was indeed one way of putting what I was doing: surveying (and preparing to sabotage) the store and home of an enemy of the Silken Order, all to gain their assistance in tracking and bringing down the Order of Argoth. The only thing keeping me from worrying I'd been set up in some manner or another was the clarity that even if I was being asked for "a bit" of sabotage, there was certainly more than a bit of difficulty and risk involved in such a public space, even if Yanner Fris's store was not a particularly formidable structure. I could see why the merchant had wondered who could do this, and whether he really needed evidence for his Order, or was taking advantage of an unexpected opportunity while getting me off of his back, I resigned myself to the task.

According to Nuraleed, Fris had made his fortune from the buying and selling of rare dyes, items which were obviously hugely important to the world of fabric and fashion—or at least that was the public story. In reality, Fris was a smuggler for hire, a buccaneer who sold his talents for moving illegal merchandise to the highest bidder. "Not that we truly care about smuggled merchandise in Tellisar," Nuraleed had said. "How the city polices its trade is its own business. But the smuggling only works in one way: to undercut the supply lines and prices of traders from outside Tellisar, and especially from outside Silarein. So we will send a message: profit off the backs of those who make the city what it is, and the price you pay will be greater than your profit."

I had no particular interest in smugglers either way, but I was not being asked to physically harm anyone, and if it would get the Silken Order firmly on our side, it was a reasonable task for me to perform, even if I had less time than I would have liked to perform it. I would normally sit for days to memorize patterns, and to observe Fris himself coming and going, both to get a sense of how to bypass any possible traps or locks and to ensure he left before I entered . . . but given the need for swift action elsewhere, I wanted to get this over quickly. So I had arrived in the mid-afternoon, and six hours of surveillance had revealed no sign of anything but an empty storefront occupied only by the "CLOSED" sign hung inside the ground floor window. With darkness now set, and hoping the man was resting his evening hours off at a tavern, I decided I should make my move on my own time and terms. So with one final survey of the street, I drew my cloak around me and moved quickly to the front of Yanner Fris's building.

Under normal circumstances, I would have preferred to enter by the second floor, but I did not relish the idea of cutting through the bars over the window above. I had done it many times before, of course, but not for quite a while, and not when the owner of the house could well be in the room with that window . . . or could return when I was occupied with it, suspended above the ground. So I went with the lower floor instead, and given the proximity of this window to the door, I assumed Fris would have seen no benefit in making the door harder to manage than the window itself. Still, I didn't want to be reckless, and so after taking a quick glance through the window into the darkened space of the room beyond, I took a minute to do a visual inspection of the door frame, and another to run my thumb and forefinger carefully around the edge of the door. Finding nothing, I pulled out two kellas, each one a long and thin piece of iron. Holding one kella in my left hand, I carefully inserted the other kella into the keyhole of the door and closed my eyes, stilling my breath and focusing all my attention on the narrow metal as I began to shift it slowly around the interior of the lock. "*Rennis,*" I murmured, and felt the kella in my left hand begin to move on its own, resonating with the kella in my right hand as it moved within the door's lock. I felt each bump and contour of the interior metal, heard the slight scrape of infinitesimal burrs on the iron as it transferred to the kella. I remembered having once explained to a bewildered Apprentice why we bothered to do things this way; using only one kella, as we had in the past, would allow us to feel aspects of the internal structure of a lock or trap too. But it was much less reliable; a single item, like a lockpick or a kella, could easily be grabbed by a trap within or beyond the lock, or break during an attempt to probe the lock's inner structure. A set of two, combined with soundshifting, allowed the Acolyte to use one kella's movement to duplicate the other, and to remember every contour and notch; even if the first kella was broken, the Acolyte could use what they had learned of the interior lock to finish picking the lock or disabling the trap with the other kella, much more efficiently than before.

As it happened, though, this was a fairly uncomplicated lock by my standards, and I was able to open it with little difficulty. I slid the kellas back into my cloak and crouched down as I entered, closing the door behind me. Although the room was mostly dark, there was enough flickering light filtering from the street lanterns outside the building for me to see that it was small, with a few simple chairs lining the walls, a counter toward the back of the room, and one door in the back wall behind that. Not very much like a smuggler's hold, but then again, this was Fris's home and public storefront; if it was meant to be the cover for his activities, he wouldn't be foolish enough to keep his stolen goods in the open. Still in a low crouch, I crept cautiously toward the counter, keeping my balance low and wide, listening for any creak from the floorboard which could give me away. But the silence remained unbroken, and I made it to the counter without incident. I thought for a moment, then moved behind the counter and put my ear to the closed door; there was no sound, and I slowly opened the door to reveal a very small room, in the corner of which was a spiral staircase leading to the second floor. Again I listened and heard only silence, and after a moment I turned away, satisfied.

On top of the counter was an unlit lantern, and I carefully rose to a standing position, looked around the room again, then opened the lantern and murmured "revelle," watching as the soundshifting word sparked the small pool of oil inside the lantern aflame. I closed the lantern door and turned the wick down as low as possible, watching as the light dimmed ... but even this small amount of extra light had illuminated much of the rest of the room. There were some small, labeled earthen pots of various colored powders on three shelves behind the counter where I stood, along with a few piles of unsorted coins . . . which struck me as a bit odd. Nuraleed never let a bit of money sit in the open; the minute a transaction was completed, the money and goods were whisked away to some belt pouch or bag within his tunic. And of all the things which could reasonably be described as "eccentric" about Nuraleed, this wouldn't be one of them— wouldn't any merchant be just as careful to keep forms of money safely tucked away?

Odd or not, my goal here was sabotage, not simple theft. I shook my head, then turned back to my work. Drawing forth a small pouch of kaltessh from within my cloak, I carefully scattered the black powder onto every shelf, over the pots and coins, and from the counter in multiple directions across the floor. Kaltessh was swift burning and completely self-consuming; when it was set alight, it would quickly burn down the building—and nothing else—leaving no trace when it was gone. I had not thought I would be able to find the ingredients to make it, but Nuraleed's contacts made it a simple matter to acquire, with no questions asked. It took about ten minutes to complete the circuit of the entire room, using the entire pouch of kaltessh; when I was finished, I put the empty pouch back into the pocket within my cloak and stepped carefully to the door, still ajar, in the back wall. Just before I closed it I again listened intently, determined not to miss anything before setting my plan in motion. Silence still reigned. But as I put my hand on the handle to close the door, my nose twitched, and I stopped. *Put too much burden on one sense,* Caoesthenes had said once, *and you will wear it out while the others atrophy*. And though I had both looked and listened, one other sense was active now. A scent was weaving its way down from the upper floor, a scent with which I was all too familiar: rotten, oddly sweet, and acrid, with a touch of copper, richly repulsive.

It was the odor of blood and urine.

It took me a moment to process what I was smelling; a moment later, I was at the foot of the spiral staircase and working my way upwards, barely pausing to make sure no wires or small glass vials had been left on the steps for the curious and unwary. But I doubted I would find anything beyond what I already feared, and as I climbed to the top step and looked out, wrinkling my nose at the stench, I saw that my fear had been realized.

I was looking at what was obviously a bedroom, with several large and colorful rugs on the floor and equally rich tapestries on the walls. The barred window I had seen from the outside was on the opposite wall from where the staircase entered the room, and a large desk stood to the left hand side of the window, with many papers scattered on its surface. In front of the desk was another wooden chair, but it was lying on its back as if it had been tossed there, and one of its legs was broken. And lying on the ground near the chair was its former occupant, legs bent underneath him, his head twisted to the side, eyes wide and staring. Underneath him, a large, dark brown patch bloomed.

I scanned the area, but neither saw nor heard anything, and climbing the last two steps I stepped into the room and swiftly made my way to the body, which was richly attired in a silken tunic of dark crimson. The livid face was clean-shaven, but the forehead was lined with the worry of many years, and an old scar extended down the right cheek. The description exactly matched what Nuraleed had told me of the owner of this home: Yanner Fris. Judging from both the smell and the state of the dried blood beneath him, he had obviously been dead for several hours. But as I kneeled down next to his body, holding my breath, I could see no obvious wounds. I carefully reached down and rolled his body onto its side—and immediately released my grip and stared as the body slumped onto its front. Around the back, the tunic was rent in six places, and in every one of those places was . . .

"Hells," I breathed. *Kushuri darts.*

I pulled one free and examined it closely. The design was slightly different than the one with which I was familiar; these were longer, with four fletchings instead of three. But there could be no mistaking the general form of the kushuri darts used exclusively by the Service of Argoth. I did not fear for the twisted use of poison as Merynne's Acolytes had done; these darts had been expertly thrown to kill, and there were no signs of poison in the body. Yet with the darts in the body's back . . . I leaned back and closed my eyes, replaying the scene: Fris at his desk, counting the day's take, while an Acolyte moves in on him silently, drawing his weapon and lifting it high . . .

Wait. Why use the darts? A simple slash would have ended Fris silently, before he could even cry out—unless something had warned him. I reimagined the scene: Fris at his desk while an Acolyte moves in on him silently. Suddenly Fris is warned, stands and turn to see the danger. He holds up his hands, then turns to run for the bed and possible cover—and the Acolyte reacts as I would have, throwing a spray of kushuri darts into Fris's back; he stumbles forward, knocking the chair and himself to the ground, then rolls in his agony onto his back, where he expires without the Acolyte having to take any further action. Conceived in this way, the encounter made sense. But there were no mirrors or silver-backed chests on Fris's desk with which he could have seen something coming in his direction; what had warned him?

Then my gaze fell on the barred window, and I noticed something odd—there was a line in the center of each bar, and if I imagined that line being connected ... I rose from my position next to Fris's body and strode to the window. With one look I knew I was right, and grasping the bars I pushed forward; the top of the window opened with ease, and in a moment I was looking at the flickering shadows on the street below. The bars had been cut; it was possible the Acolyte could have done so, but even the most skilled practitioner would have made some noise, and would have taken some time to cut through. Was Fris otherwise occupied for that entire amount of time? Or would—

I froze. From somewhere above me, I had heard a slight creak.

Silently I stepped back, and drawing my cucuri I inched back toward the stairs, eyes fixed on the open window. The only thing above this floor was the roof, and that meant if someone was waiting to finish the job they started, they would be coming through the only accessible point to the outside in the room. But I was only halfway to the stairs when I heard a whisper, soft but clear, and stopped moving.

"You won't get out that way."

It had come from the direction of the window. A moment later someone wearing dark pants and boots swung their legs into the opening, then pushed through and landed lightly on the floor next to the desk. As they slowly rose into a standing position, I could see they were wearing a dark and hooded cloak—but not the same kind worn by either the one who had attempted to ambush me several days earlier, nor one usually worn by an Acolyte in the Service of Argoth, at least not one with which I was familiar. This was made of a kind of faintly shimmering material . . . and inside the hood, I could see the person was wearing some strange cloth mask, plain and faceless. "You won't get out that way," the figure repeated. The voice was low, perhaps even a bit raspy.

I kept my expression, and my blade, level. "Because your people are covering the front door?"

The figure remained motionless. "They're not my people; they're from the Varan Guard. And they're not just at the front door. They're spread out a block in each direction down the street; probably twenty or so, ten each side. And don't worry; your pet was warned off before you were. He won't be found by the guards, if he's a little more careful than you." I couldn't get a good sense of the voice; the pitch was low and relatively unremarkable, but there was something behind the slight rasp which seemed forced, somehow.

"You know an awful lot about people who aren't yours," I said.

"I'm observant. Word is you used to be that way too, in the old days."

I barely managed to keep from frowning. "Did you get that from being observant, too?" The figure was silent behind their blank mask. "All right, then," I went on after a long moment. "How long have you been observing me, then?"

"Long enough to know you didn't do that," the figure replied, pointing with a gloved hand to the body on the floor. "You do better work, or at least you used to."

Hells. "I appreciate the compliment, even if I don't know

what you're talking about," I said. "So you're saying this isn't your doing? It's the people outside?"

They shook their head. "Don't kill unless I have to. And the people outside are guards from Tellisar ... they don't kill either, at least not usually. Too much paperwork." I thought I heard a stifled chuckle, but couldn't be sure. "But they're going to find you here, with a dead body and a house full of kaltessh, and you're going to get blamed for all of it."

"I can take care of myself."

"I know," came the surprising answer. "But taking down twenty competent fighters on their own ground is a stretch, even for you." They took one small step backwards. "You've always been a survivor. You need to survive a while longer, if you're going to find what you need."

My eyes widened a little in spite of myself. "Who are you?" I asked, almost reflexively.

"An acquaintance. And we'll meet again, if you can stay alive ... *Grayshade*." The figure took another step back, then with surprising speed and grace turned and pushed themselves through the open window. I took a step forward, but they were gone within seconds. I hesitated for a moment, mind whirling, then strode to the window. Outside, the street was silent and dark beyond the flickering lights of the lanterns, though if the mysterious figure had been right, there were guards silently waiting in the shadows. "Move," the voice suddenly said in a hissed whisper from above me. Again I hesitated. Pulling myself onto a roof on the assurances of someone who knew far too much about me to feel comfortable seemed foolish in the extreme, especially without a few minutes to think it through. But they could have gotten the jump on me several times since I entered Fris's home, even though I could have defended myself . . . and if they did know me as it seemed they did, they might have had an easier time than putting me even more firmly on my guard first.

Suddenly a noise from the floor below startled me out of my internal debate—the sound of the front door slowly opening, accompanied by a few unintelligible whispers. I hesitated a moment longer, until a slight creak on the bottom step of the spiral staircase made up my mind. Whatever theoretical danger the mysterious figure posed, the risk of being caught here by multiple guards was all too real. With a silent curse, I turned and pulled myself through the open window, reversing my grip so I could climb onto the gently sloping roof above. No cloaked figure or guard awaited me there; besides me, the roof was empty. I glanced down to see two leather armored figures in the livery of Tellisar standing outside the door to Fris's home, talking quietly. Silently I pushed the window closed, then slowly pivoted and crawled away from the edge of the roof until I could push myself into a low crouch, then a standing position.

For one moment longer I waited, remembering the last time I had stood on the roof of a home after completing a mission . . . a mission the success or failure of which I could not determine. Then I turned and was gone, hoping I could wind my way through unknown streets to Nuraleed's home more easily than I could sort through my uncertain thoughts.

CHAPTER TEN

THERE were plenty of guards in the streets around Yanner Fris's home, joined by those now evacuating at the likely discovery of the kaltessh, and I soon realized I had left by the only safe route available; going through the front door would have landed me in a nasty fight at best, and at worst I would have been overwhelmed by sheer numbers. Talking my way out of—or, more likely, stewing in—a Tellisarian prison while the Order of Argoth arranged my demise was not something I was particularly interested in doing, and I could imagine a host of even worse outcomes. On the roofs in the Sword Quarter, though, I could move fairly quickly and quietly from one to the next, and unlike the roofs in the Sabaton Quarter (or, if I was being honest, almost any of the roofs in Cohrelle), these were unlikely to send a loose tile sliding onto the street, or give way beneath my weight. I hadn't seen Caoes since leaving Fris's home, and had to hope that he had indeed escaped detection and left sooner than I had. So I moved swiftly along, my cloak close around me, moving further up the slope and dropping to a crouch when an occasional guard or Tellisarian resident passed below. At any moment I expected to see someone else on the roof ahead of me ... perhaps an Acolyte, or Rillia, or ... the cloaked figure from the house.

My thoughts returned often to that mysterious figure. Even if I believed that they hadn't killed Yanner Fris, they certainly knew something about how it happened . . . and apparently knew much more than that about me, including my name. "You do better work, or at least you used to," they had said. Of course the Order had been after me for months now, if not from Cohrelle, then from another city—I had assumed Tellisar itself, but even Arginn was a possibility, and an Arginnian could easily have ended up here. Besides, our inquiries in Tellisar could well have led to some reciprocal interest in me. But it didn't track. If it was an Acolyte, their orders would certainly have been to kill me, or at the very least incapacitate me and take me to their leaders here, not warn me of impending danger. One of Nuraleed's Silken Order, maybe? But why send me to a place and then warn me away from it? And if the intention was to frame me for Fris's killing, why warn me before the guards could reach me? Which left . . . what? A third as yet unknown organization, or someone working on their own. Either possibility meant another variable, and a variable meant more uncertainty . . . and I had already dealt with enough uncertainty in the past six months to last a lifetime.

One thing was certain, though: the Service was definitely working in Tellisar, either directly through assassinations of targets, like the ones I had eliminated in Cohrelle, or by making others believe they were involved in such actions. The kushuri darts weren't likely to be known by an ordinary guard or, I supposed, a city investigator. But anyone from the Service, or groups that had encountered them, would know. It was also possible they were being framed for something they hadn't done . . . but even if that were true, there had to be a reason to point so clearly at the Order of Argoth. Whoever had killed Fris wanted it to be clear that the Order was involved.

I hopped over a wider than normal gap between roofs, making sure to land well beyond the edge where tiles were more likely to be chipped or weakened from exposure to the weather. The spaces were getting wider, which meant I was nearing the limits of the Sword Quarter, and I slowed my pace accordingly. I hadn't seen any other guards for several minutes, but it was certainly possible that there were some stationed at the borders of each Quarter, and they would be more than a little interested in a cloaked man jumping over rooftops, even if they hadn't been sent to look for me specifically. In that I had been fortunate so far; the last thing I wanted was to be wanted and actively pursued by the Varan Guard, especially when I was busy pursuing my own targets in the Order, and at least I seemed to have escaped detection for the moment.

I reached the end of the final roof in the Sword Quarter and crouched down near its edge, looking out at the moonlit streets of the Gauntlet Quarter ahead. Only a few streets now separated me from Nuraleed's home and answers . . . or a trap I was unlikely to survive. The past months had proven I was no great judge of character; I had replaced years of caution with a reckless desire for answers, and had made nearly disastrous mistakes in pursuit of that latter goal. Rillia was even more suspicious of Nuraleed than I was, and she had spent more time assessing the inner motivations of those around her than I had. Yet Caron—and obviously Caoes—trusted Nuraleed, and I had made no mistake with my belief in either of them. And despite it all, beyond the flamboyant outfits, wide smiles, and honeyed words, something about Nuraleed seemed steady, reliable. If he hadn't killed me when he had the chance, in an alley, his house, or the home of

Yanner Fris, waiting to do it now seemed overly complicated, even in a last attempt to frame me for Fris's murder.

I sighed. Weighed all together, the evidence pointed toward trusting him. But it was far from certain, and I far from happy with my own decisions. My hand closed around the reassuringly smooth texture of the wrapped hilt of my cucuri. "No more delays, then, Grayshade," I muttered. "If you are headed to the Hells, you might as well walk in with your eyes open and your blade ready." And with one final glance around and a quick drop to the surface of the cobblestone street below, I pulled my cloak around me and vanished into the shadows of the Gauntlet Quarter.

Even at a slower and more cautious pace, it took only a few minutes for me to navigate the now familiar streets leading to Nuraleed's home, and only a minute more to make my way down the alley leading to the building in the middle of the clearing. There I waited for several minutes, watching the alley down which I had just come, until I saw yellow eyes materialize from the darkness as Caoes slowly padded up to me. I stroked his fur as I looked up and down his body for marks or cuts, but saw nothing unusual. "Well done, Caoes," I murmured. "I doubt that guards would be looking for a panther, but even you can't turn completely invisible." I sighed, looking back at the house. "I wish either of us could, though. Gods only know what we're going to do now." I took a few moments longer watching the house, eyes straining for any movement or telltale glint of blade, but all was still and dark, and after a few moments I crossed the intervening space quickly and knocked on the front door: one long, then three short, then four long knocks, as we had arranged earlier that morning. The door opened, but I was greeted not by the amused face of Nuraleed, but the worried one of Rillia, who quickly ushered me in. "You're back early," she said as she closed the door behind Caoes as he padded through, voice low. "Did anything go wrong?"

"The question is whether anything went right," I replied. "But I made it out, at least. Where is Nuraleed?"

"Gone since a few minutes after you left. He said he had to make contacts with some of his people in the Silken Order, and that he would be back as soon as he could." She caught sight of my expression and stopped. "What?"

I shook my head. "Maybe nothing. But I need to speak with him, and of course you, immediately . . . and I need Caron there." I looked around the room. "Where are they?"

Rillia sighed, the lines of worry on her forehead deepening. "Asleep. But it hasn't been a gentle rest, Grayshade. They've spent much of the time tossing and turning in their bed, and . . . I heard them crying out. Wanting their teachers, and me, and you." Her upper lip quivered. "Something about a darkness . . . all the darkness." Suddenly I heard a soft moan from the adjoining room, and I swiftly strode to the open door to see Caron lying on their bed, body contorted . . . and then saw them shift and stretch and turn, moaning again as they moved. Their forehead was furrowed, face twisted into a frown, and I thought I heard them whisper something about "shadows" . . . but I could have been imagining it, for as I listened more intently, they fell silent, though their breathing still seemed shallow. Caoes slowly walked into the room and sat back on his haunches near the bed, watching Caron as they moved again.

"How long have they been like this?" I asked, turning to Rillia, who was turned away, head bowed.

"Since they fell asleep, a few hours ago," she replied. "I wanted to wake them up when they started acting like this, but they've been so tired lately, and I thought even fitful sleep was better than none at all."

"Probably right," I said. "Rest of any kind has to be of some help to them."

"But it's not enough," Rillia said, turning to face me. "They can't continue like this. Their moments of confusion are getting more frequent. If this keeps up, eventually the exhaustion will take them."

I sighed. "I know, Rillia. But I don't know how to heal a sensate, and our problems elsewhere have just grown."

"What do you mean?" Rillia asked, her worried expression shifting into a frown. "What happened with Yanner Fris?"

"I found him at his home. No problems getting in, no issues laying down the kaltessh. I was prepared to leave." I hesitated.

"And then?"

"Then . . ." I said, remembering. "Then I smelled something upstairs. Blood and urine."

Rillia's eyes widened. "Fris?"

I nodded. "On the floor, near his desk; dead for several hours at least. The wound was on his back." I paused, watching as Rillia took a deep breath. "Kushuri darts," I went on after a moment. "Somewhat different design than ours, but definitely kushuri darts of some kind."

Rillia's lips parted. "The Service? Or someone who wanted us to think it was?"

"No way to tell," I replied. "But either way, they were familiar with the Service and its weapons, and they were thrown precisely. I even thought Nuraleed and the Silken Order could have been involved, but it doesn't make sense; why send me to a place where I can discover what they've done?"

Rillia frowned. "I wouldn't be as certain about Nuraleed as you are. You've been too trusting of him from the beginning."

I shrugged. "Maybe. But he's had plenty of chances to eliminate me, in much easier fashion than sending me to a place and notifying the guards where and when I was going to be there."

"Why? They do his work for him, and he keeps his hands clean."

"And gets directly linked to us for his trouble," I pointed out. "I wouldn't want that kind of attention if I were him. Besides, he's not the only one interested in that house." I looked back at Caron's bed, next to which Caoes had now laid down, head between his paws, eyes slowly blinking. On the bed, Caron was lying still, at least for the moment.

"What do you mean?" Rillia asked.

"I can't say I really understand it myself," I said. "But after I found the body, I also found that the window by his desk was open. Someone had cut the bars . . . an expert." Rillia's gaze intensified as I went on. "I knew things had gotten more complicated, and was headed back downstairs to leave when someone else showed up."

"The assassin?"

I hesitated. "I don't know," I finally said. "They came from the roof, through the window. They were masked and hooded, wearing a plain cloak. It didn't look like ours, or anything like the one on the person who was going after me a few days ago. But that's not much to go on. They warned me I wouldn't get out the way I came in . . . that there were guards waiting for me, and that I was going to get blamed for Fris's death if I didn't escape."

"They spoke?" Rillia said, her eyes wide. "Did you recognize the voice?"

I shook my head. "I don't think so, but they could have been disguising it. But they recognized me, for certain . . . said I did 'better work' than whoever finished off Fris. They said I was a survivor . . . and that they would see me again." I hesitated again as Rillia stared at me. "Then they left, after they called me by name. I heard the door open downstairs, and got out through the window onto the roof. There were guards on the street, all right, but I stayed on roof level all the way back to the Gauntlet Quarter. I met up with Caoes in the alley near here—they said they had warned him off just before coming to find me, though Gods only know why he listened."

Rillia took a deep breath before sitting down in one of the chairs near the entrance to Caron's room. After a minute, she shook her head and looked at me. "We're out of our depth here, Grayshade. None of this makes sense; we don't know the players, we don't know the rules. Hells, we don't even know the game."

"I don't disagree. I don't like playing games, and I really don't like them without knowing what's involved. But we may have allies we didn't expect, and that's something we can work with."

"Allies?" Rillia said, raising an eyebrow. "Where's this from? How could we know any of these people are on our side?"

"This person knew me."

Rillia made a sputtering noise. "And? Your enemies might know you just as well as your friends. If they're from Arginn, or even Cohrelle, there's a good chance of it."

"Then why not attack me? Why warn Caoes and me, instead of letting the guards find us and do the work for them?"

"Because they don't know if they'll win in a straight fight against you?" Rillia said, face tightening. "Because they're trying to find out more about your plans, your purpose?"

"They'll have a better shot of beating me if they can get the jump on me, instead of warning me of danger. And the idea they're trying to find out more about my plans is too complicated. If they know enough to know me, if they know enough to know what they're doing, they're not going to waste their time setting me up only to knock me down."

"Complicated? *Complicated?* Like staging an entire fake brigade to lure you in? You're the one always lecturing me on assumptions, to be careful of the easy answer. You spent ten years in the Service, following the instructions of the Order whether or not they made sense to you; and now some stranger whispers your name, and you're ready to dismiss options because they're too 'complicated?'"

"Rillia—"

"Did it ever occur to you," the woman said, eyes flashing as she stood to face me, "that these people might want to know about more than just you? Did it ever occur to you that they might want to know about your allies? Your friends?" Her eyes narrowed. "Did it ever occur to you that we're as much in this as you now? That whatever you do, whatever actions you take, affect us as much as they do you, that you're not a lone assassin killing for your own purposes anymore?"

"I never killed for my own purposes," I said, my face growing hot. "You should know that better than most. And the only reason we're here in the first place is so we can stop the Order of Argoth from making anyone else do what we did, or from other innocents dying because of what we did. We're here to reveal the truth and stop the slaughter. I thought you understood that."

Rillia's face grew even more pale. "I understood that we were going to do this together . . . that we were going to decide how to handle things in Tellisar as—" She broke off suddenly and looked into the room where Caron was sleeping, Caoes on the floor next to them, eyes closed. "As something more than just individuals living under the same roof," she went on after a few moments, turning back to me. "But you've been acting as a free agent since we arrived, doing your own thing, involved in your own plans which we only learn about afterward, and have no say in shaping or altering. Caron and I—even Caoes—are afterthoughts."

I stiffened. "All three of you are the first things I think about, Rillia. If I was on my own . . ." I paused, thinking back to the Repository in the Cathedral of Argoth in Cohrelle, lying on my back with my cucuri reversed, the blade over my heart . . . and then Rillia looking down at me. "I wouldn't be here."

"Neither would we," Rillia said, her jaw set.

Now my face was burning. "I have no control over that," I said, my voice rising. "I have no control over any of you. You decided to come here. You decided to throw your lots in with me, whatever the consequences. It was a stupid thing to do, and I wouldn't have done it in your place."

"I didn't know you to be a liar, Grayshade," Rillia said, voice rising to match mine. "You didn't want our help? You wanted us to let you die?"

"Better that than to risk your lives coming here, to throw away whatever hope you have by being involved with me," I replied, feeling my heart pound. "Better a life in the light than a death in the shadows."

"Slogans and platitudes," Rillia snapped, her cheeks flushing. "Even the Rites of Devotion make more sense."

"As if you know the first thing about what the Rites truly meant," I shouted.

"Well," a mild voice said, "I wouldn't know about them either. Yet I know something about making a statement sound more impressive than it is, yes?" Rillia and I turned slowly to see a man with a purple sash and bright red tunic standing in the doorway. "Your noise," Nuraleed observed, "would have woken people three houses down, if my home were right next to other buildings." He stepped inside and closed the door behind him, bending down as Caoes, wide awake again, walked over to him. "No one has ever accused me of a silent approach. But you could take a lesson from the namir," he said, stroking Caoes's neck as the panther leaned in. "He knows it is seldom time for loud action. And when the time does come, it must be swift and short. Simple shouting will accomplish nothing, except to inflame your passions and make your voices ragged."

"I don't need a lecture on how to act quietly, Nuraleed," I said, scowling, though I made sure to lower the volume of my voice considerably. "And you have some questions to answer . . . starting with why you sent me to Yanner Fris's place. The real reason, not the nonsense you fed me about smuggling and sending messages about profit."

Nuraleed raised an eyebrow in apparent surprise. "Nonsense?" He gave one last pet to Caoes, then stood slowly. "There was no nonsense about it, my friend. We asked you to sabotage a smuggler and send a message to those who would use his tactics. You, apparently, were only able to rile the Varan Guard and escape with your life, barely."

I smiled grimly. "The Guard didn't need me to rile them. They already knew that I, or someone, was going to be there ... and by now, they will have discovered what was left behind at Yanner Fris's place."

Nuraleed blinked. "What did you leave?"

"The body I found there," I replied, and watched as Nuraleed's eyes widened.

"Fris was dead?"

"You didn't know?" Rillia said. Her arms were folded, and the icy glare with which she had been favoring me was now turned squarely on the merchant. "You didn't find out when you were out just now, from your people in the Silken Order?"

Nuraleed sighed. "Clearly not, or I would not have been surprised just now."

"Or acted like you were?"

The large man rubbed the back of his neck. "As always, I admire your deep commitment to the truth. But I must confess that even in my profession, one eventually grows weary of suspicion, of half-truths and double-dealing. No, I was not pretending; I was, and am, surprised. The idea that Yanner Fris was in any physical danger, at least from an assassin's blade, is something which would not have occurred to us . . . or, it seems, to him."

"That's certainly true," I said. "But he wasn't killed by an assassin's blade. An assassin's dart, to be more precise."

Nuraleed tilted his head in apparent surprise. "He . . . was killed by a dart?"

I nodded. "More than one, actually, and long before I got there. And there was more. But before I tell you what happened, I need something from you, Nuraleed."

He blinked. "And that is?"

"Direct, straight answers. Answers you don't have to hesitate in giving me. The truth."

Nuraleed stood up straight and nodded. "I will say everything I can say."

"Then let's hit it on the head," I said. "Did you order that Yanner Fris be killed?"

"No," Nuraleed replied, shaking his head firmly. "We sent you to end his smuggling operation, not to end him. And in any case, we are not an organization of assassins; we kill only when we must, not when we might."

"I've heard that before," I said, expression serious, "and not long ago."

Nuraleed frowned as if puzzled. "If we had wanted him to be killed, we could have done so much more easily, and safely, than by sending you. No offense meant, my friend; I have some small understanding of your skill. But a failed assassination would be much more perilous to us than a failed sabotage. We would not send you on such an errand."

"Would you send someone else, then?" Rillia cut in, eyes

flashing. "Someone to finish the job if Grayshade couldn't . . . or to cast suspicion on him if he could?"

"I do not understand," the merchant said, folding his arms.

"I was not alone," I said as Nuraleed looked at me. "Right after I found Fris's body, a cloaked figure found me—someone who claimed to know me and my past work. They were the one who warned me about the Varan Guard, and, supposedly, the one who warned Caoes as well."

"Then surely that is the killer," Nuraleed replied.

"Why would the killer wait for someone to find them—or kill that person, if they did? I learned enough in my time to know that loose ends are dangerous . . . which is why I never left any. But if I had, I would have known that tying up those loose ends was an imperative. Someone good enough to get into Fris's house, stage a killing in which the blame would fall on the Order of Argoth—but only from those who knew how the Order generally worked—and get out again without being noticed would also know to tie up loose ends. This one warned me away from the danger. So no, I think it unlikely that I met the killer tonight." I narrowed my eyes. "I don't know who it is. But I find it hard to believe you don't."

"And I," Nuraleed said, his usual smooth and jovial expression replaced by a frowning, irritated one, "have told you I know nothing of this cloaked figure of yours, nor even if such a figure exists. It is much easier to believe that something went wrong during the performance of your task."

"What does that mean?" I said angrily.

"It means that you were either discovered and had to eliminate the person who discovered you—Yanner Fris, in this case—or that you planned to do so from the beginning. Killing is an easier process than sabotage, after all ... and an assassin may find old habits hard to change." He gazed at me steadily as I took a step forward.

"I am no cultist, nor some herb-addled addict who would do whatever is necessary to get what his body craves," I said, staring at Nuraleed. "I came to do what we agreed to do, and would have done it if not for the presence of Fris's body—killed before I arrived, and not by me. And your deflection proves nothing except your own unwillingness to admit responsibility."

"I will not admit to something for which I am not responsible," Nuraleed responded, standing tall. "And you have stretched the bounds of my patience, Grayshade, which is something exceedingly difficult to do."

"Not as difficult as being honest, apparently," I said, my hand drifting back to the hilt of my cucuri.

"Do not threaten me," the merchant growled, his own hand moving back to his belt. Suddenly we heard a cry, and whirling, I saw Caron at the edge of their bed, body twisted, an expression of distress on their face, though their eyes remained closed.

"Neither of you," a slow voice said, "care what happens to them." Nuraleed and I turned back to see Rillia fastening her cloak around her. "You want to keep your secrets, Nuraleed, so desperate to avoid suspicion falling on the Silken Order that you'll cover it in whatever bluster you can think of along the way. And *you*," she went on as she looked at me, "are still too driven by yourself: your doubts, your guilt, your desire to make up for whatever failures you've had. And while you both hold on to what you think matters, Caron suffers, not that either of you notice."

"Rillia—" I started.

She held up a hand. "No, Grayshade. I've had enough of your plans, and enough of Nuraleed's secrets. I'm going to do my own searching now, find my own answers, to help both Caron and me. I can't bring Caron, but I'm taking Caoes; at least he's willing to listen to something besides his own ego." She strapped her cucuri to her belt and checked inside her cloak, then pulled on her gloves. She paused and turned back to look at the bed where Caron slept, and stood watching them for several long moments. Then she turned away and walked to the front door, opening it slowly and stepping outside. Silently, Caoes rose to follow her.

"And what are we supposed to do while you're out finding your own answers?" I asked, finally finding my voice.

Rillia turned toward me slowly, her face cold white in the moonlight streaming through the door. "You," she said, "can go straight to the Hells, for all I care." And letting Caoes pad outside, she closed the door behind her, leaving Nuraleed, Caron, and me in the suddenly silent house.

CHAPTER ELEVEN

NURALEED and I said little to each other for much of the next day. I was in no state of mind to continue our lessons in the Poor Markets, and the merchant seemed none too interested in managing his stand either. Instead both of us remained in the house, he in his room and I in the main room, staring into the fire, occasionally putting out a hand to pet Caoes . . . only to remember he was gone too. Only Caron was in a reasonable mood; though tired, they had woken with no memory of the restless night they had just spent, and throughout the day they acted as a kind of go-between between Nuraleed and myself, updating each of us on the other man's condition and checking in to see how each of us was doing.

I wished I could more easily answer that question. I had not intended to be focused on myself and my own interests over the past few months, beyond the obvious fact that we were only in Tellisar because I had gone there seeking the leaders of the Order of Argoth. But I had thought I was doing that for all of us—Caron, whose life had been (and presumably still was) under threat from the Order, Rillia, who had some of the same feelings of guilt and emptiness about her time in the Service which I did, and even Caoes, who had for some reason chosen me as a companion and thus was in danger so long as I was. And then, of course, there was me. Had I deliberately mixed my own needs with those of my companions, putting them all at risk, then using their danger as a pretext for our actions in Tellisar? I couldn't say for certain. For many years I had been instructed in what needs and desires I was permitted to have; now that my will was my own, I had thought I was pursuing only those goals I must. But if Rillia was right, I had substituted the orders of a higher authority with my own desire for establishing a new order in my life . . . and my own wish for vengeance.

Justice is balance, I thought unwittingly.

I sighed, watching the fire eat away slowly at the wood which fueled it. Rillia, of course, had been right from the beginning about so much. It was easy enough to think I was making the right decisions when I looked at them one by one. But as a whole, what had we accomplished here, other than, perhaps, flushing the Order out from its safely concealed position at the heart of Tellisar? Caron's condition was gradually growing more tenuous, I was being pursued by forces whose allegiance I did not understand and in league with others I could not fully trust. And . . . Rillia. My failure with Rillia . . .

I shook my head angrily. She would say I was falling back into the habit of self-indulgent self-pity, and she would be right. I needed to act, not think. "Caron," I called, turning from the fire to see the leader of Varda's people entering from Nuraleed's room.

They smiled, though the dark circles visible under their eyes revealed their fatigue.

"Nuraleed was thinking we should go to the Markets soon. If we're not there all day, it might be noticed, and if we leave now we can still be there for the afternoon." They caught sight of my frowning expression and paused. "Rillia can find us just as easily there as she can here, Grayshade . . . we don't have to wait—"

"You couldn't sense her the last time she was gone," I interrupted them. "Can you now?"

Their expression turned serious. "Yes—well, on and off, but that's more than I could feel the last time. But her emotions are . . ." They hesitated again. "Erratic, I guess. She's feeling lots of different things."

"Like what?"

"Sadness. Anger. Nervousness." They paused. "Fear."

I leaned back in my chair. "I could have guessed those without a sensate," I said, then immediately regretted it and held up a hand. "Sorry, Caron . . . my anger isn't for you."

"I know," they said. "But it shouldn't be for you either."

I shook my head, dismissing comfort I didn't deserve. "But you can't sense where they are, besides somewhere in the city?"

They sighed. "No. My teachers say I'll learn how to do that too, in time . . . but I haven't been able to speak to them as much, and . . ." They trailed off, looking away. "I'm sorry."

"It's all right," I said. "She'll find us when she's ready. In the meantime, we need to find out more on our own. I don't like having to bring you with me right now, but leaving you with Nuraleed . . ." I trailed off, not sure myself what I could say next.

"He's just as worried as you are, Grayshade," Caron said, looking at me with an intense expression.

"Worried about what? About his plan going wrong? About the Silken Order losing ground in Tellisar?"

"Or about Rillia and Caoes," Caron said quietly.

I was silent for a while. "Neither of us can know that," I finally said. "And until we do, we can't take the risk. We have a better chance of keeping you safe if you're with me."

"Nowhere is safe," a voice said, and turning we saw Nuraleed standing at the door of his room, his usual pleasant expression gone. "Not truly so. And to return to the city streets now, when you do not know who is waiting for you, when others know more about you than you know about them, is the height of foolishness."

"I cannot learn more about them cowering in your home," I replied, stepping in front of Caron. "Especially if you are one of them."

Nuraleed's mustache twitched. "I am not, and I thought we had discussed this. The Silken Order is not behind this, and I have not betrayed you, my friend."

I looked at him steadily. "Perhaps not. But you cannot give me any proof, and I cannot afford to guess. At best, you have your own agenda, whether or not the agenda aligns with ours." I guided Caron to the front door, never letting my gaze slip from the merchant. "And you are not my friend, Nuraleed. Even if you were, I cannot afford to have them." I glanced outside quickly, then turned and exited with Caron, closing the door on Nuraleed's inscrutable expression.

———————◆———————

Although we could not stay with Nuraleed, it was true that we could not easily go elsewhere either. I certainly could not go run Nuraleed's stand without him, nor walk through the Poor

Markets as if taking the day to shop. With the looming threat of the Order of Argoth, the Varan Guard in a heightened state of alert, the Silken Order likely estranged, and the mysterious cloaked figure as a wild card, we had few options. But the threats which faced us would only increase with time, and without Rillia and Caoes, I could ill afford to take random shots in the dark. That meant going back to the beginning: tracking leads about the Order of Argoth. Whatever else they had done, my actions had at least brought the Order somewhat out of the shadows ... and perhaps that would give me an opening.

We made our way quietly but quickly through the back streets of the Gauntlet Quarter, heading for the one part of Tellisar in which we had spent little time so far: the Armor Quarter, the center of the city. This was where most of the smithies and armories could be found, and at this time of day the sounds of metal on metal hammering, bellows inflating and blowing, and fires roaring within the forges created a wall of noise not easy to penetrate. But loud noise worked both ways, as did the smoke and heat of the Quarter; there was enough sensory distraction to keep attention away from a pair of travelers journeying past the smithies ... or at least I hoped so. A few of the forges were in the open, enclosed only by a simple thin partition of stone, with enough clearance between the forge and the fairly high wall surrounding it to prevent wayward sparks from flying out into the street; but most of them were inside buildings with fire-resistant interiors and specially vented roofs, all to allow the city's massive arms and armor system to continue functioning even during the coldest Tellisarian winters. Again, this was less than optimal for the efficient gathering of information, but the separation worked both ways, and meant we could hope for fewer interested parties following our path as we moved along.

Caron had said little on our journey to the Armor Quarter; they did not look particularly distressed, but I was still worried as we came to the edge of the district. I was relying heavily on them to help with this next part of our search, and I was not at all sure they were in a condition to do so, given their fatigue and recent struggles with contacting their teachers. The leader of Varda's people had never been able to fully explain how that connection worked, or why it was so important ... but I knew that it *was* important, at least until Caron had learned what they needed to. And while that line of communication was still erratic ...

"There," Caron suddenly said, and I blinked and stopped, startled momentarily out of my own thoughts. We were standing on the beginning of Anvil Street, right inside the border of the Armor Quarter, and they were pointing at a large building on the right side of the street; it was two stories high and half a block long, made of cunningly worked stone and wood. About halfway down the street we could see the double front doors of the building, in front of which hung a wooden sign on which a shield and two crossed swords had been carved, along with the name: Tellisar Arms and Armor. "Didn't Rillia say something about that place?"

"That one, and half a dozen others," I replied, watching as the doors opened to reveal a woman in a rich green and red dress emerging, followed by another wearing a breastplate and chain leggings, sword at her belt and shield slung onto her back. They exchanged a quick word outside before the gowned woman headed off in the opposite direction of where we were standing, while the guard turned and re-entered the building, closing the door behind her. "She said that these places supply a lot of the other shops in Tellisar, along with the Varan Guard ... most of them don't sell to customers directly."

"So how are we going to get inside?" Caron asked, gazing intently at the retreating form of the woman.

"We're not, unless we absolutely have to," I replied. "There are too many buildings for us to search, and even if we could, it's too dangerous to take the risk over and over again ... at least not physically. I need you to sense what's happening in there—what you can feel about the emotional states of whoever is inside. We need something which stands out—widespread, overwhelming anxiety or fear, doubt, triumph ... anger. Anything which rises above background noise for you." I saw Caron's expression shift from intense to uncertain. "You don't think you can do it?"

Caron shook their head slowly. "I ... I can do it, probably. But I don't know how much we can trust whatever I'm feeling. My teachers are getting harder and harder to reach when I need to, and without them—" They frowned. "Without them, I won't know whether what I'm feeling is real, or whether I'm mixing things up—thinking one person's anger counts for everyone, or thinking someone is gloating when they're just happy that day."

"Caron," I said, putting a hand on their shoulder and turning to face them directly. "You told me that someday you'll have to do this on your own, right? That your teachers won't always be around to help you?"

Caron frowned. "Well ... kind of. It's not like they leave forever or something."

"Yes—but you'll have to make judgments and decisions for

yourself sometimes, without advice, without the council of others. You're training to be able to do things on your own."

The sensate nodded slowly. "I guess so."

"If you're going to manage on your own, you're going to have to trust yourself first," I said, watching them intently. "That's what this is about: learning to trust yourself, no matter the circumstances. It's not an easy lesson for anyone."

"Not even you?" Caron asked, the frown disappearing.

I sighed, remembering. "Especially me. And even now, I haven't fully learned it. But I'm trying, and you need to do the same. All right?" I watched as Caron's old smile, much too rare these days, gradually reappeared. "All right, then," I said, turning back to the building and watching as two richly dressed people in deep conversation, probably merchants, passed by the front doors. "What do you sense in there?"

"I'll need to get closer," Caron said, gazing at the building. "Right now it seems like a confused mess." I nodded, and taking several long looks around at the passersby, none of whom seemed particularly interested in us, guided Caron down the street and into an alley opposite the front doors of Tellisar Arms and Armor. As Caron was concentrating, I did my own visual scan of the building, trying to remember if Rillia had said anything specific about this place. It was certainly larger than most of the places I would expect to see in the Armor Quarter, which was the smallest district in Tellisar by total area; most of the smithies, forges, and stores were small and relatively close together, and even the residences of their owners were modest, many of them content to live in the same building as their businesses. *Like Yanner Fris*, I thought . . . *though, hopefully for them, with better security.*

Even if it was a bit larger than other buildings here, Tellisar Arms and Armor was no fortress. Several shuttered windows were visible at equidistant positions to either side of the main double-doors, and on the roof most of the small chimneys, just large enough to allow the fumes and smokes of the interior forges to vent, were pumping out light gray smoke to the outside air. I couldn't see them from here, but I had to assume there was at least one other set of doors on the far end or rear of the building to allow both incoming and outgoing deliveries. Getting in, if necessary, would take a bit of planning, but I had breached the defenses of places far more secure than this. But as I had told Caron, we couldn't afford to take unnecessary risks. If we could rule it out as a place of interest, we could move on to smaller, possibly more accessible buildings elsewhere in the Quarter.

Suddenly Caron made a strange noise, something between a grunt and a cry, and I looked down to see their face strained, beads of sweat visible on their forehead as they stared at Tellisar Arms and Armor. I looked back at the building, but saw nothing different from what had been there before. "What's wrong?" I asked, and after there was no response, I put a hand on their shoulder. They jerked away at my touch and turned, their dark eyes unfocused, and I felt my stomach drop as I saw the hollow, hunted expression on their face. I had seen it before—but not for a while, and never from Caron.

"Caron," I said quietly. The expression lingered for a moment longer, then gradually relaxed, the eyes focusing on me . . . and I was looking at the leader of Varda's people again.

"Grayshade," they said, the word both my name and an affirmation. "Grayshade. I . . . I'm sorry. I don't know where . . .

sorry." They frowned and wiped away the sweat from their brow.

"It's all right," I said. "What happened?"

"I . . . I was sensing emotions from there," they said, gesturing shakily to the Tellisar Arms. "There wasn't anything strange . . . some happiness, some sadness, not much fear or anger. Then, suddenly, there was a surge of . . . something, a really strong emotion."

"From Tellisar Arms?"

"I'm not sure, but I don't think so. It wasn't far away, though . . . definitely somewhere in the Quarter."

"What was the emotion you felt?"

Caron hesitated, an echo of the haunted expression they had a few moments ago playing over their face as they glanced at the building. Finally they looked back at me.

"Hatred."

I let the echo of their word linger as we watched Tellisar Arms and Armor for a few more moments in silence. Then I looked back at Caron. "All right. And that was all?"

Caron shook their head. "No. I felt that feeling . . . and then my teachers were just . . . gone. It was only for a moment, but they were gone, completely."

"Hasn't this happened before, pretty recently?"

"No. Not like this. Those other times I was having trouble contacting them, but I knew they were there somewhere. This time, they were just gone . . . like they had never been there in the first place." Caron's forehead furrowed. "That's never happened before, ever. It was . . . frightening."

I nodded slowly. "I understand."

"No," Caron said, voice distant. "You don't."

I took a deep breath and let that pass. "It gives us something to work with, anyway. Something in this Quarter caused your reaction, and that means we're at least on the right track. You're still not sensing anything from the Tellisar Arms and Armor?"

Caron shook their head slowly. "No. Nothing close to what I felt just now, anyway." Then they paused, tilting their head. "But there is something else . . . something nearby. Anxiety . . . fear . . . doubt . . . it's growing in strength. And it's . . ." They looked up suddenly. "It's right here. Here, right on top of us. *Now.*"

I had long since learned not to question Caron's sensitivities, nor my own instincts in reaction to them, and I drew my cucuri as I whirled around—not a second too soon. I sensed rather than saw something headed for my midsection, and I only barely managed to bring my blade up in time to deflect the weapon into the wall next to me with a crack, barely missing Caron's head in the process. The sensate stumbled back several steps as I brought my free elbow down on the wrist and hand holding the weapon, and the cracking sound immediately followed by a quickly silenced grunt of pain told me my gambit had paid off. But something else flew at me from out of the shadows, and I felt a stabbing pain in my left shoulder—the pain from, I saw as I glanced at the shoulder, a long, thin dart . . . the same kind of kushuri dart which had killed Yanner Fris.

I rolled back and out of the alley into Anvil Street, ignoring the piercing pain in my shoulder, and came to my feet as I surveyed my surroundings. Caron was on the other side of the street, near the front door of Tellisar Arms, but I had no time to gauge their condition. Two cloaked figures, one with dark hair and beard, the other with light brown hair and flashing eyes, exited the alley with weapons drawn ... though I noticed that the dark-haired man was favoring his left hand, the slightest expression of discomfort crossing his face. They took several steps toward me, then stopped, and a moment passed before I realized why: two other cloaked figures were approaching from either side of where I stood in the street, both holding weapons similar to the first two, both of them with hoods covering their faces. In just a few seconds I was surrounded by the four fighters, the five of us standing in the suddenly empty street, Caron watching intently from their position in front of Tellisar Arms. I grabbed the dart in my left shoulder and drew it free, tossing it onto the ground in front of me. The wound hurt, but did not burn; at least it didn't feel poisoned.

"I thought Anvil Street would be busier this time of day," I said, turning slowly in place, senses on high alert, watching the figures in front of me and listening for the telltale sound of running steps from behind me. "Either the market for weapons and armor has suddenly collapsed, or someone has cordoned off this street to permit us to have this ... private interaction." The figures made no reply, and I caught the eye of Caron, who nodded to me. "I certainly hope whoever it was got the permission of the city's officials, first. This is a public street, after all." Again the figures were silent, though they had each taken several steps toward me. "It would be a shame," I went on as I continued to gradually turn in place, "if we had to shut down Anvil Street more permanently. That seems like an undesirable, and very messy, outcome." Before the figures could move in any further, I drew forth a spray of kushuri darts in my offhand. "A mess it would want cleaned up, I think ... or not created in the first place."

"We were told you like to talk a big game," the brown-haired woman on the right side of the circle said in a high, accented voice. "But talk is cheap, and we're not here to play. You're outnumbered four to one, and we know all of your tricks. The word's out, and soon enough everyone in Tellisar will be looking for you ... the man who killed a well-respected merchant in his own home. Can't have something like that happen, especially by an outsider. Damn foreigners ruining the city, they'll say."

"They'll be right," one of the hooded figures, shorter and stockier than the first, said in a low, rasping voice. He sounded oddly familiar, but I couldn't precisely place his voice given how quiet it was, and I couldn't see beneath his hood.

The woman nodded. "So we're not going to shut down Anvil Street. Once we've finished with you, it will be as open for business as ever." She shifted her short sword from her right to her left hand and back again. "But don't worry. We'll take good care of that one," she said after a moment, jerking her head in Caron's direction. "We have plans for them."

I caught one sight of Caron's face, which was suddenly clouded with an expression I could only describe as fear. "You'll have to escape the Hells first," I said, voice thick with rage. And then, with heart pounding, I leapt forward, cucuri aimed for the woman's throat. She was taken aback by the fury of my assault, and only barely brought her blade up in time to keep my own from plunging into her neck ... but even with the deflection, my cucuri still slashed the side of her face, and she staggered back several steps with a yelp of pain. I strode forward to try to take advantage, but the others had reacted quickly, and I had to pivot to parry a low slash from the bearded man and duck under a high cut from one of the hooded figures, jumping back as soon as the weapon had passed over my head. It was a good thing I had moved, because the stocky figure was already charging, and it was all I could do to take his weight as he slammed into me and turn with the impact, throwing him clear. I had hoped he might hit the ground so I could neutralize him quickly, but he rolled with the momentum and came up on one knee, facing me.

Only one kind of fighter can do that, I thought. "Acolytes of Argoth," I said, stepping to the side and turning to face the others. "So you've finally crawled from your holes. Which Rites of Devotion did you speak before starting this mission? How long do you have to complete it?"

"Long enough to finish you," the bearded man said with a snarl, aiming his blade high. But I mistrusted it, and parried low instead—correctly, as his first attempt had been a feint. Still, it delayed me by a half-second, and I was only able to turn partway before something struck me hard in the side, causing me to stagger a few steps to the right . . . not a blade, fortunately, but a kick from the taller hooded figure. Still, it knocked the wind out of me, and I was only just able to roll away from another slash from the bearded man. I came to my feet and took a few steps back, watching as the bearded man and two hooded figures closed on me . . .

Wait. Where is the woman?

"Stop," a high voice said, and my heart sank as I looked in its direction—the Tellisar Arms and Armor. The woman, cut on her cheek still fresh, was standing with her arm around Caron's torso, her dagger held to their throat. Caron looked reasonably calm, but I knew their expression belied how they were feeling . . . at least now, given the situation with their teachers. "You've caused enough trouble, Grayshade," the woman said. "Drop your weapon now, if you want your child to survive the next few seconds."

Hells. Given what they had already said about knowing my tricks, I had assumed they would know me, but hearing them use my name was still an unwelcome development. The three others had stopped moving, perhaps waiting to see how I might react. I was silent for a few seconds, considering my options, but as the woman's arm tightened around Caron I knew I didn't have many. "I drop my weapon," I said, "and you'll let them go?"

The woman smirked, a drop of blood from the cut slowly making its way down her cheek. "Not quite. You drop your weapon, and I let them live."

"You said you had plans for them." Without a clear move, I had to keep her talking.

"We do, and this one is wanted alive if possible," the woman said, glancing down at Caron for just a moment before returning her gaze to me. "But our first orders are to make sure neither of you walk free from here. I'll kill them if I have to. As for you," she said, smirk shifting to a grin, "you're a dead man already. But you should be used to that feeling by now. Word is you've got the target on your back from lots of people in Tellisar. It was only a matter of time before someone got to you. At least you know we kill quickly." She wrapped her hand tightly around her blade.

I glanced around quickly, but the three others were still motionless. "You know," I said after a moment, "I've met many Acolytes in my time. Some of them were arrogant, some of them cruel. All of them were fanatics. But I only knew one Acolyte who enjoyed the killing that much—who was joyful for every drop of blood he spilled—until now." I watched the smile on the woman's face falter, and out of the corner of my eye thought I saw the stocky man shift a step or two in my direction. "Yes," I said slowly, taking one careful step forward. "You enjoy the pain, the hurt, don't you? You enjoy being cruel. But that's not what the Order of Argoth ever taught, even at its worst moments."

"Your Order," the woman spat, pulling Caron closer, the blade at their neck steady, "isn't mine. In Tellisar we follow Argoth our own way. We don't waste time negotiating with other religions, like the failed Order of Argoth did in Cohrelle. As if you could discuss truth like fiction. As if you could debate Argoth's will."

"If you believe so much in Argoth," I said, "then why do you hide? Why do you cower behind the Varan Guard?"

"No one cowers," the stocky man rasped. "I wait. Then I strike." Something struck me about that, but I couldn't quite put my finger on what it was.

"Soon, everyone will bow before us," the woman said, grinning again. "Soon, there will be a reckoning for anyone who rejects the word and will of Argoth." She drew the dagger so close to Caron's neck the blade rested against their skin. "But you won't be around to see it. You'll be in the Hells, begging for a second of cool air and a sip of clean water."

I shifted my weight carefully onto the balls of my feet, keeping a firm but not rigid grip on the hilt of my cucuri. "I've been ready for the Hells ever since I discovered the god you follow is a lie. You just haven't learned it for yourself yet. But you will."

The woman's eyes widened, and Caron had to stretch onto their tiptoes to lessen the pressure of the dagger on their neck. "Blasphemy on top of failure," the woman hissed. "It's an interesting legacy ... but it's the one you've chosen." She glanced to her right for a split second, and I knew without following her glance that her three companions would be moving toward me again. But as I brought my cucuri up, from behind me I heard a cry and the sound on metal on stone. I whirled to see the bearded man lying motionless on the ground, eyes closed, his blade lying several feet away. For a split second, no one moved. Then the taller hooded figure staggered forward and fell to one knee, cursing in obvious pain as they reached back to the hilt of a dagger, sunk deep into their leg. And standing above them was someone else, also cloaked ... but their hood was back, revealing they were wearing a dark cloth mask, completely covering their face.

Is ... is that the one from ... ?, I thought dimly. But I had no time to consider the possibilities, for the one in the mask raked the hilt of another dagger across the head of the hooded figure in front of them, who crashed forward onto the street with a grunt. With blinding speed the masked fighter threw the dagger in my direction ... but not at me. I spun back to see the woman holding Caron jerk back with a scream, the dagger embedded in her hand, which spasmed and dropped the blade she had been holding. "Caron, down!" I yelled, charging toward them, and wide-eyed, the sensate obeyed, slipping out of the woman's grasp and crawling away as she pulled the dagger free from her now useless hand. Her expression was murderous as she reversed the grip on the blade and pulled her arm back to throw, but I was already on her, and with a kick to her midsection and cucuri hilt to the back of her skull as she doubled over, I ended her threat. Without waiting to see her unconscious body hit the ground, I spun back to face the last cloaked assailant ... but the stocky figure was already halfway down Anvil Street at a full run, and I only had time to take one step to follow before I heard a familiar voice.

"Leave them," it said. "They'll lead you to more, and you won't be able to defeat all of them ... nor protect this child." I turned to see the masked figure standing next to Caron, who was looking up at them with their usual expression of curiosity. "Besides, Anvil Street is going to be full of the Varan Guard any moment, and you don't want to be dealing with them either ... at least not right now."

"The one from Yanner Fris's shop," I said, and the masked figure nodded as I went on. "I suppose that means you're going to tell us where we need to go instead ... and that we should trust you?"

"I'm not expecting trust ... not yet," they responded. "But I just saved you, and I'm not actively trying to kill you." They reached up to their mask, and with a swift motion pulled it off to reveal black hair pulled back into a bun, slightly angled eyebrows over brown eyes and copper skin. "My name is Gennovil. For now, that ought to be enough for you," she said, her voice suddenly clear and calm, no longer forced. "And if you are what I think you are—or what you should be—then yes, for the moment you'll go where I tell you to go."

"And these?" I asked, gesturing to the three unconscious bodies lying on the street.

"The Varan Guard will take care of them. Anonymous cloaked assassins aren't welcome at the moment in Tellisar, at least not openly."

I looked at Caron, a slight impression of the dagger held at their throat a few seconds before still barely visible on their neck.

After a moment they looked in my direction and, catching my gaze, nodded.

I sighed. "All right, Gennovil. We'll come with you. And if you're lying, no clever story or well-thrown dagger is going to save you."

"If I'm lying," she replied, "none of us are going to be saved. The Order of Argoth is on the move, Grayshade. You're going to need all of us to stop them." And without waiting for my reply, she turned and strode off down Anvil Street; I turned to Caron, but they were already following Gennovil, and with another sigh I walked after them. We had survived the attack from the Order, but the Gods only knew if we would be lucky enough to survive our mysterious savior next.

CHAPTER TWELVE

GENNOVIL took a winding course through the Armor Quarter, moving swiftly from street to alley and back again. I would have gone more cautiously, pausing in the shadows of an overhanging roof as a guard passed by or ducking behind a barrel or crate as a stranger approached. But the cloaked woman was either careless or overconfident, barely even slackening her speed or moving around someone in our way on the street. Yet I dared not lose sight of her. Even if we could have slipped away, it seemed likely she could find us again, and for the moment she was our most reliable guide. As she had said, she had saved us ... if she wanted to kill us, it would have been much easier to do so then, when we were facing down four Acolytes, or pick up the pieces after they had done the job. I didn't dismiss the possibility that whomever she worked for also intended us harm, if for their own purposes rather than the Order of Argoth's; her technique was not the Order's, but her skill was obvious, and that wasn't something picked up without extensive training from somewhere. Soon, I imagined, we would know who was responsible for that training. In the meantime, we would have to play along—and watch for both intention and weakness.

Whatever else she was, Gennovil was either a local or at least a longtime resident of Tellisar; she navigated the city streets easily, and in a surprisingly short period of time we had arrived at the boundary of the Sword and Armor Quarters. She had been silent ever since we left Tellisar Arms and Armor, and I had dared not ask Caron what they sensed of her emotional state, though I knew they would have given me some sign if she was suddenly consumed with some overwhelmingly dangerous feeling. For the moment they were simply walking along with me, expression calm but gaze focused on the back of our guide. The hunted, pained look they had shown in front of the Tellisar Arms and Armor seemed to be gone, at least for the moment. "Caron," I said quietly.

They looked up at me. "Yes?"

"How are you feeling?"

Caron's brow furrowed for a moment before they turned away again, stepping around a puddle on the street. "I'm . . . I'm okay. I'm not sensing what I was a few minutes ago. It only lasted for a few moments, anyway."

"I also meant what happened to you afterwards, with the woman who was holding you. I'm used to having weapons drawn on me . . . and even now, it's never pleasant. For you . . ."

"Oh," Caron said after a pause, as if slightly distracted. "Yes, that—wasn't pleasant. But it wasn't about what she was doing to me with the dagger."

"It wasn't?" I asked, confused.

"No. It was what she was feeling. Fear . . . and hatred. Not as much as what I felt earlier, but still there." They looked at me. "You said she was a member of the Order of Argoth. Was this what they all feel? Was this what you felt, when you were in the Service?"

I took a deep breath. How to explain everything I had felt when I was in the Service—something which, even though I had left less than a year ago, now seemed like several lifetimes away? "No," I said after a long moment. "And I don't think it's what most of the people with whom I served—Father Esper, Caoesthenes, Rillia, even my Apprentice Ravel—felt either. A desire for order, for peace and stability, for the sense of comfort we had from serving Argoth, yes, but not fear and hatred. But there were exceptions, like Maurend and Jant. And besides, Tellisar's Order is not Cohrelle's. They're certainly more insidious, and maybe even more dangerous. Their Acolytes seem much more cynical than the ones I knew ever were."

Caron nodded. "I noticed how different they were from you, anyway. But then, I guess you're different in all kinds of ways." They smiled at me for just a second, and for a moment they seemed like the Caron I had first met in Cohrelle, when my life path and eventual destiny was forever changed … and as the smile faded, returning their expression to the calm but slightly perturbed one they usually had now, I was struck by how very different they had become. Tellisar had changed them … whether permanently or for only the moment, I could not say. Another grievance, another evil to place at the feet of the Order: the turning of peace and calm to fear and worry, even in a child for whom that would have seemed impossible. *And until you do what you must*, I thought with a flash of anger, *this will only get worse*.

Suddenly Gennovil turned left out of the street on which we had been walking, the Avenue of Blades, and into a small side street which a faded signpost labeled Bellows Street. Calling it a street seemed somewhat ambitious; at first it was barely wider than an alley. But as we walked on, it grew wider and soon enough it was nearly as wide as the Avenue of Blades, even if there were far fewer houses and no storefronts or smithies I could see along its length. After a few moments more, we passed several fountains along the center of the street, weathered and long since dry, standing silent guard as we walked by them. They were simple enough structures, but something about their design caught my eye. They were of an older style than the ones used through much of the rest of Tellisar, and they were made of . . .

No. That's not possible. I stopped beside one of the fountains and ran my hand along the stone. Despite its age and discoloration, it was still perfectly smooth . . . just like . . .

The Cathedral in Cohrelle. Rezin stone.

I stared in wonder at the fountain for a long moment, then sensed something and turned to see both Caron and Gennovil looking at me. Gennovil's arms were by her sides, her body language almost relaxed, but she had a searching expression on her face. "You know something about fountains?" she asked after a moment.

"Not in particular," I replied, looking back at the stone structure. "But I do know something about the stone from which these ones are made . . . and how difficult it is to quarry. The Cathedral of Argoth in Cohrelle used rezin, and it was the only building to do so, a very long time ago." I looked back at Gennovil. "And that means that there's more to this street than meets the eye," I said. "This is older than most of Tellisar."

Gennovil nodded. "Much older . . . and much older than anything in Cohrelle, too. Long before it was called Bellows Street, or this area was called the Sword Quarter—before there even were Quarters in Tellisar—these were here, and many more like them. This was part of what some graybeards now call the Old City . . .

but even they only know of it from half-remembered stories told to them as children, by their grandparents." She looked up at the fountain, her brown-eyed gaze wandering over its curves and contours. "People who live here now wander past these fountains every day without even glancing in their direction. If they come down this street at all." She looked back at me. "History isn't important in Tellisar . . . only money, one way or the other."

"And faith?" I asked.

She opened her mouth as if to retort, then closed it and shook her head. "For some, maybe. And of those true believers, some may even be right, even if they couldn't explain why." She turned away. "Come on, we're nearly there. We need to get where we're going before the Varan Guard does." She strode off, and with a glance at each other, and one final one at the fountain, Caron and I followed.

Another few minutes of swift walking brought us to the end of Bellows Street, a large stone wall closing off further progress . . . or so I thought. Gennovil marched right toward it without slackening her speed, and at the last moment—vanished. Caron and I both stopped in our tracks, staring at the stone wall in front of us.

"Illusion," I muttered.

"She's still there," Caron said after a moment, their voice thoughtful, and I looked at them incredulously. "Not right in front of us. But I can sense her."

"What is she feeling?"

"Amusement."

Before I could say anything in response, Gennovil's face reappeared on the right side of the stone wall. "I see your abilities have not weakened," she said as she looked at Caron. "But as for

you," she went on, turning to me, "you still seem off of your usual
standard. Perhaps if you walked closer, you might see something
more than looking from a distance could reveal." She waited as I
took a few steps forward, then a few more ... and realized what
had happened. The stone wall was indeed real, solid, and standing
in front of us ... but it was not alone. In front of that wall were
two more walls, one to the left and one to the right, identical in
texture and appearance to the central wall. From a distance, they
looked to be all one piece; but up close, I could see there were narrow passages between the walls on both the left and right, each of
which ran several feet before turning right and left, respectively, in
the direction we had been walking.

Gennovil watched as I put my hand on the central wall,
checking for any hidden switches or levers, before turning to her
with a nod. "Clever ... but not overly secure," I said. "If I was on
my own, I would have investigated this, and whatever lies beyond.
And I would bet that if any of the, as you said, *few* people who
walk down this street made it here, at least one of them would
have checked it too."

"Maybe," the woman replied, frowning slightly. "But most of
those people are ours. And for the ones who aren't, we have an
answer as well." She turned away and walked down the passage,
disappearing around the corner as we followed. As we reached
the corner and made the turn to the left, we saw her standing in
front of a simple wooden door, closed, with no obvious keyhole
or handle. She knocked once, then three times, then again, and
finally bowed her head and whispered a few words too softly for
us to hear. After a moment, the door slid open into the side of
the passage with barely a whisper of noise, revealing two cloaked

but unhooded women holding shortswords behind it. As soon as they saw Gennovil, they bowed their heads, lowered their swords, and stepped to either side of the door, allowing her to pass. "Come," she said as she walked on. "Let us see what a system of security and trust actually looks like." I scowled but did not reply as Caron and I followed her past the two silent guards while the door closed quietly behind us.

We made our way down—and it was indeed down, as the way sloped gently but steadily in that direction—the narrow passage beyond the two guards for another minute or so, the dim light provided by several fitfully flickering lanterns set at regular intervals. This seemed odd to me; I could not see any obvious way to open the lanterns, and yet they had to be fueled by something. Soundshifting had helped illuminate the Cathedral back in Cohrelle, but even there the lamps were not inexhaustible. These lights had no clear way to be refueled, and as I looked at them more closely as we passed, I could see that the gray-tinted metalwork in their frames, featuring delicately curving lines, was both ornate and of a much older style than the rest of Tellisar . . . perhaps the same age as the stonework of the fountains we had seen earlier. I opened my mouth to ask if they were indeed made at similar times, but closed it again as we slowed to a halt. We had apparently arrived at our destination . . . and found further proof of the deeper layers of Tellisar.

We were standing at the end of the passage, which opened up into a large underground area—not a natural cavern, but a man-made chamber lit by many lanterns set in the walls, extending a hundred feet to the ceiling and several hundred feet in each direction. There were several buildings in the chamber, each apparently made of the same rezin stone as the fountains we had just seen a short while ago, cloaked figures entering and exiting each one as we watched. But the most prominent building was a tower in the center of the area, fairly thin but tall, its roof connected to the ceiling of the chamber by a ladder set within a semicircle of stone. Windows surrounded the tower, each made of some kind of stained glass illuminated from within by a steady light.

"This is all part of Tellisar?" Caron asked, their eyes shining as they gazed at the tower.

"No," Gennovil replied, looking out at the chamber. "It is from what existed here before, what we now call the Old City. Neither the people nor the government of Tellisar knows anything about this place . . . which is good, for if they did, they would either turn it into a museum of dead relics and buildings or see it razed to the ground. And we still have much work to do . . . work which must be done from a place of secrecy."

"What work is that?" I asked.

Gennovil turned her gaze on me. "You will hear that when we arrive at our destination—the Tower of Truth, there in the middle of the chamber. It is a steep climb, but safe. And the sooner we're there, the sooner we can discuss what must happen next."

"As your people see it," I said.

She shrugged. "My people have spent centuries learning to see, and I think we have clearer vision than most. But you will decide in the end." Suddenly she strode off toward the tower, and I had to move quickly to keep pace, Caron almost running to keep up with us. I tried to stay focused on the present moment, in which I knew I was going to summon as much insight and intuition as I could bring to bear, but my thoughts were troubled. I had already served an organization for which a name like "Tower of Truth" would have seemed perfectly normal ... and I had learned, at great cost, that declarations of certainty were dangerous for both believers and skeptics. "Whose truth?" I muttered. But I kept my voice low; we still had a great deal of information to gather, and we wouldn't be able to do so in the heart of a philosophical debate ... or at the end of a blade.

Within a couple of minutes we had arrived at the bottom of the tall tower, the double wooden doors to which were open. There was a short inscription carved into the rezin stone of the arch over the doors, but it was in an unfamiliar language. "What does that say?" Caron asked as we walked, now at a slower pace, toward the doors.

Gennovil answered without looking back. "It is in the ancient tongue of the Old City."

"And the phrase?" I asked.

"The Answer Lies In The Climb," she replied. I thought of the Rites of Devotion, though they were prescriptive, insistent upon one conclusion; this seemed much more up to interpretation. But either way, the tower itself was just as impressive up close as it had been from a distance, its curved stones placed together seamlessly, their surfaces as smooth as the stone of the fountains ... and unlike them, not weathered and discolored, but fully white, almost gleaming. Unless they were using some unusual maintenance technique with which I was unfamiliar, the people who occupied this tower had somehow managed to keep these stones clean and looking like new through regular, old-fashioned effort. At first I was inclined to wonder why a place like this wasn't under closer guard, but as we reached the doors and looked up

I saw movement visible in the light coming through the stained glass windows, dark shapes shifting slowly even as I watched . . . the familiar half-moon and cross shapes of crossbows.

"Guards at every window," Gennovil said as we entered the tower, and I saw a slight smile playing over her face.

"I assumed as much. And other ones we don't see, of course."

Gennovil nodded. "But you're with me, and you're expected. So long as you behave, you have nothing to fear."

I raised an eyebrow. "Behave?"

"Keep your weapons sheathed and your movements controlled," Gennovil said with a shrug. "Beyond that, just give us the chance to talk, and we should have no problems." A chance to talk was a reasonable request; whether it would be followed up with a demand for action was a whole other matter, one which I hoped we wouldn't have to consider. I had no intention of committing to an alliance with some secret cult, or following orders from the same. But fighting our way down a tower filled with armed and ready guards seemed like an almost equally unpalatable option.

So I simply nodded. "Your house, your rules. But control goes both ways. If your guards decide to get loose with a bowstring, they won't have the chance to correct their error."

Gennovil smiled but said nothing, simply gesturing us into the tower.

"Keep alert," I whispered to Caron just before we entered. "If you sense anything, I need to know about it before they can turn their feelings into action."

Caron nodded. "Do you think these people can help us?"

I sighed. "I don't know. But if they meant to harm us, they could have already. Until we know more, we watch and wait . . .

and keep our eyes open." And with one last look around, we entered the Tower of Truth.

———————◆———————

The interior of the tower was as well maintained as the exterior, though it looked like fairly simple construction. One spiral staircase, attached to the inner wall, rose from the stone floor of the tower, slowly ascending toward the tower's apex. Wide wooden platforms were set into the staircase at regular intervals, one about twenty feet up, the next at forty, and so on. On each platform a cloaked but unhooded figure waited, crossbow at the ready; none of them pointed their weapons directly at us, but their wary gazes followed us as we passed. Something else seemed unusual to me, though, and it wasn't until the third platform that I figured out what it was: all of them were women, as the guards in the passage leading to this chamber had been. *Women of all ages and builds, some in the way of Venner Kraes*, I thought, remembering the soldier's broad smile. And the higher we climbed, the clearer it became that neither Caron nor I were the usual visitors in this place. In Cohrelle there had been several religious sects which had mostly women; in the Order we had been taught that all were equally worthy of justice and responsible for maintaining it, although the Service had no leaders who were women. Still, there were a number of Apprentices and Acolytes, and several Trainers who were women—including the one who had trained Rillia—and I had viewed them the same as any other. But an organization which trained people like

Gennovil made up entirely of women was new to me. In a way it shouldn't have been surprising; Tellisar was a more robust city than Cohrelle, larger and even more reliant on trade with other countries. It certainly was more open to new ideas. Yet we were now in a part of it so old, most of the current residents didn't even know it existed . . .

I shook my head as we climbed past the fourth platform and another cloaked woman, with short cut red hair and eyebrows over green eyes which followed us as we passed. Whatever this meant, we would know more soon enough. I watched the stained glass windows as we climbed, focusing on a broad tree in various stages of growth; it grew older as we moved higher, and by the time we had reached the window on the sixth platform, its many leaves glowed emerald from the interior light. "The Answer Lies In The Climb," the phrase above the door at the entrance had read. If so, we were learning something with every platform we passed, if we could open ourselves to the lesson. The sense of awe here was inescapable.

"There," Gennovil said, pointing above us. We looked up to see the staircase taking one more graceful turn around the interior wall of the tower before ending in a final platform, beyond which was hidden from our view; below and behind us, I saw the stairs descending into the glowing light from the walls, the guards on the two visible platforms looking up at us, crossbows still at the ready. One way or the other, we were committed to the path we had chosen now.

I glanced at Caron. They were still looking up in the direction Gennovil had pointed, but their brow was furrowed, and their jaw was tense. "Caron," I said, and they flinched before looking at me, the lines on their forehead disappearing as their expression slowly relaxed.

"It's fine. They're wary, but not angry or frightened," they said after a moment.

"I wanted to know how you're feeling."

They blinked. "Oh. I'm . . . I'm okay. Just a little tired, I guess." They smiled, but it didn't have the usual ease, and I remembered their strained, painful expression outside of Tellisar Arms and Armor.

"We're almost there," Gennovil said before I could push Caron further, and with an inward sigh I turned away and climbed the last few steps to the final platform. Two more cloaked guards stood outside a somewhat larger door in the wall of the tower; above us, the tower's ceiling was now almost close enough to touch. Gennovil whispered something to the guard on the right, a blond-haired woman with piercing blue eyes, who looked at us before nodding and turning to face the door as the brown-haired guard to the left did the same. The three women lowered their heads and whispered something together, and with barely a whisper of noise the door opened inward. Suddenly I remembered a scene from the old days in Cohrelle, bowing my head and whispering the phrase to enter the Cathedral . . . and then I remembered my old Apprentice Ravel doing the same thing, and later, the way his eyes went dead right before he did, lying in the forbidden Repository beneath the Cathedral . . . killed, of course, by me. I blinked and dismissed the memory, which was my fault for indulging in the first place. Memories were never worth reliving . . . just a series of compromises and misapprehensions and double dealings, all punctuated by death. The less I dwelt in the past, the better I might be able to do in the present.

Gennovil turned and nodded, then entered the room as we followed. The roughly circular chamber was richly furnished, a sharp departure from the relatively austere decorations in the rest of the tower; a red carpet with cunningly interwoven images of two women facing each other, each one holding out a chalice to each other as blue liquid dripped from each vessel, covered the floor of the room, while three crimson and white tapestries with similar images hung upon the curved wall. At the opposite end of the room from where we had entered sat three chairs, each one upholstered in soft black velvet fastened to the chair with a series of decorative silver buttons. A woman with pale white skin and white hair, wearing a similar cloak to the rest of the people we had seen here, sat in the right chair. Her face was weathered from long years—perhaps eighty or more, if I had to take a rough guess. Yet her hazel eyes were sharp, her gaze intense and searching, and her hands did not tremble as they rested on the chair's armrests. Gennovil walked to the leftmost chair, and Caron and I drew to a halt in the center of the room as she sat down. Behind us, we heard the door close.

"Now," Gennovil said as she sat down in the chair, "we can talk."

"You seem to be missing someone," I said, nodding toward the empty chair in the center of the group.

"We are," the white-haired woman said, her voice slightly accented, thin but firm. "And you are responsible for it."

I could sense Caron looking at me as I drew myself straighter. "I don't understand," I said after a moment.

"Obviously not," the white-haired woman replied.

Gennovil watched me silently from the chair on the left as I took a deep breath. I had never responded well to mockery, but getting angry before I knew more of what was happening here would be the height of foolishness. So I simply nodded. "Then I would appreciate a bit of enlightenment. Who are you, where are we, and why have you asked us to come here?"

"It was not a request." She paused, I presumed to let that sink in. "We have interest in your survival, as you seem not to understand. If we had wished it, you would already have been dead. And if Sister Gennovil had not saved you three times, you would have been dead anyway. You have managed to make a host of enemies in Tellisar, and one of them, eventually, will slip through your guard."

I narrowed my eyes and searched her face, but the expression was inscrutable. "You stopped the one who tried to kill me in the Gauntlet Quarter a few nights ago," I finally said.

The woman nodded. "And we saved you at Yanner Fris's store, and, since you are here and not lying dead on Anvil Street, we saved you again not long ago, assassin. For one so steeped in the blood of others, it is a strange turn to have others so interested in saving your own, is it not?"

"It is a strange turn," I said, glancing at the still silent Gennovil, "to be brought to an ancient place covered by rumor and ritual, a place most in Tellisar don't even know exists, to be told at the top of a tower guarded by cloaked and armed people that I have been saved for some other purpose. I have grown used to strangeness of late. But the strangest turn of all would be to know neither the people nor the purpose behind my ... salvation." I focused my attention on the woman who had spoken first. "I would learn those things. Can I do so from you, or is this more empty theater to amuse you and the rest of your people?"

The white-haired woman stared at me, and neither of our gazes wavered as the air around us seemed to grow heavier, thicker, so thick that I barely noticed a small cough breaking the weighty silence. At the second cough, I wrung myself with some difficulty from the intensity of the woman's regard and looked to see Caron with their usual small smile. "I'm sorry to interrupt," they said, though no one had spoken for a while. "But it might be hard for us to understand what you expect of us if we don't know who you are. My name is Caron. What's yours?" The request, somewhere between innocent directness and brazen rudeness, was delivered so openly and calmly that even I, who had known Caron for quite a while now, was thrown off. But the two women reacted differently. Gennovil leaned forward in her chair, folding her hands under her chin as she gazed at Caron, while the older woman leaned back, crossing her arms in front of her.

"Why would it be hard to understand what is expected without knowing who we are?" she said at last.

"I know you are curious about us—really curious. But I can't tell if you're curious because you want to know what we're planning, or because you want to try to stop us once we've told you." Caron shrugged. "We can't know that for certain unless we know who you are."

I stared at Caron, but stayed silent. They may not have intended it this way, but this direct approach was clever; clearly neither woman had expected it, and they were obviously uncertain how to proceed. Finally Gennovil spoke. "We can't tell you everything about us . . . it's not safe, inside or outside Tellisar. We need to—"

"Wait, Sister," the white-haired woman cut in, holding up a hand. Suddenly she stood up and walked in a steady, measured pace toward Caron. My hand drifted back to the hilt of my cucuri, but I remembered Gennovil's warning about keeping my "weapons sheathed and movements controlled," and so I only watched carefully as the woman stopped only a few feet away from Caron and bent down, staring deeply into their eyes. Caron returned the gaze calmly, and after a moment the woman stood up slowly. "Yes," she said, tone thoughtful. "You are as unusual as we believed." She returned to her seat and sat down. "My name is Sister Yelinnia . . . Yelinnia to you," she said at last. "Does that knowledge help you?"

Caron nodded. "It does, Yelinnia. Thank you."

Yelinnia's mouth twitched slightly, as if in amusement. "Politeness and brazenness, in the same breath. Unusual indeed." She leaned back in her chair. "Very well. We know each other now . . . and now we must learn what that knowledge means." She glanced at Gennovil and nodded.

The younger woman cleared her throat. "We have been following you for months, Grayshade . . . since before you arrived in Tellisar, in fact, though we lost track of you when you were traveling across Silarein and only picked up your trail again when you arrived. We have been watching you since your time in Cohrelle."

"How long, exactly?"

"Many years."

What in the Hells? "My time in Cohrelle," I replied slowly, "was extensive. I grew up there."

"But you were not born there," Gennovil said, as casually as if she were commenting on the weather.

My eyes narrowed. "I don't know how you could know that. I remember almost nothing of my early childhood."

"We do," Gennovil said.

CHAPTER THIRTEEN

I looked at both Gennovil and Yelinnia, who was watching me steadily, her hazel eyes glittering. Beside me I could feel Caron's look as well, though I did not return their gaze.

Finally I let my expression harden. "I did not come here to be mocked. If that is all you have for us—"

"All we have for you," Yelinnia said, cutting me off, "is the truth. What you do with that truth is your own choice . . . as is our decision on what to do next." She watched me for a moment longer, than raised her hand and gestured to the room. "This is the Tower of Truth, and we are the Sisters of Vraevre."

I nodded slowly. "I have not heard of your group."

"You have, but not under that name. In truth, there are few alive today who know of Vraevre in her true form." Yelinnia stood and turned away from us, looking at one of the crimson and white tapestries. "But there was a time when her name was known from the western edge of the Scales all the way to the Silver Coast and beyond. She is the Goddess of Truth, and we are her servants."

I sighed, and Gennovil frowned as she leaned forward. "You don't believe us?"

"I've heard it before," I replied shortly.

"Something which sounded like it, maybe."

"I served Argoth, the Just God," I said. "For many years I

killed in his name, believing I was furthering the cause of justice in doing so. I once thought that his was the one true way, and if I had continued to follow that way without question, I would not be here ... nor would this child, whom I was sent to kill." I nodded in the direction of Caron, who was watching me with an expression of thoughtfulness ... or sadness, I couldn't quite tell. "We were never allowed to have doubts about what we were sent to do, never permitted to have uncertainty about the Rites of Devotion we recited or the superiors whose orders we followed. I learned, almost too late, that the true evil was the *certainty*—the absolute certainty that we were fulfilling the will of Argoth, who was never more than a convenient vehicle through which the Council could impose its will on the rest of us. So I have heard declarations of absolute truth before. But even if it costs me my life, I will never again serve a false god."

"Nor would we," Yelinnia said, still looking at the tapestry on the wall. "But declarations of truth are not the same as truth, and we did not write our teachings to maintain control over a group of trusting followers."

"So you believe."

"Belief is relative to experience. Or do you believe your charge there is delusional," Yelinnia said, turning to face us again, "when they claim to be able to sense the emotions of others? When they claim to be in touch with teachers who instruct them, though you cannot see or hear or speak with such people? Have they proven to be a sensate—or was that ability, too, a lie, even when it has saved you more than once?"

I glanced for a moment at Caron, who was now watching Yelinnia intensely, before turning back to her. "Whatever the truth of these metaphysical discussions, at the moment I am more interested in how you know so much about us ... and why."

The white-haired woman nodded. "A just concern. And we will tell you what we know ... though you may find that knowledge upsetting." She sat down again and closed her eyes for a few moments, taking a deep breath as if in preparation. "We are part of the Sisters of Vraevre, as I told you," she finally said, opening her eyes. "It is an organization of considerable age—older than the Order of Argoth, or almost any other group of which we have knowledge. For two hundred years we have followed the teachings of the Goddess of Truth. At first our aims were scholarly; we gathered old texts, ancient tomes and scrolls, and collated and cataloged them for the present time and for the ages to come. But knowledge, our forebears came to learn, is dangerous, and there are those who will stop at nothing to destroy it before it can be spread to a new generation. So we realized that collecting information is not enough; it must be safeguarded, not simply from the ravages of time, but from the depredations of others. We began to train in the arts of stealth and concealment, to learn how to push the athletic and acrobatic abilities of our bodies to their limits." She sighed. "Eventually, for our own survival, we had to learn how to misdirect and mislead, how to spread believable rumors and absurd myths couched as proven realities. It was not a pleasant lesson, for lying is intensely painful for us. But we had no choice ... and those as devoted to the truth as we are know the contours of a lie better than anyone else. So we went on, decade after decade, gathering and organizing and protecting information, training ourselves, and preparing."

"Preparing for what?" Caron asked.

Yelinnia looked at them. "For the moment when readiness would be needed. We knew there would be a time when many lines would converge into a single moment—when we would be forced to confront a great threat to the Sisters, and our world. That threat has arrived." Suddenly she turned to me, her gaze intense. "You are the key."

I blinked. "The key . . . for the threat?" I thought of the past few months, the swirling mist of events blurring into each other, moments and revelations and discoveries.

"Yes. Your coming is the herald of doom, if we are not prepared to heed the message your arrival has sent." Yelinnia leaned back in her chair, steepling her fingers under her chin. "We knew of this many years ago, as did our Sister. But she was the one who chose to take the next step when she deemed the time was right—when her path had become more clear. She paid for that choice, but she was right; we needed to act before events overwhelmed us."

"I don't understand."

"The empty chair," Caron suddenly said, looking at the space between the two women. "Is that what you mean?"

Gennovil glanced at Yelinnia, who nodded. "We are the Three," the younger woman said after a long pause. "We are the ones tasked with leading the Sisters, elevated to that position by them. Whenever one of the Three passes on, it is up to the Sisters to put a new one in their place, so that we may continue. But we have not done so for a while now, ever since the one who sat in that chair," she went on, nodding in the direction of the empty seat next to her, "made her decision. The Sisters have not been able to decide on someone suitable to replace her … and some say that she cannot be replaced at all. Until they can find someone most can agree upon, the chair remains vacant."

"I still don't understand what this has to do with me," I said.

"You will soon," Yelinnia said. "But it is not yet time to talk of the past. We must discuss what must happen now—now, before the Order you once served grows too powerful for anyone to stand against."

"The Order," I repeated, my heart beating faster.

"Yes. The Order of Argoth has always been dangerous. But over the last year, the threat it poses has increased … and we must act."

"How much have you learned about the Order in Tellisar?" Gennovil asked, leaning forward in her chair.

I sighed. "Not as much as I'd like. In Cohrelle, the Order was a part of everyday life, one of the great powers in the city. For a while, it wasn't easy for us to be sure they even existed here in Tellisar."

Gennovil smiled grimly. "That's how they want it, or at least how they wanted it for many years. But make no mistake: they are deeply invested in everything this city does."

"I thought Tellisar doesn't mix religion with politics, at least as much as Cohrelle did."

"Openly, no. It was not the way of the Old City, and whether Tellisar's residents know it or not, that tradition was passed on to them." Gennovil glanced at Yelinnia and sighed. "But the reality is different," she went on after a moment. "Tellisar is driven by trade, and trade has become much more difficult—the war between Arginn and Calarginn slowed things down considerably, and even if they are now in an uneasy truce, things have not returned to normal. Trade from the south has also been difficult; the weather on the Labyrinthine Sea has become unpredictable, and crossing it dangerous. Put those things together, and Tellisar is struggling to bring in enough revenue to keep the government working. If enough of Tellisar's citizens notice, it could create unrest and disruption, making trade even harder ... and increasing the unrest. So the city's officials have turned to other organizations to fulfill the services they cannot."

"Like other religions?" Caron asked. "But some of them are closer to the people than the government is. Maybe that's not so bad."

"It might not be if there were rules about what the religions could and could not do," Gennovil replied, her brow furrowed. "But since no one can publicly admit they're involved, it's all done in secret. So almost no one really knows the extent of what's being done, and by whom."

My stomach twisted. "And the Order of Argoth ..."

"... is chief among them," Gennovil finished my sentence, nodding slowly. "Like your Order was in Cohrelle for many years before their escalation, the Order of Argoth here is disciplined, focused, and competent. Their people have taken over more and more of the government's basic functions over the last few years, but it's been seamless; no one on the outside would even notice a difference. The Helm Quarter, for instance, is the public seat of government. But many of the decisions made now for the daily operations of the city come out of the Order's central complex, in the Armor Quarter."

"The Armor Quarter?" I said, my eyes widening.

"Yes. It is not well known even to most residents of Tellisar. But the Order calls it the Forge."

I looked at Caron, who looked back at me, their brow furrowed. In the Armor Quarter, when the sensate had felt that overwhelming feeling of hatred—had it been emanating from—

"You have thought of something?" Yelinnia said, bringing me to the moment.

"I don't know," I said after a moment, drawing myself back up to look at the Sister. "Or to be more accurate, yes ... but a suspicion is not reality without evidence. The Order is cautious, you say—careful to a fault."

"So far, yes," Gennovil said. "But when they do make a move, they'll do it not only with their people, but with the authority and resources of Tellisar's government behind them. By the time anyone notices, it will be far too late to stop them. And Vraevre only knows what exactly they have planned ... except that it's something big."

"A takeover in Tellisar?"

"As Sister Gennovil has told you, the Order of Argoth already has great power in Tellisar," Yelinnia said. "If they simply continued to do what they have been, they would eventually control the city anyway. But their ambitions are considerably greater." She leaned forward in her chair. "It began in Cohrelle, when the High Prelate there made a play to control the city ... and failed, thanks in no small part to you." She continued before I could ask again how she knew what had happened in Cohrelle. "Then the civil war between Calarginn and Arginn, when the Order tried to put its thumb on the scale for Arginn ... and might have succeeded, if not for you. And finally, here, where the Order seems to have decided to change from building its careful, quiet presence to challenging both the city and rival organizations in open combat on the streets ... perhaps because you've forced its hand. When put together, these elements do not suggest the Order has only limited desires. They want something greater ... and they are obviously willing to do many things and take greater risks to achieve that ambition."

I pushed back my growing feeling of dread and nodded. "So it seems. Who leads them here?"

"The captain of their Service is named Rennix, if you've ever heard of him—Father Rennix, I suppose you would call him," Gennovil replied.

"Not anymore," I said grimly.

Gennovil shrugged. "In any case, he's been around for a long time, and is highly competent and disciplined ... and, as far as we can tell, is loyal to a fault. But he's not the biggest problem. His superior, and the head of the Order, is Eparch Kaenath. The Order's involvement with Tellisar's government began steadily increasing when he came to power, perhaps five or six years ago now. We know little about the Eparch; he has stayed out of the public eye, like—until recently—the Order itself. And that makes him particularly dangerous."

I nodded again. "How far has this all gone? Are all of Tellisar's leaders working with the Order?"

"Many of them, but not all," Gennovil said. "And most of the Varan Guard has no love for the Order. If opportunity presented itself, they could be persuaded to oppose it. No matter how good the Service is, it doesn't have enough people to stand against everyone from the Guard. But the Guard is stretched thin, and preoccupied with a number of threats ... including, apparently, a mysterious cloaked stranger and his friends, causing all sorts of issues in the city."

"There were plenty of issues in Tellisar before I arrived," I replied, frowning.

"Many of which began with you," Yelinnia said, eyes narrowing. "But if—" She broke off as we heard a rapid knock on the door to the chamber, followed by the entrance of a tall, yellow-haired woman in a cloak. She went quickly to where Gennovil and Yelinnia sat, nodded respectfully, then leaned over and whispered something too quietly for us to hear. Gennovil pursed her lips as she listened; Yelinnia had no outward reaction, but after a few second her gaze shifted to me and stayed there during the rest of the murmured exchange. "Very good," she said as the tall woman finished her message and stood straight. "Inform the others. We must be ready." The woman nodded, turned, and departed.

"More trouble?" I asked.

"Perhaps," Yelinnia said, an odd tone in her voice. "But that will depend on the manner of your behavior now."

"Grayshade," Caron whispered, and I looked down to see their eyes focused on me, the gaze intense, almost strained. "I—I feel—something is—"

"They are sensing disruption," Yelinnia said. "Perhaps fear." I turned to see her standing, arms held lightly by her sides.

"You are not sensates," I said. "How would you—"

"We are scholars of the truth, and we know the feeling of Tellisar ... and when that feeling has become disrupted, disconnected," the white-haired woman interrupted. "Events are shifting quickly."

Gennovil stood. "We must move now, Grayshade."

I looked at her, brow furrowed. *What in the Hells—*

"Your friend," she continued, breaking into my thoughts. "We have found her."

My stomach twisted. "Rillia," I said, taking a step forward. "You mean Rillia? Where have you taken—"

"I said we have found her, not taken her. She has been placed under arrest by the Guard."

"For what?"

"Murder," Gennovil said after a long pause. "The murder of Yanner Fris."

Over the last six months of shocks and surprises, I had learned to adjust, to flow with the river Caoesthenes talked about so often. Or so I thought. In truth, it seemed there were still revelations which could throw me off my axis, things which I could not fit into my larger world. The idea that Rillia had been arrested and was awaiting trial—a trial for a murder I knew she did not commit—floated in my mind, a rough-edged reality which cut into the structure of my thoughts, no matter how much I reinforced them with mantras of focus and discipline. Perhaps in the old days I could have managed news like this by sinking further into ritual, girding myself with faith and a reminder of my purpose. But I had traded those familiar, safe parts of my personality for the uncomfortably bright light of truth—which, in my binary approach to morality, sometimes felt just as harsh as the Service's

Rites of Devotion ever had. It would take me longer than half a year to let that black and white harshness soften as well, if it could at all. For now I was left with the memory of Rillia's face, her dark-eyed gaze locked on mine, floating into my consciousness unbidden. Was she angry with me? Disappointed? Sad beyond measure?

Whatever she's feeling, she's trapped with her thoughts. And in the end, you put her there.

"Grayshade?" a voice said, and I shook my head to find myself on the bottom floor of the Tower of Truth, looking out the door to the steadily rising ground which led back to the door granting entrance to the complex of the Sisters of Vraevre, and beyond the door, the city of Tellisar. Gennovil, cloaked and hooded, was standing outside the door, her eyes narrowed.

"Sorry," I said. "Too many questions without answers."

She hesitated, and then nodded. "Many questions don't have answers to begin with, and others must wait. With every moment we delay . . ."

"I know," I said. After we had heard of Rillia's arrest, we had hurriedly talked through several options. Caron suggested talking to the government officials directly, to explain what we knew of Yanner Fris's death, but we quickly abandoned the idea. Even if Caron could be their usual persuasive self, we would have a hard time even seeing the people actually responsible for Rillia's fate. Gennovil explained that trials for serious crimes in Tellisar were presided over by three fully masked and cloaked figures, drawn from a pool of people representing the government, the Varan Guard, and the merchant guilds, and they were both secret and swift affairs. Judging by what we could piece together of the timeline, Rillia had been arrested yesterday; that meant her trial would likely begin within two days, and be over at least that quickly. The Sisters had heard nothing about a panther being involved in any way, so at least Caoes had probably escaped . . . but I didn't have time to track him down, and his presence wouldn't do Rillia much good in a trial anyway. I had no idea how she had been arrested, or what evidence could have been brought to bear against her . . . but she had been an Acolyte of Argoth, and someone who had known enough to use kushuri darts on Fris would have known how to link them to the Service one way or the other. Besides, neither Caron nor I would be seen as credible witnesses, particularly since the Guard was still looking for me. A frontal assault on the Guard was suicidal, and useless even if we could have managed it; Rillia would certainly be moved the minute any open attempt to free her had begun.

That left one desperate plan: a stealthy, silent rescue. We had to get Rillia out, gather evidence, and bring down Eparch Kaenath and the Order as swiftly as possible. First, though, we had to find out how to get to Rillia . . . and fast. "All right," I said. "Your people are sure she's being held in the Locks?"

"Yes. If they're going to stage a trial, and draw you toward it, they'll keep her in a predictable place. And in any case, the information we had about Rilla is as solid as we can have; she was brought to the Locks a couple of hours ago. But knowing where she's being held isn't our biggest problem."

"No, it isn't," I agreed, rubbing the back of my neck. I had heard about the Locks several times since arriving in Tellisar, and hadn't liked the sound of the place from the beginning. It was in the Helm Quarter alongside most of the public government offices, one of the oldest buildings in what the Sisters of Vraevre called the "New City"—but rather than falling apart through the natural process of time, the Locks had grown even more solid and imposing over the years, at least by reputation. There were plenty of Tellisarians skeptical about almost anything you might want to discuss about the city, from the stores to the schools, but I hadn't found one person to scoff at the Locks. "I assume the Sisters have looked in and around every nook and cranny of this place over the years?" I asked, exiting the Tower and beginning the walk up the slope toward the exit from the Sisters' complex.

"Some of them," Gennovil said, falling into step next to me. "But we haven't spent much time there. We don't fall afoul of the law in Tellisar, at least openly; we're protectors of knowledge, not assassins. As I told you when we first met, we don't kill unless we have to."

"There are many crimes short of murder. And there must have been times when you had no other choice."

She shrugged. "Yes. But even then, we keep clear of the Guard, and city officials in general, as much as possible. They don't really even know we exist, at least as one organized group."

"You might be surprised," I said, thinking of Nuraleed and the Silken Order's knowledge of what I had been doing in Tellisar—still limited, but deeper than I would have expected. We walked by two Sisters, who bowed their heads respectfully to Gennovil as we passed on. "In any case, it is what it is. What do you know about the layout of the building?"

"It's one of the strangest pieces of architecture in Tellisar, to begin with," she replied. "Supposedly it began as a simple warehouse, when the district it's in now wasn't much more than a rundown village on the outskirts of the Old City. Over time, the city grew to encompass the area around it, and at some point the warehouse became a convenient place to throw common criminals who were causing problems for the traders trying to enter and exit the city. It was still a warehouse, though, and after a few escapes it was heavily modified to be more of a formal prison, building down into the cellars. No one wanted to live near such a place, so when the city became Tellisar, that district eventually became the seat of government, the Helm Quarter."

"Not usual for a government to want its criminals nearby," I said, watching the door through which we had entered the complex of the Sisters grow larger as we approached. "The criminals tend to have long memories."

"Don't people in Cohrelle have some line about keeping their enemies closer than their friends?" said Gennovil, smiling wryly. "Tellisar's no different, I suspect. But whatever the reason, you're right that the city's leaders became nervous about breakouts and escapes, and by then they could afford to invest a lot of resources in shoring the defenses up, both with the Varan Guard and the prison. Eventually it got such a reputation that people called it the Locks. There hasn't been a breakout of any kind there in twenty years at least."

"Good to know we don't have to worry about things being too easy," I said with a sigh.

"Yes, I think we're in good shape there," she said as we approached the two Sisters standing watch by the exit. Suddenly she stopped. "Grayshade," she said, a note of intensity in her voice.

I stopped and turned to face her. "What?"

Gennovil was frowning slightly, though the lack of focus in

her eyes suggested the frown was about something other than me. After a second she took a deep breath and looked at me directly. "Getting into the Locks—even figuring out where to start—is going to be difficult, and we could use every advantage we have. Are you sure Caron—"

"No," I said firmly.

"But you were using them outside the Arms and Armor, to sense—"

"I wasn't 'using' them," I cut in, feeling annoyed. "They were helping me, of their own free will. And they were looking for distinct emotions, ones which were unusually powerful in some way."

"And they found some," Gennovil said quietly.

I hesitated, thinking of Caron's reactions in the street. "Yes," I said after a long pause. "But what are they likely to sense coming from the most dangerous prison in Tellisar, other than anger and despair? What exactly would stand out?"

"That doesn't wash, and you know it. From what we've seen, their talent is extraordinary. And we need all the help we can get."

"Not Caron," I said again, thinking of the all too common haunted expression on their face these days, the worried frowns from someone who was always an oasis of calm in a storm of uncertainty . . . and the way they had looked when the Acolyte had a knife to their throat. "They could attract unwanted attention, and we can't risk them being a target again. Besides, they need—rest. I can't explain more right now, but as important as this is, we can't bring them." I didn't mention the way Caron had looked when I explained that I wasn't bringing them, or my guilt that I was again leaving them behind, even if we agreed that the Sisters seemed to harbor no deceit.

Gennovil pursed her lips. "Then if we're heading to the Locks together, I need to know what you're planning on doing next."

I stared at her, wondering what she was playing at. "I'm planning on rescuing Rillia, and Caoes, if he's there."

She waved her hand impatiently. "Obviously. I said next—afterward, when, or if, they're rescued."

"*When*," I said with certainty. "And when they're rescued, I'm going to take the fight to the Order of Argoth—especially now that I know more about whom I'm fighting."

"Do you?" Gennovil asked, surprising me. "Do you know what is truly motivating the leaders of the Order?"

"Not completely. Neither do you, or Yelinnia, or the other Sisters of Vraevre. But we all know the Eparch is dangerous, and he, and the Order, needs to be brought down."

"Yes. But the Sisters also know what needs to happen *after* they're brought down." She sighed. "We've been watching you for a long time, Grayshade. We've seen your rise in the Service of Argoth in Cohrelle, observed you take that Service to its knees, witnessed your journey across Silarein. In all that time, you've usually reacted, not acted, responded to others instead of making your own statements from your own will."

"And I suppose you would have managed better, with the same imperfect knowledge I had."

Gennovil shook her head. "No. If I had faced what you have, I wouldn't have managed at all."

I scowled. "I'll tell you exactly what I'm going to do next, Gennovil. As soon as all of this is over, I'm going to find out exactly how you and the Sisters know so much about me, and we're going to discuss why you've—"

I stopped as Gennovil shook her head, her features softening, and put a hand on my arm. "I'll tell you well before then. You deserve to know. But we need to be focused for this, and that's why I want to know you're not going to do something foolish afterward." Her expression resumed its usual intensity. "I need you to promise that once we've found them—once we've *rescued* them—that you'll talk to me before deciding your final course of action. I need you to promise that you'll listen before you act."

"What about the other Sisters?"

She hesitated. "They—they wouldn't want me to tell you, except Yelinnia. But even she would want me to wait until the Eparch is stopped."

"And you?"

"As I said, I think you deserve to know everything, and you'll hear it when the time comes . . . if you promise you'll listen."

I thought for a few moments. More mysteries, more people I had to trust on little more evidence than Caron's abilities and my own instincts. Maybe I was reacting to others again, just as Gennovil had said. But Rillia, and perhaps Caoes too, had only days left, and I had no time to plot out all the options. And somewhere down deep, I knew I was getting closer to the answers I needed . . . and the end of all of this, one way or the other.

I looked at the Sisters standing silently at the exit, then back at Gennovil watching me, her face inscrutable. Finally I nodded. "I'll listen." I pulled my hood over my head and turned away. "But first, I'm going to get my friends back . . . no matter what it takes."

CHAPTER FOURTEEN

I had spent a good portion of my life scouting out places reputed to be impregnable . . . and, inevitably, finding the reputation to be overblown. What most people meant when they said a building was impossible to infiltrate was that it seemed overwhelming in some way: walls higher than anyone could scale, locks more complex than anyone could pick, guards more well trained than anyone could fool, and so on. But all of these were human constructions, and therefore subject to the same human weaknesses we all are. If someone could imagine it, someone else could imagine a way around it. I had never found a structure I couldn't, given time, find my way into, guards I couldn't go around or—if I had to—go through.

"Always a first time," I muttered to myself. I was on the rooftop of a minor city official—Deputy Minister for Foreign Ambassadors or something, I think the sign on the outside had read, but in truth I hadn't paid much attention—in the Helm Quarter, looking at the outer wall of the Locks. At least outwardly, it seemed to have earned its reputation. The outer walls were probably fifteen feet high and made of old, two-foot-thick stone, not rezin, but still probably quarried from the Scales and brought here for this express purpose. There was only one set of locked and barred wooden doors leading in, and I couldn't see any obvious cracks in the wall's surface, though I could probably still climb it with a fly hook. But beyond the outer perimeter, a second wall the same height as the first seemed newer and even more smoothly surfaced, and beyond that, a large, squat building sat, its walls built right into the surrounding stones of the ground. Down below it, if my information was to be believed, sat three or four levels with hundreds of small, windowless cells, only a series of thin pipes connecting those cells to the fresh air of the world above.

Three guards dressed in the livery of Tellisar passed by the front doors and stopped to talk with the four guards already on watch there. Likely part of the Varan Guard, but with lighter armor and shorter blades; not cheaper, but more tailored for agility and speed. Even from this distance, I could see their movements, swift and sure, the gestures and reactions of people in excellent physical condition, long trained for peak control of their bodies. They spoke briefly, then broke off again. *No . . . two of them headed right, one left, leaving . . . no. Now there are five guards at the gate?*

I sighed and rubbed my eyes. I had been on this and several other rooftops and alleyways over the last six hours, scouting the Locks from as close by as I could safely manage, and so far hadn't found many encouraging possibilities. Besides the high, thick walls and the limited entrances, I couldn't be sure how many of the well-trained guards I was actually dealing with. They dressed identically, and with helmets which covered much of their features, were hard to tell apart . . . and the guard shifts seemed to have no particular pattern, sometimes replacing one guard, sometimes four, sometimes none at all. It was like one of the empty mug games I had seen many times in taverns in Cohrelle, some trickster with a crooked smile hiding a coin beneath one of the three empty containers and shifting them so swiftly and erratically that their mark, convinced they had followed its path, would confidently choose one ... and be wrong every time. Whoever had designed this system had done so to prevent exactly what I was now trying to do, and quite effectively. Tellisar had gotten its money's worth from its investment into this prison.

Of course, I was tired as well ... bone-weary, in fact, though I was reluctant to admit it. I had avoided exhaustion in the past through a combination of training and routine, ensuring I would always have the energy I needed, and would have plenty of time between missions to rest and rejuvenate. On the rare occasions when those elements had failed, I could always fall back on faith and purpose to sustain me ... the first of which was now in flux, and the second only strong enough to carry me for so long. I had gained something new over the last six months: friendship, care, even compassion. But with Rillia in danger, Caoes missing, and Caron struggling more every day, I felt increasingly alone. Had I weakened so much that I could no longer be fully present in solitude?

Is it weakness to learn that you're not made of the rezin stone the Cathedral was? I imagined Caron saying, and smiled in spite of myself. It seemed I was destined to be forced into wisdom even if I didn't have the wit to learn it on my own. In any case, I was indeed tired, and that probably wasn't helping my ability to assess any possible weaknesses in the Locks.

I sighed again and refocused on the task in front of me, standing to get a better view. *All right, Grayshade. The walls aren't a real option; they're too high and too many. There aren't enough doors, and too many guards, to sneak in that way. And with the Locks set back far enough from the other buildings in the district, a roof entrance isn't possible.* I had heard of thieves using gliders to get into vaults and counting houses when there were no convenient buildings nearby to use instead, but I had no skill in flying, nor the time (or any real desire) to learn the finer arts of riding a large kite through the uncertain air over Tellisar. That left ... what? Deception? Disguise myself as a guard, try to convince the others that I had just been transferred ...

"Staring at it won't make it any easier to get in," a voice suddenly said from behind me, and I whirled, my hand flying back to my cucuri—then relaxed as I saw the brown eyes of Gennovil staring at me from within the depths of her hood. "Sorry," she said, a slight smile on her face.

"You would have been sorrier if I had recognized you a second later," I said, turning away again to look at the Locks. "Aren't you having a hard enough time replacing just one of the Three?"

"You should stick to what you're best at, Grayshade," Gennovil said, her voice strained. "Your jokes aren't funny."

"I wasn't joking."

"If you knew what had happened—" Gennovil started to reply, then stopped as she drew level with me and sank slowly to one knee, looking out at the Locks.

"Then what? What would I say if I knew what happened?"

The Sister shook her head. "Later. What have you found?"

"That what you and I both heard is right. This place has earned its reputation." I pointed to the outer walls of the prison. "Multiple walls, few doors, erratic guard shifts ... and it's not easy to tell which guards are being replaced anyway. Add that to the distance from any other building . . ." I shrugged. "A difficult place to get into if I had weeks to plan how to do it, instead of hours."

"And that's all we have. There will be no one to save in a couple of days, let alone a week."

"So you didn't find anything either?"

Gennovil shook her head. "No. I hoped there might be something on the far side of the Locks, which is the original part of the complex, but they seem to have reinforced that area recently. They have a supply wagon, but it only goes in and out once a week, always at a different time, and heavily guarded. As near as I can tell, it's already come and gone." She made what sounded like an annoyed grunt. "Maybe a distraction. If one of us could cause a commotion near the door . . . or perhaps I could talk to Yelinnia, assemble some of the other Sisters to draw the guards away . . ."

"By doing what, trying for open warfare on the streets?" I shook my head. "Any one in charge of a place that secure isn't going to be thrown off by that play. And they'd lock the place down even tighter until Rillia's fate is well decided."

"We have very few options. Even a rat would have a hard time getting in there now. If we don't—"

"Wait," I said. *A rat.* Something had flashed in my memory . . . faces . . . many faces, marked and strangely shadowed in flickering light . . . something with . . . a rat . . .

No. Not one rat.

"The Sewer Rats," I muttered.

"What?" Gennovil said, furrowing her brow.

"The sewers," I said, turning to face her. "What's the sewer system like in Tellisar?"

"I—I don't know, for certain. Most of Tellisar is kept clean . . .

even in the poorer sections like the Sabaton Quarter. It *needs* to stay clean; the city relies so much on trade that the government needs to appeal to merchants ... and, more and more, to the wealthy. Get a group of rich merchants or moneylenders to live in the city, and taxes will go up right along with them."

"Yes, but the sewers," I said impatiently. "What are they like?"

"I'm not an engineer, Grayshade," Gennovil replied, frowning. "I don't study sewer systems, nor have I made a habit of traversing them."

"Too bad," I said. "A city is only as clean as its sewer system makes it. And a good sewer system goes everywhere in the city ... absolutely everywhere."

Gennovil stared at me for several seconds. "Under the Locks," she finally said. "It could be. But there's no trade, no luxury housing there; they wouldn't bother maintaining it for the prisoners."

I smiled grimly. "And what about the guards, the warden— the officials working in the government buildings downwind?" I pointed to where Gennovil had just been. "Smell anything that way? I guarantee they'll maintain it for at least themselves. And maintenance requires entrance."

She nodded slowly. "Well, I know the sewers are old—at least the first passages are, anyway. They've been rebuilt and expanded over the years, but we can't know how well, or where they all ended up."

"Not for certain, no," I said, looking out at the Locks. "But it's a good bet that old sewer routes are somewhere near the old buildings they served ... and that prison is one of the oldest." I took a deep breath and stood. "You said the far side of the Locks is the original portion?"

"Yes."

"Then that's where we start." I rubbed my chin thoughtfully. "We can't take the time to find ferrin cloths, though . . ."

"Ferrin cloths?"

I shook my head. "I hope Tellisar's waste is more palatable than Cohrelle's was, that's all. Let's move."

———————◆———————

I was glad to have at least a plan for approach, even if it was still a long shot; any of the aboveground methods of entry were essentially impossible in the limited time we had without setting us against the entire guard. At least the sewers gave us a chance. But as we headed to the far side of the Locks, my unease grew. Even if my theory made sense, Tellisar was a sprawling, ancient city, and I knew as well as anyone how people made decisions for all kinds of reasons, most of them not sensible at all. Many years ago one of the city's leaders could have chosen to extend the sewer passages in a different direction than we needed, or cut them off from the rest of the city entirely, routing them directly to the Glacalta. Or the passages could be much too narrow for a human to use . . . and without Caoes . . . A memory of yellow eyes flashed through my mind, but I shook off the wave of sadness; if I wanted to find him, I needed to concentrate on what I was doing right now.

The houses around the far side of the Locks were short, squat affairs, so staying on the roofs, where we would be more visible, made little sense. Instead we stuck to the shadows, Gennovil leading us on a winding path through back streets and narrow alleys to our destination. It was slower going than a rooftop approach would have been, but still faster than I expected; even staying several streets clear of the building and any guards on patrol, it took us less than a half hour to arrive on the other side of the Locks. I felt even better when I saw a large circle set into the cobblestoned street, about the same size as the ones in Cohrelle, though this was made of metal instead of wood. Yet it was neither heavy nor locked, and my confidence surged as I lifted the circle from its position with ease ... only to feel that confidence vanish as I noticed gray, smooth stone covering the opening below the circle.

"A dead end," Gennovil said, standing nearby.

"Yes, but it hasn't been one for long," I said, pointing to the stone. "That's new construction. If I had to guess, I'd say they blocked this off within the last couple of months." I looked up at Gennovil, whose raised eyebrows showed she was thinking the same thing I was.

"I don't know," she said in response to my unanswered question. "The Order of Argoth is intertwined with Tellisar's government, as I said, but it's hard to imagine that it's gone so far that they can decide what to do with the Locks. It's more likely that the warden saw a danger and decided to act on it, and the city backed him up."

Now it was my turn to raise an eyebrow. "They saw a danger just now, after how many years of the Locks' existence?" Gennovil pursed her lips and shrugged. "Well, in any case," I said, "we can't go this way now. But they can't have closed off the entire sewer. There have to be access points elsewhere."

Gennovil nodded. "Then we have to find them. Do we split up?"

I shook my head as I replaced the circle. "No. If we're separated and one of us finds something, it will take too long to let the other person know. We need to stick together, and move fast." I rose to my feet and sighed. "And we need to hope that this shot in the dark has an actual chance to land."

The Sister grinned. "It won't land if it isn't taken in the first place. Let's go."

I had hoped that the blocked sewer near the Locks was a local precaution, but as we tried three more wooden circles in the streets at ever increasing distance from the prison, each one blocked with the same new stone, I began to doubt my words. Was it possible that the warden, or the city, or the Order—or all three—had decided there was such a threat that they needed to literally close down the sewers to prevent it? Would Tellisarians have noticed and asked questions? And would the city or the Order care if they had? I didn't yet know enough about the city's residents or political structure to be sure. But either way, we reached the end of the Helm Quarter and the beginning of the Sabaton Quarter with no open sewer access, and further than ever from getting into the Locks. I imagined Rillia sitting in her cell—maybe with Caoes at her feet?—looking at the same bare wall as she had been for hours. Was she questioning her path, her choices, when she could have closed her door on Caron and me that fateful night in Cohrelle and not returned to a life surrounding the Order of Argoth . . . even if this time, she was trying to destroy it?

Was she questioning her decision to take back up with me?

She should be, I thought as I stared at the new stone below another wooden circle at the edge of the Helm Quarter. *She should have walked out of my life and stayed there.* I shook my head and frowned. *Now it's all too late.* "This is useless," I said as I let the circle fall back on to the imperturbable gray surface with a bang. "We'll have to try your distraction idea after all, Gennovil. If we—" Suddenly I realized the Sister was no longer standing next to me. "Gennovil?" I said again, standing and turning to see only an empty street behind me. *Maybe she's decided to do what Rillia should have, and I wouldn't blame her*, I thought, but before I could go further with the idea, I heard a hiss from the shadows.

"Grayshade," the voice whispered—Gennovil, for certain. I looked to see her standing in an alleyway next to a small building right inside the border of the Sabaton Quarter. She was next to a sloped set of two small doors granting access into the building's basement. One of the doors was open. She nodded in the direction of the door, then slid with surprising speed into the opening and was gone. I looked around quickly to see only a couple of people dressed in ostentatious purple and gold hurrying by at the other end of the street—perhaps merchants or buyers on their way to the Poor Markets, hoping to make a few extra transactions before the end of the day—then moved to and down into the stairs below the open door, closing it carefully behind me without letting it latch.

I was standing inside a small, dusty basement, filled mostly with barrels and crates—probably preserved hardtack and cheese, judging by the partially gnawed wood on many of the containers' bottoms and the telltale droppings nearby. One small, flickering lantern lit the space, sending wild shadows around the barrels and into the basement's corners, in one of which Gennovil was kneeling, looking down at something. "That lantern doesn't have much oil left," I said quietly, walking over to her as she knelt between two crates, which from the dust-free spaces right next to them had obviously just been moved. "Whoever filled it is going to be back down here soon—"

"Shh," she said, voice intense. "We'll be gone before anyone comes down here." And she pointed down. A wooden circle was leaning against the wall, and right below where Gennovil was pointing I saw blackness—and heard the trickling of water. I blinked and kneeled down, and as I breathed in, a familiar scent drifted into my nostrils, sour, acrid, and foul.

I looked at Gennovil. "You knew about this place?"

"I guessed. The Sabaton Quarter is always changing, buildings built one place, torn down in another. This house is pretty new, and I figured it might have escaped notice." She smiled wryly. "It seems I was right. I wonder if the owner even knows this is here."

I looked back down into the blackness, listening to the gurgling water. "We're a long way from the Locks. Can you estimate the direction we need to head once we're down there?"

The Sister shrugged. "Maybe. But if the stone blocking the path from the other entrances extends far below the surface, we'll still be cut off, and this will be a short trip. And then there's the smell." Her nose wrinkled. "It's only going to get worse down there."

I nodded. "That's why I was wishing for ferrin. But I've dealt with sewer stench before. We'll block our mouths and noses with cloth, and do the best we can to limit our exposure. With luck, we'll be out of it almost as soon as we get into it."

I reached for my cucuri and pulled my cloak around.

"Stop," she said, resting a hand on my arm. "No one should cut a cloak that fine. That's Service fabric, made for movement. Look," she touched her own cloak. "Layered gauze. Indistinct, and handy for wounds." Without further comment she ran her own blade twice around the cloak, tossing one of the segments my way.

Then she rose and went to the doors leading out of the basement, and carefully lifting the one I had kept from latching, took several steps up into the open air. She drew her blade, and I heard a scratching sound as she did something to the other still closed door, then sheathed her weapon and climbed back down. "A message," she explained as she saw my quizzical expression, closing the door behind her again. "Before we left, I made sure the Sisters would be sending patrols around the perimeter of the Helm Quarter, several streets inside and outside. They'll go right past the sign I just carved on the door, letting them know where we are."

"What about anyone else?"

"To anyone else, even if they saw the marks, they would look like what you see on most of the other buildings in the Sabaton Quarter: random marks of decay and time. Tellisar likes everything reasonably clean, but new?" Gennovil shook her head. "Not likely. Even if the city had unlimited resources to fix everything up, it traffics in its history. The last thing Tellisar wants to do is make it seem like any other large city in Silarein or beyond. Of course, this is a fairly new building, but these are the doors to the basement. How many other people are going to notice the doors, the marks on the doors, and put two and two together about the building's age?"

"At least it buys us time. How long before the Sisters see the message?"

"Probably an hour at least . . . and as you said, we don't have time to wait." The last was muffled, as Gennovil was tying the strip of her cloak around her face. I nodded and, reaching for mine, did the same. Gennovil leaned over the hole, her face clearly scrunching under the wrap. "I suppose we won't be lighting any torches down there."

"No open flames," I replied as I checked the fit of my own cloth carefully. "But the lantern here should do well enough, once we refill it." I went over to the lantern, the glass sides of which were dirty but unbroken, and took it from the iron hook on the wall from which it was hanging, testing to ensure its rusty hood could still close. A small cask on the floor beneath the hook was still half full of oil, and using some of the ambient light filtering in from the outside through the slit between the closed basement doors, I extinguished the lantern, then carefully refilled and relit it with a whispered word of soundshifting. Then I returned to the sewer entrance and handed the lantern to Gennovil, who fastened it to her belt. I took a deep breath, letting the fabric-filtered air fill my lungs—no odor, though that would change rapidly within the next few moments. "All right," I said, looking at Gennovil. "The faster a path is begun, the faster it's ended. Ready?"

Gennovil nodded, and lowered herself into the sewer. I followed suit, pulling the wooden circle above us closed. Then I steeled myself, dropped down a few feet into brackish, trickling water, and followed the flickering light outlining the form of the Sister of Vraevre.

I hadn't expected a direct route back to the Locks, and so I wasn't disappointed when we almost immediately found ourselves diverted from our course by rubble and debris . . . though unlike the stone which had blocked our entrance into so many sewer entrances above, this seemed to be a naturally occurring phenomenon, along with the water which was shallower and deeper at various times. We headed left, then right, then back left again, making our way through tunnels which widened and narrowed as we went. Gennovil might not have had much experience in traversing the sewers, but she knew Tellisar much better than I did, and she managed to keep her sense of direction better than I would have on my own. The stench was more erratic than I had expected, too; in the sewers of Cohrelle, the odor was so overwhelming that it was difficult to breathe or even think, but here there were times when the scent lessened so much that it was barely noticeable, at least not through my makeshift mask. But elsewhere it increased so much that the foul air was stifling, and at these times we quickened our pace to get through as quickly as possible. We talked little; talking used up excess air, and there were times when we were both desperately in need of every breath. Even with caution, the effect of the noxious gases grew over time; it became harder and harder to focus, the ever-present odor gradually seeping into the fabric around our faces until even the most shallow breath brought with it a vague nausea.

"Tellisar may be clean above, but it makes up for it down here," Gennovil said after we had been traveling for fifteen minutes or so, winding our way wearily through the twists and turns of the sewers. "The Hells themselves can't smell this bad."

"I wouldn't test the theory," I replied, trying and failing to shift my mask to an area not as saturated with the air's stench. "Are we making any progress?"

"If you can call it that. Goddess only knows if I'm still thinking straight, but if I still have my bearings, we're under the Helm Quarter now. If we're not cut off again, we should be at an entrance to the Locks sooner rather than later—unless that's blocked too."

I shook my head, resisting the urge to cough. "They can't seal off what they're actually using. Once we're under the Locks themselves, the entrances should be clear ... of stone, anyway."

"But not of waste," Gennovil said. "There's something to look forward to. If we—"

"Wait," I said, stopping short. We had entered a wider portion of the passage—a decent size room, actually, with the ceiling a bit higher than the other passages we had traversed, though the area was still rectangular in shape; the exit was opposite the opening from which we had come. Knee-high water, foul and turgid, covered the floor; above us, a grate of crisscrossed bars, the spaces between the bars surprisingly wide, let in some flickering light, perhaps from lanterns or torches on the streets above.

"What? I don't—"

"Shh," I said, putting a finger to my mask. Something about this place felt wrong—or even more wrong than it already did. I turned slowly, trying to ignore the burning, nauseating smell in my nostrils, looking at the walls, the grate, the water. I couldn't see anything unusual ... but then ...

You must listen as well as see, I remembered Caoesthenes

saying in one of our earliest lessons. I closed my eyes and lowered myself to one knee, reaching down into the viscous water to the slimy stone bottom. I stilled my breath and reached out. There: rippling sounds of liquid moving along the stone's surface. A slow, repetitive sound—perhaps a water wheel somewhere far in the distance, or a cart being pulled along on the street above us. A faint, distorted whistling . . . maybe a guard on patrol, or a worker heading home after their shift. And rippling again . . .

Wait. More, now. Faster—stronger—and . . .

Breathing.

My eyes flickered open. "Back!" I yelled, and leapt backwards. Gennovil only hesitated for a moment before doing the same, just a second before something erupted out of the water—a large, long, slimy thing, body gray and rubbery. It swayed before us, ten feet high above the water, like a massive water worm, its open mouth a circular maw, ringed by yellow teeth glittering in the light from our lantern and the grate above, large enough to swallow one of our arms. A terrible sound of grinding came from within the body of the beast. And as I drew my cucuri, staring up at the thing as I fought to keep from retching, I knew that the sewers of Tellisar harbored much more dangerous things than stone and debris.

CHAPTER FIFTEEN

IN the sewers below Cohrelle, or at least the passages leading out of them, I had battled a creature much larger than this snake-like thing; the ralaar would tower over this beast. And in the Bloodmarsh, I had fought the krellic, wide, long, and scaled, with a mouth big enough to swallow something like this with ease. But in both those cases I had some room to maneuver, and was not weakened from nausea and lack of breath. Here I was hemmed in by walls and water . . . and barely holding down the contents of my stomach.

The waterworm—the only thing I could think to call it—was first to act, winding its body in my direction with surprising speed as its jagged-toothed mouth opened even wider, a slimy gray tongue emerging from the depths of its foul throat. I ducked right and aimed a slash at the side of its body, but sensed something wrong at the last second. I leapt up just in time to avoid the spot where its strike landed, drops of fetid water spraying up into my eyes and blinding me momentarily. I staggered backwards a few steps, and the waterworm reared up again, but before it could strike again it jerked as something slashed it from behind—Gennovil's sword, which the Sister of Vraevre brought diagonally down across the worm's body. The creature spun, its sinuous body curving up and around to face Gennovil, and as my vision cleared I could see that while her blade had scored the waterworm's skin, the wound wasn't deep enough to really damage it.

"No blood," I shouted as I stepped up, preparing to strike while the thing was facing away from me.

"I noticed!" she yelled back, voice echoing in the watery chamber as she looked up at the waterworm warily. "The skin's too rubbery for my blade to cut through."

"The surface might be thinner higher up, toward the mouth," I shouted.

"That's comforting," she responded, though the extent of her sarcasm was impossible to tell in the din of the combat. She balanced on the balls of her feet, waiting, and as the beast lifted up its mouth to strike, I leapt forward, thrusting the cucuri rather than slashing in the usual way. The point of the blade connected, and the flesh sagged inwards in response ... but as I pulled it free, I could see nothing more than another score mark along its flesh. Still, it got the waterworm's attention, and I wasn't fast enough to get away before its body whipped around and slammed into me, sending me sprawling into the dirty water of the room. I rolled left just a second before the worm's mouth struck my former position, and coming to my knees I brought my cucuri around and down on the back of its exposed head with a slash strong enough to slice halfway through a human neck. But this was not human, and it had little more effect than our other attacks had.

So much for its skin being thinner near the mouth, I thought as I rolled away again to avoid being hit by the thing's writhing body and clambered to my feet. I tried to control my breathing, but with this level of exertion I had to take in more air than normal, and combined with the filthy water saturating my cloak, I was struggling not to retch uncontrollably.

"This isn't going to work," Gennovil shouted from the other side of the waterworm. "I can hardly breathe!"

"I'm open to suggestions," I responded as I dodged another strike from the waterworm.

"We can't run; it'll take us down in seconds," the Sister said, slashing the creature's body again with the same ineffective result, then stepping back just in time to avoid the worm's reaction as its body flailed. She was a highly capable fighter, perhaps even less affected by the stench here than I was, but I could see from her eyes that she was tiring. In these conditions, neither of us would last much longer against something which was fast enough to catch us in an instant, angry enough to want to, and couldn't be hurt by our weapons. Perhaps the niscur, the finest weapon Caoesthenes had ever designed, could have cut through this beast's hide. But that weapon was a memory now, embedded in the mouth of a dead krellic somewhere below the surface of the still waters of the Bloodmarsh, and I had nothing else like it. As I stared up at the waterworm, its gray body striped with shadow in the wavering light from the grate above, I remembered seeing similar shadows on the krellic's body during that battle in the swamp, in light just like—

Wait.

I looked up again. A few feet above the waterworm's head was that grate, with large, open spaces between the bars . . . open enough for . . .

I set my jaw. *This is going to sound even more foolish when I say it out loud,* I thought, but I knew we had no other options.

"Gennovil!" I yelled, stepping to the right of the waterworm as it loomed over the Sister of Vraevre. "How high can you jump?"

Gennovil spared a split second from her concentration on the worm to shoot me an incredulous look. "*What?*"

"If you get a boost, could you reach the ceiling? That grate?" I shouted, pulling the strip of cloth from over my face.

"You sucked down too much of this latrine water?"

"Not as much as we'll both be drinking if we don't neutralize this thing," I yelled, clutching the fabric in my hand. "Can you reach it?"

Gennovil dodged another strike from the waterworm and looked up, apparently gauging the distance. "Fifty-fifty," she said after a moment.

"Those are the best odds we've got," I shouted. "When I shout, you're going to run toward me and grab this." I waved the cloth. "I'm going to give you a boost. If all goes well, this thing will come after you just as you reach the grate and hang on. You let it bite this instead of you—and then you should be able to figure out the rest."

"What if the grate gives way?"

"Then I hope you're not appetizing to sewer worms!" I slashed the side of the waterworm one last time as it lunged, sheathing my cucuri at the end of the swing as I leapt backwards to avoid the worm's recoil. As it swung toward me, I crouched down. "Go!" I yelled.

Even if Gennovil thought I was foolish and my plan more so, she didn't hesitate. Sprinting forward, water splashing up from her boots as she went, she got to within a few feet of me and leapt forward as I tossed the cloth in her direction and interlaced my fingers, lowering them to within a few feet of the water below. She grabbed the cloth in midair and landed on my interlaced hands, and with all of my strength I lifted her up. She jumped free as I lifted, and stretching her arms upwards she managed to just grab onto the grate and turn a moment before the waterworm, its mouth gnashing, lifted its head and struck at her. Holding onto the grate with one hand, she held out the cloth with the other, and as I had hoped, the worm bit down hard on the middle of the cloth. I stood, drew my cucuri, and slashed again at its body, and as the beast flailed, Gennovil wrapped her legs around the beast's neck and let go of the grate, using both hands to wrap the cloth around the thing's mouth and then grabbing onto the grate again with one hand as its body writhed beneath her. With her free hand she pulled the cloth through the grate, then swung around the head of the waterworm, twisting the cloth as the worm's body stretched to its limit.

All creatures have weaknesses; the question is how to reveal them. This was the first thing I had ever learned as an Apprentice, not from Caoesthenes but from Father Esper, and I remembered it now as I saw the hundreds of cuts and scores along the worm's body, none of them deep ... all except one. Toward the bottom of the worm was a deep scar, a cut which had been concealed by the water in which it had been sitting until now, stretched to the ceiling as its mouth was held up by the grate. Scar tissue can be tough ... but, I hoped, not as tough as the rest of the waterworm's skin. I grabbed onto the hilt of my cucuri with both hands and with a shout, slashed directly into, and through, the scar, severing the worm's body in two. The beast flailed in agony, and Gennovil was thrown off, landing with a sickening crunch in the corner of the room as the waterworm, the cloth released from the grate above, fell in ruin, landing on the floor of the chamber with a crash. I turned to avoid being hit in the face by the splash of filth, then turned back to see the waterworm thrash once, then twice more, then shudder and lie motionless in the water.

I took as deep a breath as I could manage without losing the contents of my stomach, then scrambled over to Gennovil. She was lying in the corner of the room, left leg bent awkwardly beneath her, and the cloth had fallen from her face, revealing her dirty, sweat-covered features. She coughed as I reached her side. "That—wasn't part of our plan," she managed to say before coughing again, then retching as the foul air filled her lungs.

"Don't talk," I said quietly, slashing at her abbreviated cloak to make myself a new cloth, tying it firm before carefully working Gennovil's dislodged cloth back around her mouth and nose. "Try to breathe as easily as you can." I retied her cloth, and watched as her breathing grew more regular, her forehead slightly smoother as she became more relaxed.

After a few moments she nodded. "All right," she said, then winced and gasped in pain as she slowly straightened her left leg.

"Wait," I said, and carefully felt from her ankle to her knee— swelling in the ankle and a few inches above it, at least. I shook my head. "That's not—"

"It's not broken," she cut in, still wincing. "Sprained. I can tell the difference."

"Even so, it's a bad sprain. You won't be able to move if—"

I fell silent as she held up a hand and shook her head. Reaching down with both hands, she took hold of her ankle and closed her eyes. I could hear her whispering beneath her cloth, though I couldn't make out any specific words. After perhaps a minute, she slowly opened her eyes and let go of her ankle. "Help me up," she said.

I opened my mouth to object, then saw the determined look in Gennovil's eyes and thought better of it. Even if we were not in a desperate situation, even if I were inclined to argue, I doubted I could convince her to stay where she was except by force—and that was the way of the Order of Argoth, not mine. So I stood and held a hand down to her. She grabbed it and, eyes straining, pulled herself to her feet. "So?" I asked.

She waved my question off. "I'll manage . . . much better than that thing, anyway." She nodded in the direction of the two pieces of the waterworm's body floating nearby.

"Yes," I said, looking at the dead worm. "That was quite a jump, and some good work with the grate and the cloth to follow it up. Not many Acolytes could have done the same."

Gennovil sighed. "You're just lucky I understood what you were asking me to do, and foolish enough to agree. Did the Service train you to have these fantastical ideas, or are those unique to you?"

I smiled beneath my cloth wrap. "I always take credit for my own foolishness. But in any case, we didn't have much of a choice."

"And we still don't," she replied. "We need to move. But if we run into another one of those things . . ."

"Given its size, I doubt there are a lot of those down here to begin with; they're just as likely to eat each other as anything else they find. At least I'd guess there isn't another one nearby. But in any case, we know what to look for now." I turned away from the worm. "So yes—we need to move, before this air finishes us." And with a final look around the room, we left the rippling water and the worm's body behind.

Despite Gennovil's claim that she could manage her injured ankle, from the moment we left the worm's body it was obvious that she was moving slower than before. Fatigue and sickness brought on by exposure to the fetid air could have been just as responsible, and the part of her face left exposed by the cloth showed no visible signs of pain, but I had heard the crack when she hit the ground, and no amount of whispering and silent prayers could change that. Still, I knew she would never agree to wait, and I didn't think either of us could withstand a return journey in our current state. The only way out was through. So I had to hope that Gennovil's will—which I had already seen was considerable—would keep her going until we got inside the Locks. What we were going to do once we were inside the prison, and how we were going to find and escape with Rillia and Caoes, was another matter entirely.

This was, of course, the thing which had made me most nervous about the entire plan from the start. We had no time to get a detailed layout of the building, or to track down Rillia's exact location within it. If they had her in some maximum security area behind walls and locks and guards, finding her, and getting her out, was going to be quite a challenge. Even if she was just with other prisoners, getting her out without riling the others up, who might well want to escape themselves, or sell her out to get better treatment from the guards, was going to be no easy task.

"One miracle at a time, Grayshade," I muttered to myself as I crouched down to get through a low archway leading from one passage to the next. First we had to get to the Locks, and on that score we seemed to be making steady progress; our route was slowly beginning to slope upwards, and the odor was finally starting to lessen as we climbed. At first this surprised me; the sewers were still the sewers no matter what buildings they were under, and the prisoners would have to use them as much as any-one else. But then it occurred to me that there were a lot fewer people in the Locks than in the general population, and this was, so to speak, upstream from everyone else. Whatever the reason, it was a welcome change, and after a while we were both able to lower our cloths and breathe somewhat normally. The smell was still less than pleasant, but after what we had been through, the breaths I took were as sweet as if I had been in the foothills of the Scales looking out at the Glacalta and Silarein beyond.

Immediately I remembered the dream I had back in the Bloodmarsh, the one Alarene had shared with me through the special tea she had brewed. I remembered the cold of the air, the way the wind bit through my cloak, the stinging, powdery snow blowing into my eyes. I remembered how stunning the sweeping vista was, the blue of the Glacalta and the browns and greens of Silarein beyond. And most of all, I remembered the woman with me—Alarene, young in the dream, old in the Bloodmarsh, ageless in my mind. She was from Tellisar originally. What would she think of me now, prowling through the sewers on a desperate rescue mission, preparing to strike at the heart of the Order of Argoth, no matter the cost? What would she do, or say?

What does it matter what I think, love? I imagined her saying with a cackle. *What matters is what you're going to do.*

I'm going to stop them, Alarene. I'm going to end them, no matter what.

"Hells!" I suddenly heard Gennovil curse, and with a start I shook myself free of my past. We had reached the top of another slope, and the passage forward was level and straight, with barely a trickle of water down its center, and wider and taller than any tunnel we had been in so far. But even with the lantern light I couldn't see clearly ahead of us, and it took me a moment to realize why: Gennovil was standing in front of another circular grate, but this one was vertical and covered the entire passage, with a square, hinged gate set in the center of the grate and a flat metal plate with a small keyhole placed on the gate's right edge. The Sister of Vraevre rattled the gate once, then twice more before cursing again. "Hells. We should have known they would have these passages blocked at the boundaries."

I walked over to the grate and bent down, gazing at the plate and keyhole in the flickering lantern light. The bars in the grate were thin, and it would probably be fairly easy to force ... but something seemed odd about the material, and as I leaned in to get a closer look, I almost immediately saw something glinting beneath the dull gray exterior. "Damn," I said, drawing my cucuri.

"What is it?"

I used the point of my cucuri to scratch the metal, and almost immediately the gray paint flaked off, revealing a brightly gleaming interior metal. Gennovil stared at me wordlessly as I stood up. "Revellit steel," I said. "That's the same metal my mentor used when he made the greatest weapon I've ever seen, the niscur."

"Which means we're not going to break through it, right?"

I grabbed the bars and pulled at them uselessly. "No," I said. "Revellit is almost unbreakable. It's also extremely expensive and exceedingly rare, which is why it's usually only used for small bladed weapons, throwing knives, that kind of thing. To have an entire gate made of it . . ." I shook my head. "Someone really doesn't want us getting through here, even if they still need the sewage to pass by occasionally."

Gennovil frowned. "But why cover it in gray paint?"

"I assume because most people wouldn't bother to go up and inspect the gate, even if they made it down here. If they did, they would know what it's made of . . . and how dangerous that is."

"You're talking about the Order of Argoth?"

I nodded. "Yes. Revellit first became available for use after a special refinement process, which the Order guards within its armory." I stood and stared down at the exposed metal. "This confirms the Order is calling the shots, or doing so behind Tellisar's back. Either way, the Order had this gate made. That either means they have plenty of revellit and can afford to make things other than weapons with it, even gates blocking sewer tunnels, or it means this gate and this tunnel need to be particularly secure." I looked up at Gennovil, whose brow was furrowed. "Or both," I said grimly.

"What about picking the lock?"

I shrugged, looking at the keyhole. "Unlikely. For something like this, the Service uses specialized locks with sound-sensitive keys; without the right key, the lock just won't disengage."

"Even with soundshifting?" Gennovil asked. I turned slowly to stare at her, and she raised an eyebrow. "Your Service—"

"It's not mine anymore," I growled.

She dismissed the point with a shrug. "*The* Service likes to believe all of its secrets are as closely kept as its rituals and rites. But people see much more than it thinks they can."

"I don't disagree," I replied. "But soundshifting wasn't much in fashion even among Acolytes in Cohrelle."

"It was for you," she snapped, before wincing, and shifting her weight.

"My Trainer believed any technique could be useful in certain circumstances." I frowned. "How did you—"

Gennovil shook her head as she gripped one of the bars on the gate. "No time now. So you can't get through this with sound-shifting, we don't have the key, we can't pick the lock, and the bars are unbreakable. How about the stone? Can you dislodge the whole thing?"

By now, I was believing her vagaries of knowing more about me, but as precious as whatever her secrets were, I was not going to probe them while covered in filth and trapped behind revellit. I sighed and shook my head.

"Then we're stuck. Even if we had time to go find another entrance, odds are they've blocked them all." She looked at me, her expression tense and angry. "Maybe we have to do the distraction in the streets idea after all."

"And then again, my friends," a familiar voice from behind us said, "there may be some elements you have not yet considered— and keys you have not yet tried."

We turned around to see a man in a turquoise turban, red

tunic, and purple sash, his green eyes twinkling in the flickering light of our lantern. It was Nuraleed, and he was holding a small key in his hand. But my attention was immediately drawn to the creature standing next to him, dark-furred and yellow-eyed, gazing up at me. I slowly knelt as the panther padded over to me.

"Hello, Caoes," I said softly.

PART THREE
ATONEMENT

In the end, there is only one truth, only one reality. Accept it, and you will be worthy. Deny it, and you will be cast out as a heretic, and there is no atonement for heresy. So speaks Argoth, the Just God. So must you hear, now and for all time.

—The Ninth Rite of Devotion

INTERLUDE

THE streets of the Sabaton Quarter were supposed to be as clean as the rest of Tellisar. *Get some rain on them, though, and they turn as filthy as any sewer*, Eparch Kaenath thought sourly as he made his way through the dark, wet streets of the district. *Even snow would be better, if that too wouldn't get dirty within minutes, with boots and hooves and wagon wheels crunching over it endlessly.* That was the real problem, in the end: Tellisar could be a clean and beautiful place, if not for all the living creatures which constantly soiled it. *How many things could be better without the beasts which brought them down?*

And humans, the Eparch thought as he turned onto the lane to the west of the Poor Markets and headed north, *are the worst beasts of all. They ought to know better, act better, be better, instead of rutting in the mud and squabbling over the cost of food and shelter.* His lip curled as he saw a merchant, pointing at the stand behind him and gesticulating wildly, arguing with two guards not far from the path down which Kaenath was now walking. *Why don't they have more dignity? Why don't they care about anything other than making the best deal for themselves?*

He shook his head and quickened his pace. *Useless to wonder why*, he thought. *Why does an insect crawl on even when its body has been shattered and broken? It does it because that's all it can do; it's driven by instinct to keep going until the life has been completely crushed out of it. They're all driven by instinct. Understand that and you'll understand them . . . and when you understand them, you can control them.* It was true with Acolytes, even if they were better than the average vermin in Tellisar. They were still fallible, and had to be led firmly, without pity or remorse, into a better path. Sometimes Kaenath wondered whether Father Rennix really understood that. Rennix was useful enough in his way, experienced and loyal, but too close to his people. The less he treated them as the resource they were instead of some kind of equals worth listening to, the more inefficient and unhelpful he became. *Can't get rid of him yet,* the Eparch mused, jerking his foot out of the way of a muddy puddle just in time. *But soon I'll be able to cast him aside, just like all the others.*

This was the reason Kaenath had gone to this rendezvous on his own. There could be a modicum of danger involved in meeting someone like this without guards or other backup, but he wasn't worried about that. This person needed him and what he was doing to succeed; killing Kaenath before that would work completely against their own interests . . . and their own life. Of much greater concern was Rennix's feelings, and for that matter the feelings of the other Acolytes; if they heard more details of this plan, how would they react when needed? Probably, based on everything Kaenath had seen or heard in the last week, poorly. But Rennix would always defend his own people, and Kaenath didn't have the expertise to command them directly. If they had problems with Kaenath's approach, the whole project would be delayed, even threatened.

And nothing could delay, or threaten, this project.

So Kaenath had decided to go alone, to see if he could cut

out the messenger and deal with his contact directly. But the contact had not been easy to find, and it took all of Kaenath's authority and skill to find his location without raising inordinate suspicion, either in the Order of Argoth or, more importantly, the city's officials. As inconvenient as it was to acknowledge, Tellisar still did not bow to the will of the Order in every particular, and there were those, from the Varan Guard to many of the city's governors, who disliked its influence in the city's affairs ... even actively opposed it.

Kaenath frowned as some water splashed up onto his blue robes, the lower fringe of which had grown wet and muddy. Irritating, that these people could delude themselves into thinking they had any real authority in this city. Instead of being things he could ignore, they had made themselves obstacles he would have to remove.

"And I will," he said quietly, drawing his robes around him against the chill. "Very soon, they will all be gone."

A minute later Eparch Kaenath was past the Poor Markets and into the streets beyond, and he began to count the alleyways as he went. He turned left into the fourth alley, and maneuvering around barrels and past a dead rat, he stopped about halfway down the alley in front of a dilapidated wooden door. He knocked in the ridiculous little pattern they had told him, and waited. After waiting for nearly a minute with no response, Kaenath's frown deepened. But before he could start the sequence of knocks again, a low, gravelly voice whispered in his ear, slow and halting.

"He's not here. You . . . shouldn't be either." The Eparch felt a slight touch of cold metal on the side of his throat.

"Do you always watch your own house?" he asked.

"You ... should avoid jokes," the voice rasped, the touch of the cold metal becoming stronger. "You're not funny, and I'm ... not laughing."

"You'll be laughing less when I finish you off for your arrogant insubordination," Kaenath said.

There was a short period of silence. "You ... were not supposed to find me. This isn't how ... this works."

"It is if I say it is. I wanted to contact you directly."

There was a raspy chuckle. "Such ... deep trust in your people."

"I didn't want to trust this to anyone else. That's why I pulled the Acolytes who were watching you." Kaenath looked to his right, even as the edge of the metal pushed into the skin of his throat. "And you're holding a knife to the throat of your employer ... and savior."

The cold metal remained in place for several long seconds. Then it was swiftly removed. "You're a *client*. I'm not one of ... your people," the halting voice rasped. The Eparch watched as a cloaked and hooded figure stepped in front of him, the eyes deeply shadowed in the depths of the hood.

Kaenath removed a handkerchief from a pocket within his robes and dabbed at his throat, pulling it away to reveal a single spot of red. "I'm telling you what to do. And you know as well as I do that what I'm asking you to do is necessary—especially for you."

Again the hooded figure was silent, then turned, opened the door, and entered the house. The Eparch waited for a beat, then followed, closing the door behind him. Inside the house was a small table with a candle fitfully burning, a small bag leaning against the wall . . . and that was all, without even a chair as further decoration. Even by the Sabaton Quarter's standards, this had to be the most miserably empty place Kaenath could ever have imagined.

The hooded figure walked to the opposite wall, then turned and leaned back against it, crossing their arms. "So . . . you're here."

"So are you," the Eparch said, "and I don't know why. You have one mission, and so far you have done nothing to accomplish it."

"You . . . have no idea what . . . I've done," the other replied. "And word is . . . you have your own problems."

"One of those has already been dealt with."

The figure laughed. "Because of . . . an arrest?"

"She's been taken out of the equation."

"The Locks won't stop him. And he has . . . others to help . . . now."

"I doubt it," Kaenath replied, frowning. "These others weren't able to threaten us before our power had grown. They won't be any more effective now."

"Unless their time . . . has come. And *he* wasn't here before."

"And that," the Eparch said, his frown deepening, "is why I am here now. Your job was to eliminate Grayshade, and whatever else you claim to have done, you haven't managed that one task. Nothing else can stand in our way."

The figure pushed off of the wall and stood straight. "Then . . . you'll fulfill . . . your promise?"

Eparch Kaenath smiled grimly. "I already have."

"Not all . . . of it."

"You'll get *all* of it when, and if, you take Grayshade down. I was beginning to doubt you were the right person for the job."

"I'll ... do it," the cloaked figure rasped. "In the end, I'll ... take him down, and no one else ... will stop me." They paused. "If you ... can hold up ... your end of the bargain."

"As I said, I already have. The things in motion cannot be stopped now."

"I learned to be ... confident," the other said, voice so rough that Kaenath's own throat gave a twinge. "But arrogance is ... dangerous. Anything can be stopped."

Kaenath's grin widened. "Not if it can't be seen ... and not if it's what people actually want. In the end, they will all bow to me, and make no mistake: they will do so on their own, believing this what is best for themselves and for everyone else. In Tellisar and beyond, they will all, eventually bow to me, and smile while doing it."

"Even Grayshade?"

The Eparch's grin grew tight. "He won't be there. He will come to us, and you will destroy him."

The figure's chuckle was low and gravelly. "I'll believe it ... when I see it."

"You won't see it at all," Eparch Kaenath replied, "and neither will they." From the depths of his robe he pulled forth a dark, multi-faceted jewel, as black as obsidian, and held it aloft. The blackness at the jewel's heart grew and expanded outward, overwhelming the candlelight in the room, until utter darkness filled the space.

All that was left was the laugh of the cloaked figure, a rumble of a ruined voice in the blackness of the house in the Sabaton Quarter.

CHAPTER SIXTEEN

I probably took a bit longer petting Caoes than was strictly necessary, but the panther seemed as glad to see me as I was him, rubbing his head as he nuzzled my palm. He seemed just as always, fur sleek and shiny, breathing steady, eyes bright. Wherever he had been, he hadn't been mistreated.

"I have seen many namirs over the years. But this one, my friend, is the only one I can remember nurturing such affection for someone not involved in his training," Nuraleed said with his usual wide smile.

I didn't return it. "Who says I wasn't involved?" I gave Caoes's dark fur behind his head one more stroke, then stood to face the merchant.

He shrugged. "In your own way, I suppose you were. In any case, it is fortunate you have this bond with him. I might have had difficulty in finding you if you did not."

"Is he fortunate? Or are we being deceived by the Silken Order?" Gennovil stepped forward, lips pursed, frowning as she stared at Nuraleed.

"Nuraleed," I said, indicating the man, "this is Gennovil, a . . . friend."

Nuraleed's smile grew even wider. "A most helpful one, it seems. And unusual . . . since, from my knowledge, the Sisters of Vraevre seldom have friends of any kind."

"We don't charge the ones we have," Gennovil replied, her glare intensifying. Nuraleed's smile wavered only slightly, but I had spent enough time around him to know when he was using his best methods of self-control with a particularly recalcitrant customer—or, as in this case, an obvious rival.

"All right," I said, stepping forward and raising a hand. "We don't have time for disputes or civil wars. But I do need an explanation, Nuraleed."

Nuraleed raised an eyebrow. "What explanation would you desire?"

"A truthful one. Why are you here, the only soil on your boots, waving a key? What's the game this time?"

The merchant threw his head back and laughed. "I am most glad to know some hours alone—your pardon, some hours in the inestimable company of this most worthy individual—" he said with a glance at Gennovil, who scowled, "—have not dampened your sense of caution, Grayshade ... or reduced your paranoia. Since I met you, I have begun to believe you may be right to leap at shadows." His smile faded. "As I told you, the Silken Order has not betrayed you—not at Yanner Fris's home, nor any time since. And whatever the Sisters of Vraevre may think of us," he went on, looking squarely at Gennovil, "we do not believe they betrayed you either."

"Comforting," Gennovil said coldly. "But Grayshade's question remains unanswered, and we're wasting time. Why are you here?"

"To help," Nuraleed said, bending down to pet Caoes, who arched his back at the touch. "For most of the day I have had operatives around Tellisar seeking news of Rillia or you, Grayshade, without result. About two hours ago Caoes arrived at my home alone. He was uninjured, as you see him, but clearly wished for me to follow him, and I have long since learned to listen to any message a namir brings me ... especially this namir." He smiled briefly as Caoes slowly blinked, then grew serious again. "I knew he had left with Rillia, and so it was no great leap of fancy to assume he knew where she was, or perhaps where you were. He led me to the outskirts of the Helm Quarter, and I stopped him when I saw where he was going."

"The Locks," I said.

"Indeed. I had not heard of Rillia's arrest—I must assume the Sisters had, which is why you are here—but I knew enough of the Locks to understand that if she had been taken there, walking through the front door would not be a reasonable course of action. So I brought Caoes back to the Sabaton Quarter."

"You found our entrance to the sewers?" Gennovil said, her expression startled.

"Of course not. I assume you would have carefully hidden the entrance to all but other Sisters, yes? And I do not know your marks or symbols. But yours is not the only path to use. I used one with which I was familiar ... and which would allow us to arrive in the sewers in a spot beyond the dangers and stench of most of the passages. Judging by your smell and appearance, you do not seem to have been as fortunate."

"That's putting it mildly," I said, rubbing the back of my neck. "So you know of other pathways to the Locks?"

Nuraleed's grin reappeared. "Let us say I know of a series of tunnels with mercantile applications."

"Smuggling, you mean," Gennovil said, pursing her lips.

"An unfortunately loaded term," Nuraleed said, bowing slightly to Gennovil, "but not an entirely unjustified one. There are certain goods which the city of Tellisar refuses to accept, largely because they fear it would undercut their own trade in those goods. But the population has needs which must be met, even if their rulers wish it was not so. These tunnels make meeting those needs considerably easier." He turned back to me. "I knew you would be looking for Rillia, and that either you or Caron—where is that remarkable child, by the way?"

"Back with the Sisters. They aren't doing well, and I didn't know how well I could protect them down here."

Nuraleed nodded, frowning slightly. "That troubles me, but other concerns must wait. For now, we must get through this gate and into the Locks." He held up the small key, which also looked to be made of revellit.

"I thought only Acolytes of Argoth have access to this material. Why exactly do you have this key," Gennovil asked, her expression darkening, "unless you were responsible for installing the gate it unlocks?"

Nuraleed raised an eyebrow. "A thousand pardons for the presumption, Sister. But no matter who makes a gate, given time and talent, anyone can get a key which unlocks it, and the cells which lie behind it."

"You *bought* it?" Gennovil said, her voice incredulous.

The merchant chuckled. "I prefer commerce, yes. But there are times when other methods are more . . . efficient."

"You stole it," I said dryly.

Nuraleed adopted an expression of mock horror. "Theft is dishonorable and against the code by which the Silken Order must conduct its affairs." He tossed the key up, glinting in the lantern light, then caught it again. "Besides, stealing the key would ensure any gates it previously opened would have their locks changed. But if one were to, let us say, *borrow* a certain key—then make a copy of that key, using a small supply of revellit which had been acquired in previous years, before returning the original to its rightful owner . . ." He trailed off and smiled. "Nothing stolen, nothing missing, formerly closed gates suddenly open. A wondrous development, truly."

"Truly. But none of that explains why you've chosen to come here now, Nuraleed."

The merchant pursed his lips before responding. "Because the Silken Order needs the Order of Argoth stopped, and you are the best way to stop them . . . and you need help to do it. Besides . . ." He glanced at Gennovil, whose expression had not lightened, and sighed. "Suspicion and doubt and deception dominates our chosen profession, yes? They are the stock in trade of your former Order, Grayshade, and they have come to dominate Tellisar in the same way. Perhaps that is what they desire most in the end: certainty for them, darkness and confusion for everyone else, so that they may impose their will more easily." He lifted his chin and looked directly at me. "But I am sworn to protect the Silken Order. If I may be permitted the smallest amount of self-praise, I have run it in Tellisar wisely and well. And I will not allow its name to be smeared by the filthy lies of those who would destroy those they cannot rule." Suddenly his expression softened. "And I will admit to feeling somewhat responsible for what has happened to Rillia, and to feeling somewhat fond of her, Caoes here, and Caron. Even you, Grayshade, as irritatingly, predictably stubborn as you may be, have some—let us call them redeeming qualities, yes?" He laughed as I scowled. "In fact, that stubbornness may be the most redeeming quality of all: your single-minded, ironclad will, that drive which refuses to acknowledge when you have been defeated at last. Perhaps one does not actually lose until one acknowledges the loss, to themselves and others." His smile vanished. "In this circumstance, we cannot be defeated. It is good to work with someone who feels the same."

Nuraleed turned to Gennovil. "So, Sister of Vraevre. You and the other Sisters may not trust the Silken Order, but they must surely trust it more than they do the Order of Argoth, and Grayshade more than either. Say at least that for the present moment, we have a common purpose, that we follow a common path. Walking that path together seems both logical and prudent, yes?"

Gennovil glared at Nuraleed for several seconds, then glanced at me. After a few moments her face relaxed, and she sighed heavily. "Yes. But only for the present moment, Nuraleed. I serve the Goddess of Truth, not an organization of cutpurses and shady merchants."

Nuraleed raised an eyebrow, his smile returning faintly. "Heavens strike me down, if I should ever force someone with such ... conviction into undesired service." Gennovil nodded tightly as Nuraleed stepped forward with the key and placed it into the keyhole on the gate. It turned, and with a quiet click the gate opened.

"Now we must move quickly," Nuraleed said, removing and pocketing the key before stepping through the open gate and beginning to walk down the passage. "Follow me. I will guide you to the cells, where we must hope our friend Rillia can be found."

"How do you know where to go?" I asked, stepping through the gate to follow.

The merchant paused, looked over his shoulder, and grinned. "Because, my friend, I have been here before. And my memory will be a surer guide, I suspect, than your guesses." He made a rather unsubtle sniffing noise at the two of us, then turned away and moved on, Caoes padding after him. Gennovil looked at me, mouth open, then shook her head and followed, limping slightly, with me close behind. I could only deal with one mystery at a time; unraveling the past of the leader of the Silken Order would just have to wait.

———————————————+———————————————

We did not spend much more time in the sewers. Nuraleed guided us confidently and quickly through the remaining passages, stopping us only when we got to another room similar in size and shape to the room where we had fought the waterworm. There was no grate in the ceiling, however; instead, a ladder in the center of the room led to a closed trapdoor, and Nuraleed pointed to it. "If my memory has served me correctly, this is as close to the cells as we can get from underground. Of course, what we will find once we get up there is uncertain; my knowledge is still the primary factor, and that may be suspect now. I cannot know what changes have taken place within the Locks over the last months; it is quite possible that they have altered the interior as much as they did the sewers. Let us hope that such alterations are not extensive."

"And if they are?" Gennovil asked, stepping up to the bottom of the ladder and looking at the trapdoor above.

"Then," Nuraleed said mildly, "we will be in considerable difficulty."

Gennovil snorted, but said nothing as Nuraleed climbed the ladder, the rungs creaking slightly under his weight, and used the key he had used on the gate for the trapdoor. The key turned with a quiet click, and Nuraleed slowly pushed the trapdoor open, poking his head out and looking back and forth before looking back down at us. He silently waved us up, then climbed the rest of the way and disappeared out of sight above the ladder. Gennovil followed; it seemed like she was more cautious every time she had to push up on a rung with her injured ankle, but I might have been imagining that. I went last, kneeling down next to Caoes. "All right, Caoes," I said as the panther regarded me solemnly. "This may not be your favorite method of travel, but it's the only way I can think to get you up a ladder quickly." I lowered myself to all fours and braced myself as Caoes climbed onto my back slowly, padding up to my shoulders. I reached up and grabbed his legs as I leaned back onto my knees, straining against the weight of his body; he was sleek and fit, but considerably heavier than when I'd carried him in the Bloodmarsh, and I had to be extremely careful not to stumble as I got to my feet and onto the ladder, climbing with one hand as the other held onto one of his legs, leaning close to the ladder to prevent his body from slipping off of my neck. But even carrying Caoes's weight, it didn't take me long to get up the ladder and out into the room above, letting Caoes slide off me to the floor and quietly closing the trapdoor behind us before looking around myself.

We were in what looked like a storage room in the basement of the Locks, with barrels and crates stacked against the walls; the stench of the sewer was basically gone here, replaced by a damp, musty odor of sawdust and wood. I could barely see even these things, as the room itself was mostly dark, but a faint flickering from the open door indicated a torch or lantern set in the space beyond. The large shape of Nuraleed was silhouetted in the door, and as my eyes adjusted I could see Gennovil standing right behind him. I came up behind them both, making just enough noise before speaking to keep them from being startled. "Clear?" I whispered.

Nuraleed looked over his shoulder. "So it appears," he said, voice quiet. "This is at the end of a hallway; if the layout is as it was when I was last here, we must follow this to the end, then turn right, straight on, left through a door and left again, and finally to the right through another door. Though the journey here was less than pleasant, at least our entering from below means we're close to most of the cells." He turned to Gennovil. "Did the Sisters discover which cell Rillia is being kept in?"

Gennovil shook her head. "No," she whispered. "But we're confident that she is here somewhere, or at least was a couple of hours ago . . . unless the Order of Argoth moved her."

"The namir also knew she was here," Nuraleed said. "Let us hope the last couple of hours have seen no change, and the namir can find her exactly."

"I don't know how much the Order is really in control of this city," I said quietly, peering around Nuraleed to see the hallway, walls and floors made of rough stone, extending to the left perhaps fifty feet before turning right at the end, where a single lantern hung on a hook set in the wall. "But the murder of Yanner Fris was high profile; a lot of people in the city have probably heard of it by now. If Rillia was just arrested for the murder, it's hard to imagine that they could move her that fast without Tellisar's officials giving their approval. Didn't you say the Varan Guard has no love for Argoth's people?"

"Most of them, no," Gennovil replied. "And they still basically control the Locks, from everything I've heard. But you saw the gate. If the Order was responsible for building that . . ." She trailed off and shrugged. "I don't know. But I'd still say it's a reasonable bet that she's here, at least until tomorrow. The Guard would probably hold the trial either here or in one of the nearby government buildings, quickly and quietly, then get word of the result out as soon as possible while they move her for execution."

I nodded. "Then let's finish the job. Nuraleed is our guide. Gennovil—" I glanced at her, thinking of her ankle, and hesitated. "We could use a rear guard here . . . someone to make sure the path back down is clear, if—"

"No," she said flatly. "The Sisters need to see this done. And I'm certainly not going to let *him* lead you somewhere on his own, just because he claims to have had a crisis of conscience."

"I am deeply moved by your confidence in my trustworthy nature, lady," Nuraleed said with a mock bow, turning back to the hallway before he could see her eyeroll reaction. He peered down the hall for a few seconds longer, then nodded. "All right," he whispered. "Stay close, and talk as little as possible. If all goes well, we should find Rillia's cell in minutes." He moved into the hallway.

"If all doesn't go well, we'll find our own cells just as quickly," Gennovil whispered before following him. I looked down at Caoes, whose gaze suddenly struck me as slightly mournful, before heading after the two rivals, the panther right behind me.

Despite Gennovil's worry, we had no real issues for the first few slow and cautious minutes of winding our way toward the cells; not even a rat interrupted our passage as we silently moved on. I had already seen Gennovil in action, and even with her injury I wasn't shocked to see how effectively she could move, while Caoes was never much louder than a wisp of smoke on the wind. But I was more than a little surprised at how quiet Nuraleed could be, given his demeanor and especially his size; the merchant was not a small man. Yet he was as stealthy and secret as any of us, and as he paused before opening the door at the end of a hallway leading to the cells, I was again reminded how foolish it was to judge anything based on outside appearance. *You would think you would have learned to look below the surface by now*, I thought with a touch of annoyance. But I had also learned that some lessons took longer to pick up than others.

Nuraleed looked over his shoulder and raised an eyebrow, then disappeared through the door. Gennovil, Caoes, and I followed, finding ourselves at the end of a hallway on either side of which were many iron barred doors, each with a small window in its center. The hallway was again lit by a single lantern, hanging from the ceiling about midway down the hall, and the air here was close and still. The merchant gestured to the other side of the hall as he went to the closest door on the left and slid open the shutter blocking the little window, peering inside briefly before closing it again. Gennovil went to the door opposite his while I went

to the one next to her. My cell featured a battered metal bucket
and a pile of straw, but was otherwise empty, and as Gennovil
and Nuraleed chose different doors, I moved to the next one
and found much the same thing. The third cell did have a body
within it—but it was that of an emaciated old man with wispy
white hair, face down, right hand and arm outstretched toward
the door. He could have been dead for years, or several minutes;
it was impossible to determine an age accurately without actually
going into the cell, which I had no intention of doing.

"Nothing," I said as I closed the small window on the
door. Nuraleed and Gennovil did not respond, already looking
through their respective windows, and I continued on, but after
two more windows into empty rooms, a sense of dread was starting to grow. Even if we could run through each of these cells with
relative speed, there was no guarantee we would find the specific
person we were seeking. Rillia could well have been moved by
now, and we would have no idea ... and no idea where to look
next. And if she was that important to them, would they keep
her in the general population of prisoners? Perhaps this was a
waste of—

"Guard," Gennovil hissed, and with a start I looked away
from the door in front of which I was standing to see the Sister
and Nuraleed disappearing into one of the rooms across the hallway, leaving the door open behind them. Without hesitating I
crossed the hall and entered the room; Caoes entered a second
later, and after Nuraleed gestured to the door, I closed it and
pushed against the wall, as far away from sight of the window
as I could get. For a moment I worried about our light, but then
saw Gennovil had dropped the hood on the little lantern and

tucked it under what remained of her cloak. After a moment I heard footsteps approaching outside, and then a grating sound against the window. The small frame slid open, letting a beam of flickering lantern light in to shine on the empty straw floor, and I heard some low breathing. After a long moment, the window closed, but a deep sigh of relief caught in my throat as I heard the sound of metal keys jingling followed by something clinking into the door's keyhole. My hand drifted back to the hilt of my cucuri as I saw Gennovil reach for her short sword and Nuraleed for his scimitar, though none of us drew weapons yet. There was a loud click from the door, and it slowly began to open.

"Ellix!" a harsh voice said from further away, possibly the far end of the room of cells. The door stopped opening.

"Mmm," a voice right outside the door said.

"Boss wants you," the further voice said.

"When I'm done sweeping," the close voice replied. "Can't get anything finished if we're always being told to do six things at once."

"Your funeral," the further voice said, chuckling nastily. "They're moving her soon, and boss wants the halls cleared. But you go on and do exactly what you want to do. I'm sure he won't care at all that you're ignoring him." Another chuckle faded away. We watched, hands on our weapons, as the door remained slightly ajar. After a long moment, the person outside the door muttered a nearly inaudible word—perhaps a curse—and the door closed. I listened as the footsteps faded into the distance, maintaining the silence for a good ten seconds after the sound had vanished.

"Too close," Gennovil whispered, exhaling and slowly

uncurling her fingers from the hilt of her sword. "If we're found down here..."

"We can't be," I said, standing straight. "And you heard what they said: they're 'moving her soon.'"

"Rillia?" Gennovil asked.

"We must assume so," Nuraleed replied, pulling out the key he had used to enter the cell. "And if she is moved..."

"We probably won't find her in time," I finished. "So we need to search even more quickly."

"Fortunately," the merchant said, unlocking the door and opening it just enough for him to peer out, "we don't have many more cells on this floor to check, if I have remembered the layout properly. And if the guard was being told to clear out the halls so she can be moved, that in turn means she must be on this floor, perhaps in the very next room, yes?" He looked for several seconds, then nodded to us and opened the door the rest of the way, letting us out before closing and locking the door behind us.

But the "very next room" was much the same as the first, filled with cells with either emaciated prisoners, asleep or worse, or completely empty. By the time I slid the window to the last cell in the room closed, I was convinced that we were on the wrong track. "She has to be on a different floor," I said, turning to face my three companions. "The warden probably kept her in a high security room right next to his own office, or maybe—"

Suddenly Caoes growled quietly, and I turned back to see him sniffing the door of the cell I had just been checking. After a moment he pawed the edge of the door and looked up, yellow eyes gazing at me steadily.

"I thought you just checked that cell," Gennovil said.

"I did. Maybe he's feeling the way we are, though—he's missing Rillia, and after we haven't found—"

"Shh," Nuraleed said, gaze intense as he came to the door of the cell in front of which Caoes was standing and opened it with the revellit key. The door swung open to reveal what I had already seen through the small window: an empty room with a pile of straw up against the corner. Immediately Caoes padded into the room and over to the pile of straw.

"Does he smell something?" Gennovil asked. "Maybe Rillia was in this cell to begin with, but they already moved her out."

"Maybe," I said. "But there is something strange about this room, now that I look at it again . . . something seems—"

"Wait," Nuraleed said, holding up a hand, and we all fell silent as Caoes dug into the straw with his powerful paws. After a few seconds he pulled a heap of straw out of the way, revealing bare flagstones beneath, and I heard Gennovil gasp as something shone in the lantern light. It was the top of a large iron ring set in the floor.

A second later we were all kneeling next to Caoes, and taking hold of the ring, Nuraleed and I pulled a flagstone about three feet by three feet up and out of the floor. And in the space below, lying curled up with her face filthy and bruised, eyes closed . . .

"Rillia," I breathed.

Her cloak was rent, her dark hair matted and tangled, and she had several cuts on her face and neck; for a few moments I was afraid we had arrived too late. But then I saw her chest rising and falling quickly, and a feeling of profound relief swept through me as I lowered myself into the space, knocking a dead rat out of the way. With an effort I lifted her up to Nuraleed, who slowly got back to his feet, holding her body, as I climbed out of the hole.

"Unbelievable," Gennovil said, shaking her head. "I knew about the Locks's reputation, but this . . ."

"It appears," Nuraleed said, looking down at Rillia, "that our friend was even more important to the city, or the Order, than we might have imagined." Her limp body looked tiny in the merchant's huge arms as I lowered my head close to hers, listening to the quality of her breathing. It was swift and shallow, and I thought I could hear a slight catch in her lungs, though I might have been imagining it. "How does she seem?" Nuraleed asked after a moment.

"Exhausted and dehydrated, almost certainly," I said. "But there's something else . . . something keeping her unconscious, if I had to guess."

"Poison?" Gennovil asked.

"I don't know. We never used it in Cohrelle, but who knows what the Service here might permit, especially for something like this." I put my hand on Rillia's cheek, pale and smooth. *Especially for someone like you . . . or someone like me*, I thought.

"We can treat her when we get back to the Tower," the Sister said. "It's a good thing your panther was with us; we were lucky to find her."

"Yes," I said, gazing at Rillia's face. "We were lucky—" And suddenly something about Gennovil's words clicked, and I looked at her, then Nuraleed, whose eyes were wide; he had realized the same thing I had.

"Too lucky," I said slowly. "Move!" I drew my cucuri and ran out of the cell, Gennovil, Nuraleed, and Caoes right behind me, a second before the door to the hallway flew open. Two of the Varan Guard, weapons drawn, charged through, and I barely parried the first's attack in time to dodge the second. Gennovil was alongside me a moment later, her own weapon drawn, and together we managed to drive the two fighters back through the door from which they had come . . . but only for a moment. As I swung around, the door on the other side of the hallway opened, and two more guards ran through and toward us. Caoes leapt to the attack with a snarl, and the guards, probably surprised at the unexpected combatant, gave ground . . . but I knew we were in an impossible tactical position, as had obviously been the intention of whoever had set the trap for us.

Nuraleed turned to me. "This is not a fight we can win, my friend. Take her." Before I could object, he handed me Rillia's body, then turned. "When I give the signal," he said, "run. And do not look back."

"Nuraleed—" I said, staring at him as I sheathed my blade and got a better grip on Rillia.

"Bring her to safety, and do not worry. We shall meet again, one way or the other." Suddenly his old smile, wide and dazzling, returned. "Now take our prize to safety; she is too valuable to be further damaged, yes?" He turned and faced the two guards at the end of the hallway, drawing his weapon from its jeweled sheath—a thin, curved scimitar, its edge glittering in the lantern light—as the guards took several wary steps forward, watching the panther who stood in front of them, hackles raised. "A clever trap, and we the rats," Nuraleed shouted, voice echoing through the hallway. "Now it is the rats' turn to escape!" He barked one word, and Caoes jerked forward, causing the guard on the left to stumble in reaction; then the panther sprang to the side as Nuraleed, moving with extraordinary speed, charged forward and threw his body into the other guard, who staggered back into the opposite wall. "Go!" he roared, his single blade whirling so quickly that it looked like he was wielding two. I sprang forward carrying Rillia, Gennovil right next to me, and before either guard could recover, we ran right past them and Nuraleed and through the door beyond. I looked over my shoulder just long enough to see Caoes right behind us and Nuraleed's body blocking the open door as all four guards closed in; then the door slammed shut, and Gennovil, Caoes, and I ran on.

Another notch for the Eparch's belt, I thought, centering the weight of Rillia's body on my arms.

But no matter what it costs me, it's going to be the last one.

CHAPTER SEVENTEEN

I didn't remember much of the rest of the escape from the Locks and the sewers beyond them. Most of the exodus was a blur, a mixture of the foul stench of the sewers, the sound of our boots splashing through water as we ran, Gennovil's exhortations (amid occasional gasps of pain) to move even faster, the feel of Rillia's body in my arms. And of course, Nuraleed's smile, his body blocking the guards from stopping our escape as they closed in. That image might take the longest of all to fade from my memory, if it ever would.

I ran through multiple possibilities and scenarios in my head, but I came back to the same conclusion every time: of course we had been set up, led into a trap with Rillia as the bait, either there, in the Locks, or outside, to her execution. They had counted on Caoes, but not on Nuraleed. I doubted that the Order of Argoth was fully responsible for making the trap, or they might have considered me getting through the revellit gate, and in fact that was the only cause for even a glimmer of hope; if it had been up to them, we would certainly have been killed the minute we entered Rillia's cell, through overwhelming force, poison gas, collapsing the roof, or something even worse. Instead the guards going after us acted conventionally, attacking and defending themselves competently and well, but not heedless of danger, and not with the reckless abandon of someone who has been ordered to kill their target at all costs.

I knew the type, even if I had never been one of them.

No, these were certainly regular guards—probably the Varan Guard, given their skill in combat, but definitely not Acolytes. And that meant, as Gennovil had said, that the Order did not yet have full sway over Tellisar's operations, even if its influence was still greater than it should have been.

Cold comfort to Nuraleed, I thought. *Whoever held the blade that broke through his defenses and pierced his heart or cut his throat, he's just as dead.* I knew, of course, that there was a chance he could still be alive, overwhelmed by the guards and arrested for his crimes. With the loss of Rillia, Tellisar's officials would be anxious to show they still had someone upon whom they could visit justice, and even with Nuraleed's charm, his mercantile rivals would welcome the opportunity to see him removed from the playing field. After seeing the speed with which he had moved against the guards blocking the hallway, I supposed there was even a chance he could have fought them off. But I had been in this profession for too long to believe in fantastic scenarios. The simplest option was likely to be the correct one: Nuraleed had died fighting to guarantee our escape.

As I lay on the bed in an infirmary outside the Tower of Truth, fading in and out of consciousness as I struggled for a few hours of meaningful rest, this was the thing which continued to haunt me. Why had the leader of the Silken Order sacrificed himself for us? He obviously had no connection with or care for the Sisters of Vraevre, especially after the way Gennovil had reacted to him. Caron was safe with the Sisters, and while he may have cared for Caoes, Nuraleed couldn't have the same bond with a namir that I had with the panther, given what we had been through. His fondness toward Rillia had been clear, but enough to lay down his life for her?

Could he possibly have cared enough to lay down his life . . . for me?

I couldn't see it. Even if he recognized the threat the Order of Argoth posed to the Silken Order's interests, and thought I was the best one to stop that threat, surely nothing which had happened since he made that decision would convince him he was right. He had needed to help *us* in the sewers, both with the key to the gate and cells and with his guidance to find the cells in the first place. Without him, there was a better than even chance we would still be down there, hoping against hope for something to turn in our favor, or wandering the sewers looking for an alternate way in while Rillia was moved . . . or died. Yet in spite of everything, in spite of his own annoyance with me, even the way I had left his home, Nuraleed had chosen to help me rescue Rillia . . . and, quite probably, lose his life in the process.

It did cross my mind, of course, that his convenient appearance and then apparent self-sacrifice could have all been an act, but I couldn't see it. Those guards—and Nuraleed—had been swinging to kill. And what could such a ruse achieve that taking us all there, weakened and injured, would not?

It was yet another mark to add to an ever-lengthening list of grievances against the Order of Argoth generally and Eparch Kaenath specifically, and I had sworn to bring those grievances home to them. But other than the fact that Rillia, Caron, Caoes, and I were miraculously still alive, there wasn't much else to feel good about. Whatever Kaenath was planning to do was coming to a head, and I had only one lead, one option I could reasonably consider: take the fight to the Order, right to the Forge from which they were hoping to gain power and control. But I had vanishingly few assets I could bring to bear. I couldn't expect anything from the now leaderless Silken Order, who would be unlikely to listen to me even if I could discover how to contact them. The Varan Guard was obviously out. That left the Sisters of Vraevre, who seemed too few to mount an effective assault, Caoes, an ill sensate, and a badly injured Acolyte . . . and me. *Well done, lad*, I imagined Caoesthenes saying, glaring at me with his bushy white eyebrows as I tossed back and forth in an uneasy half-sleep. *You've managed to get even weaker than you were at the beginning.*

But I didn't know, I said, staring up from a hole in the floor of a dirty jail cell. *I've been trying!* And I watched in horror as my Trainer raised a flagstone from next to him and, eyes blazing, brought it crashing down on—

I sat bolt upright in my bed, sweating, my head pounding. The room in the Tower of Truth was small and quiet, and as I gazed into the darkness, I could feel my heartbeat gradually starting to slow. But I knew the nightmares wouldn't stop until the Order of Argoth had been stopped—or I had. When I was traveling across Silarein last year, my dreams had been just as intense, deeply disturbing and often frightening . . . but then, Caron had partly been influencing them, and there were lessons and warnings within them, possibilities I could ponder even in my fear. The nightmares I was having now were just that: nightmarish.

Unless I've learned I can't go to sleep again, I thought with a grim smile, staring at my sweat-soaked sheets. *That's certainly one kind of lesson.*

The door to my room opened, and I looked up to see the form

of Gennovil silhouetted against the light from outside, her ankle tightly-wrapped, but otherwise standing with ease. "Grayshade?" she said. "You're awake, then."

"More or less," I replied.

"Good," she said. "You are called for by the Three. We must discuss what the next step is . . . and who will take it." She turned, then added over her shoulder: "Ten minutes to the Tower base, Grayshade. Sister Yelinnia thinks the Order's going to respond quickly when they find out about Rillia's escape, and she says we need to move fast." Then she closed the door, leaving me to think about when, in the last month, I had done anything other than "move fast" . . . only to end up in more or less the same place.

Ten minutes later I was ushered into the room at the top of the Tower of Truth, discovering it was much more crowded than the first time I had arrived. Gennovil and Yelinnia were in their familiar chairs at the front of the room, the middle seat still vacant. But where there had been only two guards along with Caron and myself before, now four other Sisters flanked the room, along with Caoes and . . .

"Rillia!" I said, taking several steps toward her, my eyes wide in surprise. Given the condition she had been in when we escaped the Locks, I wasn't expecting to see her conscious for several days, let alone on her feet within several hours. Her face was still drawn and pale, but she smiled as she saw me, and coming close, she put her hand on my arm as Caoes nudged my leg. "I suppose that saying you should be in bed resting, not navigating a room of ill-humored guardians of the truth, wouldn't do much good?" I asked her, too quietly for any of the Sisters to hear.

"Not much," Rillia replied, shaking her head. Then her smile faded. "Grayshade—Caron is . . ." I raised an eyebrow, but before she could say more, Yelinnia spoke.

"We are assembled, Sisters and strangers both, to set our final plans in motion. Let the room's doors be locked until our council is concluded." The two guards at the door nodded and complied, and with a click we were sealed in to the room. Yelinnia turned her gaze on Rillia. "Now, the one called Rillia. You have insisted that you be allowed to attend this council, despite your recent escape and illness. Are you certain you are well enough to do so, in body and mind?"

Rillia stepped forward and bowed slightly. "Yes, Sister. And before we go any further, I must thank you, and Sister Gennovil; I was very sick when I arrived here, and I am told I might not have survived without your help, here and in the Locks."

Yelinnia nodded. "Quite likely. You were given an herb we call twoleaf; in small amounts, it can relax and calm, but in the amount you were given—probably dissolved in water—it rendered you unconscious, and would have eventually stopped your heart altogether, had we not tended you when we did. But your thanks in this are unnecessary; you were imprisoned on a falsehood, and it is Vraevre's will that we bring truth to lies wherever they may be heard. Moreover, the organization you call the Order of Argoth must be stopped, and the one who will be instrumental in this must have all his focus on that task." She looked at me. "It is him you should most thank, for it is he who was most focused upon your return."

I frowned as Caoes curled up near my feet. "She would have done the same for me. And . . ." I looked at Rillia. "It was my fault she was there in the first place."

Rillia's eyes widened. "I made my own decision, Grayshade. It wasn't your—"

The white-haired woman cut her off with a wave of her hand. "The Order of Argoth is most to blame for your imprisonment. But whoever's fault it was that you were in that position, Grayshade felt responsible. And thanks to him, and Sister Gennovil, you have returned."

"And Nuraleed of the Silken Order," I said. "He didn't need to do what he did."

"Yes," Yelinnia agreed. "There are many who sacrificed themselves on your behalf, Rillia. I hope you will consider that as we discuss what must happen next." Rillia blinked as Yelinnia leaned back in her chair. "Since you are here," the Sister said, "we would know what information you may have gained during your imprisonment, as brief as it was. Did you hear anything of the Order's plans?"

Rillia sighed. "I was too busy being thrown into a hole in the ground and given this twoleaf you just told me about, I'm afraid. The only thing I heard was a rumor from another prisoner in the first cell I was in for a few hours, before they took me away to the place you found me."

"A rumor can be a path to the truth, if not the truth itself."

"I know," Rillia replied, rubbing the back of her neck. "But this one . . ." She frowned. "He was an old man . . . thin as paper, and already seemed witless and wandering. He kept laughing and babbling about final judgments; I was trying to tune him out. But when they came for me, he . . . he looked at me, and his expression changed. He had these blue eyes—cold, ice-blue." She swallowed.

"What did he say?" Yelinnia asked.

Rillia's lips trembled. "I'm sorry, I . . . he was just . . . I don't know. He frightened me. He said the hammer of the sky was being forged, and the one holding it would create something entirely new—and make himself a god." Her eyes became unfocused, as if she were remembering the scene. "He said," she went on after a moment, her voice unsteady, "that the hammer would fall upon Silarein . . . and its strike would reforge the entire world. Then he started to laugh again, and they took me away." She lowered her head. "It sounds ridiculous now. I was probably already affected by the twoleaf."

"Maybe," Gennovil said, musing. "But everything we've ever been able to find about Kaenath says he desires power, for the Order and himself. Whether he's found a way to get that power . . ." She shrugged. "We've never been inside Argoth's Forge. Who knows what might be in there?"

I shook my head. "It's still not much to go on."

"No, it isn't," Rillia said. "We're not making a decision based on one old man's ravings, or whatever my fears are telling me. I—I just need some time to . . . to figure out . . ." She trailed off, eyes wide in apparent doubt and anguish.

"We're not making a decision on one thing," I said, watching as she turned to me. "But if we were—if I had to make a choice based on one bit of evidence, no matter how small—I would trust it, if it came from you, and I would take whatever you had found and run with it. All the way to the Forge and the Eparch, if I had to." Rillia's mouth opened slightly, and she turned away, eyes closed.

"Enough," Yelinnia said, voice firm. "This is larger than your own personal desires, Grayshade, and larger than your own concerns with the Order of Argoth. The lives of tens of thousands are at stake—hundreds of thousands across Silarein, and the lands beyond. The truth itself is under threat, and we will not allow it to be broken, by impulsiveness or an emotional desire for vengeance."

I stiffened. "This isn't about a desire for vengeance. It's about eliminating a major threat to Tellisar and Silarein, not to mention the Sisters of Vraevre. It's about making our world a safer one."

"After," Yelinnia said, voice unwavering, "you spent ten years making our world considerably more dangerous."

I stood straighter, my hands curling into fists at my side. "With respect, Sister Yelinnia: my business with the Order of Argoth is my own. I have renounced my Service, and made every effort to pay back that moral debt since. But I will not be lectured by the head of an organization just as secretive as mine ever was, and I will not be ordered around by someone to whom I owe no allegiance nor count any connection."

"Do you not?" Yelinnia asked, eyes flaring. "You feel no connection here? Even through your family?"

I stopped short, staring, and the room grew still and silent. Finally Rillia spoke. "I don't know what this is all about, but mocking Grayshade—"

"This is about truth," Yelinnia said sharply, "not mockery."

"Sister," Gennovil said, "perhaps this is not the time."

"On the contrary, Sister, this is the only time. If he is what you believed him to be—what she believed him to be," the older woman said, nodding to the empty chair, "then he must be aware of the sacrifices made for him before we decide what happens next."

"I don't need more explanation of what I did wrong in my past. I already know, in exceptional detail, my crimes—"

"No, you don't," Gennovil cut in. "And this wasn't a crime . . . just a . . . reality. A thing that happened." She glanced at Yelinnia, who looked back imperturbably, then sighed and nodded. "Our third Sister, the most experienced of the Three, knew of you from the beginning. She lost track of you . . . but then found you again. And when the time came, she knew you would be involved in bringing down the organization you had served. She was convinced of it."

I stared at her. *What in the Hells are you*—

"She had lived a double life in Cohrelle for some time, working for the Sisters. Cohrelle was smaller than Tellisar, but growing rapidly in power and influence . . . though it was never as interested in the world outside its borders as Tellisar was. But all cities eventually desire the power of countries, and all countries the power of empires . . . and besides, the religions in Cohrelle, which had been at war in the past, were more dangerous than elsewhere in Silarein. And the most dangerous of them all, even then, was the Order of Argoth. So our Sister took up residence there, became invested in the political and religious life of the city, trying to assess the greatest threats to the Goddess of Truth, and reporting what she found to us."

I felt the room drifting away, my gaze narrowing to take in only Gennovil's face as she continued to speak, her voice slow, almost languid.

"A few years after she arrived in Cohrelle, an opportunity arose . . . a chance for her to gain access to the political elite, to learn far more than she could from the outside. She had attracted the eye of one of the most prominent money-tracers in the city, a rising star in the political fabric of Cohrelle. I was not in the Three or even one of the Sisters at the time, but I have since heard the idea was . . . controversial."

"I was in the Three," Yelinnia said, her tone flat. "And I was not in favor of it."

"Still," Gennovil went on after a pause, "she did what she said she would, and they were married. At first it seemed to pay dividends. She gave us far more information than we had received before. And her marriage, from what she described, was happy." She took a deep breath, and I could feel the eyes of Rillia and the other Sisters upon me, but I could not command myself to return their gazes, fixated on Gennovil's face and voice. Then Caoes stirred at my feet, and I held onto that movement: the feeling of a living thing in the present, a warm reminder that I had not vanished forever into the swirling fog of past revelation.

"Perhaps a year later, the Three received word that she and her husband had added another to their family: an infant she found in an alley of a small coastal village. Why she had been in that village, or gone down that alley, she never said, and perhaps did not even know herself. It was a baby boy, covered in blankets and filth . . . and at first she thought it was dead, so silent was he. She took him . . . and for five years, she took care of him." Gennovil mused for a moment before continuing. "Then one day, when the boy was five, she returned home to find him gone. Her husband would say nothing of where he had gone, nothing of where he could be found, and despite every effort she could make, he had vanished completely. Eventually she had given up hope entirely. She remained within her marriage, stayed with her work. Her personal comfort in men

as well as women and the easy nature of her demeanor allowed
her to succeed in an environment many of the rest of us could not.
Decades passed as she made herself into one of the most important
political figures in Cohrelle, and rose to become one of the Three
of the Sisters of Vraevre. She even founded a false religion to cover
her own background, one which would confuse anyone trying to
learn more about her appearances and disappearances, a small
group she called the sect of Rael. And then, one day, she heard a
rumor, an impossible one ... that a boy had become a man, and a
man had become something else. She inquired further, and added
up the years, and realized the rumor must be right."

Freedom, and a true family.

"But the Order of Argoth had taken notice, and soon it saw
the chance to eliminate two threats: a money-tracer who was now
a liability, and his wife, who had asked too many questions. She
did not realize the danger until too late."

"Even then, she could have come back to Tellisar if she
wished to, where the Sisters are much stronger," Yelinnia said, her
expression softening for the first time. "We could have protected
her here."

"That was a year ago, and I had just become one of the Three,"
Gennovil said. "I pleaded with her to return. But as one of the
Three, we could not force her ... and she said this would set a
chain of events in motion, a chain of events which would end in
the destruction of the Order of Argoth, and strike a major blow
for the Goddess of Truth. And besides ... she owed it to the boy
she had loved to let the man she still loved find the path she saw
before him, by completing the task he was assigned."

A ... true family ...

"The task he was assigned by the Order," Yelinnia said, her voice drifting through my dream. "A task which would be easy for one of the greatest assassins in all of Cohrelle."

True . . .

"But—but he couldn't have known," I heard Rillia's voice say, somewhere a thousand miles from me. "It was a mission . . . that was all it was . . ."

"Yes, he could not have known," Yelinnia said. "But *she* did. And when Grayshade completed his task, and killed the woman he knew as Lady Ashenza, he also killed a Sister of Vraevre . . . and a mother. And the chain of events that death set in motion has led to this place, and this moment, where we must decide how to end the time of the Order of Argoth."

There is a time for everyone when the past and future meet—when what we have been merges with what we will be. If we are fortunate, that time is one of celebration and hope for what comes next. If we are not, that time is one of terrifying revelation and regret. And once in a while, there is nothing on the other side of that revelation but darkness, darkness which must eventually consume the one who gazes into it.

I heard our plans being finalized. I sensed people speaking to me, words of comfort from Rillia, words of certainty from Gennovil and Yelinnia. I felt Caoes nuzzling my leg. I dimly remembered departing the chamber at the apex of the Tower of Truth, vaguely recalled descending the stairs, barely visualized my path to a small room not far from the one in which I had woken, almost blocked out my entering the room and standing above the bed within it, looking down at the small form which breathed swiftly and shallowly.

A true family.

I don't know how long I stood above the bed, watching Caron, the leader of Varda's people, sleeping ... or so it appeared. Their eyes were closed, but their brow was furrowed, and they shifted back and forth in the bed, their dark face shadowed, mouth slightly open. Once in a while they gave a quiet, muffled cry.

They were in pain. And I had caused it. *All I ever do is cause pain.*

I wasn't being maudlin. On one level, most of the last twenty years, ten in training, ten as a fully trained Acolyte, had all been in service of the same goal: to cause pain through the elimination of the Order's enemies. I could couch it in other terms, perhaps; I always acted swiftly, took no pleasure in slow and drawn out deaths, prided myself on finishing the job as quickly and professionally as possible. But in the final analysis, I was ending people's lives, concluding them in the pain of a blade or a dart. And in my wake were the lovers who would reach out to an empty bed, the friends who would never again have the person they trusted most to help them define their lives, the students who would never be taught, the parents who would never see the world afresh and with the hope only their children, no matter how old they have become, can provide ... and the children and grandchildren who would never again have their guides, the ones who separated them from the reality of a life alone.

I had done all of that, through years of blood and betrayal. What did it matter that I had misunderstood what I was doing, or why I was doing it? No one else had held my blade. I had done it. Me.

And now, I knew I had done it to myself. The memory of the

evening came flooding back to me: the smell of a light perfume, the depth of the colors in the black and purple robe Lady Ashenza was wearing, her calm expression . . .

Her gentle smile, just a second before I ended her life the way I had ended all the others.

Of course, I could never have known exactly who she was. Her words, seared into my brain, had given no warning of anything unusual in my work. *I am not a threat to you*, she had said, like so many others before, and *I am a simple person*, and on and on. It was all . . .

No. No, there was something different. Not her voice, sonorous and rich, nor her look, somehow older and ageless at the same time. But her words . . . *It is not too late to turn away from that evil*, she had said. *To do what you think you should do, not what you are told you must do. What path will you choose?*

And I had chosen—again—the path of death. The path of pain. I could not have known I was killing my mother when I fulfilled my mission. But my mission, as always, was about death and pain. And now I felt it the way the others left behind must have; in the end, pain was my only legacy, a legacy I saw etched on Caron's face as they writhed in the bed.

Dimly, I heard someone enter the room and stand next to me. "They've been like this for at least a day," Rillia said. I did not respond. I heard her voice, understood the words, but they seemed muffled, distant. Not for me. "Yelinnia thinks Caron is responding to something happening in Tellisar which is somehow connected to the Order, but she can't say exactly what it is . . . and neither she nor the other Sisters can do anything about it, other than try to make them comfortable. According to one of the other Sisters, Caron wanted to come with us when we go to the Forge . . . but Gods only know if they'll even be awake by then, let alone in condition to travel."

I was silent, gazing down at Caron as they shifted again, an expression of anguish on their face.

"Grayshade," Rillia said, putting a hand on my arm. "If we can stop them, we can stop this. We can end the threat. We can end them."

Her words were kindness, and her conclusion ridiculous. The Chief of the Sewer Rats, Rumor, Caoesthenes, Alarene, Nuraleed . . . my own mother, and a hundred more. There was no end to what I did, no end to the damage I caused, to the pain people felt around me, no matter how I tried to redeem myself, no matter what I did in an attempt to be better.

"Grayshade," she said again, her voice softer.

Suddenly I felt the grief overwhelm me, and I turned to Rillia. "I don't want this," I said. "I don't want to cause pain, I don't want to hurt. I don't want any of it. I want to leave . . . for us all to leave, to find a place far from here or any other city." Rillia's mouth opened slightly in apparent surprise, and I grabbed her hand and squeezed it convulsively. "Can we do that?" I asked, my voice breaking. "Can we run away—all of us? Can we leave this behind?"

"Grayshade," she said a final time . . . and for the first time in my life I could remember, I cried. I wept for everything I could have been before and could never be now; I wept for everything I had lost and could never regain. But most of all, I wept for everyone I had ever hurt, for every face I could never forget, for every person whose time I had ended in my arrogance and pride and dogmatic stupidity. And Rillia wept with me, as we held each other in a little room in a small corner of a massive city, two insignificant specks in an indifferent world which neither knew nor cared for either of us.

Then Rillia kissed me, a kiss of impossible warmth and bottomless sorrow, and for a moment, just a moment, I lost myself within that kiss—love and grief and hope and anguish, all mixed in a single moment of two human beings connected with each other, beyond all the rage and greed and fear of a tired world.

"Grayshade? Rillia?" a voice said, and Rillia and I broke from the kiss and slowly turned to see Caron looking up at us from their bed. Their face was still lined with exhaustion and pain, and they were still soaked in sweat. But as we gazed at them, a ghost of their old smile returned. "We need to go," they said. "We need to end this, and stop what the Order of Argoth is doing." They took a deep breath. "I can help. I'll go with you."

CHAPTER EIGHTEEN

I~~T~~ was shortly after midnight that we set off for the Armor Quarter, and, if the Sisters of Vraevre were right, Argoth's Forge. We considered bringing every able-bodied ally we could muster, but in the end decided against it: the Forge was no conventional fortress, nor was it manned by conventional soldiers, and they would be on their own ground. And the Varan Guard would also be on the lookout for us after Rillia's escape; they weren't an option either. Instead we needed to even the odds by getting as many of the Service's Acolytes still in or near the Forge away from the building. That would be the job of most of the Sisters, who would be exposing themselves in a way they had not for decades; if we failed, they would almost certainly be wiped out. But there was no other option but to hope they could hold their own for long enough while a small group—Caron, Rillia, Caoes, Gennovil, two Sisters, and myself—made its way into the Forge, to deal with the leadership which remained. From what I had been told of Father Rennix, he and any remaining Acolytes would be formidable adversaries, to say nothing of the Eparch himself. But I had dealt with formidable fighters before, and I knew that at a certain point, avoiding conflict with them is simply delaying the inevitable and introducing the possibility of error. This was the best chance we were going to get.

Still, even the best chance we could get wasn't necessarily a great one, and as we left the complex of the Sisters of Vraevre and headed toward the Armor Quarter, I wasn't sanguine about the group we had assembled. Under normal circumstances, a party of two highly trained Acolytes of Argoth, three highly trained Sisters of Vraevre, a sensate, and a combat-trained panther would have been an extraordinary team. But these circumstances were far from normal: Gennovil was injured, and no matter how she tried to conceal it, the effect was obvious; no matter what their training, I doubted that the two other Sisters knew what they were walking into, nor how they might manage it once they were there; and for all of my respect for Caoes, a single panther would have difficulty against multiple armed enemies. That left Rillia and me—one physically drained almost beyond endurance, and the other . . .

Well. In some ways I hardly knew how I felt; Rillia's kiss and Caron's words had breathed new spirit into me, but I knew I could only ignore my trauma for so long. Such things cannot be put aside forever, and when these returned, I had no idea how I would resist their effects. I had regained my outside composure. But inside, I stood upon a wire, my balance as precarious and uncertain as an Apprentice on their first mission. Caron could have sensed it almost immediately, but—

I looked at Caron, walking between Rillia and me. Their face was calmer than it had been when they were asleep, but they were far from normal. Unfamiliar lines cut into the sensate's forehead, a legacy of worry and stress totally unlike their usual feelings, and occasionally they would take an odd step and stumble before catching themselves, setting their jaw, and moving on. A few times I caught Rillia's eye when this happened, and we exchanged worried glances. Rillia was in no particular condition to be traveling either, but at least she was an adult and a trained fighter. Caron, on the other hand, was still a child in terrible shape. But we could not leave them behind again; they insisted on coming, and my gut told me we would need them before the end.

Injured, traumatized, and inexperienced was not an ideal set of characteristics for a group hoping to challenge Eparch Kaenath and the Order at Argoth's Forge. But it was what we had, and it would have to be enough.

I had been convinced that we would run into numerous Varan Guard patrols, not to mention groups of Acolytes, all searching for us. But as we made our way through the darkened streets of Tellisar, we found little other than an occasional rat scurrying by or a dockworker hurrying home, or to a tavern, no doubt after a long shift offloading crates and barrels for transfer into the city and further inland. On one occasion we did have to quickly duck into an alley to avoid a patrol, a few minutes after we crossed into the Armor Quarter. But even then, the three guards striding by seemed more at ease than I might have expected, chatting with each other as they moved past and out of sight around a bend in the street.

"I don't like that," I said quietly, peering after them.

"It could be that they haven't been alerted to what happened at the Locks yesterday," Gennovil said, kneeling next to me. "The Varan Guard is of considerable size; it's not impossible that not everyone knows yet."

"Or these are on the Order's payroll, and they know there's nothing to worry about," Rillia said grimly. Gennovil shook her head, but remained silent.

"I don't like the feel of it either way. Caron, do you sense—"
I began, but as I turned to them as they sat on the ground, back
leaning against the wall of the alley, I heard them gasp for breath
and saw their face contorted in pain, their hand reaching for their
head. Before I could say anything, their expression relaxed and
they shook their head.

"I—no," they managed after a few seconds. "I didn't feel anything . . . strange. Maybe . . . boredom. Something." They subsided
into silence, and I looked at them for a few more seconds, watching their breath slowly grow steady.

"Grayshade," Gennovil said, standing and taking a few steps
away to the other side of the alley, her gait still stiff and somewhat
halting. I stood and went to her, Rillia right behind me. "Look,"
the Sister said, glancing behind me at Caron, who was still sitting against the opposite wall of the alley, Caoes on his haunches
next to them. "I understand how important Caron is to you, and
the power you say they possess normally. When we went to the
Locks, I was the one saying we should bring them. But they're
barely able to move right now. I could send one of the Sisters back
with them to the Tower, and—"

"If you really knew the power they actually possess, you
wouldn't be suggesting sending them away," I interrupted. "I'm
worried about them too . . . that's why I didn't want them to come
to the Locks. But they've asked to come now, and no one else can
do what they can." I looked at Rillia, who was watching Caron
with an expression of deep worry; after a second, she turned back
to us and nodded tightly.

Gennovil sighed. "All right, but we can't be focused on anything but our goal. They're going to have to manage on their own."

She looked out of the alleyway in both direction, then nodded. "Let's move."

It was only a few minutes more when, the early spring moon rising overhead white and sharp, we came to an open square and the center of the Armor Quarter, facing the outside of a gated building. Two closed doors, each around ten feet high, held the gate, large iron spikes outlining the top of the entrance. Moonlit walls of the same height, made of simple but strong looking stone and topped by the same iron spikes, extended to the left and right of the gate perhaps fifty feet in either direction before turning and running away from our position a couple of hundred feet or so. The doors were unadorned and ordinary-looking, the walls unremarkable, and the size fairly insignificant. In the past I would have passed by a building like this a hundred times without a second thought, thinking of it as a small warehouse or counting facility. But now I knew, before anyone could say anything, the nature of what I was looking at. The walls were too simply designed, the gate too obviously unimportant . . . and the spikes reminded me all too well of a building I had called home for many years, in a city hundreds of miles away.

"There," Gennovil whispered, pointing at the gate. "That's—"

"Argoth's Forge," I replied. "It has to be."

"Yes," Rillia said, staring at the gate. "Although it's smaller than I would have expected."

"Passages extend below the building, I assume," I said. "And there's probably no easy way in without alerting whoever remains inside."

"Certainly not by the front entrance," Gennovil mused. "But as you said, this place isn't too large, at least on the outside. If we

do a circuit around it, we might be able to find an alternate path."
I nodded, still gazing at the structure. Something was bothering me about the area, though I couldn't put my finger on what. There were no other buildings within a reasonable distance of this structure, and the iron spikes made climbing up and over the walls an unlikely proposition at best. But none of that seemed like an obvious reason to be suspicious. There was something more, though . . . a sensation on the skin, or maybe a scent of something . . . familiar . . . but then it was gone again.

I looked at Caron, who was staring at nothing, their hands quivering. "All right, then let's not waste time," I said.

"We'll get this done faster if we split up," Gennovil said. "I'll take the Sisters and head left and around the Forge; you, Rillia, Caoes, and Caron head right, and we'll meet up on the other side, in the middle."

"All right," I agreed. "But make it quick; none of us want to be caught out here on our own."

Gennovil nodded, and turning, she and the Sisters set off to the left as the rest of us headed right. Caoes and I took the lead, with Rillia behind and Caron in the middle. I glanced back once to see Caron following, mouth slightly open as they walked on mechanically. My worry for them was growing by the second, but I knew our only chance to really help them lay somewhere in this building; the sooner we were in and dealing with the Order, the sooner we could get Caron better.

The sooner we can help them with their pain. I shut my eyes for a split second, just enough to hold back the reminders of my failures for a little bit longer.

I hadn't expected to see any obvious point of entry to the

Forge, so I wasn't overly disappointed to find nothing all the way down the rightmost wall. The stone was simple and unadorned, but surprisingly smooth and unmarred by cracks or pits—not rezin, but not ordinary granite or sandstone either, nor decades old. But whatever it was made of and whenever it was built, most important for us was that it was going to be difficult to get over or through.

"Maybe they don't want anyone getting in *except* via the front gate," Rillia said quietly. Rillia and I were moving along in a crouch, reducing our noise and, I hoped, our profile for any nearby Acolytes on watch; Caoes was already low to the ground, and Caron . . . well. Caron was smaller to begin with, and seemed to be stumbling along slowly through sheer will; I had no idea how they would react if I broke through their determined trance.

"Only a fool leaves themselves only one entrance and exit," I replied. "It might come out elsewhere nearby . . . maybe even into the sewers, even if this building isn't as old as the Locks. But there has to be another way in."

"Maybe," she said, a trace of doubt in her voice. "But this isn't the Service we knew. At the Cathedral in Cohrelle, we would have been accosted at least twice by now. Where are the Acolytes guarding this place?"

I did not answer, mostly because I had the same thought she did. If this truly was the center of the Order's power in Tellisar, it seemed inconceivable that there would not be more people protecting it, even if the Service was stretched thin. Soon most of the rest of the Sisters would arrive, and perhaps their "frontal assault" on the gate, intended as a feint, would pull the snakes from their holes. But even then, we would still need another way to get in, and in the meantime, I was growing increasingly suspicious of the ease with which we were scouting the perimeter, without a single note of challenge. I had just about decided to suggest we change tactics as we reached the rear corner of the wall, when Caoes drew back, a low growl rumbling in his throat.

Immediately we dropped from a crouch into a kneeling position, and I peered carefully around the corner, seeing nothing more than the same kind of wall we were next to now. "What is it, Caoes?" I asked. "Do you—" And then I stopped, because I had heard something—a quiet, small sound, so small most would either not hear it at all, or would immediately dismiss it with one of any number of normal explanations for sounds in a city at night. But as I looked at Rillia, I saw from her wide eyes and set jaw that she had heard the same thing I had: several quiet *thunks*, with one quiet cry suddenly cut short, sounds only Acolytes would truly understand.

Kushuri darts.

"We need to move," I said as I glanced at Caoes, whose ears were raked back against his head, his eyes narrowed, then at Caron, who was swaying slightly back and forth on their feet. "Take them," I told Rillia, and not waiting for an answer, I stood and ran around the corner and down the rear wall, Caoes running easily next to me. For a moment I had a flash of memory, running with Caoes through the Bloodmarsh, toward the sound of a keening cry . . .

Faster. Run faster.

I could move quickly when I wished, but no matter my training or experience, I had never been able to outrun my memories. But I made a heroic effort that night, and I arrived at the opposite corner of the rear wall in record time. I maintained enough of my composure to keep from running out into the open, as I dropped into a crouch again at the corner. Caoes padded up to me, but I barely noticed him, because another noise was competing for my attention: the sound of running water, trickling and splashing on stone. As I slowly looked around the edge of the wall I saw a fountain not unlike the ones I had seen near the home of the Sisters, but newer, and with one particular feature those fountains did not have. In the middle of the fountain there was a huge, cunningly carved stone hand holding a hammer lifted as if ready to strike . . . perhaps slightly different in cosmetic decorations, but unquestionably the Hammer of Argoth. Water was flowing in a shallow arc from the top of the hammer into the basin of the fountain, glittering in the moonlight as it splashed up from the stone.

For a moment I saw nothing else besides the fountain and the street beyond, and relief filled me. "Must have heard something else," I muttered to Caoes. "I'm on edge, and—"

Then I saw the light outlining something else, a dark shape extending past the edge of the fountain, and I knew that my doubtful nature had again been proven correct. Taking another quick glance around, I crossed the space between the wall and the fountain quickly, kneeling down next to the shape I had seen. It was the boot of one of the two Sisters lying on her back, sightless eyes staring up at the sky. I shook my head and pulled down the cloak around her neck. Four kushuri darts were embedded in her throat.

A quick inspection revealed the second Sister, lying facedown, was also dead, more kushuri darts in her back. But where was Gennovil? Could she have—

"Grayshade," a voice suddenly hissed, and I looked behind me to see Rillia and Caoes at the corner of the wall, Caron nearby, even more unsteady on their feet than before. But a second later I saw Rillia was pointing at something on the other side of the fountain. I moved around it to find . . .

Hells.

It was Gennovil. She was lying on her side, looking as if she had crawled here from the other side of the fountain, but as I took a closer look, I could see she was still breathing. I pulled aside her cloak to see a couple of kushuri darts embedded in her torso—but not enough to kill, unless poison was . . .

Suddenly she convulsed and grabbed at my hand, grunting in pain. "I—uh—no, no," she said, eyes rolling back in her head.

"Lie still, Gennovil," I said quietly. "Somehow you avoided being hit by the full spray of darts, but these could still kill you if—"

"Shut up," she cut in, coughing. "I . . . never mind me. The fountain . . . darts . . ."

"I saw."

"No, they—said . . ." Another coughing fit overtook her, and she clutched my arm until it passed. "Devotion," she finally said.

"What?"

"Devotion," she said again. "Needs . . . devotion . . ." With a final effort she threw her arm out toward the fountain, then fell backwards with a crash.

"Will she make it?" a voice whispered, and I looked to see Rillia next to me, staring down at Gennovil's unconscious form; Caoes and Caron were right behind her.

"I don't know," I replied. "She was hit in the side with two darts; the other Sisters got four each, both in more dangerous locations."

"Where did they come from?"

I shook my head. "I don't know that either. She pointed to the fountain, but . . ." I looked up at the hammer. "I couldn't make sense of it. But we have to; the Sisters of Vraevre should be arriving to start their distraction any minute."

Rillia pursed her lips. "What did she say?"

"Darts . . . the fountain, and devotion. Maybe a trap, I suppose." I rose and moved carefully to the basin of the fountain. "But she didn't say to leave." I moved slowly around the front of the basin, peering intently at its surface, but careful not to brush against it. Suddenly I stopped. There, attached to the block of stone on top of which stood the arm, hand, and hammer, was a marble plaque. Engraved on the plaque in flowing script was the following phrase:

FOR THOSE WHO SEEK JUSTICE
DEVOTION IS REQUIRED

I stared at the words, only dimly aware of Rillia coming to my side. "There," she said quietly, pointing to the corners of the plaque. There was a small hole in each corner . . . small, but evident if you knew what to look for . . . and if you knew the size of a kushuri dart. "And on this side," she went on, walking to the side where the other two Sisters lay, "four more holes right at the base of the marble block. I'd wager we'd find the same on the other two sides of the fountain. Touch it on any side and this would trigger . . . and since no one comes to the Forge unless they have business with the Order, they could leave this in place for anyone else who got too curious about the area. Although ... I don't know why they would only put this on this fountain."

"It's not just a fountain," I said, still staring.

"What do you mean?" Rillia asked, walking back to me. "And why are you still looking at that plaque?"

"I'm looking at the words," I said. "And I'm thinking of what Gennovil said." I looked at Rillia. "*Devotion.*"

Rillia looked again, then grew very still. Finally, slowly, she looked at me again. "It couldn't be," she said, a strange expression on her face.

"Yes, it could. With everything the Order believes—everything it's ever taught us—it may be the *only* thing it could be." With a sigh I knelt in front of the fountain and lowered my head. I no longer believed the words I must say, but they had been burned into my memory, and I could no more forget them than I could forget my own name. Quietly but steadily, I recited the Nine Rites of Devotion:

"By hating death, you become its servant; by loving it, you
  become its master.
You must always choose love.

Justice is neither love nor hate, neither mercy nor vengeance.
Justice is balance, and you will bring it to the world.

And who will not rejoice when he knows his life is a
  righteous one?
Who will not weep for joy as he brings justice to the world?

There is no room for indecision, or uncertainty, or
 hesitation.
When the Hammer falls, it falls with absolute conviction,
 and forges the metal it strikes whether it will or no.

The smith shapes the metal to his will as the Just God
 shapes the Acolyte to His Service. Both metal and
 Acolyte will bend or be broken.

There is no fate, or chance, or coincidence.
There is Argoth's will, or darkness.

Do not seek alternatives.
One will never find the way after turning from the straight
 path of righteousness.

The path of truth is straight, unbroken, and undeniable.
To deny, to doubt, is to be deceived. You must believe, or you
 will fall.

In the end, there is only one truth, only one reality. Accept it,
 and you will be worthy. Deny it, and you will be cast out
 as a heretic, and there is no atonement for heresy.
So speaks Argoth, the Just God. So must you hear, now and
 for all time."

As I spoke the last word, I heard a grinding sound from
above, and looking up, I saw the arm, the hand, and the hammer
slowly begin to descend as the bottom of the fountain split in

two, sliding into the sides of the basin walls as the collected water drained away into the space beneath. I quickly got to my feet and backed up several steps, watching as the hammer continued its downward path into the empty space. It took perhaps twenty seconds, and when the process was completed, the entire structure had vanished into the newly open area—all but the head and handle of the hammer, which now formed a kind of ramp descending into the darkness.

"Devotion," I heard Rillia say, her tone a mix of wonder and fear.

"Demand for control," I responded. "But we're past that now."

Suddenly Caron gripped their head and shrieked, face contorted in terrible pain. For a moment I thought they had been hit by more darts, and I whirled as Rillia grasped Caron's arm . . . but nothing else moved in the shadows, and the darts had certainly not come from the fountain. I turned back to see Caron swaying badly on their feet before slumping into Rillia's hold, eyes closed and face still contorted. After a moment Rillia looked up, saw my questioning glance, and shook her head. "No, nothing hit them. And they're still alive . . . breathing, if a little shallowly."

"Then what happened?"

"I don't know. Maybe the—"

Suddenly a great shout went up from the front of Argoth's Forge, accompanied by cries and the sound of metal clashing on metal. "The Sisters," I said. "The distraction's begun, and it won't last long. We need to move."

"What about Caron? And Gennovil?"

I hesitated. We didn't really have the time or resources to bring anyone along who couldn't bring themselves, as Gennovil

had herself warned, and bringing both of them would be suicidal—we had no real idea what we were walking into, and
we wouldn't be able to protect both them and us. But to leave
them here ... I thought for a few seconds longer as the sounds
of combat grew louder. "We may still need Caron ... and they
won't be able to survive in this state, if anyone tries to take them.
With Gennovil, one of the Sisters might find and be able to treat
her—and if she regains consciousness, at least she can fight."
Foolishness, and more pain, I thought, but dismissed it and set my
jaw. "We have to hope for the best for Gennovil, and she would
understand. But bring Caron."

Rillia paused, then nodded and picked the child up—and, to
my surprise, blinked back tears. "I'm fine," she said before I could
ask. "They're just ... so light." Then she shook her head angrily
and stepped up onto the basin of the fountain, then onto the head
of the hammer, and began descending the sloped handle into the
darkness. I took one last look at Gennovil, then back at the ever
increasing sounds of battle, and followed, Caoes padding behind
me.

I had been concerned about the lighting at the bottom of the
fountain; we had brought a hooded lantern like the one we had
used in the sewers under the Locks, but I wasn't sure what attention such light might attract, and I wasn't sure how long we might
need it; the oil would eventually burn out, and finding more
would be a risky proposition. But as we descended the ramp, I
soon noticed that the darkness I had seen from above was only
relative to the bright moonlight bathing the fountain; right as we
entered the darkness, we saw a small sparkle of light from below,
which grew brighter as we got closer to the bottom. Despite the

need for haste, I knew that a fall here, especially with Caron in
their current condition, would be disastrous. So we went at a
steady but maddeningly slow pace down the stone slope. After
about a minute we were nearly at the bottom when we heard a
grinding sound from above, and looking back I saw the circle of
moonlight, now a good distance away, narrow and vanish. Behind
me, Caoes watched the circle disappear before turning to look at
me and tilting his head slightly, blinking slowly.

"Hells take it," Rillia muttered, half turned to look as she held
Caron's body. "So much for escape."

"We wouldn't have found one through there anyway," I said.
"That area is about to be flooded with Acolytes, Sisters, fighters
from the Varan Guard, and who knows what else."

"So how do we get out?"

"You know what they say," I replied with a grim smile. "The
only way out is through, right?"

Rillia's expression did not change. "Right. Through—whatever's next." She shifted Caron to a different position in her arms.
"Grayshade," she said after a moment. "Neither of us really know
what's down here except, probably, Acolytes of some type or
another. But even if we're at our best, you know the odds as well
as I do."

I nodded. "We both knew them coming down here."

"Yes. But we talked about chances and possibilities then, in
front of many others. It's just the two of us now—well, two of us
plus Caoes," she qualified, nodding at the panther, who turned his
gaze to her. "So before we go any further, I want to know exactly
what you're thinking with this."

"What do you mean?"

Rillia sighed. "I mean, are we going to survive this? Any of us?" She frowned as I hesitated. "And don't make the answer pretty, Grayshade. I want this to be real."

I looked at her steadily, trying to read the real inquiry at the heart of her question. Then I realized there was nothing else, no shadows I had to penetrate with the light of logic. She was deadly serious. So I took a deep breath. "I don't know what happens to Caron, or Caoes," I said. "But this isn't about odds; this is about going after an enemy prepared for our arrival, in his own place."

"You don't think we're going to make it."

I sighed. "No," I replied. "For us, I think this is a one-way trip. And if it gets us an end to the Order, I'll take that trade with both hands."

Rillia nodded slowly. "So will I. If it comes to it. But ... for them ..." She looked at Caoes, standing squarely on his four paws, then at Caron resting in her arms.

"I know," I said. "I know, Rillia. Caoesthenes always used to say you either fight the river's current helplessly, or you swim with it and help shape where it takes you. He never told me what happens when you reach the end of it. Every river I know ends in the ocean at some point ... and I guess that's where we'll be, too."

"There are worse things, I guess," Rillia said, voice catching slightly.

"Yes. And there are worse people to be with, too."

She smiled, and, for the first time in an age, I suddenly felt an overwhelming surge of a different emotion than anger or sadness or grief.

Love, at the end of the river, I mused. *Did Caoesthenes always know that was where this led?* But I said nothing, simply allowing the briefest echo of my love to pass into a simple, peaceful smile.

Suddenly Caron moaned, and we saw their face contorted in pain. Rillia looked at them, then me, and I nodded. "Let's finish the job."

CHAPTER NINETEEN

AT the bottom of the ramp, we found ourselves in a well-lit passageway, illuminated by lanterns, hung at regular intervals, reflected by walls formed from the distinctive white substance of rezin. I had seen more rezin over the last few days in Tellisar than in all the years of my life put together, but even that paled before this: walls of rezin extending into the distance. Rillia whistled softly as we walked. "This doesn't look that old," she said. "How did the Order get this much rezin into Tellisar and down here? How much money do they really have?"

I shook my head. "Much more than they should. And getting the rezin down here couldn't have been easy either. All the Acolytes of Tellisar and Cohrelle put together wouldn't have been enough to build this on their own."

"No, they must have brought in outside workers," she agreed, musing. "I wonder what stories they could tell about it."

"Assuming you could find any of them alive now," I said, "or more than a couple of weeks after the work was done. You think the Order wanted any of them to talk about what they saw here?"

Rillia did not reply, and was silent for a few minutes afterward as we walked along.

The passageway was straight for a little while before it started to wind slightly, first left, then right. After a minute I noticed a kind of low hum, barely audible but still vaguely irritating, like a phantom itch on the skin . . . and at the same time, Caron's moans became more frequent and slightly louder, growing in volume as the hum did. But we all felt something growing in intensity; even Caoes's hackles were slightly raised as he padded along. At first I thought it was just nerves, my anxiety growing as we approached our goal, but when I felt sweat beginning to bead on my skin, I knew I wasn't imagining things.

The air was growing hot.

We walked along for several more minutes in this way as the passageway wound back and forth and the hum, and temperature, increased. Rillia, Caron, and I were all sweating profusely now, and Caoes's hackles were raised even higher than before, growling slightly now and again. The sense of irritation seemed also to have progressed to a vague sense of pain . . . for all of us except Caron, who was now moaning and squirming in Rillia's arms in a way which made clear their pain was not even remotely vague, even in their unconscious state. The hum had also begun to increase and recede at regular intervals, creating a pulsing sensation, and I was unpleasantly reminded of the way my head had felt in the hours leading up to my revelation at the Cathedral's Repository, back in Cohrelle—as if something was pounding on the inside of my head. If Caron was feeling even a bit of that same thing . . . well, I only hoped they were as unconscious in the realm of dreams as they were in ours.

After another minute, we saw we were coming to the end of the passage and a large room beyond it, brightly lit—but not just with reflected lantern light. The light from the room seemed to glow at least partially red, flickering like the ashes of a dying fire. And even here, several hundred feet away, we could feel a great heat rolling out of the room, flowing over and around us like water. Rillia and I looked at each other, and I knew from her grim expression that she had the same thought I did: we were almost there. We slowed our pace slightly to avoid the most obvious traps, but realistically I knew we were well beyond that stage. We had come to seek whatever awaited us in that room; if it was a trap, then they had wanted us to reach it.

A few moments later, Rillia, Caoes, and I stepped into the room and stopped. It was a kind of antechamber, a large, square room connected to a larger one on its far end by an archway, with walls made of the same rezin as the passage we had been walking down for several minutes. But there was one substantial difference: there were no lanterns on the walls here, and indeed none were needed, for the entire room was bathed in the glowing red light coming from the room to which this one was attached. The heat in the room was stifling, and the hum from the passage had become a dull rumble here, punctuated by metallic *thunks* at regular intervals. Caron stirred and cried out quietly with the sound of every impact, and I opened my mouth to suggest we hurry into the far chamber. But before I could speak, three cloaked figures stepped through the archway, the two on either side hooded and with blades drawn. Something about the build and movement of the one on the right struck me as familiar, but I couldn't determine why.

The person in the middle had no hood, and robes were visible underneath his cloak in the reddish light. He looked to be of middle years, with flat-combed hair and thin eyebrows to go along with a thinner goatee, and he was observing us steadily. "So," he said after a few seconds of silence, his voice slightly higher than I might have expected. "I did not know if you would come. But it seems there is nothing you are incapable of, if given the opportunity, even if that involves a suicidal challenge to an established authority. In that regard your reputation was well-earned."

"I appreciate the compliment," I responded, scanning the three for weaknesses. "But your authority is hardly established, by anyone except yourself." I paused to look him up and down slowly, noting the way he held his sword—slightly curved, but longer than my cucuri—in his right hand. His posture and position were practiced, the grip on the hilt of his blade firm but flexible . . . but it was a bit too stiff, a bit too training-perfect. Not in regular practice, then—but from the way the others stood behind him, he had to be more than an Acolyte. "Although," I said after a moment, "you do have authority over these people, at least . . . Father Rennix?"

The man smiled thinly. "A reasonable deduction for a former Acolyte in good standing. But you're not at liberty to call anyone from the Service 'Father' now, Grayshade. You've left all of that behind."

"I only had liberty," I said, "once I left the Service, and its lies, behind." Behind me, I heard Caron cry out again in pain, and turned enough to see Rillia looking up as she knelt by them; she must have laid them on the floor in preparation for what was to come.

"Ah," Rennix said, raising an eyebrow. "And you've brought the child, I see. Unfortunate that you have no other safe place to keep them. Unfortunate for you, I mean." Something clicked in my mind at that, but I couldn't take the time to figure out what.

"They will only have use when well," I said. "Your concern is with me, and mine is with the Forge behind you."

Rennix chuckled. "You have no idea what our concern truly is, apostate. That's another unfortunate truth, one you won't live long enough to understand. But I don't enjoy my security being breached, so perhaps I can make one offer. If you stand down now, lay down your weapon and explain exactly who is working with you, we'll make your end quick, and even spare *both* of your friends here. Play around ... well, I'll still have the other to use as leverage."

Both friends? I thought. *What happened to ... ?* Still, I managed to keep my confusion out of my face as I answered, fighting the urge to wipe the sweat from my eyes. "That's most generous of you. But I hope you'll understand if I say I'm out of the habit of believing anyone from the Order, much less one of their attack dogs. So I'll make you a counteroffer. *You* stand down, and we won't kill you."

Rennix laughed, in some twisted mirror of joy. "Those trainers never disappoint on the 'fight to the death' front, do they? Two ex-assassins wander in with an unconscious child and you still think you have a way through."

I smiled. "My trainers were exceptional. And I would think the Head of the Service would be better at his job. But perhaps standards have lowered since I was an Acolyte."

Rennix's smile vanished. "Your arrogance certainly hasn't. You're outnumbered and out of your depth here. This isn't your city, and you're alone."

"He isn't alone," Rillia said, and I looked to see her step next to me, her cucuri drawn. "And this isn't your city, any more than Cohrelle was. You're parasites, leeching off of the weak and desperate. You don't belong here, and it's time for you—all of you—to leave."

Rennix pursed his lips and nodded slowly. "Brave words from a dying soul. I'll say a prayer for you both to be granted Argoth's justice when you're gone . . . but I doubt you'll get it." His cloak flew open, and I dodged left, Rillia to the right, as a spray of kushuri darts flew between us. Snarling, Rennix charged, the two cloaked figures right behind him, and I brought my cucuri up just in time to parry a strike from the Head of Tellisar's Service, then spun away from a slash from one of the other Acolytes and backpedaled to give me time to assess the situation. Rillia and the Acolyte I had found familiar were trading slashes with their cucuris, the sound of clanging metal echoing through the chamber, and that left me with my two, because—where was Caoes? I didn't have time to consider the possibilities as the nameless Acolyte pressed their advantage, carving down and across my body in an effort to break through my defenses. The technique wasn't entirely familiar to me, more driven by strength and stability than agility and pinpoint accuracy, but the Acolyte I was facing was good, and most would have been hard pressed to defend effectively against their attack.

Most, but not all.

I relaxed and let my body curl out of the way of the slash, then suddenly tightened my muscles again and took a step forward into my assailant's space, so they could neither lift their sword or throw more darts in my direction. Their eyes widened as they sensed what I was doing, and they tried to step back, but I was already crouched and slashing low. They stumbled out of the way just in time, but their balance was off, and as I leapt up and forward from my crouch, they fell backwards, their head impacting the ground with a thud. I reversed my cucuri and brought my handle across the head of my assailant, but before I could get back up, I hesitated. Their hood had fallen, and in the reddish light I could see the sweat on their clean-shaven face, their eyes rolling as they fell unconscious. He was young ... much too young. Suddenly I remembered another scene: me staring down at the face of a young man, one whom I had known very well ... my Apprentice Ravel, whose only crime was belief, his only sin a misplaced faith.

Pain. Gods, why do they do this?

It was only my deeply seated training which allowed me to sense the danger, and I managed to pull away just before a slash from Father Rennix, whom I had stupidly ignored in my reverie, would have ended my life. As it was, it slightly bit into my right shoulder—only a superficial wound, but one that stung as I staggered backwards. But I was momentarily defenseless, and I saw Rennix's set and staring expression as he stepped up and started to bring his blade across my body. But the blow never landed, as a dark blur slammed into him from the side, and his weapon flew to the ground with a crash. I shook my head to clear it, and blinking away the drops of sweat from my eyes, I saw Rennix on one knee, staring at what had hit him.

Caoes had come.

The panther stood in front of me, a low growl in his throat, gaze fixed on the Head of Tellisar's Service. But even as I watched, I saw the expression on Rennix's face shift into a sneer, and I knew something was wrong. "Caoes, watch—" I started to yell, but before I could complete the warning, his body jerked, and he fell with a crash. Standing on the other side of the room was the other cloaked Acolyte, who almost immediately turned to parry another strike from Rillia. But Caoes was motionless, with three kushuri darts in his side.

The pulsing sound of metal on metal was loud, but the roaring in my ears was louder; the room was red, but my vision was redder; the space was hot, but my body was aflame. Father Rennix closed in, having retrieved his weapon from the floor, but I was standing tall, taller and stronger than the rezin walls which made up this cursed Forge, and as my cucuri met his blade my anger felt great enough to consume us both. I threw back his assault with ease, the pain in my shoulder barely even a pinch now, and with a guttural roar I kicked him with such force that he flew back several feet before landing on the ground, gasping for breath on his hands and knees. He looked up as I strode toward him, opening his mouth to speak—but I kicked him in the face, hearing a sickening crack as he fell onto his back, blood spurting from his nose.

"Use ... useless," he gasped through the blood, eyes wide. "Just ... just a brute ... an animal ..." He stared up at me with a terrible red grin. "*Heretic*," he spit, his voice ragged, contemptuous.

Heretic. Yes. I believed nothing; nothing except hate, and blood, and death, mattered. I was a heretic, and I would bring my unbelief to the world.

"Welcome to the void," I said, and with my eyes wide I drove my cucuri directly through his chest into Father Rennix's heart, watching as his expression faded from awareness into whatever lay beyond.

"Grayshade!" I heard someone cry, and I looked up to see

Rillia on the ground, holding her side, pointing to the far side of the room. There, the remaining Acolyte was dragging a body through the archway into the room beyond.

Caron.

Perhaps it was only Rillia's voice and the sight of Caron's body which could have broken through the red veil of blood which obscured my vision, the pounding of rage in my skull. But whatever it was, I suddenly felt the sting of pain in my shoulder and the sweat dripping from my face, and with an effort I stood up, yanked my cucuri from Father Rennix's lifeless torso, and stumbled after Caron and the remaining Acolyte.

There were two steps right past the archway, descending further into the deep red light of the room beyond. By the time I had navigated both stairs I was, except for the pain in my shoulder and the horrid depths of hollowness in my stomach, recovered enough that I could look up to take in the space—and in spite of the situation, took a deep breath as I saw the heart of the Order, hot and pulsing before me. An enormous semicircle, at the center of which was a large, elevated platform surrounded by a wide channel, with only a narrow bridge of stone from the far side of the room granting access to the platform. Thick, viscous, red liquid flowed slowly into the channel from two large pipes, one set over each end of the channel; stifling heat was radiating from the liquid. And sitting on the center of the platform was a great anvil, behind which stood a man holding a large hammer in two hands. He had no cloak or hood, and his robes were purple in the red light; he was clean shaven, and his face almost ageless. He stood smiling, staring down at me as the Acolyte dragged Caron's body toward the bridge.

"Stop!" I shouted, my voice wavering in the heavy, almost incandescent air. The cloaked Acolyte stopped and looked up at the man with the hammer.

"Why?" the man said in a deep, sonorous voice, and I was immediately reminded of the High Prelate of Argoth from Cohrelle. "Why would you have us stop, when you have helped our cause immeasurably so far?"

"You have no cause," I said, breathing heavily, watching as the red outline of his body wavered in the waves of rising heat. "All any of you have ever had is a lie, a lie you used to poison the minds of people who wanted truth."

"Ah, yes," the man said, nodding slowly, shifting the hammer in his hands. "I had heard of your strange self-absorption, this tendency to moralize. It's hard to imagine how one so efficient could spend so much time lost in the waste of one's own mind. But then, maybe your efficiency is just a reflection of your innate brutality. Just animal, savage instinct, with a blade and a cloak."

"I am what the Order made me," I said, blinking to keep my vision clear.

The man laughed, the sound rumbling in the heavy air of the room. "No, Grayshade," he said after a moment. "The Order just refined what you already were. We could never make people into killers unless they were halfway there themselves. Or did your High Prelate pretend differently, in your little city of Cohrelle?"

"I wouldn't know," I said, taking a step toward the platform. The Acolyte had now turned toward me.

"Of course you wouldn't," the man said, his mirth vanishing in an instant. "You never *knew* anything; that's how he kept you in line, like baby birds waiting to be fed their next morsels of belief.

But he was an idiot, an idiot worthy of the city he should have easily commanded as his own. Little Cohrelle," he said, chuckling. "So in love with its own petty squabbles, its own small shadows, vermin fighting over vermin."

"And you're different—Eparch Kaenath?" I said, taking another step forward, the pounding in my head relentless, the heat overwhelming. The Acolyte stepped in front of Caron's lifeless body.

"I'm glad you know my name, though soon it will matter little to you," Kaenath replied. "And yes, I am different. We created the Order in this city, piece by piece, story by story—and then we sent it out, to Arginn, Cohrelle ... even Sullbris, though it never took hold there. They all had their moments. But this was the only place where it became what it was always meant to be: a way for those who must rule to gain the power they need to do it."

"No one," I said, stepping forward again, "*must* rule."

"Of course," the Eparch said with a sneer. "Because it would be *wrong* to tell others what to do. But when there is no one to do so? When you're left to your own devices? What's left? Theft, murder ... war? Did you change when you left the Service? Or did you kill just as many people ... but now for you, instead of someone else?" He gestured to the bodies in the antechamber behind me. "Then I suppose congratulations are in order for your new moral clarity. Your ... *evolution*."

My vision swam, and my head was fire. I stepped forward again, and the Acolyte's body grew tense, but Kaenath did not seem to notice. "It's unfortunate for you that your process of change will come to an end here, in the Forge," he went on. "But it's also fitting, I suppose, don't you think?" He directed this last question not to me but to the Acolyte, who nodded.

"If the Head of your Service couldn't stop me," I said, my voice sounding distant and muffled in my ears, "why do you think an Acolyte under him can?"

Kaenath smiled but said nothing, and the Acolyte stepped forward. "Because," they said, their voice a low rasp, "I don't work for Rennix . . . or even Kaenath. I work . . . for me." He pulled back his hood, and my world suddenly twisted, distorted. I shook my vision to clear it, but the image in front of me—completely, totally impossible—remained. His face was scarred almost beyond recognition, twisted and burned. But even through the ruin of his features, I could never forget the man beneath.

Maurend.

It was Maurend. Maurend, my rival, the greatest assassin besides myself in all of the Service of Argoth. Maurend—whose life I had ended in the home of the Governor of Cohrelle.

"I see you have recognized your old friend," Eparch Kaenath said, though I only heard his voice dimly, my gaze fixed on Maurend's face, expression twisted in a terrible grin.

"This . . ." I said with difficulty, trying to corral my racing thoughts, "is not a friend. It's . . . a phantom. A trick."

Maurend laughed, his voice a horribly ragged croak, like a rusty blade being drawn across rocks. "I'm no phantom, Grayshade. But then you never . . . were very smart . . . never saw what was right in front of your face . . . even in Cohrelle. Ask Rillia whether I'm real. Or the Sisters upstairs . . . the ones not getting slaughtered right now by Acolytes. The ones already . . . dead." He laughed again, showing a mouthful of blackened, broken teeth. "I should have ... been dead too. But you never finished the job ... just like you never finished the one ... before it. Always leaving messes ... for the rest of us to clean up. Didn't think I'd have the chance ... to clean up this last one ... back in Jarrett's house. But things ... have a way of coming around." He laughed again, but nothing he was saying made sense; nothing fit, nothing clicked into place. *I saw him die—I killed him myself—*

"I suppose it wouldn't make sense to me either," the Eparch said, his voice raised in near delight, "if I was as limited as you. Dogs get confused if you teach them too many tricks." He lowered the hammer to the ground, head first, and put both hands on top of the handle. "You know the basics of soundshifting—parlor tricks for you, little games and toys to confuse the vermin you're sent to exterminate. But it's much, much more powerful than that, once you understand how it works, and what it works with." He tapped the handle of the hammer. "Have you ever wondered why the Cathedral in your city, or the Forge here, is made of rezin—so expensive, so difficult to extract and send to other places? It's strong, yes, but there is other stone nearly as strong, and much cheaper to get and work with. Have you wondered why cities might even begin to fight over the stuff?" He raised the hammer, the head still facing down, and whispered something as he tapped the anvil with the handle. Immediately a low, resonant sound echoed through the chamber, and a pain shot through my head, causing me to take a step back before I could catch myself. On the ground Caron twisted, and they cried out in obvious pain.

Kaenath smiled. "Yes, indeed. Stone doesn't create this effect. But rezin—combine rezin with soundshifting, and the effect is multiplied tenfold. Infuse rezin into metal, and you have something even more powerful . . . and portable."

"Another . . . weapon," I gasped, the pain in my head fading slowly. "I've seen them before."

"No, vermin," the Eparch said, tapping the handle against the anvil again, sending another wave of pain through my skull as Caron's body twisted terribly. "This isn't like anything you've seen before—and it's not just a weapon. Think bigger."

"Much bigger," Maurend rasped.

"We found him," the Eparch said, "in a mass grave outside of Cohrelle. A fitting end for a cutpurse, or petty thief. But for one of the Service's most skilled Acolytes? Like throwing a priceless vase into the gutter on the street." He gazed at Maurend, an owner looking proudly at a prized horse in his stable. "Bringing him back would be difficult. He had been gone for some weeks. But I had studied the history of your Service. Two among you stood out, the greatest servants of the Order: Grayshade, the renegade, the heretic—and the one you killed, Maurend, whose cruelty was legendary, whose hatred toward the one who killed him would have held him close enough to life that something might still be salvageable."

I stared dumbly at Maurend and Kaenath, trying to will the world back into a recognizable form, sweat pouring down my face, my head pounding.

"Difficult, but not impossible . . . and I needed to know for sure if my idea had merit. We brought his broken body here. Then, the soundshifting technique of binding blood—but enhanced, multiplied, expanded by the rezin, and the Forge." The Eparch's eyes glinted in the red light surrounding him. "Then it was done, and I knew I could do it again, and more."

"You ... you brought him back," I said, struggling to articulate my whirling thoughts.

"Yes," Kaenath said, voice full and pleased. "I brought him back to life. And I will do more. With the Forges I will build across Tellisar, and eventually all of Silarein, we will build more rezin-infused hammers, and more powerful relics still. Soon enough, the Order will control the power of life and death itself."

"Why ..." I slurred, taking an unsteady step forward again, "why ..."

"Why you?" Kaenath said, his smile widening. "That has always been your real problem, Grayshade: your belief that you are the only one who matters in your story, or anyone else's." He looked at the handle of the hammer. "This item is more power-ful than any other ever seen in our world. But its effects are ... temporary. When I first began my experiments, they lasted only a few seconds. After many—sacrifices," he went on, pursing his lips, "I extended the duration of its abilities to a few months. Even Maurend, with all his strength, will only last another week or two." Maurend said nothing, but I could see his scarred, crooked hand tightening around the hilt of his cucuri. "But I have discovered the way to make the effect permanent, for Maurend, or anyone else I bring back to life ... or kill beyond saving," the Eparch went on. He leaned forward, his voice lowering. "I never wanted *you*, heretic. But you wanted *us* ... and you would need someone to help find us. Someone who can sense emotions ... communicate through dreams ... and, when they become old enough, can harness the power of the mind, their own or others." His gaze shifted to the motionless body of Caron, and suddenly, like the clicking of a sprung trap, everything fell into place, and the world made sense again—the terrible logic at evil's heart.

"You," I breathed, swaying slightly. "You wanted . . . Caron . . ."

The Eparch laughed softly. "A sensate of enormous power. Combined with this hammer, their ability will give us what we need to forge others . . . and to make what those relics do permanent, creation and destruction. Imagine it, heretic: a world shaped in our own image." Suddenly I remembered Jant's words again: *We are the gods you thought you prayed to.* "It is unfortunate, though," Kaenath said, raising an eyebrow as he looked down at Caron, then to me. "Like all the others, they will not survive. But they will have contributed to a new world, and that itself is a reason to rejoice. You should rejoice with us, even now, Acolyte."

Joy, and pain. Perhaps those things had always danced in my soul, like love and hate, or compassion and cruelty. But in the end, if all I could do was wait for the dance to conclude, at least I would do it on my terms.

"I am not an Acolyte," I said, holding my cucuri in a position of readiness, given to me by false gods and power-crazed prophets. "I am a heretic. And you will not hurt them, or anyone else, again."

Kaenath stared at me, then nodded to Maurend, who stepped forward. "If you are indeed a heretic," the Eparch said, "then you will die like one." And with no warning, Maurend leaped to the attack.

I had fought many Acolytes, some in training when I was an Acolyte myself, some since becoming a renegade, including Maurend himself . . . once several days ago, when I had not realized who he was. Some had been more difficult in combat than others. But none were as Maurend now. He had obviously been holding back when I had encountered him outside of the Tellisar Arms and Armor; now he was fighting without limit. Whatever the enhanced soundshifting technique Kaenath had used, it had granted Maurend incredible strength and speed to go along with his training, and I was already exhausted and injured. And something else was happening; a weight was pressing down on me, the heat increasing around me, and within several parries, I knew I had little time left. I feinted left with my cucuri, then kicked right—but he was nowhere near my boot, having moved out of the way so rapidly it felt as if I had attacked the empty air. I swung in that direction wildly, but he was again out of the way, his sunken scowl twisting in hatred. With a contemptuous swing, he hit my blade so hard it flew out of my hand and clattered onto the floor behind me, and before I could recover, he brought his blade down upon my exposed leg. Pain exploded in my knee and flew up my leg into my torso, and I fell backwards with a crash.

Maurend stood over me with a terrible grin twisting his features, as I struggled to hold on to consciousness, my vision swimming, body racked in pain. "You've lost . . . a step," he said in his halting voice. "But maybe . . . you were never that good . . . to begin with."

"Finish the job, Maurend," Eparch Kaenath commanded. He had come down from the platform and picked up Caron's body during my fight with Maurend, and was now halfway over the bridge to the platform with the waiting anvil and hammer.

"With pleasure," the Acolyte replied. "I heard you say something . . . about the void back there, Grayshade. It's time for you to find it . . . yourself." He reversed his cucuri, and with his fixed, awful grin, raised his blade. I felt sadness flow through me—sadness for those I could not save, especially Caoes, and Rillia, and Caron. *I'm sorry*, I thought through the pain. *I'm sorry I didn't learn in time*.

Suddenly, as I stared up at Maurend, I heard the twang of a bowstring, and I watched in shock as an arrow struck him in the middle of the chest. His eyes widened, and he staggered back, but two more twangs sounded, followed by two more arrows striking him in the torso, sending him stumbling back further. His mouth opened, and he gave a scream of unrestrained hatred. Then a final arrow pierced him through the throat, and he fell backwards into the red liquid. There was a terrible hissing, gurgling sound—and that was the final end of Maurend, Acolyte of Argoth.

Every part of my body was screaming in pain, but I managed with extreme difficulty to roll over and see what had happened. Standing in the archway of the room were at least six members of the Varan Guard, three with bows, flanking two men dressed in bright tunics—one of whom I knew quite well. It was Nuraleed, his thin, curved blade in his hand, and his accustomed smile was gone. He pointed past me. "Stop him!" he bellowed, and the archers raised their bows—but just as suddenly as he had pointed, everything in the room seemed to stop, and the weight I had felt increased until I felt crushed beneath a ton of stone. Slowly, painfully, I managed to turn myself enough that I could see what was happening within the room.

Eparch Kaenath was standing in front of the anvil, his robes billowing behind him, and in the red light and my dimming vision he seemed like a creature from the Hells, grown enormous in his wrath and triumph. On the anvil lay Caron, eyes closed, arms flung back in the position they must have landed when thrown onto the anvil's surface. I tried to pull my arm forward, but it was useless; under the crushing weight I could barely move it, much less my entire body. Only Kaenath seemed to be moving at his normal speed. "Good," he cried, his voice rumbling throughout the chamber. "All of you here in one place makes this considerably easier." He reversed the hammer so the handle was now in his hands, the head of the hammer in front of him. "Finally," he shouted, "the time has come for our new world." And with an awful smile, his teeth glinting red, he lifted the hammer above his head with two hands.

Suddenly, everything—the gurgling liquid, the pulsing within the room, even the pounding within my head—seemed to sink into silence. I blinked, convinced my mind had finally given way, but my vision cleared enough to show that it was true: Eparch Kaenath was himself frozen, or at most moving extremely slowly, the hammer still above his head. Sitting up on the anvil was Caron, gazing at Kaenath curiously. And next to Kaenath and the anvil was a lone figure, shimmering in the heat. She was of medium height, wearing a long dress and hood, which she pulled back as she looked at me. Her face was drawn and pale, with long, dark hair ... and she looked like ...

No. No, this is a dream, a dream before dying.

The figure smiled at me, and when she spoke, I seemed to hear her voice everywhere in the room—and in my head—at once. "In life, I sought redemption. And I have found it ... here."

It was Lady Ashenza. Sister Verencia. My mother.

I could not speak, and simply stared at her mutely. And

even as I did, another figure to the right of Kaenath appeared, also wavering in the reddish light—an older man, clean-shaven with wispy hair, and even more familiar to me. "We have found redemption," he said, his voice echoing everywhere. "You have made it possible, lad."

Caoesthenes.

I looked at the shade of my long-time Trainer and mentor as another appeared behind him, young, wearing a cloak of the Service. It . . . it could not be . . . and yet . . .

"Redemption," the shade of Ravel said—Ravel, my Apprentice, whom I had killed in the Repository of the Cathedral of Argoth, back in Cohrelle. "At long last, it is here."

Another figure appeared behind Sister Verencia, stepping into view long enough for me to note their features. "Gray one hurt," he said. "But we hurt too, and now, we were redeemed." Even if I could not have seen his deliberate, pointed features, I would have recognized the speech pattern of the Chief of the Sewer Rats in Cohrelle, who had sacrificed himself to help me reach Cohrelle's Governor Jarrett in time to save him and stop the High Prelate.

One final figure appeared in front of me, bending down toward me with a crooked smile. "Strange days indeed, love," the woman in a ragged cloak said, "strange days when our redemption comes through you." She cackled a laugh, and even in my trance I knew I was looking at the shade of Alarene, whose body lay in the Bloodmarsh near the hut where she had healed and nourished me. Her laugh eased again into a smile, and with a slow turn she floated to the front of the anvil, her body suspended over the red liquid. Kaenath was now surrounded by the shades, his hammer beginning to move down, centimeter by centimeter, toward the anvil and Caron's body.

"There is powerful magic here," my mother said, her body rising above the ground as well, "magic which resonates with the room and the people within it. The Eparch's hammer is powerful enough to summon the dead, even if he did not realize that himself. But it only became possible to summon us because you gave us time . . . and because Caron was able to break through the haze of Kaenath's rezin-enhanced soundshifting. It is they and their teachers who have summoned us."

"Is there no other way?" Caron asked, and their voice was filled with sadness.

"No," Sister Verencia replied. "There is no redemption for Kaenath, and no chance to explain. Perhaps his people—the Acolytes he trained—can yet be saved, retrained. We have seen it happen once." She looked at me, and smiled as my heart seemed to break in longing and grief and wonder. "But he himself must be stopped, and this Forge of hatred and malice destroyed."

Caron nodded. "Then it must be done," they said, their voice strong.

Sister Verencia raised her hands. "Peace, and redemption," she and the other shades said at once. Then she and the shades of Caoesthenes, Ravel, the Chief of the Rats, and Alarene began to circle Kaenath, a white light glowing as they moved. Faster and faster they went until I could no longer see him, and the light grew more and more intense until I had to close my eyes to block out its glare. Suddenly the weight in the room was gone, and I heard a terrible shriek. I opened my eyes to see the shades gone and Eparch Kaenath, still holding the hammer, staggering back and forth, eyes wide and staring. He stumbled into the anvil, then a step right, and finally stumbled a few steps to his left. His foot touched air, and with another awful scream, both the man and the hammer fell into the red liquid. There was a great rumbling, the room itself shaking, and I felt the pain in my body overwhelming me.

As my consciousness fled I thought I saw, for one brief moment, my mother bending toward me, a kind smile on her face.

No. That was a dream, and it, and my life, is ended now.

Darkness took me, and I knew no more.

EPILOGUE

"THE truth is, my friend," Nuraleed said, his smile broad, "that I will need my guest room back soon. I do not wish to run an inn in Tellisar, yes?"

I was sitting up in bed, my back against the headboard, eating some greenselle soup. It was the first time I had felt strong enough to eat in days, and it was good enough that I did not feel it necessary to argue. I simply raised an eyebrow, and was gratified to see Nuraleed laugh in response.

"Fine, then," he said. "Perhaps I can give you a bit longer, even if it bankrupts me."

"You won't be bankrupted," Gennovil said, leaning against the wall of the room in Nuraleed's home where I had been convalescing. She had a sling around her left arm, and several scars on her face and neck, but they were healing. "The Silken Order will always find a way to make money."

"I have no doubt that if we demonstrate too great a level of greed, the Sisters of Vraevre will be there to offer ready correction," Nuraleed said with an exaggerated bow. Gennovil snorted, but her expression did not harden. It had been Nuraleed himself who had found Gennovil, who regained consciousness long enough to tell him what she had discovered about the fountain, and both he and the healers he had brought with him had saved her ... though not in time to save her other Sisters, nor the ones who fell in battle in front of the Forge. Still, she remained grateful—and, though I imagined she would never admit it, impressed with the merchant . . . as was I. Few others could have convinced the guards in the Locks not to kill him immediately, or to summon the commanders of the Varan Guard to explain the situation to them. And only someone of Nuraleed's charm and cunning could have persuaded *them* not to kill him, and to recognize the danger posed by Eparch Kaenath and Father Rennix . . . even if he had to give up some of the Silken Order's secrets to do it, which I knew was more of a blow to him than the merchant would ever admit.

"How have the Sisters fared?" I asked between sips of soup.

Gennovil sighed. "We are in mourning. The Acolytes of Argoth knew their business. We lost fifteen Sisters, and another five are injured badly enough that they will probably never recover enough to be effective fighters again. Even when we have finished grieving, it will take a while to find and train replacements."

"I can't think of anyone better to lead the recovery," I said. "And perhaps you will have some time now, with the Eparch defeated and the Order of Argoth broken."

Gennovil snorted again, but her smile showed there was no heat in it. "Even now I still don't fully understand what happened down there, even after it's been explained to me."

I nodded. "I don't either, and I was there to witness it. But . . . I know it happened, somehow."

"That makes sense, since you were a big part of it," another voice said, and I looked to see Rillia, her side still heavily bandaged, sitting uncomfortably on a chair.

"Eh, a small part, maybe," I said, shaking my head. "But

without you, I would have been finished long before I kept Maurend and Kaenath busy for a minute."

"Without you," Rillia said, "we all would have been finished. Without you and that stubborn neck of yours. You never did know when to give up." She smiled, but a shadow passed over her face a moment later. "And Maurend . . ." She shook her head. "I never fought anyone like that. He was—more than human, somehow, at least in strength and speed."

"He was more than human, and less," I said, remembering the look on his scarred face before toppling backwards into the liquid. "Who knows what he would have become if Kaenath had been able to finish the process with the hammer? All I know is he was beyond any of us individually."

"Maybe," Rillia said. "But then we weren't just individuals then, were we? We fought together, in a way the Service had never prepared us to do. Kaenath only trusted himself, in the end. We trusted each other . . . and that made a difference." She smiled at me, and a feeling of warm contentment filled me as I rested the bowl of soup on my lap, trying to ignore the rising aroma demanding more attention to my appetite, and let my right hand drift down to my side where I could stroke the fur of Caoes, who had been mostly asleep on the bed next to me for the better part of the last few days since we had been pulled from the Forge.

Nuraleed grinned. "Your namir may never be useful again, friend Grayshade. He seems to like this softer living."

"You have no one to blame but yourself, since you saved him," I responded, returning the smile . . . though we both knew it was true. Only a member of the Silken Order with long knowledge of namirs could have known how to help one tap into their own healing capacity, especially one who'd been hit by three kushuri darts. His side was heavily bandaged, and one leg was badly sprained; it would be weeks before he was recovered. But he was alive, and that was more than enough.

Nuraleed nodded. "To lose a namir is a serious thing among my people, and it speaks well of you that you feel the same way." His expression grew serious. "I wish we could have saved more. But in the end, we all did what we must. Yet even with all of us, it would not have mattered without Caron."

"You mean without me to help bring you all together," a calm voice said, "in saving me?" I looked over to see, sitting in a chair near Rillia, the leader of Varda's people. Of all of us, Caron was the healthiest, for they had been freed with the destruction of the hammer and passing of the Eparch. Indeed, they had never looked healthier, their calm and pleasant expression restored, but with wisdom and peace added to it.

"None of us would have been saved," I said with a frown, "if you had not broken through the soundshifting haze Kaenath had created. I still don't know how you were able to do that in your state."

Caron nodded slowly, their smile fading. "I stayed in the dream," they said at last. "A dream like the ones you had when you were traveling across Silarein. But here, I was visited by my teachers ... and, in the end, by some of the shades you saw, Grayshade, especially Caoesthenes and Sister Verencia. They showed me the path, and you gave me the time I needed to tread it back to the light."

"Did you know what they would do?" Rillia asked, looking at Caron softly.

"Not until I saw what the shades were doing. I ... wasn't

happy about it. Even Kaenath deserved something, a path out of his hatred and fear. It flowed from him in waves, like the heat in that room." Caron shuddered. "But there was no other way. And when he fell from the platform, and took the hammer with him . . . everything became completely clear."

"And so you are now, truly, the leader of Varda's people," Gennovil said with a smile.

Caron nodded. "Yes. I have my full senses now. I can feel everything . . . but filter out what I do not need, what would be overwhelming otherwise." They smiled again. "My teachers have left . . . but I know now I will always be able to find them if I need them. And I may need them again. There are many people to be helped, many overwhelmed by sadness and grief and rage. All of them need to be led to their own paths. But," they said, their smile widening, "we finally have time. Time to do what we must." They looked at me, their grin wavering only a bit. "And what of you, Grayshade? Now that your own duty is fulfilled?"

"Is it?" I said, sighing. "We have done what we had to do . . . but I cannot take back my own past."

"You can rethink your present, and future," they replied.

"For what good it may do me," I said, indicating my leg, splinted and immobilized. "This injury is too severe, Caron. I'll survive, but I won't be much good at any of the things I was trained to do. All I am now is the heretic Kaenath called me."

"You're not an assassin or a heretic, or what anyone else called you," Caron said seriously. "You're Grayshade. You will decide what and whom to believe, and what to build your life around now. About your injuries . . . I am . . . sorry. But your skills and your knowledge haven't gone."

"Or your redemption," Rillia said gently, and I looked at her, deeply moved.

"I—maybe," I said after a moment, swallowing my tears. "But I'm not sure what I'll do with those things."

Nuraleed cleared his throat. "It seems to me," he said, "that Tellisar now has a group of highly trained fighters with no one to serve and no one to guide them. The Order is bereft and leaderless, and a tremendous waste of talent and resources. Such a group could be turned to a more . . . positive purpose, yes?"

I stared at him. "You think a group of assassins could somehow be changed? Redeemed?"

"Yes, my friend," the man replied, straightening his purple sash, "for I have seen it before." I opened my mouth to reply, then saw his expression, and turning, saw Gennovil, Rillia, and Caron with the same smiles, looks of curiosity . . . and of kindness.

I closed my mouth again. Indeed there was work to do in rebuilding here; Argoth's Forge would have to be permanently destroyed, and the situation in Cohrelle resolved, and . . .

I shook my head. "Maybe. But before I take on another mission, there's one last thing I must do first—in a day or two, when I'm strong enough to leave this nook you call a place to house guests." I picked up the bowl from my lap again. "And if you can all let me finish my soup in peace."

In the end it was closer to a week than a few days when I finally stood at the edge of the Glacalta, its deep blue surface rippled by a gentle breeze from the south. Spring was in the air, and the mid-day sun warmed me as I limped slowly to the edge of the water. I could have done this at the Docks, but I wanted to be outside Tellisar's walls, and so the trip here had taken some time. But for the first time in many years, I was in no hurry. At my feet stood Caoes, limping as severely as I was, but otherwise holding the same imperturbable expression he always did. The last time we had seen this, we had not been nearly as close . . . or understood nearly as much.

I drew forth my cucuri, visually tracing the etched design in the blade as it glinted in the sunlight. Next to me, Rillia, her right arm through my left, sighed. "Are you sure about this, Grayshade? You don't have to on my account, or Caron's, you know." I looked at her, again rendered almost breathless by her beauty in the golden light, and smiled. "I know," I said. "But most of all, I'm doing this for me." I looked at Caron, whose hand I had held all the way for the entire trip here. "You told me once that just because the path you're on has ended doesn't mean you can't make a new one."

"I remember," they said, smiling. "Are you making a new path now?"

"In a way," I replied, disengaging myself from Rillia and undoing my cloak, letting it settle on the shore near the water. "Although for the first time, I don't fully know where I'm going."

Their smile widened. "That sounds like the best way to begin an adventure, don't you think?" I looked at them, then Caoes, then Rillia. Somewhere in the wind, I thought I heard a distinctive laugh—maybe the laugh of a healer and friend I had once known, or maybe just the wind itself. Then, with Caron, Caoes, and Rillia giving me space, I reached back and with all my might threw my cucuri into the waiting waters of the Glacalta. It landed on the surface and rapidly disappeared. I watched it sink out of sight. Then I turned with a smile and, arm in arm with my family, began the slow trip back to Tellisar, and my new life.

It's amazing how long it can take someone to die ... and, as I finally learned, even more amazing how long it can take someone to truly live.

And now I will.

ACKNOWLEDGEMENTS

Milestones are a tricky thing to process when you're in the midst of passing them, especially for authors who are always looking to the next project. But occasionally it's important to really take stock of how far one has come, and this is such a situation for me: the completion of my first full trilogy. If you've read my acknowledgments in the previous books within *The Gray Assassin Trilogy*, you'll know that this entire series has gone on a long and complex journey from first conception to final publication, and with this book, that journey finally comes to an end…thanks to many people who helped out along the way.

As I've discussed before, I will always be grateful to Marie Bilodeau, the original editor of this series, and Ed Greenwood, who first gave the series a chance with his publishing company years ago. But the people most involved with seeing this through to its conclusion are the ones I most want to focus upon here. Emily Bell, whose edits have played a critical part in shaping *Heretic* and the series as a whole, has been both supportive and insightful throughout, and I am deeply thankful for her input, assistance, and friendship. Beta reader Dimitris Tzellis was again thoughtful and encouraging with his feedback, and his unwavering enthusiasm for the series has been a genuine pleasure. Patricia E. Matson was again both detailed and helpful in her copyedits, and I'm grateful to her for her work here.

I remain thankful to Brandon O'Brien (also the designer of the forthcoming *Grayshade* TTRPG), Brad Beaulieu, and Julie Czerneda for their friendship and support of this series, to Chris Bell for more wonderful work on layout and design, and to Peter Tikos for extraordinary cover work throughout *The Gray Assassin Trilogy*. Thanks are again due to my students for helping me learn even as I'm teaching them. And for everyone in the larger SFF field who supported me in any of this process: thank you for your belief and encouragement, both of which have mattered a lot in writing this book and series.

As always, I'm most thankful to my friends and family who support me in everything I do—especially my parents, whose inspiration remains, my wife Clea, who has supported me through a journey I sometimes thought wouldn't end the way I hoped, my amazing and inspiring daughter Senavene, and my son Calen, who seems to love acrobatics just as much as Grayshade does.

Again, thank you for reading this book, and if you've been with *The Gray Assassin Trilogy* since it began, for reading the whole series. It will always be a privilege to be able to publicly share a world I have long imagined privately.

Connecticut
2024

GREGORY A. WILSON

Gregory A. Wilson is Professor of English at St. John's University, where he teaches creative writing and speculative fiction, and is author of Clemson UP's *The Problem in the Middle: Liminal Space and the Court Masque*, book chapters, and journal articles. Outside academia he is author of the epic fantasy *The Third Sign*, the award-winning graphic novel *Icarus* and dark fantasies *Grayshade* and *Renegade*, and the 5E adventure/sourcebook *Tales and Tomes from the Forbidden Library*, plus many short stories. Under the moniker Arvan Eleron he runs a Twitch channel focused on story and narrative, with many sponsored TTRPG campaigns.

He lives with his family in a two-hundred-year-old home near the sea in Connecticut; his virtual home is gregoryawilson.com